DECADENCE AND SYMBOLISM: A SHOWCASE ANTHOLOGY

Brian Stableford has been publishing fiction and non-fiction for fifty years. His fiction includes an eighteen-volume series of "tales of the biotech revolution" and a series of half a dozen metaphysical fantasies set in Paris in the 1840s, featuring Edgar Poe's Auguste Dupin. His most recent non-fiction projects are *New Atlantis: A Narrative History of British Scientific Romance* (Wildside Press, 2016) and *The Plurality of Imaginary Worlds: The Evolution of French* roman scientifique (Black Coat Press, 2016); in association with the latter he has translated approximately a hundred and fifty volumes of texts not previously available in English, similarly issued by Black Coat Press.

SNUGGLY BOOKS

DECADENCE AND SYMBOLISM:
A SHOWCASE ANTHOLOGY

Edited, Introduced and Translated by
BRIAN STABLEFORD

THIS IS A SNUGGLY BOOK

ISBN: 978-1-943813-58-2

Contents

Introduction

1.
Preliminary Definitions

Symbolism is everywhere in literature, as it is in life; it could not be otherwise, language and thought being impossible without it. In the narrower meaning of the term to which the present anthology of Symbolist prose refers, however, the "Symbolist Movement" was a phenomenon that emerged in Paris in the mid-1880s, reached a swift heyday in the 1890s, and gradually faded away thereafter as familiarity began to breed a certain contempt and other rallying cries became fashionable; the torch that the Symbolists had carried for a while in the great relay of French literature was eventually handed on to the Surrealists.

The Symbolist Movement never died entirely, the carriers of literary banners often being old soldiers in that regard, and it could still have been regarded as not-quite-faded-away until the 1960s, when the last of its once-active participants, Paul Fort, "Gérard d'Houville" and "Tristan Klingsor," finally expired. As a vigorous active entity, however, it only survived the nineteenth century by a few years, and by the time of the Great War of 1914-1918, "Symbolism" had effectively become mere symbolism again, still everywhere in literature, as in life, but with only a few advocates still trumpeting its credentials as the distilled essence of literary creativity, and sounding increasingly like voices in a wilderness.

The concept of Symbolism-with-a-capital-S, as defined and described by the Movement's various manifestos—most famously the one published by Jean Moréas in *Le Figaro* on 18 September 1886—was inevitably formed by means of its relationship to various other perceived Movements, partly in a spirit of pillage and partly one of defiant opposition. Four such Movements were of particular importance in that quest for definition, two of them old and allegedly passé, which the Symbolists wanted to replace—the Romantic Movement and the Parnassian Movement—and two of them more recently born: the Naturalist Movement and the Decadent Movement.

Symbolism can be seen as an evolutionary successor of the Parnassian Movement, which can itself be seen as a species of neo-Romanticism, but its relationship with the two contemporary schools was necessarily more complicated. Throughout its lifetime of loud publicity, Symbolism tended to be seen as a crucial opponent, and perhaps even a polar opposite, of Naturalism, their adherents engaged in a struggle for prestige whose outcome might determine the future of French literature, at least in terms of the key location of reputation. Distinguishing between Symbolists and Decadents, however, was a much more problematic matter, and throughout their parallel lives, the two Movements overlapped to such an extent that only a few diehard pedants claimed to be able to tell their adherents apart.

Naturalism was primarily associated in France with the novelist Émile Zola, who had issued a "Naturalist Manifesto" of sorts in the second edition of his novel *Thérèse Raquin* in 1867, the argument of which he had elaborated further in an 1880 essay, "Le Roman experimental." He defended his work on the grounds of the realism of its representations, which, he argued, was informed by a spirit of objective analysis akin to that of contemporary science, in a search for the essential truth of human relationships and behavior. Symbolist literature was, by contrast, routinely seen as something inherently unnaturalistic in its representations, characterized by imaginative artifice—but the matter was by no means as simple as that capsule distinction implies. Symbolist Manifestoes also claimed routinely to be seeking an essential truth, with the aid of a different notion of what constitutes "truth" and how best to grasp it.

The relationship between Symbolism and Decadence was even more complicated. The best-known characterization of literary decadence in the 1880s was Théophile Gautier's definition of "decadent style," set out in his introduction to the 1868 edition of Charles Baudelaire's *Les Fleurs du mal*. From Gautier's perspective, which makes literary decadence a matter of stylistic ornamentation and exoticism, literary symbolism becomes one of its most important devices, so that all symbolist art would, by definition, be a subcategory of Decadent art. "Decadence" was, however, a heavily loaded term, which had very different implications in other contexts, and it was, therefore, difficult to separate the idea of literary decadence from what common parlance called moral decadence—a carelessness of social convention, especially in respect of sexual and alcoholic promiscuity—and what intellectual parlance called cultural decadence: the historically observable tendency of civilizations, once having flowered, to decline and fall.

Gautier argued, with his tongue slightly in his cheek, that literary decadence had no necessary connection with moral decadence, but the idea that artists—especially artists addicted to stylistic ornamentation and exoticism—have a natural tendency to moral decadence had been around for a long time, and Gautier knew perfectly well that both he and Baudelaire, along with such peers as Arthur Rimbaud and Paul Verlaine, were widely reputed to be symbolic paragons of moral decadence. On the other hand, he argued that there was a definite empirical connection between literary decadence and cultural decadence, because civilizations in decline tended to produce decadent literature, just as, notoriously, they tended to produce copious moral decadence.

Just as "Symbolism" in the title of the present anthology refers to the Symbolist Movement, much as defined by the Moréas Manifesto, which was very largely based on the esthetic theories of Stéphane Mallarmé, so the term "Decadence" in that title refers, essentially, to Gautier's notion of "decadent style." Both terms, however, require more elaborate explanation, in terms of their evolution and their historical context, if the works contained in this anthology are to be fully understood and appreciated, and that is the purpose of the present introduction.

2.
A Brief Preliminary Symbolist Observation on the Supposed Opposition between Symbolism and Naturalism

The symbolism of common parlance, with its customary stupidity, routinely uses the example of an unreplete glass of beer as an illustration of the difference between an optimist and a pessimist. Whereas a pessimist, so the argument goes, would see the glass as half-empty, an optimist would see it as half-full.

The argument, of course, assumes that people are idiots. Any reasonable person, seeing the glass in question, would know that it is far more likely that a person engaged in consuming it had paused half-way than it is that a person engaged in filling it had paused half-way, and would take the implication that the glass is half-empty, not half-full.

A stern Naturalist might, I suppose, approach the question in a different way. He might say that the distinction is false, a half-full glass and a half-empty glass being exactly the same thing, because it is the level of the beer in the glass that determines the value of "half." And that would be true, in terms of one particular notion of the truth.

A Symbolist, on the other hand, would consider concentration on matters of measurement and the quantification of "half" to be missing the point. For the Symbolist, what matters is the implication of the half-emptiness of the glass in terms of the reality of the drinking process, even though we cannot see the drinker, because all we have before us in the framework of the enigma is the half-empty glass; the drinker is not included in the description, and is thus invisible. Nevertheless, the image of the half-empty glass, and the manner in which we choose to describe it, does communicate impressions. Unless he is a lunatic optimist who might describe the glass as "half-full," the Symbolist would consider that a half-empty glass is an intrinsically sad thing, because it inevitably recalls to mind that which has gone, leaving behind nothing but a bitter aftertaste and a hint of intoxication, symbols in their turn of entropy and universal decay. And that would be true, in terms of one particular notion of the truth.

The glass itself, of course, is the just way it is, but the sight of it inevitably implies a time factor and a process. One does not have to be a pessimist to have that consciousness, but one certainly would have to be an optimist to think that the beer in the glass might have been interrupted in mid-replenishment. Insofar as the unreplete glass symbolizes the wider reality of optimism and pessimism, therefore, it represents the fundamental truth that optimism, properly understood, is the only true mental illness—if we mean to imply by that phrase, as we should, a disease of reason—whereas pessimism, properly understood, is a telling symptom of sanity.

However, the two truths of Naturalism and Symbolism are complementary, and not detachable from one another. It is not the case that a Naturalist *only* cares about the accuracy of measurement, even though he might consider accuracy of depiction primal and paramount. Unless he is an idiot, he will be fully aware of time's arrow and entropy, and the sight of the half-empty glass will sadden him as much as it saddens the Symbolist. We need not quibble in this instance about the possibility of his being an optimist; no one has ever seen an optimistic Naturalist, and no one ever will, because accuracy of measurement eliminates any such crass psychological possibility.

In the same way, even though it is not his primary concern, and not his immediate focus, the Symbolist is not unconcerned with accuracy of measurement. He is fully aware of the fact that the symbolism of a half-empty glass is significantly different from one that is three-quarters empty, or one that that has only just begun to be consumed. The implied aftertaste might be much the same, but the degree of intoxication will differ, as will the imminence of the expectation of emptiness, annihilation, disappointment and regret. It makes perfect sense, therefore, to speak of accurate symbolism, even though there might be a very large number of symbols capable of representing the essential sadness of time's passage far better than a momentarily neglected half-pint of beer.

The Symbolist, of course, would prefer to be drinking champagne or absinthe, figuring, for symbolic reasons, that beer is the sort of thing that only Naturalists drink, but that, as they say, is another story.

3.
The Symbolism of Decadence

It is a routine feature of the evolution of language that words continually acquire new symbolic connotations, over and above their simplest literal meanings. The French word *décadence* made an important acquisition of that sort in 1734, when Charles-Louis le Secondat, Baron de La Brède et de Montesquieu, published *Considérations sur les causes de la grandeur des Romains et de leur décadence*. The idea that the historical fate of the Roman Empire had been a long decline toward oblivion, accompanied by striking symptoms of moral decline on the part of its Emperors, many of whom seemed to historical hindsight to have been both mad and despicable, was not new, but Montesquieu was one of the first scholars to argue cogently that the disintegration of the Roman Empire was not simply a series of unfortunate accidents, but the inevitable unfolding of a pattern governed by a quasi-scientific law, applicable to all empires, and all civilizations. In that way of thinking, civilizations are doomed by their intrinsic nature to follow a life cycle that guides them inevitably from infancy to virility, and from virility to decrepitude.

Whether that hypothesis is true or not remains open to question, but its intellectual popularization had inevitable corollaries. Symbolism is everywhere in science, as it is in art, and all hypotheses are energized by their symbolic examples. The idea of the inevitable decadence of civilizations changed the symbolic value of actors in history and the scripts written for them by legend, reportage and fiction. For Montesquieu, as for those who took his ideas seriously, the decadence of Rome came to be symbolized, quintessentially, by the images of its vicious and crazy emperors, especially Caligula and Nero. That was, of course, not new; the Roman fabulists who passed themselves off as historians saw things in much the same way, and had also supplied a vast cast of minor characters to add to their own apologues of perceived decadence, in which women such as Cleopatra and Messalina played important antiheroic roles. Such is the power of fabulation that all those roles, starring and subsidiary, were handed down to the literary movements of the nineteenth century, ripe for refurbishment.

History, of course, being essentially an exercise in symbolism, only pretends to be about the past; what Montesquieu was really theorizing about, and the true but covert purpose of his investigation, was the current condition of France, seen from his perspective as repeating the inevitable life-cycle of civilizations, with Louis XIV and Louis XV playing Caligula and Nero (not necessarily in that order), with the aid of their own subsidiary cast of Cleopatras and Messalinas. The catastrophe was already looming, and it was widely assumed to be only a matter of time before the barbarians stormed the Bastille—which, of course, they did in 1789, thus forcing a slight change of perspective on the writers of the nineteenth century. It was, however, by no means difficult to cast Napoléon as Julius Caesar, or Alexander the Great, by fiddling the imaginary chronology a little, thus resetting the clock in order to discover the decadence of contemporary France still in the full evil flow of its decline, with the real catastrophe still looming.

In anticipation of another pseudoscientific law of history, however, the theory of inevitable decadence did not go unopposed, and another symbolic schema for the interpretation of the historical situation of France emerged toward the end of the eighteenth century, just in time for its chief popularizer, the Marquis de Condorcet, to become one of the victims of the Revolution: the philosophy of progress. Like the idea of decadence, the idea of progress was not new, but what Condorcet and like-minded thinkers added to it was the notion that technological progress—the increase in scientific knowledge and its practical spinoff—and social progress, by which they meant a movement away from brutal tyranny toward liberty, equality and fraternity, were, in fact, two faces of the same coin, moving through time and happenstance hand-in-glove, by no means smoothly, but nevertheless relentlessly.

From the viewpoint of nineteenth-century believers in progress, the symbolic storming of the Bastille was not a matter of barbarians hammering another nail into the coffin of decadent France, but an admittedly-stumbling step in the direction of a more liberal and egalitarian society. It was in the context of that broad opposition of ideas that the Romantic Movement in French literature slowly took form in the early decades of the nineteenth century, provided with a label by the exiled Madame de Staël and enthusiastically brewed in the cauldron of *cénacles* headed by Charles Nodier, Victor Hugo and Théophile Gautier.

4.
Romanticism and the Idea of Decadence

Romanticism was a complex, sprawling phenomenon, mostly defined by what it was not. Primarily, what it was not was "Classicism"—a theory of art that held, broadly speaking, that excellence in artistic endeavor was to be sought by the intellectual application of rules of construction and etiquette that had been discovered in Classical times, and set out in such works as Aristotle's *Poetics*. Opposition to that stance had been brewing for a long time among the eighteenth-century *philosophes*, but had been somewhat muted—in terms of his work for the stage, Voltaire had made money by following the perceived rules, not by breaking them, and it was only in such despised genres as prose fiction that he gave his iconoclastic spirit free rein. That slow progress left undone the work of knight-errantry that Victor Hugo deliberately set out to accomplish by starting a belated theatrical Revolution in 1831 with *Hernani*, having formed a literal army to assist him, fully prepared, if necessary, to engage in fisticuffs on the opening night, to which Gautier turned up symbolically clad as a redcoat.

The backlash was not long in coming, and the particular symbolic form that it took played a significant role in determining the terminology inherited by the literary movements of the *fin-de-siècle*, and hence by this anthology. One of the self-appointed defenders of Classicism against the assault mounted by Hugo and the members of his cenacle was the critic Desiré Nisard, who began in 1834 to call Romanticism "decadent"—by which he meant that it was a backward step in what he saw as the progressive march of literature toward greater order and decency. Nisard's sniping reached a crucial controversial junction when he launched an all-out attack in an article entitled "M. Victor Hugo en 1836," cast as a demolition of Hugo's *Les Chants de crepuscule* [Twilight Songs] (1835), although it could easily be read as a general blast aimed at the entire Romantic Movement, on the grounds of its supposed "decadence."

According to Nisard, the key symptoms of the literary rot that was supposedly setting in as the discipline, elegance and etiquette of Classicism were tragically undermined, were a liking for profuse description, a preoccupation with detail, and—most important of all—a rebellious elevation of raw imaginative force over the stern restrictions of rule-bound reason and etiquette. All those trends were, according to Nisard, direly unhealthy. He admitted that they were also seductive—especially the elaborate employment of the imagination—but that seductiveness only added to the danger, in his view.

Nisard's lightning-strike had various effects. Victor Hugo simply dismissed the assault, including the notion that his work was in any way "decadent," as ridiculous. Some others, however, soon began to take a different tack, deliberately turning the intended insult into an ironic compliment by affecting to construe the word "decadent" as an item of praise. The most vociferous of the writers who adopted that stance was Charles Baudelaire, always a lover of seeming paradox and champion of seeming perversity. He began to use the term in his own critical writings as a compliment, employing it not only to describe the literary work of Victor Hugo and other Romantic writers, but also practitioners of the other arts, championing the Romantic painting of Eugéne Delacroix and the Romantic music of Richard Wagner. He was more than content for his own poetry to be considered and described as "decadent," and took ostentatious pride in the appellation.

It is worth noting, however, that Nisard's rant about "decadence" did not arrive completely out of the blue. In the pages of the *Revue de Paris*, the chief organ of the Romantic Movement in the 1930s, the concept of cultural decadence, and the alleged cultural decadence of contemporary France, had been much discussed in recent years, including articles by Charles Nodier declaring forcefully that the philosophy of progress was a myth, and that all civilizations were fated to decline and perish. Interestingly, one of Nodier's acquaintances, "X. B. Saintine" (Xavier Boniface) published a remarkable item of documentary satire in the *Revue*'s pages in 1832: "Histoire d'une civilisation antédiluvienne" (tr. as "The Story of an Antediluvian Civilization"), which dramatized that thesis in graphic symbolic fashion.

Historians elaborating or contesting Montesquieu's thesis had no examples to study of a civilization starting from scratch—all those remarked by history had emerged from the ruins of previous civilizations—and it was arguable, too, that all of them had failed to complete their natural life-cycle, being murdered rather than dying of "natural causes." Saintine set out to fill in the gaps by presenting a hypothetical account of the first ever human civilization, tracking it all the way from its birth to its ultimate decrepitude. His account of early human evolution—imagined long before the advent of any paleontological evidence—is an interesting exercise in the imagination, but where the story became a *tour de force* was in its scathing satirical account of the supposedly-inevitable decadence and collapse of the civilization: a tacit prognosis for the fate of contemporary Western civilization.

In Saintine's representation, all of modern literature, as well as all of modern science, becomes a direct product of cultural decadence, having originated as a way of employing the excess of leisure produced by civilization, and having evolved greater intricacy as the perpetuation of leisure inevitably generated an appetite for ever-more-intense and ever-more-exotic stimulations. Amour too, in Saintine's view, is another symptom of the disease of decadence: a mythology refined and elaborated as a way of filling time, in close collaboration with literature, subject to the same process of complication and intensification.

Like Voltaire, Saintine made a living sticking to convention, while maintaining his iconoclasm as a sideline, but instead of writing tragedies he wrote vaudevilles, and thus was never regarded by his fellow Romantics as a serious writer; none of them ever cited him, but Baudelaire and Gautier must surely have read "Histoire d'une civilisation antédiluvienne" in the *Revue de Paris*, and are unlikely have been unaware of the relevance of its argument to their own notions of what literature was, in its ultimate essence. Baudelaire's key notions of *ennui* and *spleen*, are merely labels for Saintine's pessimistic representations of the inevitable effects of excessive civilization.

It is important, in considering Gautier's definition of "decadent style," to remember that he and Baudelaire had previously been at odds regarding the nature of art, and that his introduction to *Les Fleurs du mal* was, in part, a conscious attempt to smooth over that difference. Gautier, famously, had formulated the doctrine of "*l'art pour l'art*" (usually translated as "art for art's sake"), whose central claim is that art does not have to justify itself with regard to any purpose beyond its own existence—by which he meant, of course, that it did not to have to justify itself by service to any moral or political cause. Baudelaire, who was not a man ever inclined to agree with anyone about anything, as a matter of instinct—although he made an exception for the late Edgar Poe, whom he considered to be his only soul-mate, and whose French voice he became—answered Gautier by arguing that art did, in fact, have a profound psychological and educative utility.

In fact, as any pedant will readily point out, the disagreement was illusory. Gautier was not arguing that art had no utility, merely that it did not have to justify itself by reference to any external or further utility. Naturally, he chose not to take the argumentative tack of claiming that he really agreed with Baudelaire, but proposed instead that Baudelaire—safely dead by then—really agreed with him. It is worth remembering that Baudelaire would have disagreed, on principle, with Gautier's interpretation of his work. Nevertheless, that interpretation remains the canonical account and analysis of decadent style.

According to Gautier, "the style of decadence" is "Art arrived at the point of extreme maturity that determines civilizations which have grown old; ingenious, complicated, clever, full of delicate hints and refinements, gathering all delicacies of speech, borrowing from technical vocabularies, taking colors from every palette, tones from all musical instruments, contours vague and fleeting, listening to translate subtle confidences, confessions of depraved passions, and the strange hallucinations of a fixed idea turning into madness."

Such a style is, Gautier affirms, "summoned to express everything and to venture to the very extremes" and is "the necessary and fatal idiom of peoples and civilizations where an artificial life has replaced a natural one and developed in a man who does not know his own needs." Casting a severe glance in the direction of Nisard, he adds: "Contrary to the Classical style, it admits of backgrounds where the specters of superstition, the haggard phantoms of dreams, the terrors of night, remorse which leaps out and falls back noiselessly, obscure fantasies that astonish the day, and all that the soul in its deepest depths and innermost caverns conceals of darkness, deformity and horror, move together confusedly."

A cynical observer might have thought that Gautier was talking about his own work rather than Baudelaire's, but that would be a trifle unjust, bearing in mind that the two of them did, indeed, have a great deal in common, and that insofar as they spoke in harmony, theirs was the voice that set the tone for their era. Whether or not Saintine was right about everything mistakenly considered to symbolize "progress" actually being a symptom of terminal decay, the work of the decadent Romantics really did constitute a fine symbol their era, extracting and concentrating its essence. And—symbolically speaking, at least—it was Gautier's depiction of Baudelaire's endeavor, and the argument he offered in support of that depiction, which provided the theoretical cake for which Stéphane Mallarmé and the Symbolist Movement subsequently provided the icing.

5.
The Prelude to the Symbolist Manifesto

The cradle of the Symbolist Movement was the series of weekly meetings that Stéphane Mallarmé began hosting in 1880, his "*mardis*" [Tuesdays], which he employed as a forum for developing his ideas about the essential nature of literary creativity. His obsession with literature had developed much earlier, in his teens—he was born in 1842—when he had been an avid and unusually attentive reader of Hugo, Baudelaire and Gautier, the three writers who played the leading role in formulating his tastes and his attitudes, Like Gautier he believed in *l'art pour l'art*, but he did not believe that art, seen thus, had no utility; quite the reverse.

In Mallarmé's view, art—like philosophy and its handmaiden, science—was a means of seeking knowledge, but it was crucially different from, and superior to, empirical philosophy, especially the positivism developed by contemporary philosophers in the wake of August Comte, the first step of which was the reification of the world as an object of study by rigorous observation. Like the pioneering philosopher of esthetics, Alexander Baumgarten, Mallarmé saw art as "secondary creation," a recapitulation of the work of God, which arrived at understanding not by clinical observation but by participant action, more a matter of "knowing how" than "knowing that."

Unlike Baumgarten, however, Mallarmé did not think that artists ought to be aiming to imitate God's handiwork as closely as possible by mimicking it with the greatest possible accuracy; indeed, he thought that the whole point of having the freedom to create was to have a license to experiment freely. Baumgarten had considered "heterocosmic" creativity—the creation of worlds within texts different from the world as observed and presently understood—to be intrinsically bad. In Mallarmé's view, such work was very valuable, precisely because it challenged vulgar observation—a flawed process, in his thinking—and created possibilities for new and better understanding.

That was the framework of consideration with which Mallarmé attempted to infect the acolytes who gathered in his home, with a considerable degree of success. Mallarmé was a poet, and his own attention was focused primarily on poetry, but his theories were applicable much more broadly than that, and one of the first significant group ventures of his coterie, in 1885, was the founding of *La Revue wagnérienne* (1885), which applied his ideas to analyses of and commentaries on the operas of Richard Wagner, still the object of a fanatical cult following in France and a subject of fierce controversy long after their initial championship in Paris by Baudelaire. Created by Édouard Dujardin and Téodor Wysewa, both regulars at the *mardis*, the pages of the short-lived periodical were filled by Mallarmé's associates, including articles by himself and Jean Moréas.

As well as a perceived kinship with Wagner's experimental operas, the Symbolists also had a perceived kinship with Impressionist artists following in the footsteps of Delacroix and, more immediately, Édouard Manet, and a school of Symbolist art soon developed in France and Belgium, exemplified in France by such artists as Félicien Rops, Odilon Redon and—most crucially and most spectacularly—Gustave Moreau, and in Belgium by James Ensor, Jan Toorop and Jean Delville. All those artists were influenced by Symbolist writing, and they influenced writers in their turn, in a virile cross-fertilization: an expectable, and perhaps necessary, consequence of Gautier's theory of decadent style.

By 1885 other periodicals were also beginning to take an interest in Symbolist work, although they did not adopt the label immediately. In 1883 the anticlerical *Nouvelle Rive Gauche*, founded by "Léo Trézénik" [Léon Épinette] tried to broaden its niche market and changed its name to *Lutèce*; it published work by Paul Verlaine, Jules Laforgue, Jean Moréas, Paul Adam and Charles Morice before disappearing in October 1886. By then, Gustave Kahn had founded a periodical that he initially co-edited with Léo d'Orfer, *La Vogue*, which made its début in April 1886. In October of that year, just as *Lutèce* died, Kahn, Moréas and Paul Adam founded *Le Symboliste*, but the latter only ran for four issues, while *La Vogue* published thirty-one before dying in 1887 (although it was resurrected twice thereafter).

Both of Kahn's periodicals featured previously-unpublished work by Arthur Rimbaud as well as contributions by Jules Laforgue, Francis Poictevin and Édouard Dujardin, all of whom had recently published books that could be claimed for the cause, and *La Vogue* also published work by Charles Morice and several new recruits to the cause from outside Mallarmé's clique, notably Joris-Karl Huysmans, Jean Lorrain and Paul Bourget—all of whom, significantly, were also reputed as Naturalists, illustrating the degree to which the two Movements overlapped. 1886 also saw the publication of two volumes written by Moréas and Adam in collaboration, *Les Demoiselles Goubert* and *Le Thé chez Miranda*, and it was in the midst of that sudden flood of publications that Moréas' Manifesto appeared in *Le Figaro*.

It is necessary to remember that although it was heavily dependent on Mallarmé's theoretical perspective, the *Figaro* Manifesto was the work of the splinter group formed around *La Vogue* and *Le Symboliste*. One of its idiosyncratic argumentative purposes was an attempt to draw a line between the Kahn/Moréas version of Symbolism and the simultaneously burgeoning Decadent Movement, which already had a mouthpiece of its own in *Le Décadent littéraire et artistique*, a periodical launched alongside *La Vogue* in April 1886 by Anatole Baju, who was ambitious to found and head his own school, and wanted to distance himself from Mallarmé's clique. Mallarmé, however, was equally content to be labeled a Decadent or a Symbolist, and was widely regarded as the effective figurehead of both overlapping Movements.

Baju might well have taken his own inspiration from the publication in 1884 of Joris-Karl Huymans' novel *À rebours* (tr. as *Against the Grain* or *Against Nature*), which became, almost instantly, the symbolic Bible of Decadence, in its elaborate analysis of the world-view, attempted lifestyle and artistic tastes of its protagonist, Jean Des Esseintes. At any rate, the success of *À rebours* and the boost it gave to the notion of literary decadence undoubtedly had a good deal to do with the temporary success of *Le Décadent*, which survived longer than the majority of periodicals of the era. Full of admiration for Baudelaire, and crammed with flamboyant symbolism, Huysmans' novel was a dramatic change of direction within the work of its author, previously renowned as a Naturalist and acolyte of Émile Zola and the Goncourt brothers; but Huysmans, like Victor Hugo before him, certainly did not think of himself or his work as "decadent," refused the label, and did not contribute to *Le Décadent*.

Baju had better luck, however, in recruiting Paul Verlaine, who had made his own symbolic contribution to the idea of Decadent literature in 1884, when he published his combative critical study of *Les Poètes maudits* [The Damned Poets], championing poetic outsiders who had allegedly swum against the grain of contemporary fashion and had suffered a sort of martyrdom in consequence. Verlaine's archetypal symbol was Rimbaud, whom he mistakenly assumed to be dead, and with whom he had once had a famously stormy and scandalous relationship, but he also included Mallarmé on his core list of damned poets, as well as the flamboyant Auguste Villiers de l'Isle Adam, author of a significant collection of Decadent prose, *Contes cruels* (1883), which completed a kind of triptych of key Decadent exemplars.

Verlaine was more than happy to be hailed as a symbolic archetype of Decadence in both literature and lifestyle, considering that his alcoholism, drug addiction and tertiary syphilis were as many badges of that entitlement, complementary to his poetry. He became a regular contributor to *Le Décadent*, before also becoming a contributor to *Le Symboliste*. His was the kind of disreputable renown that Gustave Kahn and Jean Moréas did not really want to become exemplary of their Symbolism, but honesty compelled them to admit that Verlaine's poetry made him an important precursor. Mallarmé, although he had an exceedingly sober lifestyle himself, also appreciated Verlaine's work, recognized a definite kinship with his own, and was doubtless proud to find himself included, with lavish praise, in a definitive study of *poètes maudits*.

6.
The Figaro Manifesto

Jean Moréas' Manifesto, begins, as most Manifestos do, in a fashion that is simultaneously aggressive and defensive, proudly declaring what it is against (the list includes, perhaps a trifle quirkily, education, declamation, perverted sentiment and objective description) and then defending its opposition to those things, prior to asserting what it wants to achieve instead. Symbolism, Moréas dutifully points out, is everywhere in literature—he offers examples—but his justification for making it the primary focus of literary endeavor is not merely a matter of emphasis. His argument is partly esthetic, borrowing extensively from both Gautier and Mallarmé, in lauding not merely creativity but a kind of creativity that is various, elastic and prolific in its appropriations—which he carefully refrains from describing as "decadent"—but it is also partly metaphysical.

The metaphysical aspect of Moréas' argument is understandably numinous, but crucial. It is basically Platonic, contending that the world we observe with our senses is best regarded as a kind of simulacrum, a mere shadow of a superior world of "primordial ideas." Because those primordial ideas are inaccessible, at least directly, they can only be suggested by analogy, and can only be grasped—to the extent that they can be grasped at all—via symbolic representations that always retain an element of uncertainty and mystery. Whereas Zola's Naturalism wanted to go behind superficial appearances to search for explanations of the human behavior in material terms, via heredity and physiology, Moréas' Symbolism wanted to look more deeply and more profoundly into a metaphysical reality that was impersonal and elementary, perhaps divine.

It is worth noting that the Moréas Manifesto appeared shortly before an intense redirection of interest in psychological science toward "the unconscious," whose theorists rapidly developed a model of the mind in which the inaccessible contents of the unconscious fraction of the mind could make themselves suggestively accessible to the conscious fraction via symbolic imagery, especially in dreams. Had Moréas had access to a theory of that kind, he might well have recruited it to his notion of the further reality toward which Symbolist art was reaching rather than falling back on Plato. In any case, the intensive interest in dreams and dreamlike forms of narration developed by Symbolist writers not only anticipated but provided useful fuel for the investigation of the unconscious—most obviously by Sigmund Freud and Carl Jung—as well as providing for their own eventual supersession by the Surrealists, who wanted to establish direct channels to the unconscious in the production of their works.

The Moréas Manifesto includes a curious interlude, which casts part of its argument in dramatic form, exploring the idea of poetic creativity, as developed in an essay by the Parnassian poet Théodore de Banville, *Petit traité de poésie* (1872), by representing Banville as a character in a symbolic dialogue. As previously noted, it was relatively easy for critics to interpret the Symbolist Movement as the latest in a series of evolutionary developments of Romanticism, in which the Parnassian poets were seen as intermediates; the dialogue is Moréas' way of trying to explain the differences between his thesis and Banville's, while paying due homage to the accomplishments of those predecessors who could be regarded as precursors.

The heart of the Parnassian Movement was a series of three showcase anthologies entitled *Le Parnasse contemporain*—Mount Parnassus being the mythological abode of the Muses—published in 1866, 1869 and 1876. Mallarmé and Verlaine were both contributors, although the work that came to be seen as centrally definitive of Parnassian poetry by later critics was the lushly exotic mythologically-themed poetry of Charles Leconte de Lisle. Another core member of the Parnassian Movement was Catulle Mendès, whose short-lived *Revue fantaisiste* (1861) had anticipated the philosophy of the showcase anthologies. The Parnassians distinguished themselves from prior Romanticism by an attempt to adopt a more impassive and impersonal voice, allegedly more appropriate to the positivist era, while retaining a fascination with heterocosmic imagery that Naturalism refused. Parnassianism can be seen in retrospect as an awkward hybrid that never really gelled, but it undoubtedly laid significant ground-work for Symbolism. Several of the contributors to the Parnassian anthologies went on to become significant fellow-travelers of the Symbolist Movement, and the salon hosted by the ex-Parnassian José-Maria de Heredia, became a significant Symbolist *cénacle*, second in importance only to Mallarmé's *mardis*.

In Moréas' Manifesto, Banville is cast as a champion of the ideas that had been brought to perfection by the Symbolists, but who did not carry his mission through, and abandoned the Movement. Needless to say, Banville would not have seen his role in that fashion, seeing the relative modesty he retained in his ideas and his work as a sane moderation, whereas the Symbolists often took audacity to a dubious extreme in the extravagance of their language, in a manner that often seemed chaotic to un-sympathetic observers. Committed Symbolists, of course, would not have apologized for their audacity, considering it a virtue in itself, and—perhaps more importantly—would have argued that a recognition of the element of chaos in the nature of things was essentially more honest and truthful than an attempt to discover or impose an artificial order.

In any case, Moréas' criticism of Banville as a defector from the cause came back to bite him when he defected from it him-self in 1891, while Symbolism was commencing its brief heyday, in order to set himself up as the figurehead of his own "École Romane," which preached a return to ancient traditions in search of a lost ideal, in order to achieve an alchemical marriage between Symbolism and Classicism. For once, however, it was the rat that sank while the ship sailed triumphantly on, at least for a while.

7.

The Marketplace

Literary history generally considers the commercial aspects of literary production to be essentially vulgar, and often refuses to grant them any significant causative force or evolutionary influence. From the perspective of the esthete, the current of literary creativity flows downwards, like the Pierian spring from the heights of Parnassus, bearing the inspiration of the Muses. The reality is very different. Literary Movements are born of the economics of publication; when there is no money, there is no movement.

The great majority of those who follow a literary vocation are notoriously poor, and notoriously content in their poverty; sometimes, they take an ostentatious pride in their lack of wealth, as an important symbol of their superiority to the moral corruption of filthy lucre. They have to live, but they do not have to live on their writing, and throughout history very few followers of the vocation have ever been able to do so; even those who are content to starve materially, however, cannot thrive artistically without publication, and publishers cannot thrive without a paying public. Literary historians often seem to assume, tacitly, that publication and paying publics materialize spontaneously—if sometimes a trifle belatedly—in response to genius, but in symbolic terms, that is putting the cart before the horse. It is when paying publics generate a partial vacuum of demand that publications proliferate, and it is when publications proliferate that literary endeavor blossoms in search of viable niches within that partial vacuum of demand. Alas, the process is essentially self-defeating; as vacuums are filled in, the pressure they exert always drops, so they are always ephemeral.

Seen from one point of view, it is true that the Symbolist and Decadent Movements—and the Naturalist Movement too—were responses to the intellectual ambience of the approaching *fin-de-siècle*: a hyperconsciousness of its symbols of social and moral decay, and the mysteries inherent in the attempt to understand the paradoxicality and perversity of that reality. Seen from another viewpoint, however, they were responses to a situation in which printed books and newsprint were becoming much cheaper to produce, because of developments in the technology of paper production and the technology of automated printing machinery, which permitted books and periodicals to reach much larger audiences, much more prodigally. Without that, Stéphane Mallarmé's *mardis* would have remained a series of cozy chats between friends, faint voices in a wilderness. As things were, the expansion of the potential audience created abundant room for innovation and experimentation, as publishers cast their bait and fished for custom, only getting bites occasionally, but sometimes leaving printed legacies that, although unappreciated at the time, remained potentially interesting to posterity.

The *fin-de-siècle* was particularly notable for a new boom in newspaper production. The first such boom in France, in the late 1830s and early 1840s, had secured the fortunes of the Romantic Movement, and had played a major role in shaping its products, by virtue of the invention of the *feuilleton*: a line separating a section of the newspaper page, usually at the bottom, from the news items and the ads. It soon became conventional to run long serials in that space, which often became important factors in boosting and maintaining circulation, and made the fortunes of writers like Alexandre Dumas and Eugène Sue. The *feuilleton* serial became a central institution of nineteenth-century French literature, routinely despised on esthetic grounds but of vast economic importance.

The *feuilleton* serial was still an important economic factor in the major daily newspapers of the *fin-de-siècle*, but even there, particular in *Le Journal* and in the "literary supplements" produced at weekly or monthly intervals by *Le Figaro* and other dailies, there was a very noticeable trend toward replacing the serials with short fiction. In much the same way that the gauge of railway tracks had been determined by technical inertia carrying forward the specifications of horse-drawn carriages, the dimensions of *fin-de-siècle* short fiction were determined by the volume of the space that had long been typical of the sectioning of the page by the *feuilleton*: a space that usually contained between 1,400 and 1,800 words. Weekly periodicals that were structured like books rather than newspapers could, of course, accommodate much longer stories, and frequently did, but their editors, wanting to balance the assortment of articles, poetry, criticism and short fiction, very often gave preference to stories in the same sort of range.

The history of the Symbolist Movement is, in large measure,

the history of the periodicals in which it thrived, most of which were short-lived, but some of which survived long enough to exercise a powerful influence over its development. *Lutèce*, *La Vogue* and *Le Symboliste* led the way, but many others followed, and *Le Décadent* must also be recognized as a significant if slightly displaced pioneer. All three had, however, been anticipated by Félicien Champsaur's *Panurge*, founded in 1883, which published early work by several writers later to become prominent as Symbolists. Champsaur, in fact, became one of the Movement's earliest journalistic defenders, but his truculent personality enabled him to offend virtually everyone in the Parisian literary community in the space of a few years, and he was subjected to occasional resentful diatribes by Symbolists, as well as adherents of other causes.

As previously noted, *La Vogue* was revived twice, by Kahn and Adolphe Retté in 1889 and then by Tristan Klingsor and Henri Degron in 1898, that third incarnation dying with the century in 1900. One of Kahn's associates, G. Albert Aurier, founded *Le Moderniste Illustré* in 1889, although it did not survive that year, while another, Felix Fénéon, associated himself with *La Revue Blanche*, founded in Liège in 1889, which did survive, and became a significant market for Symbolists under his influence when it moved to Paris in 1891. There, it entered into competition as the principal voice of the Symbolist Movement with the *Mercure de France*, edited by Alfred Vallette with the assistance of his wife, Marguerite d'Eymery, alias Rachilde, Remy de Gourmont, Pierre Paul Roux, alias Saint-Pol-Roux, and Jules Renard. Subsequent entries into the marketplace, notably *Le Centaure*, founded in 1896 with an editorial committee including André-Ferdinand Herold, Pierre Louÿs and Henri de Régnier, found it difficult to compete.

The *Mercure* proved by far the hardiest of the Symbolist periodicals, surviving long into the twentieth century, although it widened its scope considerably after the turn of the century, when a few new Symbolist periodicals, including *Vers et Prose*, edited by Paul Fort and founded in 1905, occasionally materialized, but proved ephemeral. While they lasted, however, those periodicals constituted the beating heart of the Symbolist Movement, publishing a good deal of its poetry, a substantial fraction of its critical commentary, and almost all of its short fiction—and the short fiction they published was very largely shaped, quite deliberately, to fit the size of the slots they offered.

8.
The Adaptation of Symbolist Prose to its Primary Marketplace

The market slots provided by the various Symbolist periodicals did not require any substantial adaptation of the Movement's poetry, but they were the cooking-pot in which Symbolist prose took on its characteristic narrative forms and taste sensations, with relatively few prior recipes that could be adopted for modification or variation. There was, however, one very significant fortuitous convergence of esthetic and economic forces.

One of the chief distinctions between Naturalism and Symbolism was visible in their typical formats, which were a logical corollary of their different philosophies of procedure. At its inception, Symbolism was primarily a genre of poetry, because it was in poetic imagery that Symbolist analogies seemed comfortable, and where they already existed in the greatest abundance. Naturalism, by contrast, was primarily a prose genre, and its principal vehicle was the novel, which was pre-adapted to the kind of detailed analyses that Zola and his disciples wanted to carry out. It is not the case that there is no such thing as a "Symbolist novel," but there are relatively few, and most of them are novels whose narrative development is largely naturalistic, but which contain and frame crucial symbolic intrusions or interludes. On the other hand, when Naturalists wrote poetry or short fiction, they found symbolic representation invaluable as a summarizing or encapsulating device, and ostensibly Naturalist novels very often contain Symbolist elements or interludes.

There was, however, one prose genre that was extremely hospitable to Symbolist methods, and that was the prose-poem.

As long ago as the 1850s Baudelaire had given a tremendous exemplary boost to the relatively new genre of the "poem in prose," and before the advent of Symbolism, several of his admirers had dabbled in what was still a rather fugitive genre; Joris-Karl Husymans's first book was a collection of prose-poems, *Le drageoir aux épices* (1874), and Huysmans went on to characterize the prose poem as "the osmazome of literature," osmazome being a term coined for application to a distilled and concentrated essence of flesh (Bovril made its debut in the same era).

The Symbolists, several of whom were enthusiastic champions of "free verse" liberated from the restrictions of rhyme and scansion—Gustave Kahn was particularly vocal in that cause—inevitably found the extra step from free verse to prose poetry very attractive, and began to dabble in its almost as soon as they began to call themselves Symbolists. Several writers active in providing key exemplars of Symbolist literature, including Mallarmé, Saint-Pol-Roux and Hugues Rebell, produced hybrid texts intermediate between free verse and prose. The poem in prose proved to be an ideal format for the deployment of Symbolist imagery, and also very convenient for deployment in the Symbolist periodicals, all of which took it up enthusiastically.

Many Symbolist poems in prose are exactly that, but it did not take long for some of the leading members of the Movement, and its fellow travelers, to realize that, with the aid of a further slight modification, the format also offered an attractive entrée to the market slots opened up by the trend to replace *feuilleton* serials, at least partially, with short stories. That opportunity was taken up with particular profusion by Catulle Mendès, Villiers de l'Isle Adam, Remy de Gourmont, Jean Lorrain, Bernard Lazare and Gabriel de Lautrec. The pages of the early issues of the *Mercure de France* were largely supplied with prose by four writers: Gourmont, Jules Renard, Saint-Pol-Roux and Gaston Danville, and while Renard and Saint-Pol-Roux retained a stern allegiance to the basic principles of prose poetry, the work that Gourmont and Danville did for the magazine soon evolved into a kind of short fiction more reminiscent of Villiers' *contes cruels*.

An entire battalion of specialist writers soon emerged to supply the short story slots in the newspapers on a quasi-industrial basis, by calculated mass production, and many of those writers either emerged from or retained significant links to the Symbolist and Decadent Movements. The writers who developed a genuine expertise in that kind of craftsmanship included Marcel Schwob, Léon Bloy, Henri Ner (who changed the orthography of his name to Han Ryner), Jean Richepin, Octave Mirbeau and Edmond Haraucourt, all of whom had some affinity with the Symbolists, or at least with the Decadent world-view, although none of them would have described himself as a Symbolist with the same commitment as such purists as Stuart Merrill—who edited a showcase anthology of English translations of French prose-poetry, *Pastels in Prose* (1890)—Saint-Pol-Roux or Ephraïm Mikhaël.

The effective hybridization of Symbolist poems in prose with short fiction designed for periodical slots whose basic design was set by the space beneath a *feuilleton* was arguably the most striking feature of the Symbolist's Movement's achievements, and the present anthology is essentially a cabinet of curiosities illustrating the spectrum of that hybridization. The exhibits it contains range from straightforward poems in prose to substantial stories, some of which—but only a few—would have overflowed a standard *feuilleton* slot by some measure.

The longer items, including those adapted to fit the space beneath a *feuilleton*, often employ the narrative strategies and story-arcs typical of short fiction, especially of the *conte cruel* species, but many of them also take advantage of the additional narrative space to elaborate their symbolic imagery, by adding detail and complexity, sometimes to a phantasmagorical extent. It is arguable that all Symbolist prose now seems akin to dreams, or the product of similar alternative states of consciousness, because we have now been educated to see dreams and hallucinations as exercises in spontaneous symbolism, but in their day—from the late 1880s to the early years of the twentieth century—they were not produced with the aid of the kind of hindsight that we can now bring to bear; their visionary quality is more spontaneous, and, in a sense that is not at all insulting, naïve.

The prose poems and stories in this showcase, therefore, are drawn from the well of the unconscious without their extractors having many prejudices as to what the dark waters in question might contain; they are journeys of exploration, not exercises in explanation, and, as such, they have a particular value that became increasingly difficult to reproduce as the twentieth century progressed and all writers and readers became more aware of what the familiar symbols of literature and life might "really mean."

The items in the showcase are, of course, far from being all alike. They range from simple and straightforward descriptions of everyday sensory experience to exercises of stylistic complexity that sail deliberately close to the edge of syntactical and lexical chaos. A few are entirely naturalistic in their substantial content, their Symbolism being subtle and delicate, while some are full-blown fantasies, flamboyant or grotesque. Many of them—especially those adapted for sale to newspapers—are apologues or parables of a sort, although they are usually subversive of conventional morality, sometimes extremely and aggressively so.

The assumed reality behind superficial events that the stories herein attempt to signify elliptically is very various, and in most cases, the suspicion that even the author does not know precisely what it is must be fully justified; but not only is that inevitable, it is by no means a bad thing. If we already knew the truth that we are trying to grasp, there would be no point in groping, and no surprise in brushing or clutching it. Symbolist art always attempts to be surprising, and somewhat mysterious, and the one thing Symbolist prose ought never to be, in the vulgar sense of the term, is prosaic. That is not a paradox, any more than the concept of a poem in prose is an oxymoron. Only a brutal Naturalist could think otherwise, and none of the Naturalists writers who were sometimes viewed as being in opposition to Symbolism was that crass.

Because it was always surprising and always mysterious, the injection of Symbolism into the newspaper *feuilleton* slots of the 1890s enriched them considerably, and in return, the newspapers whose editors made those slots hospitable to Symbolist prose enriched the writers, at last to the limited extent that writers ever are enriched, in a marketplace that is only rarely modified in its routine hostility to the vast majority of its entrants.

9.
The Lexicon of Symbolism

Inevitably, the writers of the Symbolist Movement inherited a vast lexicon of existing symbols, but the whole point of there being a Movement was to develop that lexicon, to adapt the relationships between the symbols and their traditional meanings to a new era, by a process of calculated challenge and transfiguration, and also by augmentation.

To some extent, of course, the entire history of literature is an adaptation of that kind, both in its subjects and its techniques, so what the Symbolists did was merely a process of concentration, a matter of intense focus. Their dealings with a particular set of symbols are of particular interest in terms of the illustration provided by the present anthology, and it is worth running rapidly through a few of them and offering brief comments on the adaptations made in the context of the Movement.

One of the most prolific sources of symbols ripe for modification was, of course, legend, which routinely converts the actors in history into emblematic heroes and villains, and augments them with an additional cast of fictitious characters, who—precisely because they are invented and custom-designed for the purposes of symbolism—often come to seem more real than actual individuals, who rarely stick as faithfully or as effectively to their symbolic scripts.

The mad, bad and dangerous Emperors of Rome have already been mentioned as exemplary symbols of decadence, as well as the *femmes fatales* with whom they were near-contemporaries, but the spectrum of similar emblems of decadence extends much further; even historians, aware of the inadequacies of real emperors, found it politic to invent Sardanapalus and Semiramis to exemplify the fallen Assyrian Empire. All kings, however, tend to be symbolically transfigured by legend, that being the price of being remembered, while their subjects can only achieve a legacy in posterity by becoming heroes, villains or *femmes fatales*—in which capacities real individuals are even less well-adapted to compete with their entirely fictionalized counterparts. (Not all symbolic women of legend are *femmes fatales*, of course, but almost all of the remainder are martyrs, that being the essential sexism of history: beauty dooms or is doomed, and lack of it is synonymous with a lack of symbolic status, save for a few antithetically symbolic hagwives.)

The slight confusion of real events, with which the symbolic investment of kings and warriors routinely has to contend, does not, of course, apply to preachers and priests. All religion is entirely symbolic, from its rites to its theologies, and where living individuals were involved in their creation or propagation, those individuals were swiftly and completely overwhelmed and eclipsed by their symbolism. The force of that process is such that the symbolism of dead religions routinely survives the complete loss of any belief to they might once have played host. The gods of paganism did not lose their symbolic energy when they lost their worshipers; they still remained a rich source of inspiration in the 1890s—certainly richer than they were in the days of sincere belief—and the Symbolist writers had little difficulty in finding new variations of the symbolism of old gods.

There are, of course, all kinds of objects that have been handed down through the ages with a cargo of symbolic values. Most of them are natural: particularly flowers, but also trees and many species of animals, not to mention mountains and gemstones. The sexual symbolism of flowers was highly developed long before biologists provided a sophisticated account of their role in the sexual reproduction of plants and their crucial role in plant evolution. Attempts to analyze nature added a more fundamental layer to that symbolism; early natural philosophy was, like religion, almost entirely an exercise in symbolism, and the Classical theory of the four elements works far better as an exercise in symbolism than it ever did as a theory of physics—which is the reason why its components have survived and thrived, alongside all the no-longer-worshiped gods of paganism, as a convenient apparatus of thought and art.

Even the most superficial glance at Symbolist art, however, and especially its prose, will demonstrate that the starring role in the lexicon of the Symbolist Movement, more important than the goddess Aphrodite/Venus and her son Eros/Cupid, more important than Heaven and Hell, and more important than all the roses, narcissi and other kinds of flowers put together, with the birds, bees and beasts thrown in for good measure, is the weather, particularly the changes induced in it by diurnal and annual cycles. The symbolic frame of almost every Symbolist rhapsody is supplied and energized by winter or summer, dawn or dusk, and the condition of the clouds. The crude symbolism of weather as Nature's emotions—the so-called "pathetic fallacy"—is a foundation-stone of almost all situated narrative, but it is in Symbolist prose that the narrative strategy in question is taken to its extreme.

Anyone who doubts the fundamental pessimism—and hence the fundamental sanity—of Symbolist prose has only to count the sunsets featured in this anthology, and see how far it outweighs the number of dawns. The balance between springs, summers, autumns and winters is more nearly equal, which offers interesting evidence of the symbolism of the various perceived time-scales of our experience of human life. Precisely because the role of the weather is the leading role, however, it is caught in something of a straitjacket, without much scope for variation. The same is true of other natural symbols, such as hearts and tears, whose significance is innate and hence relatively inflexible to variation.

It might seem surprising, given the Symbolist mission, that there is relatively little evidence herein of modern technology, which, being largely innocent of innate symbolism, offered much more scope for invention and complication. The preliminary psychological labor necessary for such explorations takes time, so it would be easy enough to construct an apologetic argument for the relative scarcity of telephones, bicycles and even railway locomotives, steamships and telegraphs, but it would probably not be the correct explanation. Such artifacts were probably seen, at least by the majority of Symbolists, as aspects of the superficial details of life, possessed of insufficient metaphorical depth to provide routes to deep meaning.

Symbolists did not ignore the objective any more than Naturalists ignored the subjective, but it was not where their priority lay. They were, in general, more interested in the past than the present, and more interested in the mythical past than the historical past, because that was where they imagined the best and most easily navigable routes were located to the realm of "primordial ideas"—or, as their Manifesto was not yet able to put it, to the unconscious. They were probably right, but if they were not, it was a difficult mistake to avoid in the *fin-de-siècle*.

It had been possible for a long time, in the nineteenth century, for interested parties to buy guides to the symbolic meanings of flowers, items of clothing and jewels, as well as lexicons of omens and presages, and, of course, almanacs purporting to discover the future by means of the symbolist science of astrology. The other hardy perennial among symbolist sciences, alchemy, still retained its grip on medicine to a large extent. All of that provided grist for the Symbolists' mills, but all of it added together would probably not have countered, in the balance of significance, the interpretation of dreams.

The extent to which psychology and psychiatry still remain symbolist sciences, only a little more sophisticated by injections of naturalism than astrology or alchemy, is controversial today, as is the matter of whether Sigmund Freud's *Die Traumdeutung* (1899; tr. as *The Interpretation of Dreams*) is anything more than a symbolist fantasy. Freud's ideas were not popularized rapidly enough to have any direct influence on the writers of the Symbolist Movement, but the synonymy of their production is surely no coincidence, and the importance of overt and covert dream narrative—whether visionary, hallucinatory, delusional or merely representative of a quirkily altered state of consciousness—in Symbolist prose can hardly be over-estimated.

In spite of Freud's best efforts, and those of his one-time associate Carl Jung, we still have little or no certainty as to what dreams are and what their precise existential significance might be, but we do have every reason to think that dreaming is a psychologically necessary process, the typical forgetfulness of the dreamer notwithstanding. It is at least arguable that literary symbolism also participates in psychological necessity—or, at the very least, that literary activity would be a great deal poorer without it.

If that is accepted—and it is surely difficult to deny it—then the relationship between Symbolism and Decadence acquires an extra dimension of interest. One of the most interesting studies of the European *fin-de-siècle* and its literature was written in Paris by a German, Max Nordau, and published under the title *Entartung* (1892; tr. as *Degeneration*), which adopts a viewpoint not so very different from Desiré Nisard in considering contemporary art to be "degenerate" and mentally unhealthy. Nordau attacks Symbolism specifically, and his key examples of degenerate artistry include Wagner, the Symbolist's musical idol, Huysmans, the author of their prose Bible, and Oscar Wilde, the principal English recruit to the Symbolist Movement, although he does not spare Zola and the Naturalists from inclusion in the same slop-bucket.

Perhaps equally interesting, in juxtaposition with Nordau's analysis, is a major study of the development of a particular set of ideas and symbolic images from the Romantic Movement to the Symbolist Movement by the Italian critic and historian of interior design Mario Praz, *La Carne, la morte et il diavolo nella letteratura romantica* [The Flesh, Death and the Devil in Romantic Literature] (1930; tr. as *The Romantic Agony*) which tells a very similar story from a very different viewpoint, seeing "the Romantic agony" not as a matter of moral degeneracy and madness, but as a kind of torment and martyrdom: a distilled essence of pessimism, rendered graphic by its necessary and necessarily flamboyant symbolism.

The reader confronted with the productions of the Symbolist Movement can still make a choice between the attitudes of Nordau and Praz, deciding to see it as a symptom of mental disease or as a testament to difficult and desperate psychological heroism, although both attitudes tend to downplay its brighter aspects—not all of its *contes* are cruel and not all of its humor black—as well as the fact that many of its practitioners were in search of a genuine ornamental beauty of expression. There is, however, no room for compromise, and no middle course. Even at its quietest and most pensive, Symbolist literature is never anodyne. It is very often laconic, but that is merely a rhetorical device in which to dress its relentless cynicism. It would not be accurate to say that symbolist fiction never has happy endings, but the few items that qualify as exceptions to the rule are invariably infected with irony.

The Symbolism of the Symbolist Movement—which is essentially Decadent, though not necessarily decadent—is not only a fundamentally pessimistic art-form, but one that strives to demonstrate, perhaps more effectively than any other, the fundamental sanity of pessimism. That, in a nutshell, is the central truth at which it aims, and which this eclectic exhibition aspires to display, as the bull's-eye at the heart of its gaudily colorful spectrum.

—Brian Stableford

DECADENCE AND SYMBOLISM:

A SHOWCASE ANTHOLOGY

Part One:
Precursors

CHARLES BAUDELAIRE
(1821-1867)

Charles Baudelaire produced one of the landmark works of French literature in his collection of *Les Fleurs du mal* (1857) famously prosecuted for obscenity; it was reissued in 1861 with the poems suppressed from the first edition restored, and again in 1868, with the introduction by Théophile Gautier that hailed it as an archetypal example of "decadent style." In 1848, a year before the American writer's untimely death, he began translating the works of Edgar Poe, whom he regarded as a kindred spirit, and his translations made Poe into a key exemplar for later Decadent writers. He intended to produce a definitive collection of his prose poems as *Le Spleen de Paris*, but died before doing so, and the work in progress was issued posthumously in volume IV (1869) of the first version of his *Oeuvres complètes* (7 vols 1868-70).

"L'Invitation au voyage" first appeared in *La Présent* 24 août 1857. "An Invitation to the Voyage" was originally published in *The Second Dedalus Book of Decadence: The Black Feast* (Dedalus, 1992).

An Invitation to the Voyage

There is a wonderful country, the so-called land of Cockayne, which I dreamed of visiting in the company of an old friend: a strange land, lost in the mists of our North; one might deem it the Orient of the Occident, the European China, so heated and capricious is the fancy which has free rein there, so enduring and obstinate is the wise and delicate greenery which decorates it . . .

A true land of Cockayne, where all is beautiful, lush, tranquil, authentic; where the luxury of pleasure is reflected in nature; where life is full and every breath is sweet; where disorder, turbulence and the unforeseen are excluded; where happiness is wedded to silence; where the cuisine is poetic, rich and flavorsome all at the same time; where everything reminds me of you, my dearest angel.

You know the feverish malady which takes possession of us in our chilly miseries, that nostalgia for lands unknown, that anguish of curiosity? There is a country made in your image, where all is beautiful, lush, tranquil and authentic, where fancy has built and furnished a western China, where life is full and every breath is sweet, where happiness is wedded to silence. It is there that we ought to live, it is there that we ought to go to die!

Yes, it is there that we must go to breathe, to dream and to overfill the hours with an infinity of sensations. A musician has penned an "Invitation to the Waltz"; who will likewise compose an "Invitation to the Voyage" which one might offer to the woman one loves, to the bosom companion one chooses?

Yes, it is in that atmosphere that one must seek the good life—out there, where the leisurely hours have room for more thoughts, where the clocks sound their good humor with a more profound and more significant solemnity.

On illuminated panels, or on gilt-edged leather of a somber sumptuousness, complacent pictures live discreetly, as calm and profound as the souls of the artists who created them. The light of the sunsets, which so richly colors the dining-room or the salon, is filtered by beautiful curtains or by tall leaded windows with many panes. The furniture is heavy, curiously-wrought and fantastically-formed, guarding with locks the secrets of delicate souls. Mirrors, metallic surfaces, drapes, gold jewelry and porcelain perform a visual symphony, silent and mysterious; and every object, every nook and cranny, including the cracks of the drawers and the pleats of the curtains, breathes out an exotic perfume, a Sumatran forget-me-not, as if it were the very soul of the place.

A true land of Cockayne, I tell you, where all is as rich, tidy and bright as a clear conscience, as a well-stocked kitchen, as a gorgeous golden necklace, as a gaudy display of precious stones! All the treasures of the world are accumulated there, as if it were the house of a man of achievement, to whom the world owes everything. A strange land, as far superior to all others as Art is to mere Nature—which is here remade as a dream: corrected, ornamented, transfigured.

Let them search, let them search even more, let them unceasingly push back the horizons of their happiness, these alchemical gardeners! Let them offer rewards—sixty or a hundred thousand florins—to the man who can achieve their problematic goals! For myself, I have already found my black tulip and my blue dahlia . . .

Incomparable flower—rediscovered tulip, allegorical dahlia!—it is there, is it not, in that beautiful land which is so calm and so dreamlike, that you live and flourish? Would you not find a perfect frame in your own analogue; would you not be mirrored there, as the mystics would have it, by your archetypal counterpart?

Dreams . . . always dreams! The more adventurous and sensitive the soul is, the further dreams transport it from the possible. Every man carries within himself an appropriate measure of natural opium, incessantly secreted and replenished . . . and yet, between birth to death, how many hours can we count to the credit of positive pleasure, or of actions planned and carried out? Shall we ever dwell within—shall we ever even enter—the scene which my imagination has designed . . . the world made in your image?

All this treasure—these furnishings, this luxury, this perfect order, these perfumes, these miraculous flowers—it is you. More than that; you are the great flowing rivers and the tranquil canals; the huge ships which ply them, laden with riches, whose sailors work to the monotonous rhythms of their chants, are the thoughts stirred in my head as it rests on your rising and falling breast. You lead them gently towards that sea, which is the Infinite, mirroring meanwhile the profundity of the sky in the clarity of your beautiful soul . . . and when, wearied by the swell, and heavy with the produce of the Orient, they return to their port of origin, they are still my thoughts, immeasurably enriched, returning from the Infinite to you . . .

ARTHUR RIMBAUD
(1854-1891)

Arthur Rimbaud traveled from his provincial home in Charleville to Paris in 1871 at the invitation of Paul Verlaine; the latter abandoned his family and the two took refuge for a while in London. After their first separation in 1873 an attempted reconciliation in Brussels went badly, and Verlaine shot Rimbaud, although he only wounded him slightly. Rimbaud went home and wrote the collection of prose poems *Un Saison en enfer* (1873), which he published himself. He returned to England with the poet Germain Nouveau, where he compiled his poetry collection *Illuminations*, but could not publish it. He gave up writing and enlisted in the Dutch Colonial Army, but soon deserted, living on the run thereafter in various far-flung places, until he was forced by illness to return to France in 1891. In the meantime, Verlaine, assuming that he was dead, had made him the star of his study of *Poètes maudits*, and obtained publication for various works; *Illuminations* was partially published in *La Vogue* and other items in *Le Symboliste*, thus placing Rimbaud albeit belatedly, at the heart of the Movement.

"Nuit en enfer" first appeared in *Un Saison en enfer*. "A Night in Hell" was originally published in *The Second Dedalus Book of Decadence: The Black Feast* (Dedalus, 1992).

A Night in Hell

I have swallowed a prodigious draught of poison—thrice blessed be the counsel which has come to me!—and my guts are afire. The violence of the venom torments my limbs, deforms me, and casts me down. I am dying of thirst, suffocating, unable to cry out. This is Hell, eternal suffering! See how the flames leap up! I burn, as one must. Ho, demon!

I have caught a glimpse of that conversion which leads to goodness and happiness. Let me describe the vision; the atmosphere of hell cannot tolerate hymns! It was of millions of charming creatures, a sweet spiritual harmony, strength and peace, noble ambitions and I know not what.

Noble ambitions!

And yet this is life—if damnation is eternal! A man who wishes to mutilate himself is certainly damned, is he not? I believe that I am in Hell, therefore I am in Hell. That is the fulfillment of the catechism. I am the slave of my baptism. Parents, you have secured my misery and your own. Poor innocent! Hell has no power over pagans—I am still alive! Much later, the delights of damnation will become more profound. A crime, quickly, that I might fall into oblivion at the behest of man-made law.

Shut up, shut up! This is shame, and reproach: Satan himself says that fire is ignoble, that my anger is utterly foolish—enough! Errors have been whispered to me, magic spells, false perfumes, puerile music—and to think that I grasp the truth, that I see justice: my judgment is sane and settled, I am ready for perfection. Pride. My scalp is dry. Pity! Lord, I am afraid. I am thirsty, so thirsty! Ah, childhood, grass, rain, rocks in a pool, moonlight as the clock struck twelve . . . the devil is in the belfry at such an hour. Mary! Holy Virgin! . . . the horror of my stupidity.

Down there, are they not honest souls, who wish me well? Come . . . I have a pillow over my mouth, they cannot hear me, they are phantoms. Anyway, no one ever thinks about anyone else. Let no one approach. I smell something burning, to be sure.

The hallucinations are innumerable. That is surely what has always afflicted me: lack of faith in history, obliviousness of principles. I shall keep quiet about it: poets and visionaries would be jealous. I am a thousand times richer than they are; let us be as mean as the sea.

Ah, look there! The clock of life has suddenly stopped. I am no longer in the world. Theology is to be taken seriously; hell is certainly below—and Heaven on high. Ecstasy and nightmare slumber in a nest of flame.

What mischief is performed while one waits in the country-side . . . Satan, Ferdinand, runs riot with the wild seeds . . . Jesus walks on the purple brambles without trampling them down . . . Jesus once walked on troubled waters. The lantern showed him to us standing up, white-skinned and brown-haired, flanked by an emerald wave . . . I will unveil all mysteries: mysteries religious or natural, death, birth, the future, the past, cosmogony, the void. I am a master of phantasmagoria.

Listen . . . !

I have all the talents! There is no one here and there is some-one: I do not wish to spread my treasure far and wide. Do they want negro songs or belly-dancing? Do they want me to disap-pear, or to immerse myself in the quest for the ring? What do they want? I will make gold, or sovereign remedies.

Have faith in me, then; faith is a solace, a guide, a healing. All of you, come—even the little children—that I may console you, that one might pour out his heart to you . . . the marvelous heart! Poor men, laborers! I do not ask for prayers; with your confidence alone I shall be happy.

And let us think about me. I have scant regret on behalf of the world. I am lucky that I no longer suffer. My life, regrettably, was naught but tender folly.

Bah! Let us make all the faces we can.

Decidedly, we are outside the world. There is no longer any sound. My sense of touch is gone. Ah, my chateau, my Saxony, my wood of willows! Evening, mornings, nights, days . . .

How tired I am!

I ought to have a Hell of my own for wrath, a Hell of my own for pride, and a Hell to cherish; a concert of Hells.

I am dying of lassitude. This is the tomb; I am going to be with the worms, horror of horrors! Satan, joker, you wish to melt me with your charms. I protest. I protest! One prick of the fork, one gush of flame.

Ah, to climb again to life! To stare upon our deformities. And that poison, that kiss a thousand times accursed! My weakness, the cruelty of the world! My God, have pity, hide me, I am still too bad! I am hidden and I am not.

It is the fire that rises up again with its damned soul.

THÉOPHILE GAUTIER
(1811-1872)

Théophile Gautier was one of the stars of the Romantic Movement and began a memoir of his involvement with it that was published posthumously as *Histoire du Romantisme* (1874). His novel *Mademoiselle de Maupin* (1835), the preface to which expounded his doctrine as *l'art pour l'art* was originally intended as a quasi-documentary account of the seventeenth-century cross-dressing opera star and duelist Julie d'Aubigny, who used the stage name Mademoiselle Maupin; Gautier transfigured her into an archetype of his own in one of the first great Symbolist novels. The novella "Une nuit de Cléopâtre" (1838), a similarly flamboyant transfiguration, launched a tradition of lush historical fantasies that became the backbone of the Symbolist novel, carried forward magisterially by Gustave Flaubert's *Salammbô* (1862), Anatole Fracc's *Thaïs* (1887) and Pierre Louÿs' *Aphrodite* (1896). Gautier's introduction to the 1868 edition of Baudelaire's *Les Fleurs du mal* crystallized and popularized the notion of decadent style, providing a heart to complement the backbone.

"Babylonian Dreams" is excerpted from a translation of the fictionalized essay "Paris futur" (Le Pays, 20-21 decembre 1851), which was originally published in *Investigations of the Future* (Black Coat Press, 2012).

Babylonian Dreams

Often, when I stroll in some somber plain at dusk, and the livid horizon is cluttered by great banks of cloud, heaped on top of one another like the blocks of an immense aerial city fallen into ruins, Babylonian dreams come to me, and phantasmagorias in the style of Martin[1] pass before my eyes.

I begin by carving gigantic trenches out of the flanks of distant hills for the foundations of edifices; soon, the angles of frontons are sketched in the vapor; pyramids cut out their marble faces; obelisks rise up in a single jet, like granite exclamation marks; immeasurable palaces are elevated in superimpositions of retreating terraces like a colossal staircase, which only giants of the pre-Adamite world could climb.

I see stout columns extending, as strong as towers, fluted with spiral grooves in which six men could hide, friezes made of sections of mountains and covered with monstrous zodiacs and menacing hieroglyphs; the arches of bridges curving over a river that gleams throughout the city it traverses like a Damascene sword in a half-cut pass; lakes of salt water in which domesticated leviathans leap, shining in a radiant light, and the great golden circle of Ozymandias sparkling like a wheel detached from the chariot of the sun.

Bathed at its base in the ardent russet mist thrown up by the restless activity of the city, seething with the work of pleasure, the temple of Belus[2] invades the sky, where it challenges the lightning, by means of eight convulsive efforts, each of which produces an enormous tower taller than the steeple of Strasbourg or the pyramid of Giza; the cloud cut its sides with their stripes

---

1 John Martin (1789-1854), famous for vast paintings of Biblical and mythological scenes unparalleled in their mystic grandeur, such as the *The Fall of Babylon* (1818).

2 Belus is the Babylonian god also known as Bel or Baal; but Gautier has in mind a legend said by secondary sources to have been recorded in a book by Artabanus, in which Belus was a member of a race of Titans who escaped their destruction by the gods and built a tower in which to reside in the city that became Babylon.

and the entablatures of the final stage are blanched by threads of eternal snow.

Other temples also inscribe their severe and magnificent forms on the horizon, whose grandeur only serves to make the enormity of the temple of Belus stand out more sharply; and in the background, in the incandescent redness of the sunset, one divines the dismantled silhouette of Lylac,[1] the colossus of pride, the walls of which the Ancient of Days has caused to crack by setting his hand on its summit as on an excessively weak staff. The flames of the evening filter through the cracks, through which behemoths and mastodons pass without brushing their carapaces, and create the most bizarre plays of light; one might think that a conflagration was trying to devour the formidable ruin that the wrath of God has not entirely cast down, and whose summit still rises above the waters of a new Deluge.

Here and there, the black chaos of buildings lights up; basalt sphinxes display their hindquarters and stretch out their claws on granite pedestals, forming an avenue a league long at the door of some palace. Above the rooftops, in the midst of the crowns of palm trees and baobabs, surges the trunk of a bronze elephant, blowing a jet of water into the air, which the wind scatters into fine pearls and silvery mist. Ramps go up and down, tracing angles on the flanks of terraces; the prows of ships, the tips of masts and antennae betray the presence of canals; staircase-streets bring daylight into the crowd of edifices, and in the distance, according to the hazards of perspective, the girdling walls appear, creating a roadway three hundred meters from the ground, on which six or eight teams of four might gallop abreast.

That, at least, bears some resemblance to a city, and stands out jaggedly against the background of the sky. Cause the shadows of passing clouds to soar over it, in order that the scene might be complete, like prodigious black eagles; strike with unexpected gleams the formicary of the multitudes that crowd the squares, the crossroads and the external doorways; cause caravans to un-

1 Gautier also refers to a place called Lylac in a book about travels in Spain, where he couples it with the tower of Babel, but there does not seem to be any reference to it outside his work.

furl in the plains of sand, like the coils of infinite serpents, laden with the treasures of all the worlds, and enthrone, in the center of the grandiose city, a king as powerful as a God, as feared as a God, and invisible as a God, by the name of Tiglath-Pileser, Merodach-Baladan, or Belshazzar, who, by his enormities, will force the Eternal to write on his walls!

A city like that plunges as far into the ground as it rises into the air; its roots go in search of the nucleus of the world and only stop when they arrive at the surfaces of interior lakes or the furnace of the central fire. Beneath the living city extends the dead city, the black city of motionless inhabitants. Broad ventilation-shafts, gaping like the mouths of Hell, lead to the region of crypts and syringes.[1] Funereal tribes labor in the vomitory cities, tribes of gravediggers, the slaves of death; those who melt the natrum and the bitumen in boilers; those who weave the mortuary bandages; the coffin-makers, the painters, the gilders and the sculptors of tombs—all those whose works will never see the light of day, and who trace inscriptions by the yellow light of a lamp that lacks air, which are immediately covered by shadow and will only ever be read by sightless eyes.

That crepuscular population, which has no communication with the upper city except for the corpses that it receives, could fill a city larger than Rome; they are born, they marry and they die in that obscurity. There are vanquished nations there, forced to re-enter the earth and cede their place in the sun to the victorious people; the necropolis whose threshold they inhabit is the work of vanished races, and its immensity frightens even the most audacious Babylonian architects.

There are interminable corridors, all lined with panels of hieroglyphs and cosmogonic bas-reliefs, leading to pits as black as the abyss and as profound, into which one descends by means of bronze crampons. There are chambers hollowed out of the living rock, the center of which is occupied by enormous sarcophagi of basalt and porphyry, without anyone being able to comprehend

---

1 The term syrinx, of which syringes is the plural, refers in this context to a kind of Egyptian tomb hollowed out of rock.

how they were brought here; rooms in which torches cannot illuminate the depths, where entire cycles of generations, complete reigns with their princes, their mages, their poets, their soldiers, their horses and their war-elephants sleep, with their backs to columns sustaining ceilings that one cannot see, so high are they.

The further one descends, the more the mummies take on gigantic proportions and strange physiognomies. Under the pale brown of balm unknown profiles are designed, with features as if carved with blows of a hatchet in blocks of stone; faces reminiscent of the muzzles of primitive animals; foreheads in which the wrinkles seem to be streaks of lightning or the beds of torrents; unvanquished limbs that corruption dares not attack, and the muscles of which are tangled like the beams of a scaffold. One can see there the companions of Nimrod, primitive hunters who drew bows made from the jawbones of whales, and fought hand-to-hand with the mastodon, the paleotherium, the dinotherium and all those colossal and monstrous beasts produced by an earth intoxicated by strength and youth, which, if they had lived, would have ended up devouring the world.

The contemporaries of Chronos and Xixuthros[1] repose in the inferior circles into which no one ever descends, because it requires lungs more powerful than those of present generations to tolerate the air, impregnated with the bitter perfumes of the sepulcher. The secrets that envelop those mysterious tombs are lost, or only known to the old men of the subterranean people, so laden down with years that no one any longer understands their archaic language. Below them are couched the kings who lived before Adam, but the crust of the earth has thickened so much since their death that they lie at an incalculable depth, and it is as if they had become the bones of the world.

Is that not a necropolis superior to Père-Lachaise, the cemetery of Montmartre, etc., etc?—where we cannot leave our dead

---

1 Chronos is a common misrendering of Cronus, the name of the leader of the Titans who rebelled against his father Uranus but was eventually overthrown by his own son, Zeus. Xixuthros is a Hellenization of the name of the Sumerian king Zuisudra, who was said to have ruled immediately before the Deluge and to have survived it, much as Noah did in Hebrew mythology.

to sleep peacefully for more than seven years, where the phrase *concession à perpetuité* is a true derision and signifies no more than the "always" of lovers;[1] where the tombs are veritable playthings devoid of sadness, dignity and grandeur, and which give rise to the belief that a population of dwarfs is interred there, so meager are their proportions and so miserly the space allotted to them. But we have no greater understanding of death than of life, and, under the pretext of progress, we shall soon have gone back four or five thousand years. The imprint of Adam's foot, which can still be seen in the rock of the isle of Serendip, is nine handbreadths long! We have degenerated somewhat since.

XAVIER FORNERET
(1809-1884)

Xavier Forneret lived in Paris from 1837-40, and was enthusiastic to participate in Théophile Gautier's *petit cénacle*, but Gautier and Gérard de Nerval never accepted him, deeming him to be an eccentric bourgeois devoid of talent; he allegedly became a recluse living in a Gothic folly. He could afford to publish his own writings, and did, but he remained obscure until his work was rediscovered by André Breton, and he was hailed as a significant precursor of surrealism. Had the Symbolists ever noticed him, he would have been hailed as an important precursor of their own Movement.

"La Diamante de l'herbe" first appeared in 1840 in the collection *Pièce de pieces, Temps perdu*, published by the author. "The Diamond in the Grass" is original to the present volume.

---

1 Paris developed an acute shortage of graveyard space in the eighteenth century, which eventually led to the remains they contained being dug up and removed to ossuaries in the catacombs in order to make way for new graves. Famous people sometimes obtained a "concession of perpetuity" for their tombs, but prestige is fleeting in a society continually overturned by revolutions, so many such concessions were subsequently overturned.

The Diamond in the Grass

According to what is said, I believe, the glow-worm announces its appearance, more or less renewed, more or less adjacent to a particular place, more or less multiplied, because, still according to what is said, it moves under the influence of what is going to happen, the glow-worm presaging either a tempest at sea or a revolution on land, in which case it is somber, reilluminates and is extinguished; or a miracle, in which case one scarcely sees it; if a murder, it is ruddy; if it is going to snow, its feet turn black; for cold, it is incessantly bright; rain, it changes location; public festivals, it quivers in the grass and pours out innumerable little jets of light; hail, it moves jerkily; wind, it seems to sink into the ground; fine weather for the following day, it is blue; a fine night, it stars the grass almost as for public festivals, except that it does not quiver. For the birth of a child the worm is white; finally, at the moment when a strange destiny is accomplished, the glow-worm is yellow.

I do not know to what extent these sayings ought to be believed; but here goes: I shall tell a story.

One evening, when all the breath of the angels was blowing over human faces—one of those evenings when one would like to have a thousand lungs in order to give them to that air, which seems to come from the gardens of heaven—under enormous and old trees planted in the blades of grass, a detached house displayed to the moon its oblong and dilapidated wings.

There was water there, which wept in passing over a bed of thorns. There were also many green-tinted stones, in which the fingers of time had made big holes; a great deal of moss round the stones; a great many dried leaves, perhaps accumulated over three or four years; a great deal of mystery, a great deal of silence; a great deal of distance from anything that was human life. There, a man might have believed himself to be the first man or the last, at the creation or the judgment of God. Oh, how the moon appeared to offer to every leaf of the old trees, to every stone of the detached house, to the water that went away, to the branches that stayed, her grave melancholy and her white tears! But soon she wearied of gazing at the earth, covered herself momentarily with an almost black veil, and then there was no longer anything to illuminate the things of the abandoned place except a slight fire in the grass. It was a little glow-worm springing from all sides in stars; it was predicting a fine day, after the night that was passing.

Honeysuckle came over the roof of the house, sliding through the windows, twisting and letting itself collapse of old age; and when the moon reappeared, the house resembled a white head, having at its summit long tresses of green hair that came to caress the stone with eyes full of tears.

On the pavement, sprinkled with dust and old plaster detached from the ceilings and walls of the ruined dwelling, were the freshly made imprints of a man's feet, and fine light marks that announced that a woman's feet had also brushed that place of profound solitude.

A bronze lamp, retained by a cord of pink silk, was vacillating imperceptibly in the heart of the building. Its wicks were in a state to give light, and it was easily recognizable that they had been burning since the previous night.

Over that lamp there was a shade, like that of a hooded lantern, and from that shade a brown-colored ribbon was attached to the only remaining arm of an armchair, the other doubtless having lost the battle of years.

On the very broad armchair, clad in a fabric that had once been amaranth velvet, two places were marked; the interstice allowed it to be observed that the two people who had been sitting there had clung to one another very closely. Many places on the armchair were covered in dust, while elsewhere, everything was shiny, rubbed, waxed, and almost worn away by the bodies that seemed to have taken possession of one another frequently.

The armchair was facing the lamp, which was hanging a short distance from the ground and from it.

In addition to the water that was flowing outside, something could be heard inside the house that was quivering in all its corners; and when the gaze of the moon illuminated some of them, the eye distinguished objects similar to large patches of exceedingly black ink, to which hazard gave paws, against the whiteness of a piece of paper: objects moving and stopping, then moving again, and marking out beneath them trials of reflections, like those launched by the wings of joyful cicadas, or soap bubbles in the sunlight, or the scales of fish seen at a certain time of day; a clan of spiders, gathered together, with a trousseau of webs, the despair of flies and the rescue of cut fingers.

The spider was displaying her independence proudly there, having nothing to fear, neither the screams of the child nor the woman who might detect her presence, nor the duster of the valet that might stun her, nor the soles of shoes or slippers that might crush her, nor even the tongue of a candle that might burn her. The spider lived there in complete security in her dusty domain. The glow-worm would not have to put on for her its hue of strange destiny, its yellow hue. The spider spun herself a silken good fortune, soft and uniform, any day, at any hour, any minute, any second or any fraction of a second.

Flowers had shed their petals on the armchair and throughout the house. A little bench, covered by a cushion, touched the front feet of the set of repose, and only served the right-hand place; at least, one could suppose so; the remaining arm was also on the right.

Under the support of the little bench, disposed in the form of a drawer, there was an ussassi box that had often been disturbed and replaced in its case; its corners were softened, splintered and rounded out by dint of being touched and retouched repeatedly.[1]

Nine o'clock chimed at the moment when the moon was giving her gaze, when the spider was spinning, when the glow-worm was shining.

The water, like the time, was still passing.

Soon, a young woman appeared in the line of earth and sand of a path. Her dress was white, and flying under the mouth of the wind. Her hair was agitating like gilded waves over her bosom, as pale as her dress and as breathless as her hair. Her mouth, oh,

---

1 In François Raymond's 1824 dictionary of the arts and sciences, "ussassi" is defined as a species of fruit-tree growing in India.

her mouth! You might have thought that she was posed on her lips, so much was she quivering, so much was the voluptuous agitation applied there that only exists when lips are on lips, when hearts are upon hearts. In all of her features there was all of hope; in the most covert of her gazes there was the death that a happiness often gives: you know, the death that arrives by means of a frisson that overtakes you, by means of a tightness that binds your veins, by virtue of the ecstasy that halts your life and leaves you the warmth of your blood; do you know?

That is because, you see, the woman was going to an amorous rendezvous. She believed in God, of course: in God, the saints, the angels, in everything. Oh yes, she believed. If you had been able to see her heart leaping in her breast in the midst of her holy beliefs you would have said to yourself: "What's the matter with that woman? Oh, what's the matter with that woman?"

And no matter how strong and well-armed you might have been, if she had been able to read your thoughts through your face, she would have replied to you: "Get back! Get back! Let me pass! I'm going to my amorous rendezvous, and even if, in passing, I have to leave you a part of my body on your sword, and several of my broken bones molded to that part of my body, provided that I still have enough to carry my heart to my lover's, provided that I have enough to give a breath to his kiss, a smile to his mouth, a gaze to his eyes, a tear to his soul, well, let my blood flow afterwards under the point of your weapon, let my flesh separate and spread under its blade, it doesn't matter to me, you see, it doesn't matter! But please, my God, my God, let me go to my amorous rendezvous, let me go to the paradise of Heaven!"

And she went, she went, the young woman, caressing the earth with her feet, as if she had kissed it, perfuming, by her passage, the flowers and the air; leaving everywhere a little of her gaze, a little of her breath, a little of her soul.

She said: "So I'm going to look at him, to speak to him, to hear him, to touch him! Oh, yes, I shall have all that. My voice will mingle with his; but his is a thousand times softer. Oh, if you heard him, truly he makes me die with the words of his heart, truly. You can't imagine how he says: 'I love you!' No, for he never says it, and I hear it incessantly. The sun warms the veins of the earth; he burns mine. My God, how can I tell you what I feel? I'm very embarrassed. There's something, when he's there, utterly transparent, utterly illuminated, utterly suave, which rejoices, which astonishes, which overwhelms. I hear sounds, which bite the ear at first, and then caress it afterwards, and then envelop it with melody. I hear kisses, that silver of the lips, which ring all around me, then cries that begin, continue, swell, undulate and go away, fading out. Is that what I feel, what I hear, what I see? No, perhaps that's still not it. Sometimes images, thin leaves of gold, seem to pass over my head; whirlwinds of spirits, with wings that make no shadow anywhere, come to brush my face; ribbons in shades infinite in number unroll, spread out, crumple, shine, and fall who knows where; a Genius, which God alone knows and sends, surrounds me with an impulsion that sometimes bumps me, retains me, chills me, reanimates me, melts me. It's as if I were receiving life three or four times, and death three or four times."

The young woman looked at the stones, the bushes, the grass, and murmured to them whatever was agitating in her.

Soon, the path was lost in the location of the detached house and took the young woman away. She listened to its water, felt something very soft, very soft, and smiled at its little worm, which had just hidden the moon.

She went in.

The little worm turned yellow.

Immediately, she fell to her knees, made the sign of the cross and appeared open-mouthed before one of the places of the armchair. Her fingers mingled softly with bunches of violets and jasmine, separating their white and blue flowers from their stems; then she threw them on the armchair like a petty priest sprinkling incense at Corpus Christi. A barrier weighed upon her breath, and a veil of tears was over her eyes.

That adoration lasted almost as long it takes to say five *Pater nosters* and four *Ave Marias* . . .

After that, the young woman got up, sat down, and did not light the lamp, because she was no longer occupied with anything; already, she resembled nothing more than a machine still moving slightly. She was anxious breathless, surrounded by frissons, for she was waiting, and no one came. She only brought the ussassi box out of its hiding place in order to kiss all its faces, all its sections, all its corners.

We shall not attempt to say what she felt during an hour, not seeing anyone enter the house. It would be as difficult to describe as the world is to remake. We only believe that a heavy smoke stifled her, that teeth gnawed her, that ropes of fire bound her heart, that she struggled, languished and died under something frightful.

Suddenly fear seized her when she saw, a little above the obscure lamp, eyes that were gazing at her.

For some time she remained fixed to the armchair by those two moving nails, but a sudden effort grabbed her by her dress and made her flee, sowing with her hips: "Oh, what if he were dead! Oh, what if he were about to die!"

And she ran, she ran, and fell over her lover, who had just been murdered.

There was an owl on the lamp in the detached house, which was swaying gravely, and which, at the moment when the young woman went out, was mirrored by the glow-worm.

The next day, at the same hour, that glow-worm, which had turned yellow for the man, turned yellow for the woman; she had poisoned herself where she had fallen.

THÉODORE DE BANVILLE
(1823-1891)

Théodore de Banville was a late recruit to Romanticism, and a dedicated disciple of Gautier's doctrine of *l'art pour l'art*. His *Odes funambulesques* (1857) was heavily influenced by Victor Hugo. He then became one of the prime movers of *Le Parnasse contemporain*. His highly-regarded analysis of the forms and methods of French poetry, *Petit traité de poésie française* (1872) became one of the key reference-points of Symbolist theory in Jean Moréas' Manifesto, calling for a purification and perfection of art that the Symbolist poets were ambitious to provide.

"La Vie en rêve" first appeared in volume 1 of *Le Nouveau décameron* (Dentu, 1884)—the first of ten, featuring works by various hands. "Life in Dream" is original to the present volume.

Life in Dream

One day in October, during the hour of recreation, in the Mesdames Olliver's celebrated boarding-school for demoiselles, situated in a silent quarter of the Vieille Estrapade, the gardens of which—thus far respected by the new constructions—occupied an immense area, two young girls, Blanche de Castan, aged fourteen, and Jeanne de Meslide, aged thirteen, disdaining their companions' games, were taking pleasure in admiring the rosy and gilded furnace of the setting sun, while dead leaves carried by the wind swirled at their feet.

"What's the matter, my dear?" said Blanche, stopping suddenly. "Your eyes are shining with an unaccustomed gleam; your voice is tremulous, you're marching with a more agile step than usual, and a joyful expression is bursting in all the features of your face. What's the matter? What's happened? Have you, by any chance, found a treasure, or a pearl the size of a hazelnut, in that forsaken grotto where a little spring murmurs, and into which no one except you ever goes?

"Oh," said Jeanne, "you're right to interrogate me, for I need to make you my confidences, and my heart is burning to pour itself into yours. Yes, I'm mad, I'm in ecstasy, I'm happy. That torment, that happiness, that unknown enchantment about which we've spoken so often, I now know. I'm in love."

"You?" said Blanche.

"Listen," said Jeanne. "He's a young man of seventeen, handsome, with short black hair, dark pensive eyes, with red lips above which a slight black moustache is scarcely born, very slender and almost invisible. His neck is robust, but as white as ours. His name is Henri; he's studying to enter Saint-Cyr, because he's going to be a soldier, and he adores me. When he thinks about me, his eyes shine and become very moist, and he scarcely dares to name me, Jeanne, and pronounces my name in a whisper."

"But where is he?" asked Blanche, quite astonished. "Where have you seen him?"

"I haven't seen him," said Jeanne, "but I suddenly remembered him; his image has been traced distinctly in my memory, with the most fugitive details; I recognized the flash of his exceedingly white teeth, his long eyelashes, eyebrows as if traced by a paintbrush, and his proud mouth, which only softens for me."

"But if you haven't seen him," said Blanche, her surprise reaching its culmination, "how do you know he exists?"

"Well," said Jeanne, excitedly, "I know him, I see him, I sense him. If he didn't exist, how could he be present in my thoughts? How would I have learned his name? How would I have divined that he loves me? Where he is, I don't know; perhaps behind the high wall that encloses this garden, for we don't know who lives there; perhaps it's his parents. But what I'm certain of is that I sense that I'm in his presence, before his eyes, very close to him, and he'll surely find a means of showing himself, of writing, of cheating the absence that separates us."

"Well, my dear," said Blanche, cheerfully, "all of that is a simple chimera, and I advise you frankly to renounce that dream."

"Oh, you bad girl!" said Jeanne, whose breast rose violently, whose gaze became wild and whose cheeks were flooded by large tears.

Blanche immediately strove to console her, but also to cure her, and make her understand the childishness of her dream of amour. Far from convincing her, however, she only succeeded in rendering her desolate and wounding her. The recreation ended; the bell was already ringing to recall the girls to study; Jeanne was still weeping, unable to stifle her sobs, and trembling in case one of the mistresses might hear them. Blanche had a fatal idea. Since she could not persuade her friend that Henri did not exist, why should she not play that character, whom she would cause to act and would govern at her whim, in order to suppress him as soon as possible?

In fact, she settled on that project, which she thought sage, and which was to lead to irreparable misfortunes; for passion is never so redoubtable as when it marches in spite of all obstacles, guided by terrible childish logic.

Two days later, having gone to sit down in the grotto that she had adopted, Jeanne found a letter there bearing the address *Mademoiselle Jeanne de Meslide* on the envelope. She hastened to open it, certainly without astonishment; on the contrary, she thought that the expected letter was arriving very belatedly. She read it and devoured it, all the way to the signature, to the name *Henri* that she always had in her heart and on her lips, delightedly savoring the joy of believing herself to be loved.

Written by Blanche de Castan, who, with her fourteen years, did not know much more about it than her young friend, the letter was one of those that a little girl might have written to her doll; it was all the more dangerous for that, and attained its goal more accurately, being exactly within the range of its reader.

Jeanne found it natural that her lover would not only praise her beauty but the details of her attire as a boarding-school pupil; it seemed to her quite simple that Henri knew the details of her classes, her studies and her walks; the contrary would have astonished her. As she had implored the communication, she replied without hesitation, without regret, like a woman—every young girl is a woman!—who had immediately given herself forever, and she left her letter in the same place where she had found Henri's pretended letter.

And that correspondence continued thus, foolish, ardent and intoxicated, all the more plausible for Jeanne because she plunged more docilely into the traditions of tales of enchantment, and, in talking to her about conquering worlds for her, of sitting her on thrones, and of putting diadems on her forehead, Henri seemed to be remaining in the strict measure and saying exactly what he ought to say.

But Jeanne was not alone in being enfevered and burned by those pages full of ecstasy and folly; in reading them, and in writing them, Blanche was also infected by the contagion, and savored a thousand delights and tortures in her turn. Was she also in love? Was she that Henri whose role she was playing and who, invoked by the imagination of the two girls, had ended up becoming really alive between the two of them? She did not know; she would have found it very difficult to assign an object to the passion that was devouring her in her turn, but she had played too imprudently with amour not to be burned by the flame that spares nothing. Prey to a delirium that was no less violent for being born of a simple fiction, having imprudently awakened in herself the thirst to love and be loved that is dormant in every feminine soul, it was now with aimless but unsimulated ardor that she wrote the letters whose incendiary language excited her as dangerously as her friend Jeanne.

Nevertheless, Blanche was the first to recover her reason, because she found herself facing a material embarrassment that she had not foreseen. That was because, at a moment when the reckoning was approaching very rapidly, she was not at all sure how to make the character that she had audaciously taken on go into action. Jeanne de Meslide, who, like all young girls, could very easily find what Agnes found, wanted to see her Henri and oblige him to show himself—an embarrassing summons for a lover who did not exist.

Twice a month, Jeanne went to spend a day with her mother; on two other occasions she went for a walk with the pupils of the school; it was necessary for Henri to be cruelly devoid of imagination not to succeed in finding himself in her passage and exchanging a glance with her. She gave him a thousand means, which Henri eluded with a timidity that resembled bad faith. But in the end; it was necessary to do it. Not admitting obstacles, as imperious as a conqueror and a little girl. Jeanne commanded the presence of her lover, who had no more good or bad excuses to offer in order to dissimulate himself.

Blanche de Castan found herself driven back to the wall, so she was seized by the ferocity of the dramatic inventor—the worst of all, for the maker of plays, embarrassed by one of his actors, kills him off with less remorse than a professional assassin would suffer. Blanche did not take malevolence as far as killing Henri, but he was sent to the Midi by his parents, as the necessity of a severe chest infection. In Cannes, where he dreamed under the laurels while gazing at the blue sea, there was no longer a medium-sized wall to climb in order to deposit letters in the little grotto where the spring murmured, so Henri was obliged to maintain silence, to the great relief of his young poetess, who was at the end of her tether.

Blanche hoped that, no longer having anything to write or read, Jeanne would console herself naturally, and forget an Henri who no longer manifested himself in any way.

On the contrary, however, the girl reread the old letters, nourished herself thereon, and incessantly recommenced savoring the deceptive intoxication.

Soon, as if hallucinated, devoured by an invisible and profound illness, she grew thin, became as pale as wax, and ceased to eat and speak. She went for walks alone, no longer even confiding in Blanche, and nothing was any longer to be seen but her immeasurable wide eyes. When consulted, the school's physician could not hide his anxiety; he was dealing with a malady that he could not explain, and was watching a charming young girl perish without knowing by what ailment she was afflicted.

Madame de Meslide was obliged to come to fetch Jeanne and take her home, but there too she was mute, estranged from everything and tottering. Soon, she no longer had the strength to stand upright, and was confined to bed. Then, holding her icy hands in her own, Madame de Meslide begged her to confide in her.

Without a struggle, without resistance, without having to be begged, as had been feared, Jeanne recounted her love for Henri, the letters, the entire little school romance. There was no advising her to be reasonable; she did not ask for anything, she did not want anything, she was dying; and willingly, in order to delay the death of a child devoid of will, the unhappy mother set forth in search of Henri, the sight of whom was the only thing that could save the child.

But how could one find a lover whose very name was unknown, and who doubtless had his letters carried by sylphs? For the Mesdames Olliver demonstrated very easily that it was impossible to sneak into the school, that its neighbors had no young son, and that if some audacious individual had attempted to scale the high wall he would infallibly have been devoured by Tom, the giant dog that was released into the gardens at night, almost famished, to sharpen his ferocious fangs.

That uncertainty did not last long, however. Frightened, Blanche de Castan confessed everything to her mother, who enlightened Madame de Meslide. It was thought then that Jeanne might be cured by telling her the whole truth, and making her understand that she had loved a dream, and Blanche, from whom that sacrifice was demanded, made a complete confession to her friend, shedding tears of repentance in floods.

But the pale invalid only saw in that belated confession a pretence, a ruse contrived in order to render her calm, and she, to whom the love of the invisible Henri had seemed so real, saw nothing in the reality but a chimera, so true is it that only illusion seems sincere to the winged aspirations that torment our souls.

They no longer had a choice. In order to make one last effort, it was necessary once again to have recourse to lies, and on the advice of the illustrious practitioner who was caring for little Jeanne, it was decided to show her a fake Henri. A young nephew of Madame de Castan, who had arrived from Guadeloupe in order to finish his studies in Paris, and who bore a sufficient resemblance to the character created by Jeanne's imagination, seemed appropriate to play the role, for which the desolate and repentant Blanche provided him with the necessary indications.

Very emotional, and very troubled by the tragic event into which he was entering, the enthusiastic and kind young man was brought to the bed in which Jeanne, already white and transparent, was only any longer alive in her gaze, and, seizing the little girl's hand, he tried to speak; but she looked at him with sad eyes and in a voice that was no longer anything but a faint breath, she said, despairingly: "It isn't him."

And she plunged into the pillow, and turned her head toward the wall, in order to die. And at the moment when she exhaled her poor soul, the young man fell unconscious at the foot of the bed, shattered and broken, mad with amour for the dead girl.

PAUL VERLAINE
(1844-1896)

Paul Verlaine published the Parnassian *Poèmes saturniens* (1866) and two other collections regarded as significant precursors of Symbolism before enlisting in the National Guard after the collapse of the Second Empire and becoming head of the Paris Commune's press bureau. He was fortunate to escape arrest when the Commune was suppressed, and shortly after he emerged from hiding he met Arthur Rimbaud and ran away with him. After being imprisoned for shooting Rimbaud—while in prison he wrote the lachrymose poems collected in *Romances sans paroles* (1874)—he returned to England for some years, where he wrote the poems subsequently collected in *Sagesse* (1880). His colorful life made him legendary long before he drank himself to death in the perpetuation and celebration of his reputation. He included an account of himself, anagrammatically disguised as "Pauvre Lelian" in his classic study of *Les Poètes maudits* (1884), one of the foundation stones of the Decadent Movement.

"Un de mes rêves" first appeared in *Le Décadent*, 20 novembre 1886. "One of My Dreams" is original to the present volume.

One of my Dreams

I shall attempt to describe as minutely as possible a few of my recurrent dreams: those, of course, that seem to me to be worthy of it by virtue of their fixation or their evolution in an atmosphere scarcely breathable by people who are awake.

I often see Paris. Never as it is. It is an unknown city, absurd in all its aspects. I surround it with a narrow river, tightly enclosed between two files of some sort of trees.

Red roofs glisten between exceedingly green foliage. It is heavy summer weather, with large, extremely deep clouds, with branches, as in the keys to historic landscapes, with the most intense yellow sunlight between them. A peasant landscape, you see. However, when I cast a glance in the direction of the city, on the other bank, there are still houses, courtyards and blocks, where laundry is drying on lines, and from which voices are coming: the horrible plaster houses of the true suburban Paris, reminiscent of the Saint-Ouen plain and the entire military road to the north, but more scattered and uneven. I am always frightened by that, and I sense there the tradition of nocturnal and other attacks. Might it be an excessively vague remembrance of a phantasmal Canal Saint-Martin?

I do not know how one penetrates into the city properly speaking, and it is without transition that I am in three successive squares, all the same, with small, angular white houses with arcades. On the sidewalk and the roadway not a cat is to be seen, but there is a commissionaire who is talking to me, I don't know why, and pointing with his finger to the indicative plaque in the corner of one of the squares. He is laughing, thinking it stupid; I no longer remember for what reason, and I forget the name of the square, although I was able to read it. He points out the English Embassy to me and I go there. It is on a square in one of the low houses with arcades. A red-clad grenadier is mounting guard, in a fur hat without any accessories, no plume, cockade or gold braid. A short tunic with white trimmings, black trousers with a thin red stripe. I go in, I climb an official staircase of white granite with a high banister.

On the steps and on the banister Scotsmen and Scotswomen are sitting or sprawling in more or less abandoned poses. On a kind of entresol to which the stairway leads, the scene changes, or rather, is accentuated. What a bizarre species! It is a kind of guard room: shiny weapons are arranged in a corner and on the camp beds, on the parquet and the flagstones; almost naked, always with some characteristic item of costume, a cap with an eagle-feather, a short red and green striped skirt, or brodequins, men and women, chaste, and so white, so nimble, are moving around in proud games and courageous badinage, brightly punctuated by laughter, showing beautiful teeth, and the loud songs of their highlands . . .

The vision fades away in a semi-awakening, and slumber finds me again striding along one of those streets that are new and not new—do you know what I mean?—broad, devoid of shops, bearing the names of entrepreneurs with names ending *ier* or *ard*; plaster dust and gritty sand; the shutters and the window-panes of houses, the bronze and green of lamp-posts, and everything else there, has that badly-wiped appearance that sets the teeth on edge and makes the tips of the fingernails cold. It slopes upwards, that street, and the cause of my haste is a funeral procession that I am following, in the company of my father, dead himself for a long time, but whom my dreams represent constantly.

I must have stopped somewhere in order to buy a wreath or flowers because I can no longer see the funeral carriage, which must have turned at the top of the hill into a narrow avenue that intersects it to the right. To the right and not the left. To the left there is waste ground with the backs and sides of large terraced houses, all on the same level, a hideous perspective!

My father makes me a sign to go more rapidly, and I soon catch up with him. A one-second lacuna in my memory leaves me ignorant of how and when we climbed on to the top deck of a vehicle that is traveling on rails without any apparent agent of locomotion. What is that vehicle? In front of us, traveling along the rails like scuttling bugs, are oblong boxes about two meters high, painted a dirty bright blue; they contain coffins, and it is a train for the cemetery. I know that; it is conventional; the system has been functioning for a long time. The avenue is still slanting to the right. Large trenches in the clay soil are gaping, green and yellow in layers.

Gravediggers leaning on their implements watch us go by, the train of the dead and us. Those men are gray in the gray air. It's cold. It must be November. We keep on going.

X. B. SAINTINE
(1798-1865)

X. B. Saintine was one of the pioneers of Romantic prose in the story series launched in 1823 in *Le Mercure du dix-neuvième siècle*, allegedly narrated by the immortal "Jonathan le visionnaire," who was subsequently credited as the hypothetical author of "Histoire d'une civilisation antediluvienne" (1832), a striking dramatization of the theory of cultural decadence. Best known as a prolific writer of vaudevilles, Saintine also achieved success as a novelist with the classic *Picciola* (1836; tr. as *Picciola; or, The Prison Flower*), one of the core works of the Romantic Movement, in which the life-enhancing symbolism of a flower growing in an exercise yard enables the psychological survival of a desperate political prisoner. Saintine's last collection of short stories, *La Seconde Vie* (1864) consists entirely of accounts of dreams and visions, and is a significant precursor of Symbolist prose.

"Prométhée" first appeared in *La Seconde Vie*. "Prometheus" is included in the English translation of the collection, *The Second Life* (Black Coat Press, 2018).

Prometheus

What is the significance of the punishment inflicted by the master of the gods on the individual who stole from the heavens the celestial fire—which is to say, the flame of knowledge and intelligence—and imparted it to the human species? Why, in our sacred books, is God seen to expel the first man from Eden, only guilty of having tasted the fruits of the tree of knowledge? Why is Lucifer, the angel who bears light, according to ancient tradition, the genius of evil?

I also recall that the ancient sages of India and China forbade the people the knowledge of reading and writing; a prohibition that our old druids, their disciples, did not fail to propagate throughout Celtic Europe.

Are humans only down here in order to admire, and not to know: spectators, not commentators? A big question!

Sitting in my garden, listening to the murmur of my spring—or, rather, not listening to anything, lost in the vagueness of reverie—I have no idea how a mountain suddenly surged forth before me. That mountain was the Caucasus, and on the Caucasus the unfortunate Prometheus was nailed, in the company of his vulture, occupied in gnawing his liver. Hence the train of thought to which I was letting myself go; and I said to myself:

God, however, created humans with all the instincts of sociability, and what social condition can exist without scientific progress? Is it not knowledge that has extracted us from brutishness, and from barbarity? But perhaps the distance between knowledge and science is infinite. Let's examine the case . . .

Is it probable that humans emerged from the hands of God without the notions of the just and the unjust, already perverted, like wretches escaping from a prison camp? I find it repugnant to make humans, in their origin, idiots or ferocious beasts. No, the savage state is not a state of nature; barbarity is born of our vices; at the beginning of the ages a society must have existed of simple people—ignorant, if you like—but directed by honest instincts that I would like to believe innate in the beings of my species.

While I was arguing thus with myself, Prometheus, his mountain and his vulture had disappeared, giving way to lush fields strewn with small primitive huts. Swarms of handsome young men and beautiful young women, not under the orders of a master but a father, were devoting themselves to their rustic labor without any great excess of strength. Humans, not very numerous then, had been able to choose the place of their settlement in a suitable, salubrious terrain on the edge of a lake or a river, already shaded by fine trees bearing fruits. I supposed them to be installed in some Oriental region, the Orient reputedly being the birthplace of society; at any rate, I could see palm leaves serving as covering for cabins.

Among all the laborers, united by family ties, the father or ancestor—in sum, the elder of the tribe—was both chief and judge; he accumulated the three powers in his person, everything emerged from him, and the book of the law was only written in his consciousness. People did without other books then.

It was the patriarchal age, the Golden Age, which, in order for there to be so much talk of it, must have been more than a word. But that primitive civilization, scarcely sketched, where no one was able to fathom any other science than that of wellbeing, could only count as the first stage in the progress of humankind.

Once again, the scene before me changed; a surprise that I was able to give myself at will—in that regard, reverie is more accommodating than dreaming.

The population had increased; the families had become populations, and then peoples. The land being unable to occupy so many arms; there had been territorial disputes. War had mingled and disciplined races, bringing in its wake many dolors, but also new ideas of heroism and devotion. Although Jupiter, Moses, the philosophers of India and the Celts had been able to think of it, the law of progress was also the law of God. The need to occupy so many inactive arms had given impetus to commerce, industry and the arts.

There, where I had seen—with my mind's eye—wretched cabins of pastors and cultivators, stood palaces, temples and splendid monuments. Only a few centuries had gone by, and science had removed the stopper from the source of all the forces of nature put in the service of humankind. Humans, in an unlimited expansion of their power, were enthroned in the midst of a paradise of delights that they had made themselves.

The image of that prodigious civilization, which our Occidental civilizations might never attain, then passed before my gaze.

In the midst of a cortege of soldiers clad in brilliant armor, on gilded chariots, young women showed themselves with coiffures laden with rubies, emeralds and diamonds. Between the chariots and the troops, a double row of slaves were shredding flowers or singing, accompanying themselves with harps, not songs of love and triumph, as one might have thought, but tender and plaintive mewls.

Then, beneath an awning sparkling with gems, a shrine rather than a shelter, one could scarcely make out a sort of human appearance, so much was the air obscured by clouds of myrrh and incense.

In its wake marched the college of astrologers and all the other academic societies, extending endlessly as far as the eye could see.

It came to a halt in front of a palace as large as a city; a man, in the prime of life, with a royal ribbon around his head, emerged from beneath the awning, and, with a smiling gesture, dismissed his cortege of soldiers and scholars.

In a vast courtyard, with porticoes of jasper and marble, a platform was set up. There, by his order, fabrics and the most magnificent carpets had been disposed along the steps, as well as his jewelry, his gold, and all his treasures. His favorite slaves, his odalisques and his women took their places there, adding the splendor of their costumes, their ornaments, their youth and their beauty to the spectacle of all those splendors. Soft music was heard; golden cassolettes cast their perfumes into the air; slaves threw flowers, and women smiled. Then the representative of that civilization, the king of that people, the possessor of that palace and those riches, the master of those women and slaves, put his lips to a cup full of delicious wine, and drank: to Oblivion!

And at the same time I saw flames spring up on all sides and mount from step to step. The stage was nothing but a pyre.

That Assyrian, Babylonian, Ninevite civilization had for its ultimate name *Sardanapalus*.[1] After having spent nearly a thousand years attaining the culminating point of human science and glory, it suddenly collapsed, leaving nothing behind but ashes.

Sardanapalus, that sated son of Prometheus, was, like his people, softened, depraved by contact with the sensualities of the body and the mind; he was no longer able to occupy himself with anything but pleasures, touching spectacles, passionate discussions of the arts, cuisine, perfumes and philosophy; his weapons had fallen from his hands, and he no longer had the strength to pick them up, although the enemy was howling at his gates. After

---

1 Sardanapalus, the mythical last king of Assyria, who did not exist, seems to have been an invention of the Greek writer Clesias, although that writer's account is only known second-hand via Diodorus Siculus.

having cast a glance around, seeing no one there but poets, scholars and the voluptuous, and voluptuous himself, he had come to savor death in one last illusion.

Looming up before me in the wake of those tableaux, succeeding one another like dazzling flashes, came the towers of Notre-Dame, the Tour Saint-Jacques, the column of the Place Vendôme, the Luxembourg, the legislative Chambre, then the Rue Vivienne, the Rue Saint-Denis, the Boulevard de Sebastopol . . . in sum, the entire city of Paris, as great as Nineveh, similarly populated with scholars, skeptics and Epicureans. I shivered at the mere idea of that analogous connection.

It seemed to me that during my itinerary from Nineveh to Paris, abrupt and rapid as that change of location and time had been, I had seen passing along my route the sinister shadows of Tyre, Sidon, Athens, Rome and Byzantium, all powerful cities that had lain down in their turn on the pyre of Sardanapalus.

Was Paris, my dear Paris, menaced, in the imminent future, with dying like them of a plethora, of an excess of science and material wellbeing, infallible generators of the languor of races and the extinction of the moral sense?

The progressive march of our century frightened me. Our industry seemed to me not so much to multiply our wealth as our artificial needs; I feared that our arts, in perfecting themselves, would succeed in softening even more than charming the present generation. Science—science, above all—with her everyday miracles, caused me more fear than all the rest.

In a final tableau she appeared to me, not, as before, with a book or compasses in hand, but terrible, noisy and formidable; she was a giant sorceress with muscles of steel and a face smudged with coal-dust; around her was accumulated a frightening materiel of bronze and iron, enormous tubes, engines of war and machines even more terrible.

Alas, I said to myself, *has human intelligence any need to arm itself with such means? Steam and railways risk making human beings nothing but incessant travelers, who will soon no longer have any family or fatherland. The human brain is enlarged, but the human heart is desiccated; we are in decadence!*

What means can ward off the peril? A return to the patriarchal era, to the Golden Age? Fourier has thought of that. Although seductive, his phalansterian ideas have been declared utopian and unrealizable. Opposing to the scientific, progressive barbarity that is invading us, the true barbarians, those who have already transfused their vigorous blood into the veins of sickly and decrepit Rome? Today, the Teutons and the Germans have become metaphysicians and philosophers; they could only add to the evil; the Cimbrians and the Scythians are reputed to be the most artful diplomats in Europe . . . Let us search elsewhere.

But why do we not appeal to the class of people who, among us, have remained closest to nature, to the primitive state, who witness our improvements without understanding them, who oppose to our forward march their routine and immobility: the peasants?

A voice goes up that replies to me: "The peasants? They have conserved their customs of old without the mores of old, the traditions without the virtues; rejected violently, perhaps arbitrarily, to the bottom of your social hierarchy, they have become jealous, envious, full of rancor and covetousness. Besides which, have they not been able to take their place, broadly, without waiting for your appeal? They have done it so well and so wholeheartedly that they will end up invading everything.

"The French nobility has disappeared since it stupidly decided to teach the peasants to read; ignorance protected them so well! They did not suspect their rights then! A narrow paltry, bourgeoisie, which speculates from day to day, which imposes economically the number of dishes that ought to figure on its table, and the number of children that can be permitted, has succeeded them; it has taken their employments, their land, even their titles; but where has that bourgeoisie, high or low, financial or mercantile, been recruiting its ranks for fifty years, and still is, and where will it necessarily recruit tomorrow? Among the peasants, who produce innumerable offspring in swarms and send them to assault the cities. There, they fill in the enormous voids that are made in superior circles; they populate the workshops and the boutiques; from workers they become masters, entrepreneurs, capitalists; from merchants they pass on to become landowners and even castellans. A few are sent to the Chambre to represent their départements. You see that you have nothing more to desire in that direction."

Well, then, I was alarmed too quickly. I'm reassured now; the barbarians have arrived; the transfusion of blood will be operated without violence; progress will find someone to negotiate . . . Blessed be those barbarians, since we find in them, instead of enemies, compatriots. But it was just in time!

"You don't believe in Providence, then?" the voice went on. "Your peasant parvenus, scarcely uncrushed, cast aside all their good and honest prejudices along with their blouses and satchels, only to take them up again when indefinite progress threatens their shops or their castles; but the cause—of which they ought to have been the faithful servants, by virtue of their right to ignorance, thank God—can count on other, more constant defenders. Among all people, in all latitudes, since the beginning of the world, that retrograde party, so jeered and so shamed, has always existed, and even counts among its most fervent adherents a large number of sages and the learned. It always will exist, because it is a necessity.

"In mental matters as well as physical matters, life is movement; movement is flux and reflux, action and reaction, affirmation and negation. Those two contrary principles, which dispute the world, serve mutually as checks and balances; if one disappears, the other dies of its excess. A bird needs its two wings, a boat its two oars, a chariot its two wheels, a steam engine its two pistons, a railway its two rails; the opposing part, no matter what side it is on, is the second wing, the second oar, the second wheel, the second piston, the second rail. It completes the machine and gives it, if not thrust, at least the equilibrium that prevents it from veering to the right or the left.

"If revolutions are aborted, if a day comes when they turn violently against themselves, it is because, after having broken their second wing, their second oar, they necessarily experience the need to replace it, to bisect the vanquished party in order to create an opposition.

"Since antagonism is one of the essential laws of nature, as of society, since both only arrive at their normal development by means of struggle, refrain in your political debates from hating your adversaries; they are useful to you—indispensable, even. A fortunate modification has taken place among you, in any case; for those furious duels of contrary parties, in which the earth drinks blood, you have substituted struggle by speech, battle by sitting down and standing up; today, in our diets, the projectiles of war, instead of being thrown at the head, are dropped into the ballot box.

"That is better; that is good! On that legal route, progress can advance for a long time yet, without danger to anyone, thanks to the great law of antagonism that moderates it; live in peace, then, and no longer doubt Providence; God, in mingling the two elements of fire, hydrogen and oxygen, has made water, which extinguishes fire; trust in him, let things take their course and reconcile yourself with your two neighbors, whom you have ceased to see because they wounded your moderationism with their two opposed poles, the right and the left."

The voice ceased to make itself heard. Where had it come from? I looked around. I only saw Lalagé. Sitting on the edge of the stream, watching it flow, her head inclined, her legs crossed, her arms extended toward her knees and linking them together, she was meditating, and scarcely seemed to be thinking about me.

"Oh, Lalagé," I said to her, "thank heaven you interrupted me in the fastidious colloquium in social philosophy that I've just been having with myself! Why did I, who was with you a little while ago, smiling at flowers, birds and the sun, suddenly preoccupy myself with the state of modern society, our legislative chambers, our peasants and our railways, all of that in comparison to the Golden Age, Nineveh and Sardanapalus? I remember . . . it was Prometheus who appeared to me first. But why did I think about Prometheus rather than someone else?"

Lalagé smiled, and pointed to a little daisy, white and pink, on the same grassy mound where we were sitting.

"A little while ago," she said, "you were looking at that little flower, a charming reduction of the large ox-eye daisies of our meadows; an insect with gaudy wing-cases came to settle on it, in order to drink from the cornets of its florets. Do you remember? Then the daisy received a shock, and swayed for some time on its stem; it was a tiny bird—a wren, I think—that had just touched it with its wing—and when the bird flew away, it had the insect in its beak."

I remembered the event perfectly, but could not understand as yet that it might help me to recover the first cause of my great philosophical, political and palingenetic reverie.

Lalagé added: "Then you followed the wren in its flight, and your thoughts, rising above it, went into the upper regions of the air, searching for the bird of prey of which, in its turn, the raider might become the victim; you thought about a kite, and then a vulture; you were led to wonder what mystery of wisdom the ancient tradition contained; the rest followed naturally.

"The drop of water that falls from the rock covers the surface of the lake with spreading ripples, which connect one to another; likewise, the highest human inspirations sometimes have no other primal cause than the cry of a cricket or the sight of a blade of grass; an atom of the air is sufficient to put in motion and cause to radiate in its immense orbit a thought that can simultaneously embrace God, time and space."

For as long as Lalagé spoke, I did not think either of interrogating her again, or even of responding to her. Only one thing preoccupied me, which was the fact that, at that moment, her voice resembled the one that had resounded in my ear during my reverie.

AUGUSTE VILLIERS DE L'ISLE ADAM
(1838-1889)

Auguste Villiers de l'Isle Adam, whose father spent much of his life trying to prove that he was a hereditary Comte—a delusion he inherited—idolized Baudelaire and threw himself into the Bohemian lifestyle he thought befitting a poet, which did not prove helpful to his actual production, several of his novels and plays remaining incomplete. He found it easier to finish short stories, his first collection being *Contes cruels* (1883; tr. as *Sardonic Tales*), which certainly did not invent the genre in question—the Romantic writers S. Henry Berthoud and Petrus Borel had pioneered it more than half a century earlier—but provided it with its definitive label and offered an important exemplar to Decadent prose writers. He followed it with his much-rewritten novel *L'Ève future* (1886; tr. as *Tomorrow's Eve*), but died almost as soon as the Decadent Movement began, according him a heroic status.

"Lord Lyonnel" first appeared in the *Mercure de France* in May 1891, one of a number of fragments published posthumously in that periodical; it evidently comes from one of the earliest drafts of the text that ultimately became *L'Ève future*. The translation is original to the present volume.

Lord Lyonnel

Often, by night, when awakened by the first north winds of October rattling the blinds, Lord Lyonnel considered his sleeping mistress, and began to wonder obscurely whether he really had the right to lend himself to the work, at least strange, that Edison was attempting; whether he, Lord Lyonnel, was not guilty of a tacit duplicity—and, even more seriously, whether it was not, in fact . . . yes whether it was not tempting God?

A singular event—one of the thousand coincidences, doubtless fortuitous, that become at length something worthy of attention, which are always produced in some fashion around those whose minds are prey to that sort of occult anxiety—of the most gripping nature—occurred one night, when he had expressed that thought for the first time, in a low voice, as if speaking to himself. He had formulated it in precise terms, hoping that the very precision might dissipate the vagueness and excessive heaviness of a conjecture of that order.

As it persisted, his consciousness suggested to him the idea of writing to Edison right away. He wanted to suspend the execution of the terrible work. He could not bear the idea of going to sleep with that obsession. Having got up, therefore, he put on a dressing gown, went to his writing desk and dipped his pen in the inkwell. At that precise moment, as he half-closed his eyes, gazing at a fixed point on the wall in the corner of the room, like a man seeking his expressions and weighing them before writing, he perceived, vaguely at first and then distinctly, an object that first astonished him, then stupefied him, and then chilled him with an unknown impression.

It was the simplest thing in the world, merely a skull, very gray, of ancient appearance, which seemed to be making an effort to appear upon the weave of the obscurity in that corner. A detail of sinister absurdity, it seemed to be wearing a sturdy pair of spectacles in front of its two eye-sockets.

Lord Lyonnel was not only a courageous man but also an intrepid one. The strength of a proud motto was amalgamated with the blood flowing in his veins by the action of centuries. He pulled himself together, although a trifle pale, and considered the object in silence.

By trying to analyze the provenance of his sensations, he convinced himself very rapidly that his hallucination was due to a certain nervous lassitude that pleasure sometimes induces, and which then determines, if not a visual perversion, at least a sort of intense excitation of the pupils. At those times, in fact, if the eyes are half-closed, the retina is subject to a sort of memory, which resuscitates objects and magnifies them, as under the influence of opium. Panoramic landscapes, trees, rocks and distant avenues are evoked beneath the eyelids; great dead cities, Pompeiis, Atlantises and Palmyras are prolonged resplendently; Thebaids extend to the limits of vision, over which strange caravans pass; the spangled golden waves of Pactoluses flow and sparkle under shady banks—and all those visions are fleeting.

This one was of a funereal order, that was all. It reflected the coloration that the imagination had had at that moment. That was all. Certainly, that was all. Nevertheless, he did not dissimulate the fact that the vision was less fleeting and more intense than the others. Yes, but that might also come from the intensity engraved in his mind just now, and which fixed the image more profoundly in its visual correspondence.

In sum, he told himself, it was nothing but a hallucination, like any other; and he was still gazing at the skull, which persisted.

At that moment, Miss Evelyn, whom he saw asleep in the alcove, and who had her back turned to him, called out, in a voice that was somewhat sleepy and banal: "Oh! Lyonnel! If you knew . . . it's odd . . . I can see a heap of things, since a moment ago . . . look! A skull! Oh, how gray it is! It's odd, eh? One might think that it's wearing spectacles! Oh, but . . . that's annoying! It doesn't want to go away . . ."

The young man had dropped his pen as he listened to those horrible phrases and stood up, but without pronouncing a word . . .

He seized a candlestick and marched toward the corner.

The movement had doubtless dissipated the vision; the skull had disappeared.

"Well, what's the matter with you?" said Miss Evelyn, drawing aside the curtain. "What's the matter? You've been very singular for several days. What! You're getting up at night to write?"

And the mischievous young woman was seized by a fit of mad laughter, which resonated in the corner of the alcove.

"Your laughter is inappropriate, this evening, dear," said Lord Lyonnel, in a tone that suddenly calmed the untimely gaiety of the frivolous child.

Leaving the candle lit, he rejoined her, without adding anything, turned his back on her, propped himself up on his elbow and set about meditating on the incident.

"What a pity," said Miss Evelyn, yawning and going back to sleep, "that such a handsome fellow, and so rich, should be a trifle mad!"

After a few minutes, Lord Lyonnel rendered an account of the event in the following terms:

It's a curious phenomenon, even very curious, but it's only a phenomenon of the order of magnetic hallucinations. That's all. It's the simultaneity, the ubiquity of the vision shared between Evelyn and myself that impressed me just now. And it's because of my state of mind, that the nature of the vision—the skull—combined with those two ulterior circumstances, impressed me so much. In fact, I had the hallucination first, of which I believe I had clarified the probable origin

Now, a very intense magnetic current, a chain of affinities, reinforced by a sort of somnambulism, was still established between Miss Evelyn and me—in sum, it had not yet dissipated—at the moment when the phenomenon was produced for me. The sensorial emotion that it caused me, by its suddenness and the character of almost supernatural solemnity that my mind, then under the influence of the thought of God, attributed to the objectified skull—or, to put it better, clothed it—in its unreflective state, almost of prostration, passed, by virtue of its very violence, into the intimate and occult current uniting our two nervous systems. That's certain . . .

The event is in the magnetic domain—not yet elucidated, but in that domain. I have been contagious for her, I have been electric; in brief, she saw, like me, by means of me, that skull, who terrifying spectacles must have originated from my lorgnon. She has seen it, I say, for the same reason that two people living together often have the same idea at the same time, which is sometimes very difficult to trace back to an appreciable point of departure.

Having thus explained the phenomenon scientifically, Lord Lyonnel, still submissive, involuntarily, to a residue of nervous anxiety, stared fixedly between his eyelashes at the candles burning in the candelabrum until dawn. He smiled at the idea that they took on, for him, the aspect of candles burning in front of a catafalque. He knew now where ideas of that sort came from.

At length, he went to sleep too, thinking that the rising sun would dissipate his tiresome nightmare—which was the case,

In his subtle and very reasonable analysis, however, Lord Lyonnel had not paid attention to one small thing, which is that the phenomenon, wherever it came from, by distracting his consciousness, had caused him to forget to write the letter in question. The days succeeded one another, and, whether by virtue of human respect, forgetfulness or negligence, he let matters take their course.

ERNEST HELLO
(1828-1885)

Ernest Hello was a Catholic polemicist who dabbled in literary criticism and produced a volume of his own fiction, *Contes extraordinaires* (Albin Michel, 1879), much of which makes extravagant use of symbolism in a similar manner to Villiers de l'Isle Adam.

"La Recherche" appeared in *Contes extraordinaires*; "The Search" is original to the present volume.

The Search

He was the greatest of the kings of Asia. Compared with his magnificence, the tales of the Orient you have heard are like stories of suburban life; it was beyond the scope of your Western imagination. Set beside his, the splendors of your world are a dung-heap. Every single column in the courtyard of his palace would have added luster to the capital of a huge empire.

The servants who knelt before him placed their foreheads on the ground when they approached him, and did so willingly, instinctively, as if they were not acting under constraint but honestly overwhelmed by the redoubtable majesty of their master. The idea of beatitude was inextricably mixed, in the minds of his subjects, with the spectacle of his power and wealth, and they dared not use such expressions as "happy as a king" because the beatitude of their sovereign was incomparable. The people seemed always to be festive, because they had such a king; the mere contemplation of such beatitude generated happiness.

Alas, the sky had been darkened for some time; the sun was less brilliant, and the people less happy—but no one dared inquire as to how it had come about that a cloud had dared to pass before the face of the sovereign.

The king was usually not to be seen. Entrenched in the depths of his palace, he only saw those grandees of his court whom he had expressed a desire to see, and the offence of catching sight of him without his instruction or permission was punishable by death.

One day he called an assembly of all the grandees of his court and all the sages of the realm, and said to them: "My mind is occupied by a new need, which troubles and importunes me. The honors due to me and the government of my realm are tedious. I want to know where God is. I want to know His name."

Every grandee and every sage proffered a name. While the assembly was in progress an indefinite noise was heard in the courtyard of the palace.

"What is happening?" the king asked.

"Pay no attention, highness," was the reply. "It's a dog that your servants are chasing away."

Actually, it was not a dog but a mendicant, but the mendicant in question was known throughout the land as the Dog—everyone called him that because he was so wretched. Compared with him, other mendicants seemed like oriental monarchs; one got the impression, on seeing him, that he went on all fours, and one would hardly take him for a man at all.

The assembly in the palace continued. The discussion was long and knowledgeable. Many arguments were put forward.

Even so, during the days and nights that followed, the king's brow became more deeply furrowed, and the cloud cast a shadow upon the faces of his people. One evening, however, the mood was lightened momentarily, when it was announced that the Dog had asked to see the king—the king of kings who was not to be approached by anyone. This tentative request, amusing in itself, was all the more amusing for having arrived at the most solemn and preoccupied moment of the monarch's existence, when his brow was furrowed.

He convened for a second time the assembly of grandees and sages, and told them to gather into their company the mages who studied the stars. And the king, seeing them arrive, rose from his throne with a sad gesture and said: "I have not found peace. Do any of you know the name of God?"

Each one made his reply. The discussions, more elaborately prepared than the first time, were full of the most profound erudition—but each one was saying within himself: "If it falls to me to tell the king the name of God, the king alone knows how my fortune will be increased, and what throne will be given to me."

Then a noise was heard in the courtyard of the palace. It was the Dog, who had returned, and who was being chased away for the second time. The sound of voices was mingled with numerous bursts of laughter, because he had insisted on speaking to the sovereign. The insults and stones that were hurled at his face and the laughter that greeted his request attracted the attention of the monarch himself, who watched the performance through a window—and his brow became unfurrowed when he saw that it was the creature in question, dog or man, who had dared to desire to enter his presence.

The sovereign immediately burst out laughing—and the grandees and sages, who had had the same scene before them, but had not dared to laugh, having now been given permission to do so by the laughter of the king, burst out laughing in their turn.

But their gaiety was short-lived, and the sadness which succeeded it was so fatal that the words died on the lips of the wise men—and they went away, one after the other, as terrified in the moment of their departure as they had been prideful in the moment of their arrival, in mortal dread of the king's anger.

At the parting of that day, people who passed by in front of the palace thought that they saw a black flag starred with gold hung outside the doorway. The death of the king was the subject of every conversation. Sleep had fled his bed as the smile had fled his lips, and he had ordered that his portrait be covered by a veil; tired of himself, he had tired of his image.

Nevertheless, a third conference was announced, and the steward took measures to ensure that the Dog's burlesque could not possibly be played out again.

Mages were summoned from the remotest regions of Asia to assist the others. Persia and India sent their own overlords and their retinues. All of the grandeur, luxury, wisdom and magnificence of Asia was mounted upon elephants and camels. They all prostrated themselves, foreheads to the ground, at the appointed hour of the appointed day, kings seeming like liveried servants in the court of the king of kings.

But the king of kings was pale, for sleep was not numbered among his subjects. Sleep would not obey him; when he bade it come, it came not. Everything was allowed him, except sleep, and his fury burst forth in response to that rebellion. The more it insulted him, the more he begged for release.

Since the moment when the steward had given orders for the complete removal of the Dog from the environs of the palace—which he was forbidden to approach, for fear that his barking might disturb the silence of the king's repose—sleep, in its turn, had also fled from the palace. Sleep, laughter and forgetfulness had fled the royal palace like three refugees, and then had departed the dwellings of the people. Insomnia, sadness and preoccupation were camped on every threshold of the palace, and they sent forth their daughters and their servants to camp on the thresholds of the meanest hovels.

This was why the king was pale when the kings of Asia arrived, followed by their grandees, their sages, their elephants and their camels. The elephants and camels were loaded with the most sumptuous gifts, but the pallid king barely spared a glance for the magnificent offerings, as if his eyes were saying: "Is sleep numbered among your gifts? Do you know the name of God?"

The whole of Asia spilled into the palace of the sovereign all its treasures of eloquence and erudition, just as it had spilled the produce of its industry. And the kings and the mages looked at one another, and looked at the king's face, and their gazes fell once again from the face of the king upon other faces—and, jealous of one another, they sought to prevail one against another, every one desirous of reading his own triumph in the face of the king. But the king of kings got up without replying, without even sparing them a glance, not even a look of disdain. He got up, and disappeared. The door closed, and no one dared follow him. And when, after the surprise had died down, someone asked, "Where is the king?" each one of them found on the lips of another, instead of a reply, a question. Everyone was asking of everyone else: "Where is the king?"

Night fell on the palace at the usual hour, but the king was not seen again. A strange and singular competition developed among his servants. Who could solve the mystery? They searched here, they searched there. They investigated the corridors, the coverts, the most improbable hiding-places. The king was not there. While the night wore on they searched in vain, and the search became increasingly panic-stricken. Everyone doubted his own senses, and those of others.

In the end, the palace took on the appearance of a lunatic asylum.

Meanwhile, a caravan set out across Asia, bound for Africa.

Donkeys and camels were transporting pilgrims; all of them were talking about their destination but one. The exception was truly singular: magnificently dressed, surrounded by servants who did not come from the same country as himself, whom he had taken into his service when he set out, he had not told anyone his name. There was a suggestion of authority in his expression, and his staff resembled a scepter. He called himself "the pilgrim", and if anyone asked where he was going, he replied: "I don't know".

Everywhere that an illustrious man had left evidence of his passage, the pilgrim paused. He spent long hours there, studying the places and the inscriptions, questioning people and rummaging through things.

Wherever a celebrated foot had left its print upon the sand, he stopped on the shore of the sea and sat down on a stone, his head in his hands, looking neither to the left nor the right. And when the sun set upon the Ocean, setting its reflection ablaze, and the moon rose, serene and tranquil, on the opposite horizon, he passed yet again through the memories of the researches, labors and studies he had conducted in the course of his journey.

The tombs of the illustrious, visited by multitudes, attracted him. In the places where they had lived, and the places where they had died, he searched for traces of wisdom. He wanted to breathe in their inspiration; he meditated upon their tombs. Sometimes he also thought about his own.

His own funeral ceremony sometimes appeared in the distance of his thoughts: he saw himself conducted to his last resting-place, escorted by kings and wise men—but there was no place for the poor within that final procession. They were left out of his dream. Whether they were glorious or funereal, the dreams of the pilgrim were full of powerful things and powerful men.

In my capacity as narrator, I am permitted to examine them! I see them full of heroes. They are possessed and shot through by power. They admire those who are vigorous, bold, and enterprising. They admire those who assert themselves, and—without knowing it—those who are wealthy.

I see the pilgrim himself depicted within his dreams. I see him contemplating himself, first a king, then a pilgrim. I see him preoccupied with his grandeur and rambling amid his glory. It seems to me that in his own eyes, the pilgrim is more important than the king.

It seems to me that his journey appears to him to be more important than his throne. His investigative tour of the world appears to him as the greatest proof he can afford himself of his wealth and power. He adorns his interior life with the splendors that he contemplates; it seems to him that he eats and drinks the substance of the great men who lived there in the past.

I dig deeper into those dreams with the indiscretion that characterizes the story-teller and the rights attached thereto. In these hollowed-out dreams, excavated and sifted, I cannot see the tears of those he has left behind, unhappy and inert, in the regions from which he departed. I cannot see any place of grief. I see no memory of women searching for bread while their husbands lie sick. I see no ships and camels. I see no acknowledgment of the misery of his empire.

Everything down here has its term, though, and a tour of the world is soon concluded. One cannot walk forever. A point of departure always threatens to become a point of arrival.

One day, the king was seen again in his palace.

There was an indescribable commotion. There was hurrying, shouting, trembling, even running away. Who could distinguish, among such transports, which fraction was sincere and which dishonest? He who had returned was master again, and he never asked anyone whether he had done well to depart. He came through his gardens, which were as magnificent as his palace, and he re-entered his magnificent apartment. The crowding courtiers competed to attract his eye, and awaited a smile.

As for him, he sat down on his throne. Everyone looked at him, trembling. His hair had gone white. His proud figure was strangely bent. His eyes were untroubled, fixed and cold. A singular pride—the pride of having done what he had done, even though it had been futile—dressed his despair in vestments of disdain and insolence.

His forehead was creased by a particular sorrow, gloomy and unacknowledged, which nothing had touched. The pomp that surrounded him was full of luxury but empty of majesty. A certain irony, ill-defined in its cause and its effects, strayed vaguely over his lips, and if they had opened it seemed that they would have said: "I have not found the name of God, but if my search has to begin again, I shall begin it again, so that I and no other will accomplish it."

All of a sudden, the king uttered a slight sigh, collapsed, and slid down from his throne on to the carpet on which the throne was set.

The chief physician of the court approached, as none of the other spectators dared to do so, and applied his finger to a place where a pulse ought to have been detectable.

"He's dead," he said.

On the next day, the kings of Asia, followed by their grandees and their mages, formed the funeral procession of the king of kings.

Now, it happened that the distance to which the Dog had been chased away from the palace, on the orders of the steward, was exactly the distance at which the cemetery lay. And when the final cortege of the king of kings passed along the length of its route, the mendicant of mendicants was seen kneeling at the cemetery gate.

Four letters were inscribed at the bottom of the wooden bowl which he extended to the people who passed him by. They were the name of God.

CATULLE MENDÈS
(1841-1909)

Catulle Mendès came to Paris in 1859, and was taken under the wing of Théophile Gautier. He began to cultivate a scandalous reputation when his first novel, *Roman d'une nuit* (1861), was prosecuted for obscenity, landing him in prison for a month. He fell out with Gautier over his marriage in 1866 to the latter's daughter Judith, whom he left for the composer Augusta Holmes in 1869. He became a central figure in the Parnassian Movement, but proved extraordinarily adaptable and prolific thereafter, producing an enormous amount of short fiction for periodicals. His calculatedly scabrous novels *Zo'har* (1886) and *Méphistophela* (1890) were crucial contributions to the Decadent Movement. He was found dead in a railway tunnel, somewhat mysteriously.

"Le Petit Faune" first appeared in *La Revue populaire*, novembre 1882 under the pseudonym Jean-Qui-Passe, which Mendès employed for his work while he was the editor of the periodical. The translation was made from the version in the collection *Pour lire au bain* (Marpon et Flammarion,1888) and is original to the present volume.

The Little Faun

At the bend in the path, on his terracotta pedestal, the little faun was laughing boldly. Horned, swollen-cheeked and pot-bellied, he laughed, the lubricious, naked young god, being the one who presided over the fluttering couplings of sparrows in the sand, the crepitant caresses of dragonflies over the heather, the rapid and fleeting marriages of squirrels along the branches.

But it was not sufficient for his triumph to show that bestial joy. Brazen to the point of cynicism, disdainful of all modesty, like a drunken Eros, he affirmed in broad daylight, like a sign of supremacy, his arrogant virility, like a young king holding the scepter of command. With the result that the faun in question was an object of scandal for the honest passers-by, and that many strollers could not see him without blushing beneath the eyelashes or concealing a little laugh behind the rosy trellis of their interlaced fingers.

But she, Berthe-Marie, the demoiselle of the château, charitable and devoted, so good and so pure, who went every day to the church where people pray and the cottages where alms are distributed, passed by without blushing or averting her eyes from the bold simulacrum; she considered it, smiling, with a complacency that was slightly astonished but not at all fearful, in the peace of an inviolate innocence, neither pensive nor anxious, the depths of her blue eyes reflecting the perfect ingenuousness of a child taking pleasure in looking closely at the pictures in a missal, and touching them with her fingertips. For she was candor itself, ineffably ignorant of evil; and if lakes of immaculate azure exist on some Alpine plateau, which have never even been traversed by the shadow of a white cloud, it is one of those lakes that her soul resembled.

One morning, she went into the woods with her lover, who was her fiancé. Yes, with her lover. Why not? Virgin hearts have their affections too; one can give oneself without giving oneself, and a betrothal ring is not the ring of Hans Carvel.[1]

He was almost as young as her, and they were as naïve and tremulous as one another; it was to be an exquisite day! They did not hold hands, and were careful not to allow their elbows to touch, both aware as if by instinct of their sensitivity. But their souls were united in spite of their bodily separation.

Wordlessly, they exchanged thoughts in immaterial conversation, the alternating distichs of an angelic eclogue. It was in

1 The story of Hans Carvel seems to have been first committed to print in a collection of lewd tales, *Liber Facietarum,* by the papal secretary Poggio Bracciolini (1380-1459); it was retold by Rabelais and than recast a fable in verse by Jean de La Fontaine. Carvel, an old doctor with a young wife, dreams that the devil gives him a ring that will prevent him from being cuckolded as long as he wears it. When he wakes up he finds that his finger is stuck in her vagina, with the result that "Hans Carvel's ring" became a common euphemism for that anatomical feature.

vain that around them, in the sunlit air where ardent odors were vaporized, branches brushed one another with gentle caresses, and flying green-gold beetles traced redoubtable magic circles, the voice of the nightingale faded away, ecstatically, beside its nest, and the entire wood, full of love, enveloped them, gave them the culpable advice of embraces and united lips; they went through the perils, without paying any heed to such sweet wicked temptations.

Not once—not once!—did he press her to his heart; not once did they look at one another too closely, sighing. In the paradise that they did not want to lose, they were like an Eve and an Adam who were not thinking about forbidden fruit. Yes, such would be, all day long, the slow excursion beneath the trees of those two pure children, and I would even swear that they did not linger to search in the moss for the little fresh strawberries that are reminiscent of kisses, nor to interrogate the daisies, those providers of troubling answers.

It was after dark, in the moonlight, when they returned. Certainly, in the depths of her large blue eyes, Berthe-Marie still had—and why should she no longer have had?—the ingenuousness of ineffable ignorance . . .

When they passed before the faun, horned, swollen-cheeked and pot-bellied, who was even more boldly triumphant, the lubricious little god, like a young king holding the scepter of command, however, she turned her head very swiftly, and started to laugh, stifling her laughter in her friend's neck.

JORIS-KARL HUYSMANS
(1848-1907)

Joris-Karl Huysmans published two overlapping collections of prose poems, *Le drageoir aux épices* (1874) and *Croquis Parisiens* (1880; tr. as *Parisian Sketches*), producing two Naturalist novels, *Marthe* (1876) and *Les Soeurs Vatard* (1879) in between. *À rebours* (Charpentier, 1884) represented a dramatic change of direction, and became the handbook of Decadent lifestyle fantasy. *Là-Bas*

(1891), based on the author's flirtation with the Parisian Occult Revival, became equally archetypal in its fascinated but horrified account of contemporary Satanism. The author dressed as a monk for the rest of his semi-reclusive life.

"Des Esseintes' Dream," a translation of chapter 8 of *À rebours*, was originally published in *The Second Dedalus Book of Decadence: The Black Feast* (Dedalus, 1992).

Des Esseintes' Dream

Des Esseintes had always been infatuated with flowers, but this passion—which, during his sojourn at Jutigny, had extended to all flowers, no matter what species or genus they belonged to—had eventually been purified and narrowly focused on a single kind.

For a long time now he had despised the commonplace plants that bloomed in Parisian markets in moistened pots, beneath green awnings or red parasols. While devoting time to the refinement of his literary tastes and his aesthetic preferences, preserving his affection for no works save those finely sifted and distilled by subtle and tormented minds, and while simultaneously hardening his distaste for widely-held notions, his love of flowers had also been purged of its dregs and superfluities; it had, as it were, been clarified and rectified.

He was fond of comparing the stock of a horticulturalist to a microcosm in which all the social classes were represented. There was wretched floral riff-raff—mere weeds like the wallflower, whose true milieu was the window-box, their roots crammed into milk-cans or old earthenware pots. There were also pretentious, conventional and stupid flowers, like roses, whose place was to be bedded down in porcelain pots painted by young ladies. Lastly, there were flowers of noble descent such as orchids, charming and delicate, thrilling and sensitive—exotic flowers which, in Paris, had to be exiled to the warmth of glass palaces. These were the princesses of the vegetable realm, living apart, having nothing at all in common with the plants of the street or the bourgeois blooms.

Although Des Esseintes could not help experiencing a certain interest, born of pity, in the flowers of the lowest class as they wilted by the exhalations of the sewers and sinks of the slums, he loathed utterly the bouquets which matched the cream and gilt of the new houses; the delight of his eyes was entirely reserved for the rare and distinguished plants brought from afar, maintained by careful artistry in tropical conditions faked by the controlled breath of stoves.

Once his definitive choice had settled on hothouse flowers, it had to be further modified by the influence of his general philosophy of life and the specific conclusions at which he had now arrived; previously, in Paris, his natural penchant for the artificial had led him to forsake the real flower for its image, faithfully reproduced by virtue of the miracles of rubber and wire, cotton and taffeta, paper and velvet. Consequently, he possessed a marvelous collection of tropical plants fashioned by the hands of true artists, who had followed Nature step by step while creating anew.

They had taken each bloom from the time of its birth to the fullness of its maturity, even simulating its withering, making note of its subtlest nuances, the most transient aspects of its wakefulness or repose. They had observed the tenor of its petals when ruffled by the wind or crumpled by the rain, sprinkling its unfolding corolla with drops of dew or glue, presenting it in full flower when the branches are bowed by the weight of sap, and with a withered stem and shriveled head to reflect the time of discarded petals and falling leaves. That admirable art-work had long held him in thrall, but now he dreamed of another kind of floral display; having had his fill of artificial flowers aping real ones he wanted natural flowers which would imitate fakes.

He brought his intelligence to bear on this problem; he did not have to search for long or go very far, because his house was situated in the very heart of the horticulturalists' territory. He took himself off directly to visit the greenhouses of the Avenue de Chatillon and the vale of Aunay, returning exhausted and broke, wonderstruck by the vegetal extravagance which he had witnessed, unable to think of anything except the species which he had acquired and the haunting memories of bizarre and magnificent blossoms.

Two days later, the carriers arrived. With his list in his hand, Des Esseintes went forth to confirm his purchases, one by one.

The gardeners brought down from their wagons a collection of various species of the genus *Caladium*, which bore upon their turgid and hairy stems enormous heart-shaped leaves; although they maintained a general appearance of kinship no two of them were exactly alike. There were extraordinary specimens among them. Some, including the Virginale, were roseate, and looked as if they had been cut out of oilcloth or English sticking-plaster: others, such as the Albane, looked as if they had been fabricated from the pleural membrane of an ox or the diaphanous bladder of a pig. Others, especially the Madame Mame, had the appearance of zinc, parodying bits of stamped metal tinted with imperial green, splashed with paint and streaked with red and white lead. There were those, like the Bosphorus, which produced the illusion of starched calico flecked with crimson and myrtle green; while there were others, like the Aurora Borealis, which displayed leaves the color of raw meat, purple-streaked along the sides, with violet fibrils and tumescent leaves sweating blue wine and blood.

The Albane and the Aurora presented the two extremes of temperament to be found in this kind of plant: chlorosis and apoplexy.

The gardeners brought in more new varieties. These affected the appearance of simulated hide criss-crossed by counterfeit veins. Most of them bore livid fleshy patches mottled with pink spots and flakes of scurf, as if they were being eaten away by syphilis or leprosy. Others had a vivid pink hue like scars on the mend, or the brown tint of coalescing scabs; others were blistered as though they had been cauterized by burning irons; yet others displayed hairy teguments pitted with ulcers and embellished with cankers; finally, some appeared to be covered with dressings—plastered with black mercurial lard or green unguents of belladonna, dusted with the powdered yellow mica of iodoform.

Riotously reunited with one another before Des Esseintes, these flowers—more monstrous now than when they had first surprised him—were mingled with others as if they were patients in a hospital, behind the glass walls of their hothouses.

"Sapristi!" he exclaimed, enthusiastically.

A new variety related in its general appearance to the Caladiums, *Alocasia metallica*, excited even greater admiration. This one was endowed with a ground-color of greenish bronze glittering with flecks of silver; it was a masterpiece of artifice—one might easily take it for a length of stove-pipe made into a spearhead by some practical joker.

Next, the men unloaded bunches of bottle-green lozenge-shaped leaves. From the midst of each one rose a sturdy stem at the tip of which quivered a huge ace of hearts as polished as a pepper. As if to defy as the norms of plant life, fleshy and fleecy tails jutted from the middle of the bright vermilion hearts, white and yellow in color, some of which were straight, others spiraling forth like pigs' tails. That was *Anthurium*, an araceous plant recently imported into France from Colombia; it had been assigned to the same family as *Amorphophallus*, a plant from Cochin-China with leaves shaped like fish-slices and long black stems as checkered with scars as the maltreated limbs of a Negro slave.

Des Esseintes was exultant.

Fresh batches of monstrosities continued to descend from the carts. There was *Echinopsis*, thrusting from beds of cotton-wool wadding pink flowers like the stumps of amputated limbs. There was *Nidularium*, opening its sword-like petals to reveal a chasm of flayed flesh. There was *Tillandsia lineni*, trailing its broken ploughshares the color of unfermented wine. There was also *Cypripedium*, whose complex, incoherent colors might have been devised by some demented inventor; it resembled a shoe or a pin-tray, on top of which a human tongue curled back tautly, exactly as depicted in medical works dealing with diseases of the throat and mouth. Two little wings, as red as a jujube, which might have been borrowed from a toy windmill, completed the baroque assembly: a combination of the underside of a tongue, the color of wine-dregs and slate, and a glossy wallet whose lining secreted viscous glue. Des Esseintes could not take his eyes off this unbelievable Indian orchid; the gardeners, impatient with his slowness, began loudly to read out the labels stuck in the pots which they were bringing in.

Des Esseintes watched, somewhat startled, savoring the sound of the forbidding names of the verdant plants. *Encephelartos horridus* was a gigantic iron artichoke painted with rust, like those put on the gates of grand houses to keep trespassers at bay. *Cocos micania* was a kind of palm, slender and toothed, completely surrounded by a crown of leaves which looked like paddles and oars. *Zamia Lehmanni* was a huge pineapple, a monumental Cheshire cheese planted in a bed of heather, bristling at the top with barbed spears and primitive arrows. *Cibotium spectabile*, the most highly-prized of its genus by virtue of the craziness of its structure, outdid the wildest products of the imagination by projecting from its palmate foliage the enormous tail of an orangutan, hairy and brown and contorted at the tip like a bishop's crosier. But he scarcely paused to contemplate these items, awaiting with impatience the group of plants which he found most fascinating of all: the ghouls of the vegetable world, the carnivores. The Antillean fly-trap with the furry stem secreted a digestive fluid, and had curved spines upon its leaves which folded over, interlocking to form a cage around the insects which it caught. *Drosera*, from the peat-bogs, was garnished with glandulous hairs. *Sarracenia* and *Cephalotus* opened voracious maws capable of dissolving and absorbing whole pieces of meat.

Nepenthes, last but not least among these, was a fantasia surpassing the familiar limits of formal eccentricity. He could never tire of turning back and forth in his hands the pot in which this floral extravaganza was arrayed. It resembled a rubber-plant in that it had elongated leaves of dark metallic green, but from the tip of each leaf there extended a green thread, a dangling umbilical cord supporting a greenish urn dappled with purple, like some sort of German porcelain pipe, or a singular bird's-nest swinging gently to and fro, displaying an interior carpeted with hairs.

"This one is truly extraordinary," murmured Des Esseintes.

He had to interrupt his voluptuous indulgence because the gardeners, in a hurry to depart, were emptying their carts as fast

57

as they could, scattering tuberous Begonias, and black Crotons like sheet-metal spotted with red lead.

Then he noticed that there was still one name on his list: the Cattleya from New Granada. His attention was drawn to a winged bell-flower, of a lilac hue so delicate as to be almost mauve; he took it up and held it to his nose, but quickly recoiled; it had an odor like varnished wood, like a toy-box which he had once owned, and gave him the horrors. He decided that he must take care to avoid it, and almost came to regret having admitted to the midst of so many odorless plants one which evoked such disagreeable memories.

Alone once more, he surveyed the tidal wave of vegetation which flooded his hallway; the species were all mingled together, crossing swords, spears and curved daggers with one another in a massive display of green weapons, above which floated, like barbarian battle-standards, harsh and dazzling flowers of every color.

The atmosphere of the room was becoming rarified; soon, in a shadowed corner, at floor-level, a light shone, whitely and softly. He was drawn to the spot, where he found that it came from certain Rhizomorphs which sparkled like night-lights as they breathed.

"These plants are utterly amazing," he said to himself, as he stepped back again to take in the entire assembly at a glance. His objective was achieved; not one of them looked real. Cloth, paper, porcelain and metal had seemingly been lent by Man to Nature in order to permit her to create these monstrosities. When she had not been able to imitate the work of human hands she had been reduced to copying the internal organs of animals, or borrowing the vivid hues of their putrescent flesh and the hideous splendors of gangrene.

"It is, after all, only syphilis," thought Des Eseintes, as his gaze was drawn and held by the horrible stripes of the Caladiums, caressed by a ray of sunlight.

He had a sudden vision, then, of humankind in its entirety, ceaselessly tormented since time immemorial by that contagion. From the beginning of the world, all living creatures had handed down from father to son the everlasting heritage: the eternal malady which had ravaged the ancestors of man, whose disfigurations could be seen on the recently-exhumed bones of the most ancient fossils!

Without ever weakening in its destructive power it had descended through the centuries to the present day, cunningly concealing itself in all manner of painful disguises, in migraines and bronchial infections, hysterias and gouts.

From time to time it clambered to the surface, preferentially assaulting those who were badly cared for and malnourished, exploding in lesions like nuggets of gold, ironically crowning the poor devils in its grip with diamond-studded head-dresses, compounding their misery by imprinting upon their skin the image of wealth and well-being.

And here it was, brought forth once again in all its unparalleled splendor, upon the colored foliage of plants!

"It is true," mused Des Esseintes, returning to the starting-point of his argument. "It is true that, for the most part, Nature, on her own, is incapable of producing species as depraved and perverse as these; she simply supplies the raw materials, the seed and the soil, the nourishing matrix and the elements of the plant, which man then raises up, shapes, paints and sculpts to suit himself.

"As stubborn, confused and narrow-minded as she is, she is in the end submissive, and her master has succeeded in changing the components of the soil by means of chemical reactions, in developing hardier subspecies and carefully contrived hybrids, in skillfully and methodically taking cuttings and grafting stocks so that nowadays the same branch may put forth blooms of different color, and in devising new shades and modifying structures as he wishes. He chisels her blocks of stone, finishes off her sketches, puts his own stamp upon them, and imprints them with his hallmark."

It went without saying, he realized, as he continued his reflections, that Man could achieve within a few years a process of selection that sluggish Nature could not contrive even over centuries. Decidedly, as time went by, the world's horticulturalists were becoming the truest artists of all.

He was a little tired, and he felt stifled by the atmosphere of the hothouse; the excursions he had undertaken during these last few days had exhausted him; the transition between the sedentary life of a recluse and the activity of liberated existence had been too sudden. He left the hallway and went to lie down on his bed.

Absorbed as he was, however, by his unique fascination, he was wound up like a coiled spring. He carried into his sleep a train of thought which soon rolled on into the dark madness of a nightmare.

He found himself upon a path which led through the depths of a twilit forest; he was walking beside a woman he had never met, nor seen, before. She was lanky, with stringy hair and a bulldog face, with freckles on her cheeks and irregular teeth jutting out beneath a snub nose. She was wearing a white apron like a maid's, and a long scarlet sash was draped across her breast; she had calf-length boots like a Prussian soldier's and a black bonnet with a plaited frill and a ribbon rosette. She had the manner of a foreigner and the appearance of a fairground hawker.

He asked himself who that woman was, feeling that he had known her for a long time and that she was somehow intimately involved with his life; he sought in vain among his memories for her origin, her name, her occupation, her relevance to him; he could not remember anything at all about his inexplicable yet undeniable association with her.

He was still searching his memory when, all of a sudden, a strange mounted figure appeared before them, trotting ahead for a few minutes before turning round in the saddle.

His blood ran cold, and he stood as if rooted to the spot by horror. The ambiguous and sexless rider was green of face, and it opened its purple eyelids to reveal eyes of a terrible, luminous cold blue; its mouth was surrounded by pustules; its extraordinarily emaciated arms, like the arms of a skeleton, bare to the elbows and shivering with fever, projected from ragged sleeves; and its fleshless thighs shuddered in their over-large riding-boots.

Its frightful and penetrating gaze was fixed on Des Esseintes, chilling him to the marrow; the woman with the bulldog face, even more terrified than he, held fast to him and howled loudly enough to wake the dead, with her head thrown back and her neck taut.

He was immediately able to interpret the meaning of the terrifying vision. He had before his eyes the incarnation of the Great Plague.

Spurred on by terror to remove himself he ran along a narrow side-path until he came to a pavilion surrounded by laburnums; he went inside and flung himself down into a chair in a corridor.

After a few seconds, when he was beginning to get his breath back, the sound of sobbing made him raise his head; the bulldog-faced woman was before him. Grotesque and lamentable, she wept hot tears, wailing that she had lost her teeth while she fled. She began taking clay pipes from the pocket of her apron, breaking them up and embedding the white pieces of the stems in the gaps in her gums.

"All well and good," said Des Esseintes to himself, "but she's very silly—those stems can't possibly take hold." In fact, they all dropped out of her jaw, one after another.

At that moment, the sound of a galloping horse became audible. An awful terror seized Des Esseintes. His legs turned to jelly as the sound of hoof-beats grew louder, but desperation brought him to his feet nevertheless, like the crack of a whip. He threw himself upon the woman who was by now stamping her feet on the bowls of the pipes, pleading with her to be quiet, and not to betray them by the sound of her boots. She fought against him, and he dragged her to the end of the corridor, strangling her cries in her throat. He suddenly perceived a tap-room door, with green-painted shutters; it was unlocked and he pushed it, prepared to leap through—and abruptly caught himself up.

Before him, in the middle of a vast moonlit clearing, gigantic white clowns were hopping about like rabbits.

Tears of discouragement welled up in his eyes; never, never could he bring himself to cross that threshold. *I'd be flattened*, he thought—and as if to justify his anxieties the number of gigantic clowns was multiplied; their somersaults now filled up the entire horizon and the entire sky, which they bumped continually with their heads and their feet, turn and turn about.

Then the sound of the horse's hooves stopped. It was there in the corridor, behind a round window. More dead than alive, Des Esseintes turned round, and through the circular aperture he saw two pointed ears, an array of yellow teeth, and two nostrils breathing vaporous jets which reeked of phenol.

He sank to the ground, abandoning all thought of fight or flight. He shut his eyes so that he would not meet the frightful gaze of Syphilis, which stared at him from behind the wall. It penetrated his closed eyelids anyhow, and he felt it slide down his clammy back, while all the hairs on his body stood on end in pools of cold sweat. He was ready for anything, even hopeful that it might be ended by some *coup-de-grâce*; a century—which doubtless lasted less than a minute—went by, and then, all a-quiver, he re-opened his eyes.

It had all vanished without trace; as though there had been an abrupt change of scenery wrought by theatrical trickery, a desolate stony landscape now extended into the remote distance: pallid, empty, split by ravines, utterly lifeless. This desolate place was illumined by a soft white light, reminiscent of the glow of phosphorus immersed in oil.

On the ground something moved; it became a woman, very pale, naked save for her legs, which were clad in green silk stockings.

He looked at her curiously. Her hair was curled with split ends, as though it had crimped by irons that were too hot. Two urns like those of *Nepenthes* hung from her ears. Her half-flared nostrils displayed the color of boiled veal. Her eyes were enraptured. She called to him in a low voice.

He had no time to respond, for the woman was already changing; flamboyant colors lit up her eyes and her lips took on the vivid red of Anthuriums; the nipples of her breasts flared up, as glossily varnished as two red peppers.

A sudden intuition came to him. *This is the Flower*, he told himself. His obsessive reasoning persisted even in his nightmare, drawing an analogy between vegetation and infection just as it had done during the day.

Then he observed the frightful irritation of the breasts and the mouth, and discovered that all the skin of her body was stained with sepia and copper. He recoiled in horror, but the woman's eyes fascinated him and he advanced slowly towards her. He tried to dig his heels into the ground to stop himself, and fell to the ground, only to rise up again and continue to move towards her.

He was close enough to reach out and touch her when black *Amorphophalli* sprang up all around them, stabbing at the belly which rose up and fell again like the swell of the sea. He thrust them aside and pushed them away, utterly disgusted to see those warm, firm stems swarming between his fingers. Then, suddenly, the odious plants had disappeared and two arms were trying to wind themselves around him. A frightful anguish set his heart pounding—for the eyes, the frightful eyes, of the woman had become blue, bright, cold and terrible.

He made a superhuman effort to free himself from her embrace, but with an irresistible grip she seized and held him. Haggard and horrified, he saw between her uplifted thighs the blossoming of a cruel *Nidularium*, which opened wide its bloody maw, surrounded by sword-blades.

His body brushed the edge of that hideous wound, he felt death come to claim him—and awoke with a start, choking, ice-cold, mad with fear, sighing: "Ah! Thank God! It's nothing but a dream!"

CHARLES CROS
(1842-1888)

Charles Cros was a poet and inventor, a pioneer of the phonograph and color photography—historically eclipsed by his failure to obtain patents—and the first person to propose a method of communicating with the inhabitants of other planets. He was a prominent member of Émile Goudeau's literary drinking club, known as the Hydropathes, a close friend of Villiers de l'Isle

Adam, with whom he wrote dramas for performance in Nina de Villard's salon, and he also did a double act in Le Chat Noir with Alphonse Allais. His literary work included monologues for the stage adapted by Ernest Coquelin and a good deal of *avant garde* poetry and prose.

"Le Caillou mort d'amour" first appeared in *Le Chat Noir*, 20 mars 1886. "The Pebble that Died of Love" was originally published in *The Supreme Progress and Other French Scientific Romances* (Black Coat Press, 2011)

The Pebble that Died of Love:
A Story Fallen From the Moon

On the 24th of Chum-Chum (Vegan calendar, 7th series) a terrible moonquake devastated the Sea of Tranquility. Horrible or charming fissures opened up in that virgin[1] but infertile ground.

A flint (definitely not from the epoch of chipped stone, more probably that of polished stone[2]) chanced to roll down from a doomed peak and, proud of its roundness, lodged about a *phthwfg*[3] from fissure AB33, commonly known as Moule-à-Singe.[4]

---

1 Cros inserts a footnote: "We cannot put any credence in the infamous slanders that have been put about regarding this region."

2 Early French anthropologists subdivided what the English called the Stone Age into three divisions: the era of *pierre éclatée* [chipped stone], the era of *pierre taillée* [carved stone] and the era of *pierre polie* [polished stone], although the first two were never clearly distinct and were eventually merged into the *paléolithique* [Paleolithic] while the third became the *néolithique* [Neolithic]. The chronological order of the two eras is reversed here, in the interests of euphemistic reference.

3 Cros: "The *phthwfg* is equivalent to a length of 37,000 meters of iridium at seven degrees below zero."

4 This now-obsolete argot term combines two words, *moule* [mussel] and *singe* [monkey], that are both used abusively to signify something similar to the English "fathead"; it is relevant to note, however, that the fissure presumably resembles the narrow opening of a feeding mollusc, which is cited analogically in the slang of other languages, notably the Australian euphemism "spearing the bearded clam."

The rosy appearance of this region, entirely new to a flint scarcely chipped away from its peak, and the black manganese moss that overhung the new abyss, frightened the audacious pebble, which stopped dead, foolishly.

The fissure burst into silent laughter—the silence peculiar to the Beings of the Planet Without an Atmosphere. Far from losing its grace in the course of that laughter, its physiognomy gained a certain exquisite modernity therefrom. Enlarged, but more elegant, it seemed to say to the pebble: "Come on then, if you dare!"

The latter, whose name was actually *Skkjro*,[1] judged it appropriate to preface its amorous assault with an aubade, sung into the void perfumed by magnetic oxide.

It employed the imaginary coefficients of a fourth-degree equation.[2] It is well-known that in ethereal space, one obtains unparalleled fugues in that fashion (Plato vol. XV, ch. 13).

The fissure (whose Selenian name means *Augustine*) seemed at first to be appreciative of this homage. It even softened, welcomingly.

The Pebble, emboldened, was about to take advantage of the situation, rolling further, perhaps penetrating . . .

At this point, the drama commences—a drama brief, brutal, and true.

The dry surface of the moon, jealous of this idyll, was subject to a second quake.

The frightened fissure (Augustine) closed again, forever, and the pebble (Alfred) exploded with rage.

That was the beginning of the Age of Chipped Stone.

1 Cros: "This forename, common on the Planet, is an exact translation of 'Alfred'."
2 Cros: "The original lunar text has 'a fourth-floor landing'—an obvious typographical error."

FÉLICIEN CHAMPSAUR
(1858-1934)

Félicien Champsaur was also a prominent member of the Hydropathes before embarking on a successful journalistic career in the early 1880s, in the course of which he alienated most of his friends, many of whom resented their portrayal in his *roman à clef Dinah Samuel* (1882). His short-lived periodical *Panurge* (1883) was a significant precursor of the Decadent and Symbolist periodicals. He built a highly successful career as a popular novelist after the best-selling *L'Amant des danseurs* (1888), although it never recovered its early impetus after the interruption of the Great War.

"Le Dernière homme" first appeared in the booklet *Les Deux singes* (Éditions de l'Hydre, 1885); "The Last Human" was translated from the version in the collection *Entrée des Clowns* (Jules Lévy, 1886) and was originally published in *The Human Arrow* (Black Coat Press, 2011).

The Last Human

It is a fact that Charles Bergheim, of Stephenson & Co., Stellar Publicity, after dining at a tavern with his blonde girl-friend Alice Penthièvre, had demonstrated a remarkable enthusiasm, at the Exhibition of Incoherent Arts, for a shocking drawing by Mademoiselle Valtesse representing two coherent lizards.[1]

That adorable composition, in which two amorous little animals were about to confide in one another tenderly, gives evidence of a patient and continuous study of nature on the

---

1 Émilie-Louise Delabigne, alias Comtesse Valtesse de la Bigne (1848-1910) was a famous courtesan, who rose to fame as the mistress of the composer Jacques Offenbach, was ennobled by Napoléon III and was said to be a model for several notable literary figures, including Zola's *Nana* and Goncourt's *Chérie*. The absurdist Exhibition of the Incoherent Arts, founded by the publisher Jules Lévy, was held every year from 1883 to the mid-1890s, anticipating Dada and surrealism.

part of the witty red-haired woman who is its author. Nearby, Dinah Samuel, on the arm of a young man, was reproaching the lounge-lizard for not having sufficiently hospitable paws and the lizard for lacking coherence (on examination.) Bergheim, on the other hand, was not criticizing. His eyes full of perverse flames, he loudly declared, contrary to the opinion of Penthièvre, that Mademoiselle Valtesse was charming and babahissant, her drawing marvelous.

Since then, Alice had been sulking.

That same evening, they had taken the train to a château, an Angevin bachelor establishment where a jolly hunt for game of every sort had been organized, for they had only gone to the crazy exhibition to amuse themselves while waiting for the departure time.

Alice had not addressed four words to him. She had slumped in a corner of the compartment while he had huddled in the opposite corner. The lamp up above gazed at them like the moon.

Bergheim had given some thought to an idea he was working on: the illumination of Paris by a formidable source of electric light at the top of a lighthouse, a competitor with the sun, a tower of stone and iron erected in the center of the city. He read two pages of a new novel and went to sleep.

As he did not have a tranquil conscience with respect to Penthièvre—for, so far as affairs were concerned, he had not felt any remorse for a long time—his slumber was full of dreams.

He dreamed that instead of being on a train, they were back at home in the Avenue de Messine. His girl-friend, still pouting, had locked her bedroom door. Anyway, he liked solitude just as much. He installed himself in the drawing-room, on a soft divan. At the back of the room, under a palm-tree, a parrot was asleep in its cage.

At about two o'clock, Bergheim suddenly opened his eyes and sat up on his elbow. He heard a great tumult and saw, through the windows, that it was as if the air was on fire. What could be the cause of such an anomaly? Was there an earthquake, in which Paris would collapse? Were the drains finally in revolt?

He looked outside.

A current lashed his face, as if he had put his head out of the window of a fast-moving carriage. A crazed population was running around the boulevard, in great confusion. Everyone, nevertheless, seemed to be devoting himself to his normal occupation, but with an activity overexcited to the thirtieth power. There were cries that were almost savage; Bergheim thought he was in the Bourse.

Without further anxiety, he reflected that it was only a dream, and that there was no point disturbing himself—needlessly, in any case—if there really had been an earthquake. He lay down on his divan again and, draped in a Japanese silk sheet embroidered with silver and gold monsters, he said to himself: "Before me, the end of the world."

What had happened during the night was quite simple. A comet, arriving from infinite space, without any warning, with a velocity of several million leagues a minute, having deviated from its orbit in consequence of a celestial cataclysm, had traversed the solar system. Its immeasurable tail—a wake of oxygen, hardly anything at all—encountering our atmosphere, had run prodigiously around the world. The drawing-room in the Avenue de Messine where Bergheim was lying down had been, by a freak of chance, the center of that monstrous whirlwind; the financier and his parrot had been the only ones spared.

When the former went into the bedroom the next morning, having broken down the door, Alice Penthièvre, clad only in her black stockings, otherwise naked on the carpet and the cushions seemed to be sleeping peacefully, but neither her pulse nor her heart was beating; she was dead.

Bergheim did not know that she had fallen down after having danced a frenzied jig, for the comet, with its tail of oxygen, had strangely multiplied the vital force on Earth during its passing.

On their sudden awakening, it was as if all the people and animals alike had been possessed by demons. They had surrendered themselves, with prodigious faculties, to their habits, their desires, their instincts and their passions. In the first moments, everyone had produced the potential, good or evil, that he bore within him; it had increased to the extreme in that abnormal atmosphere.

Soon, life, exhausted by such a chimerical self-manifestation, had ceased entirely. All creatures had died in the cataclysm, from giants to microbes. The subtlest germs of animal life had been annihilated, with the result that putrefaction was impossible for a long time.

Bergheim went out. Although the comet had moved away, the air was still very rich in oxygen, and he felt a great vigor. Strongly overexcited, and content—for he despised the human race—he strolled like a madman through the bizarrely quiet streets.

Walking was difficult, however, because of the cadavers, maintaining the appearance of life, with which the streets were strewn. It was frequently necessary to step over a corpse, as one has to do with the beggars on an Italian dock.

Carriages of every sort gave the impression of having been traveling at high speed when the horses been stopped in their tracks, their lungs burned by an excess of vertiginous life. The coachmen were leaning forward, their eyes open, their lips seemingly ready to utter an insult, holding firm to the reins. Passengers had stuck their heads out of the windows; they had doubtless expired while shouting "Faster!"

Their muscles magically tautened, individuals who had been clinging to some sort of support at the supreme moment had retained the attitudes they had adopted in life. Animals were on their feet; at the Senate, Monsieur de G*** was standing like a wax statue, his hand clenching the podium.

The ear was no longer aggravated by the continual noise of city life. A frightful silence weighed upon the Earth.

And that evening, Bergheim, certain that he was alone, rejoiced.

He began roaming idly around Paris. He realized a dream that he had had at the age of twelve, before entering into business: the dream of possessing the ring of Gyges, which would render him invisible and permit him to acquaint himself with intimate human life.

Without the mysterious ring, he could now penetrate the populous houses of workers, bourgeois apartments, the boudoirs of courtesans, the homes of politicians and artists. He went into the most private feminine worldly milieux. (What is love? An exchange of electricity, a bringing together of opposites.)

In this way, Bergheim discovered many vile acts in a life interrupted in its acuity.

From time to time, Bergheim experienced a desire to talk to someone; then he addressed himself to his parrot, the only other being that was still alive. But he soon wearied of that companion and set the bird free. It continued living in Paris for several months.

The parrot always asked its former master for news whenever it encountered him. "How are you?"

"Not bad, old chap. And you?"

The parrot was an adequate replacement for the numerous friends that one meets in the street and with whom one politely exchanges vain remarks.

Every day resembled the next. Existence scarcely varied. Bergheim ate lunch and dinner in taverns, where he drank vintage wines. He also invited himself to private houses.

One of his pleasures, after dinner, while smoking his cigar, was to admire the vegetation produced by the passage of the comet and the new warmth of the atmosphere. After some hesitation, he abandoned his English suit.

Nature had become almost what it had been in the antediluvian epochs before the central fire, breaking through the thin crust that imprisoned it, had abruptly raised up chains of mountains—the Alps, the Cordilleras, the Andes—and new lands in the midst of vast oceans.

In the overheated atmosphere, vegetable life was extraordinary. The Seine flowed beneath a tangle of lianas, an exuberant and capricious verdure. The hills of Sèvres and Meudon, and the windmills of Montmartre, Orgemont and Sannois, were covered by a boom of arborescent ferns, lycopodendrons and giant horsetails.

In Paris, blades of grass lifted paving-stones as they grew and became slender and flexible trees, with infinitely undulating foliage. On the Boulevard des Italiens, around the Opéra, the vegetation climbed toward the roofs like a flood of the sap of primitive forests.

Sometimes, Bergheim, who now swung from branch to branch like an ape, perceived a large green bird with a hooked beak. It was the parrot, which was slowly being modified. It had only retained one of the choruses it had previously known, and sang it often:

Coco, Coco,
Scratch me . . .

It was the sole lyrical evidence of the vanished civilization.

Was another organic life about to be born? Would enormous and superior beasts soon appear: the gigantic dinotherium, the prodigious iguanodon, and pterodactyls with horrible wings in the sky? Sometimes, Bergheim was afraid, thinking that he had suddenly perceived terrible eyes amid the tangled foliage of the virgin Parisian forest, with pupils a foot in diameter, seeking the light.

Was humankind about to accomplish a retrograde evolution and be annihilated, like the trilobites of the Silurian period, when the seas were hot and pale sunlight scarcely pierced the thick atmosphere? Was humankind about to come to an end, like the saurians of the Lias,[1] and the mastodons and megatheria of the Tertiary Epoch?

Charles Bergheim, of Stephenson & Co., Stellar Publicity, was transformed into a quadrumane.

Suddenly, as he tumbled pitifully in front of the Café Riche from the top of a fern, he perceived, through the glass of his compartment in the express train, the pale light of dawn.

Alice Penthièvre, exquisitely modern, in this year's blouse, with a Tyrolean hat on her exceedingly blonde hair, the color of maize, said to her lord and master, with a smile: "Did you sleep well, you naughty monkey?"

---

1 The Lias was a geological designation roughly equivalent to the early Jurassic era.

Part Two:
Pioneers

STÉPHANE MALLARMÉ
(1842-1898)

Stéphane Mallarmé was the archetypal Symbolist poet and the chief theorist of the Symbolist Movement, which was incubated in his *mardis*. He was a contributor to *Le Parnasse contemporain*, but remained relatively obscure until his most famous poem, "L'Après-midi d'un faune," apparently begun in 1865, was published in 1876. His definitive collections *Poésies* (1887) and *Divagations* (1897) did not reach print until the Movement was well under way. He never finished his "Hérodiade," begun in the 1860s, but its exposure in the *mardis* assisted its protagonist, more usually known as Salomé, to become one of the key Symbolic figures deployed in works by other hands, including the play written in French by Oscar Wilde.

"Le Phenomene futur" dates from 1864; it was reprinted in *La Revue blanche* in 1891 and Mallarmé's collection *Vers et prose* in 1893, "The Future Phenomenon" was originally published in *The Second Dedalus Book of Decadence: The Black Feast* (Dedalus, 1992).

"Le Démon de l'Analogie" was first published in 1874. "The Demon of Analogy" is original to the present volume.

The Future Phenomenon

A pale sky above the world at the end of its decrepitude might disappear within the clouds: the threadbare purple tatters of sunsets fade into the dormant river at the horizon, drowned by rays of light and water. The trees languish in *ennui*, and beneath their blanched foliage (blanched by the dust of the ages rather than that of the roads) the Showman of Past Things has erected his tent. Many streetlamps await the dusk, retouching the faces of a miserable crowd of men, conquered by the undying malady and sin of centuries, beside their puny accomplices pregnant with the wretched fruits by which the earth shall perish.

The showman's patter spills into the unquiet silence of all those eyes, imploring with a despairing cry the descending sun that slides into the water. "The spectacle inside has no signboard to advertise it, for there is nowadays no painter capable of displaying a pale shadow of it. I bring with me, alive—preserved over the years by superscientific means—a Woman of the olden days. Some novel and naïve madness, an ecstasy of gold or I know not what, which she called her *hair*, is draped with silken grace about a face illuminated by the blood-tinted bareness of her lips. Instead of the conceit of clothing she has a body; and even her eyes, which have the semblance of exotic stones, cannot surpass the glare emitted by her blissful flesh: from the breasts uplifted as though they were replete with eternal milk, nipples towards the sky, to the lithe legs which guard the salinity of the primal sea."

Mindful of their paltry spouses—bald, ghastly and full of horror—the husbands press forward. Their wives, too, moved by melancholy curiosity, desire to see.

When all have contemplated the noble creature, a relic of some earlier accursed age—some indifferently, for they will not have the power of understanding, but others heartbroken, their eyelids moist with tears of resignation—they will look at one another. Then the poets of those times, sensible of the rekindling of their extinguished eyes, will make their way towards their light-source, their brains intoxicated for a moment by an ambiguous glory, haunted by Rhythm, forgetful of the fact that they exist in an era that has outlived beauty.

The Demon Of Analogy

Did unknown words sing on your lips, accursed shreds of an absurd phrase?

I left my apartment with the appropriate sensation of a wing sliding over an instrument, slowly and lightly, which replaced a voice pronouncing the words: "The Penultimate is dead" in a descendant tone, in such a fashion that

The Penultimate

finished the verse and

Is dead

was detached from the fateful suspension, quite unnecessarily, in a void of significance. I took a few paces along the street and recognized in the absence of sound the taut string of a musical instrument, which had been forgotten, and that the glorious Memory had certainly come visiting with a wing or a palm and, with a finger on the artifice of the mystery, I smiled and implored a different speculation from intellectual prayer. The sentence came back, virtual, disengaged henceforth from an anterior fall of the pen or branch, through the extended voice, until it was finally articulated in isolation, alive in its personality. No longer contenting myself with a perception, I went on reading it at the end of the verse, and once, as a trial, adapting it to my speech, soon pronouncing it, with a pause after "Penultimate," in which I found a painful enjoyment: "The Penultimate." Then the string of the instrument, so taut in the forgetfulness of the absence of sound, doubtless broke, and I added in the manner of a prayer: "Is dead." I did not stop attempting a return to thoughts of predilection, alleging, in order to calm myself, that *penultimate* is certainly the term in the dictionary that signifies the next to last syllable of vocables, and that its appearance was the poorly abjured residue of a linguistic labor by which quotidian sob my noble poetic faculty is interrupted, the very sonority and the air of deception assumed by the haste of the facile affirmation being a cause of torment. Harassed, I resolved to let words of a sad nature wander through my mouth of their own accord, and I went along murmuring with an intonation susceptible of condolence: "The Penultimate is dead, it is dead, quite dead, the desperate Penultimate," thinking by that means to satisfy anxiety, and not without the secret hope of burying it in the amplification of the psalmody, when, what!—by virtue of a magic easily deducible and nervous, I sensed, my hand reflected in a shop window making the gesture there of a caress descending on something, that I had the voice (the first one, which had undoubtedly been the only one).

But where the irrefutable intervention of the supernatural installs itself, and the commencement of the anguish under which my once lordly mind is agonizing, is when I saw, raising my eyes, in the street of antiquaries instinctively followed, that I was in front of the shop of a maker and seller of old musical instruments, which were hung on the wall, and, on the ground, of yellow palms and the wings, buried in shadow, of ancient birds. I fled, a bizarre person probably condemned to wear mourning for the inexplicable Penultimate.

JEAN MORÉAS
(1856-1910)

Jean Moréas was born in Athens, but came to Paris in 1875 to complete his education and joined Goudeau's Hydropathes. His early poetry, collected in *Les Syrtes* (1884) and *Les Cantilènes* (1886) was strongly influenced by Verlaine, but his association with Gustave Kahn led to his becoming a central member of the Symbolist Movement, collaborating with Paul Adam in the prose collections *Les Demoiselles Goubert, moeurs de Paris* (1886) and *Le Thé chez Miranda* (Tresse et Stock, 1886) and writing the 1886 Manifesto published in *Le Figaro*, which defined the Movement, albeit rather controversially, before he departed to found his own École Romane in 1891.

"Le Lévrier" first appeared in *Lutèce*, 18 mai 1884; it was reprinted in *Le Thé chez Miranda*, where "L'Innoucento" appears to have been published for the first time, and from which the translations of the two stories were made, both of which are original to the present volume.

The Greyhound

I

Since the death of her husband—it would be a year ago at the time of the grape-harvest—Comtesse Diane de Gorde had lived alone and inconsolable in the old château sadly situated on the edge of the pool. Served by taciturn domestics, assisted by her confessor, who preached evangelical resignation to her, but in vain, she spent her life mourning her irrevocably vanished happiness, her heart pierced by seven swords.

Of noble lineage and a delicate beauty of old pastels, she had married a trifle belatedly, at twenty-four, the Comte de Garde, a handsome young man of thirty, gallant in the exquisite fashion of old, a fervent lover of hunting, a true French gentleman and no anglomaniac.

Courted more than any other, because of her rank and her beauty, the Comtesse de Gorde was able by virtue of a subtle tact and an irreproachable conduct to discourage the fatuity of men and disarm the malevolent speech of women. The beautiful Diana did not hide, however, beneath her divinely molded cleavage, the glacial indifference for amorous ecstasies of her namesake, the ancient huntress.

Sensing the blood of a bacchide in her veins and too much pride and devotion to sully herself with adultery, she preferred to kill her husband, literally, by means of her inexorable caresses. For five years there was a life of alarms and delights: the torches of amour burned all the way to the candles around the catafalque. She watched him extinguish, her heart ulcerated by remorse, but impotent to command the rebellion of her senses. And he, already touched by death, still came back, a melancholy smile on his pale lips, and from the happiness in the depths of his eyes magnified by fever, he came back, again and always, to respire the lilies of that body of a goddess, those lilies deadlier than the flowers of the manchineel tree.

Thus, in an autumnal dusk, as the dead leaves were beginning to curl along the jaundiced hedges, he rendered his soul in a final kiss.

II

During the first months that followed the Comte's death, Diane's despair was such that there was anxiety for her reason. Gradually, however, her dolor was appeased, and a mute prostration followed the delirious exaltation. With the relative calming of regrets, nature resumed its right; the exasperated fermentation of nagging desires began to beat again in her hot veins, her nights were haunted by hideous nightmares that extenuating monastic mortifications had not succeeded in exorcising.

Often, waking with a start, the victim of tempting hallucinations, she fell to her knees before the Madonna's niche, sobbing and imploring absolution from the unconscious frenzy that was burning her blood, or even, after having wandered like a desolate apparition through the somber corridors of the château, she spent the night until the first rosiness of dawn in the broad peripter open over the pool where the teal wept, upright, her feverish forehead against the marble of the colonnades, avidly breathing in the wind charged with mist.

Ashamedly, she surprised herself coveting the muscular arms of gardeners or the fleshy calves of valets de chambre. Sometimes, she also thought of remarrying. Then a familiar phantom, very pale, with a soft smile full of reproaches, loomed up before her frightened eyes, to remind her that she had sworn to him at his deathbed never to allow her couch to be sullied by another man.

Thus, her eyes circled by bistre, her features tortured by nervous spasms, she languished and etiolated, that mimalone condemned to celibacy by an irrevocable oath.

III

It was an afternoon at the end of spring. The sky, in the torrid heat, resembled a white-hot furnace; dragonflies were marauding over the nympheas on the still waters, nests were twittering in the bright foliage; an amorous languor passed through the heavy air.

Comtesse Diane, melancholy, leaning on her elbows at a window, allowed her distracted gaze to wander over the verdant countryside. Suddenly, an unexpected scene attracted her attention. Behind a squat caryophyllea bush, her favorite greyhounds, Tom and Giselle, were copulating freely in the sunlight.

The Comtesse closed the window and went away, pensively.

From that day on, Tom, the handsome Scottish greyhound, gorged with treats, no longer quit his mistress. Diane had almost recovered her fresh colors of old. And when she went, twice a day, to ornament her husband's tomb with the thyrsi of white roses, she knelt down and prayed, repeating with conviction: "I swore that no other man would ever sully our couch."

The Innoucento

Very upright, and tall, tall and dusty under the ardent sun, she went along the only street in the village, with its border of buildings as white as chalk and roofed in thatch, with its exceedingly dilapidated church at the very end, where the fake dial had always marked the same hour for many years. Above it was the mountain with its pine forests, as woolly as a negro's head, and its background blue-tinted by virgin glaciers; beyond, the stream full of trout, persevering against the accumulated rocks of its bed under the little bridge that the weight of carts overflowing with forage caused to tremble.

She had grown up there, the innoucento,[1] as she was familiarly called, among the pigs and the chickens, grunting and clucking with them on the dung-heap and in the mud. A large deformed head, hunched between the poorly-squared shoulders, excessively small eyes gleaming uncertainly, the eyes of a cretin, a mouth slit to the ears, with thin lips and teeth already mossy; excessively long arms, excessively large hands, and flattened feet in espadrilles: thus, gamboling in the fields of maize and vegetable plots, her body deformed and her mind clouded, the poor idiot reached twenty years of age.

Her parents being dead, an old woman, Madame Lafont, had taken her into her service. She guarded the livestock and went to wash the linen in the stream. The village lads mocked her, taking her by the chin with comical mimes, and the girls asked her confidentially, in order to chuckle, whether she had a lover: *As oun galan, Innoucento?* And the poor idiot widened her little eyes, not understanding, and clucked like a chicken.

It was an afternoon in July. A fierce sun was darting its red rays in the white sky. Flies were buzzing over the stagnant waters, wasps gleaning over the hedge, hazel-grouse cooing in the branches, and little green lizards crawling in the hollow bushes. The innoucento, who was grazing her livestock in the fields sensed her head becoming heavy with somnolence and went to sleep in the shade of poplars.

At that moment, the gamekeeper Miquelas was going along the path, drunk. He saw the innoucento asleep under the poplars, and a baroque idea traversed his head, heavy with drink.

"That'll be funny!" he said to himself.

Then he woke the poor idiot up with a kick. She rubbed her eyes, grunting. Then he took her in his arms and carried her into a nearby thicket, where the grass was long. And the flies were buzzing over the stagnant waters, and the wasps gleaning over the hedge, and the little green lizards crawling in the hollow bushes.

From that day onward, when the girls asked her *As oun galan, Innoucento?* the idiot no longer clucked like the chickens, and her gaze became serious.

---

1 The Occitan word *innouncento*, the equivalent of "innocent," was generally used to mean "mad."

A few months later, her figure thickened visibly, and the village lads, when they encountered her, said with bursts of laughter: "How fat you're getting, Innoucento. Are you pregnant?"

But she did not reply, and fled at a run over the plots of beets.

Often, in the evening, when she undressed, she fixed her anxious gaze on her swollen belly and remembered, blushing, the day she had gone to sleep under the tall poplars.

In the village, people smiled when they saw her go past, and the housewives whispered, with astonished expressions: "But who the devil can have done that?"

Old Madame Lafont, very intrigued, summoned a passing empiric and had him examine her servant. The empiric declared that the young woman was pregnant.

Then the old woman entered into a frightful anger and told her servant to get out of her house as quickly as possible. "I don't want a whore in my house," she said.

The poor idiot made a bundle of her clothes and left, weeping, across the country, without knowing where she was going. At nightfall, she stopped, exhausted by fatigue, on a little bridge over the stream, which plunged into the depths with a lugubrious din over a bed of sharp rocks.

The night was delightful. The silver-haloed moon was shining over the peaceful mountain. Dogs could be heard howling in the distance and water splashing under the bridge. A soft breeze perfumed by strawberries rustled in the pine-needles. The mind of the poor innoucento went back again to the day when the gamekeeper had carried her into the thicket, and a smile that was sweet and bitter at the same time passed furtively over her thin lips. She looked at her swollen belly and palpated it curiously.

Then, as if a flash of light had suddenly traversed her darkened brain, she started to sob.

The moon had hidden behind the tall forest trees.

The innoucento gazed for a moment at the brown-tinted water plunging into the depths with a lugubrious din over a bed of sharp rocks; then she climbed over the parapet and threw herself into the river, without uttering a cry.

GUSTAVE KAHN
(1859-1936)

Gustave Kahn founded the first wholly Symbolist periodical, *La Vogue*, in 1886. His pioneering collection of *vers libre*—a term he claimed to have invented—*Palais nomades* (1887) also included prose "Interludes" and he became one of the most prolific writers of Symbolist prose, extending his work in that vein well into the twentieth century.

"L'Ombre sur la rose" appeared in *Vieil Orient orient neuf* (Fasquelle, 1928). "The Shadow on the Rose" is original to the present volume.

"La Maison natale" appeared in *Le Conte d'or et du silence* (1898); "The Natal House" was originally published in the translation of that volume, *The Tale of Gold and Silence* (Black Coat Press, 2011).

The Shadow on the Rose

In the dull and violet shade of the garden, Gadi waited. The somber mass of the fig-trees hid him. The monotonous footsteps that glided over the terrace above his head did not frighten him, for old Ahmad, when he walked like that, was only thinking about the glory of Allah, without anything being able to distract his thoughts, his eyes or his ears. In the fading night, nothing was making a sound but the foliage. Sometimes, very softly, a distant song or the rhythm of a flute embroidered the blue-tinted silence with gold and silver.

It seemed to Gadi that he recognized those sparse fragments of music, for his métier as a poet and musician was to furnish the amorous with songs they could sing, or brief chants for those whose voice was hoarse and had recourse to instruments. Those songs and chants served lovers to announce their presence to the objects of their love, who replied to them from the terraces of houses where they were captive, married or maidens. It was with the letters that he traced, like a public scribe, for gallants who did not know how to write, that he earned his paltry pittance: Gadi, the poor poet of Shiraz, a great sufi before Allah, whose grandeur and essence he penetrated, and of which he sang for himself, with his wife and wine, in triple and delightful ecstasy.

Apart from a low beat of drums and a strumming of guitars in the far distance, signaling a celebration, the silence became denser. Ahmad had gone back into his dwelling and bolted the doors.

Above Gadi, a soft voice imitated the trills of a nightingale. Gadi climbed into the fig-tree. "Leila," he murmured. With one bound he was on the terrace. Leila drew him toward an empty watch-tower, where they embraced; but the still-nocturnal hour at which prudence parted the lovers arrived so rapidly.

Gadi slid down the smooth wall nimbly and disappeared into the back-streets, muffling the sound of his footsteps, in order to return to the little house of cob in the most distant of the outlying districts of Shiraz, where his shop was, to which an old negress had come one day to bring him to Leila, and Gadi held in his fingers and raised to his lips a fresh crimson rose he had just been given by Leila.

And the days went by in the little house of cob, and Gadi spent the long hours of the day beside a little rose-bush that he had planted in his exceedingly narrow garden, and which only bore a single fresh crimson rose, like the one that Leila had given him.

On many evenings he returned to hide in the fig-trees, under his beloved's terrace, and Ahmad's footsteps glided over the terrace, and then, in the silence rhythmed by distant amorous music, he waited, and waited in vain. Neglecting all prudence, he often murmured the appeal well known to Leila, whistling a nightingale's trill, chosen by him rather than the verse of a poem as a simpler interpreter of a more ample passion. The night remained silent and closed. He went up on to the terrace; the little windows closed, one after another, like eyes with lowered lids. A watchman's arrow vibrated in his ear, and that night, he had difficulty escaping the dog launched in his pursuit.

It seems to him that in a cortege of people going away, followed by carts loaded with baggage, toward some village in the country around Shiraz, he recognized the rich Ahmad, and that the woman enveloped in a long pink and sulfur-yellow robe was Leila. He is sure that they were Leila's eyes shining behind that veil, like twin stars. He runs, but the armed guards drive him away with sticks. And he is in love! He is in love!

Is it the same negress who slipped a short note under his door: *Wait and love?* Oh, let misfortune fall upon the client who, at that moment, had made him come, in order to hide amorous mottoes in a basket of fruits! Let Sheitan persecute him, whom lucre and the vanity of a poet enabled him to forget his dolor that day. He suffered, for he knew nothing about Leila but her name, the supple shoot of her body, and her taste. What was she in Ahmad's eyes? A wife, his daughter, a servant, a slave? If Leila had loved him, Gadi, it is because she could love. Since she had loved him, in that amorous nocturnal refuge, it is because she could steal a moment of amour from a master. But might she not have recovered her amour for that master?

In the rapidity of their brief meetings, their ardent kisses had always been their dialogue, and, knowing Leila entirely, Gad knew almost nothing about her. If a day came when he went past her, and the veil parted, would he even recognize, in its indifferent aspect, the amorous face that she had shown him? For a woman's face is no longer the same, and her gaze attains a beauty so intense in the caress that her habitual expression is only a pale and uniform reflection of it.

While Gadi remained sitting facing the rose-bush, on which a single rose trembled similar to the one Leila had given him, he incessantly imagined different Leilas, amorous or perverse, ingenuous or guileful, desolate or infidel, curbed under the yoke or radiant, and the images precipitated alternately between a Leila crowned with gems and a Leila covered in sordid rags, a Leila enchained or a Leila spread upon another terrace, over other lovers, and to the quivering of all those songs of appeal that he, Gadi, had animated with his tenderness, delivering a rain of fiery kisses.

Gadi's mind weakened under the continuity of his suffering. He no longer opened his door when it resonated under the fists of visitors, and by dint of searching for Leila's face, on the scabby ground and beneath the blazing skies, when his gaze returned to the rose on the venerated rose-bush, he saw a motionless shadow there.

The other poets of Shiraz were delighted by his melancholy. In the evenings, he no longer came with them into the little inns and the gardens planted with vivacious rose-bushes to empty cups of wine, or to throw quoits on to the square traced on the ground with the point of a knife. For their audience of scribes, notaries, illuminators of manuscripts or merchants who liked good stories, the poets sang in the gaiety of the evening; Gadi, in love, was a slave of the shadow on the rose, of the shadow of a single rose on a single rose-bush. A sort of bizarre glory surrounded Gadi, whose mind had been unhinged, it was claimed, but some people, especially women, did not feel any tenderness for a man haunted by such an entire amour.

And Gadi became gradually weaker and more desperate. An old potter, his neighbor, had acquired the habit of placing beside him a pitcher of water, pancakes and the few fruits of a meal that Gadi scarcely touched, and as the potter was good, he attempted to cure the invalid.

"Gadi, the shadow that you claim to see on that rose, I, Memdouck the potter, do not perceive!"

"That is, Memdouck the charitable, because you only perceive the appearance of things."

"But Gadi, what appearance is there, since everything passes and flies away, dusk succeeding dawn, and the gilded shadow proceeds incessantly and regularly from this wall to the other, that a shadow can remain motionless over a rose?"

"And yet, Memdouck, the shadow is in the heart of the rose."

"Gadi, is it not in yours, and does it not cover your eyes like a blindness?"

"Memdouck, everything is similar beneath the veils with which Allah incessantly dresses and undresses himself before us."

"Are you incurable then, Gadi?"

"Yes, Memdouck, so long as that rose does not blossom in its original clarity."

Discouraged, Memdouck got up in order to leave, and he was picking up, in order to take them away, the pitcher, still full, and the basket, scarcely touched, when a veiled form slipped through the door that he had neglected to close.

Memdouck was about to exclaim in surprise, when the form put a finger to its lips to command silence, and the astonished potter sat down again, amazed and charmed, for beneath the gray veil, which fell, a white veil was revealed, and then a yellow veil, and then a pink veil, and then the light veil of the face fell, and before the rose-bush, before Gadi's closed eyes, there was the most graceful apparition of a peri with brown hair and gilded eyes, with a snowy complexion mingled with pale gold, and from the peri's lips sprang the trill of a nightingale.

Gadi awoke, as if from a long dream.

"O Leila, Leila, the awaited and the beloved!" And his arms closed around her.

Memdouck went away softly, closed the door, and remained on the alert; but no sound troubled the sunlit street, and the potter went take his siesta, while Gadi, certainly, lavished his Leila with caresses, who would perhaps soon slip away from the cob house on tiptoe, and about whom he might never know anything, while knowing everything; and the crimson rose scintillated beneath the bright sky, clear and sunlit, until the expelled shadow came to settle upon it again.

The Natal House

A young man had left his city, his father and his mother—not that he did not love them, but his soul contained all the crazy flames of curiosity and aspiration. He had formed an image of the world according to the tales of travelers who had returned to their hearths long before—which is to say that they were embellished. He believed that at the gates of cities, wise old men, touched by his fatigue, would interrupt their conversations to give him good advice, and that adventurous young men like himself would help him to discover everything about their corner of the earth.

He saw himself thus associated with all experiences and all the songs of youth, and believed that tresses would be unbound for a stranger who knew tales from far away and had seen other climes.

His route was long and no part of his hope was satisfied. The old men sitting at the gates of cities questioned him thoroughly, asking his name, his age and his origin, and then shook their heads and proclaimed the benefits of stability in the natal house, deploring before him ancient misfortunes whose victims he did not know. The young people were impassioned by their own adventures, some absorbed by hatred of the local tyrant, others living in a great desire for travel and fortune; the latter sometimes accompanied him as far as a bend in the road, but that was all. And the young women laughed together at the spring, no longer astonished by one more passer-by; so many of them disappeared before their large eyes among the caravans that went through the city without stopping.

Sometimes a tax-collector, alone in his tollbooth, entertained our young man for a little longer, but that was to hear fresh news. Everyone demanded a little of that from him, but no one gave him any—and to his saddened mind, the foreign earth seemed monotonous. As he clung stubbornly to his chimera, however, he continued on his way, with the result that one day he found himself direly impoverished, exceedingly weary and a long way—a very long way—from home.

He also fell ill, and one evening, exhausted, he fell down by the roadside. It was a road almost devoid of trees, and the sky above his head, palely violet, was impregnated with such total calm and such negative nonchalance, and the silence of the place was so deep, that the young man had the impression that he was going to die there, alone and far from any human assistance.

As the invincible somnolence overwhelmed him, he seemed to see—and did indeed see with the eyes of his soul—a peri. The merciful goddess wanted to know the cause of his distress.

"Oh," he said, "if only I might return to my father's house. It is in my native land, beside the tranquil river, where the clear water passes over white pebbles; there grow the reeds that I cut, as tall as my childish stature, and that is where I poured out my confused and ignorant songs.

"White room where I played on the carpet, which I always saw as high and colossal; fountain in the interior garden, always filtered by the minutes of the maternal smile; maternal house, original basin of the springs of my life; high window from which I discovered for the first time the red, yellow and brown caravans of the infinite plain; fig tree with the first-rate figs, in whose shade I often slept; little garden wall, the first obstacle I was able to overcome; you live on, silent friends whose advice I did not understand, perhaps awaiting the one who wanted to go wandering and would like to become one of you again, and participate in your static calm. Doubtless, today, my father has asked the criers and guides returned from afar whether they have seen me."

And the merciful peri enabled him to see his father's house once again, in spirit.

They both departed, and the road was beautiful—much more beautiful than it had ever seemed to the young man when he was traveling it at first, even with the joys of adventure.

The landscapes recognized him. A tree said: "He's far less sad than he was a little while ago, and his tread is lighter; he's undoubtedly returning to his father's house, having got his wish, and the person who is accompanying him is very beautiful."

A stream that was making a mill-wheel turn tuned its song to his footsteps, joyfully, and the young man realized that it was possible, with that clear accompaniment, to accomplish thousands of joyful strides.

Night rang numerous silvery bells; they were the peris who were going to visit one another in seductive apparel. Their hair is the color of the fraternal night; on their foreheads they bear the lucid amber color of the plumes of celestial fire that seem to humans to be shooting stars. Their dresses are of every beautiful color, but they pass by so quickly that mortals only see white veils, which they mistake for little clouds; at close range, however, they are exquisite robes whose fabric is made of pearly grains—and to run from one celestial terrace to another they launch themselves forth on exceedingly rapid little horses, which furrow space with their wings, as iridescent as those of the butterflies of the realm of gods and genies. Bells suspended from their necks emit a harmonic confusion of clear notes, infinitely.

On fine evenings, the peris visit one another, or occupy themselves with helping a human in his misery, or devote themselves to embellishing flowers and young women, whose features they retouch while asleep, by presenting them with dreams of happiness, or spread long trails of perfume through the world, which drift the following day, idly circulating over the earth, astonishing with their unexpectedness and complexity the humans who are able to perceive them, without fixing them clearly in memory.

Our young man, his eyes open to all that joyous enchantment, followed his protectress ardently, even though, intoxicated by the perfumed course, he could no longer remember the objective of their journey—and he was very surprised when, in the evening of the city still lit up by a few torches and tambourines, he perceived his father's house, black and enormous. Only one window was lit, so meagerly that it seemed a crack in the wall, and that mass of masonry was so gray, mute and enclosed that he felt a chill in his heart.

"Oh, Peri, kind Peri, is that really my natal house?"

At that moment, in the only lighted room, he saw his brothers. Thanks to the peri, he could hear them; they were calculating the use that they would make of their future fortune. Their father's fortune would surely be divided into three parts, since one of them had left and not returned.

"However," said the eldest, "I can certainly not oppose that. Our brother wasn't one of us; he didn't understand the language of our hearth; so far as we are concerned, he was born a stranger. And such is the opinion of our father—but our mother will defend him. Anyway, he's undoubtedly dead."

That was certainly their desire, but, because they were young and their senses still keen, they had a vague notion of some divine presence, and separated without formulating their thoughts.

The peri then took him into the room where his aged parents were sleeping, and thanks to her, he visited their dreams. He saw himself there, still small and frail, amid all the things that he loved and had once seemed to him to be so large, but as if diminished, dried-out and frayed—and his father and mother saw him too. They both spoke about him often.

The father said: "Infinite justice will bring him back to us; I shall be clement, but he must immediately, not humiliate himself, but take his place at our counters and share in our labors."

And the mother said: "Infinite generosity will bring him back to me; when he comes back I shall heal his wounds and make sure that, for at least three full days, his father will not force him to lend himself to his labors—but he will resume them; feeble as I am, I shall demand that of him."

And their dreams filled with slow minutiae, hollow-eyed cares. Examining crevasses in the walls, laborious ants ran in all directions.

"Let's go," said the young man. "Let's go."

As soon as he pronounced those words, he found himself alone on the bend in the distant road where he had fallen down. The sky was brighter and the dawn indulgent. A great calm penetrated the marrow of his bones, like the gentle, still half-broken awakening that follows the fatigues of a long and difficult journey.

He got up and went on his way, into more distant lands. As he knew old chronicles, he told their tales; as he knew songs, he sang them; as he had beautiful handwriting worthy of ancient manuscripts, he applied his calligraphy to documents or copied exemplars of poets for rich people who liked to display books— and he made a living. It transpired that during these years the young man became a man, and, if the cares of his existence were diminished by that, the uncertainties and troubles of his soul became heavier.

One summer's day, the countryside was scorched by the terrible aspect of the sun, and the distant hills smoked at the summit like a white fire of mists, and the paving stones of the town, as white as chalk, burned the feet like bricks heated in a Turkish bath. He went in search of a shady corner in one of the side-lanes of a bazaar.

It was so hot, although the alleyways were cooled by their high vaults, and little black slaves were pouring trickles of perfumed water on to the ground, that all the merchants were asleep on their cushions, without keeping watch on their open coffers full of colored scarves and silk mantles, and carpets embroidered with marvelous golden birds, and leaving their caskets rippling with the fires of precious stones wide open. Although their sleep was heavy, their tranquility and security were complete, for the boldest of thieves would not cross the ring of torrid streets that surrounded the bazaar.

Our man sat down on the threshold of a humble shop selling paltry foodstuffs and cheap beverages, and went to sleep. No sound vibrated in the covered streets of the bazaar, save for the words of dreams, and the black slave responsible for sprinkling water yielded to fatigue and went to sleep.

The man's dream told him that his temples were going gray, and that he was even further away than the day when he thought he had visited his father's house, his birthplace. It seemed to him that he was sinking, but very slowly, sliding not through the streets but into the gray mirror of a lake.

He thought he heard a vague sound of weeping, and the peri of the former vision reappeared to him, who knew wrinkles, still cheerful and light-hearted in her immortal youth—and as he wanted to see his father's house, she took him away so that he might see it via the mind's eyes.

The road glittered like a furnace; where he had seen trees, the area was cleared, and further away, near clumps of woodland, teams of woodcutters were asleep beside their axes. The stream that made the mill-wheel turn accompanied him again with its song, so lively that one might have believed, and even desired, that one could take thousands upon thousands of strides to the enthusiastic accompaniment to its laughter—but the man understood that the stream was so cheerful because it recommenced the same circuit indefinitely, and that its apparent gaiety was only movement.

The atmosphere was still. The peris did not show themselves in that raw daylight, in which only the leaders of caravans stayed awake, waiting in the shade of walls until it was time to get under way again.

The natal house seemed even grayer to him; once, a few flowers had appeared at the barred windows; now heavy shutters supplemented the stone in the upper part of the house. Down below, his brothers were supervising slaves, counting money, filling orders.

Alone in the interior courtyard the father was now dreaming alone, and thinking: "Those, by their presence, and the other, by his absence, have rendered me more solitary than death."

The old man understood that he was worn out, that the best of his dreams now looked forward to a sealed tomb, devoid of care, devoid of hope, devoid of regret, devoid of confidence and devoid of movement.

Things no longer had any of their natal appearance. They were old and sullen, attentive to the avaricious dreams of three new masters. The old man's head was slumped on his breast. The things around him did not recognize him, and he had forgotten them. Momentarily, he had the presentiment of a divine presence, but as he was very old, and his thoughts often followed the same course, he thought he saw Azrael and shivered from head to toe.

And the traveler's heart ached. "Let's go," he said. "I see, dear goddess, that there is no natal house for a man, but only a banal corner of a city that is everywhere the same, that only a child naively believes that he is discovering. And I see that a man soon forgets the tree that he had planted himself, if it does not produce basketfuls of fruit every season. My father's fig-tree is desiccated, and its bark is hollowed out, and my father is growing old beside the fig-tree like a decrepit, exfoliated tree. There is nothing beautiful in human life but the memory of some dream that fills us with joy and even that is the memory of the beginning of a dream.

"Oh, when you came to find me in my near-mortal fatigue, when I perceived your eyes, which are divans for a god, and the ebony forest of your hair, and the scintillating plume of your eternal youth, I thought I was seeing the battens of heaven opening, in order that beauty and truth could explain to me what the dream of happiness was, and the meaning of the dogged pursuit of life. And the bells of beautiful adventure rang out for me—but it was only the consolation and remedy of a single day.

"Peri, beautiful Peri, is there no longer any happiness?"

And the Peri replied: "Your rose-bushes are flowering again, and I like your misfortune enough to save you from it. My love, made of pity for the children who weep at ground level, will save you. In a land that I know, where the dawn is perfumed and the evening full of fans, we shall live; the water of the profound spring will make you forget who you were, and I shall be your beloved and loving guardian, and only smiles will illuminate your face, for, no longer recalling suffering, you will no longer remember your life.

"Would you like to come with me to the land without mirrors; the noisy springs there are invisible, the valley resounds throughout with an indolent concert, and the shady corners are so profound that one might sleep for years without perceiving a hint of the sky between the trees . . ."

"But what about you? Won't you be losing anything?"

"I will be like a dream enchained for long years yet, before your breath expires in blessing me. The matrix of my mortal love will deprive me of my wings, but later, ennobled by a regret and a dolor, I shall joyfully travel through the air again in quest of some new unfortunate. As generous as the evening breeze, momentarily captured, I shall come back beautiful, like the free and errant evening breeze."

And the man replied: "That will be my whole life, then—the murmur of the stream that I can hear, cheerful and rhythmic because it is scarcely larger than the breadth of the basin in my father's house? I prefer my troubles and cares. Let's go."

And he woke up in front of the humble shop in the market.

The next day he left that city. As he knew old chronicles and new songs, and could draft documents, he made a living. When he grew very old he stopped in a humble side-street of an even more distant city, and awaited his final slumber in a low room. He wished that the Peri would return to him, to show him one more time the perfumed heavens and his father's house, but he was so tired that when she brightened the air he shivered from head to toe, as if he had seen Azrael.

When one has traveled too far one can no longer see one's father's house, one's natal house, ever again.

JULES LAFORGUE
(1860-1887)

Jules Laforgue was born in Uruguay of French parents, but from 1866 onwards he was raised by cousins in Tarbes, until his father moved the family to Paris in 1876. In 1880 he was taken under the wing of Paul Bourget, editor of *La Vie moderne*, and began to frequent Le Chat Noir with the Hydropathes, but he got a job working for the Empress Augusta and lived in Berlin from 1881 to 1886. While there he published a pioneering collection of Symbolist verse, *L'Imitation de Notre-Dame de la Lune* (1885), dedicated to Gustave Kahn, and when he returned to Paris he threw himself into the burgeoning Movement wholeheartedly, publishing in *La Vogue* and *Le Symboliste*. He died of tuberculosis a year later, leaving behind a classic collection of Symbolist prose, *Moralités legendaries* (1887) as well as a considerable body of poetry. He was one of the most extravagant contributors to the Movement and would probably have become its brightest star had his career not been cut short.

"Bobo" first appeared in *Le Symboliste*, 15-22 October 1886; the translation is original to the present volume.

Bobo

A creole capital where there is never snow, and never skating, but what afternoon romances of exile!

Ah, the young woman . . .

A muddy capital in the North, under a downpour (O hotel central heating!) on the edge of the sea where Hamlet mocks the untamable seagulls.

Ah, the young woman . . .

Then a capital in the sands, a furiously undisciplined wind

protesting against the discipline of well-organized administrations, three beatific Rembrandts agonizing under ambered leprosy in a Greek museum whose precise acroteria are soiled by passing crows

Then a little Parisian capital, posters by Chéret, coffee in glasses, brilliant tips in the air, an absolute but disarming void.

Then Paris, a salad of arrondissements, divine and human consummations all dirtying the depths of the heart; a hundred societies of foresight, but no operation of definitive life, no signs in the sky.

Then the sea, the sea devoid of capitals, the blue and spring-like sea of the last fine days, and, leaning on an old cannon, at the very end of the jetty, whose beams are engraved with the names of lascars with a knife that could do more exotic work, the beautiful and comfortable boat that takes thirty-five minutes to disappear in the glory of the horizon.

Ah, young woman, dolor and old age! rings the Angelus. Eh! What do they matter to me, a solitary amputee, those bells, and the marriage or burial of brothers that they might be sounding today with so much importance? On a railway station shed: *Fire pump*. O mundanity! Oh, let everything burn! My cat wouldn't lose the caress of an inhuman hand thereby . . .

Oh, the coast of France, the works of maritime defense and the dunes . . .

I shall have passed through this life,
Like a crow above cities,
For I mistrust;
Idylls;
In this life, I shall have passed
Like an insensate who mistrusts.
I shall have passed, padlocked.

The piano remains, the piano at home, and a few fugitive fragments of poetry . . .

And the young woman . . . Ah, bobo, bobo.[1]

Follow me carefully.

---

1 "Bobo," a baby-talk corruption of "bébé," is also the exclamation little children make when they have hurt themselves, appealing for consolation.

Woman is our companion, a worthy being, quotidian, very terrestrial, who never torments herself with the beyond, created by religions consolers of death, as man does.

(O woman of the clay
You had your god in your bed,
But he had to go away,
And so far from your head!)

Woman is an associate of the other sex, a very ordinary sex. We ought not to occupy ourselves with her any more than our other brethren, only associated with at certain hours, certain half-hours, because of the objectives of that sex. Step forward, step after. Association, toil, progress, getting up and going to bed with the sun. (A little Boër wine, if you like.)

But no! Man has been impelled to want words and gods in the half-hour of amour, and as the half hour was brief and disappointing every time, he has put the instrument in a hothouse (gynaeceum, chivalry, salon) and he has searched everything, invented everything, and corrupted his religions, in order to sharpen her, electrify her.

She has therefore been left in idleness, mirror, slavery, with no other occupation than her sex, her sole weapon and currency. And she has, therefore, by virtue of centuries in the hothouse, hypertrophied her sex. And she has become the Feminine, the Eternal Feminine (as if there were an Eternal Masculine!), a freemasonry of false brethren, what.

Ah, young women, I forgive you for not fighting fair with us. Oh, we let our little sister make a humanity apart. One reaps what one sows.

Everything that she can give us, fundamentally, is contained in half-hours; she has therefore found ways to fill the voids, in order to join the two ends . . . of the garland. (And there are inventions! every year, every season, a fashion, a hairstyle that renews her lure of the ideal, and it is the geniuses that she causes to suffer particularly, in order to make them produce masterpieces that also renew her, transfiguring her, alimenting the prize-fund of the lottery, and are the varieties of amour, of the head, the flesh, the heart, etc.)

And all that leaves man in sole charge of human history (a lame history by virtue of Woman having retired to her tent), in which we see Pessimism (the Phylloxera of Progress, as Victor Hugo put it, having understood it.)

Man has died with his gods; long live Woman, brave little being, quotidian and beautiful and very terrestrial. Eve will save the world.

Henceforth, Man will occupy himself with the arts and scientific intuitions; Woman will do the housework of the Planet (sciences, industries, catalogues, cleanliness, hygienic caresses.)

It is as clear as a debt to be paid.

In the meantime, there remains the piano, the piano at home, and the fugitive fragments of poetry. I've done a few of those . . .

CHARLES MORICE
(1860-1919)

Charles Morice was born into a devout Catholic family, but split with his relatives when he eloped to Paris in 1882, and lost his faith. He began writing for the anticlerical *La Nouvelle Revue gauche*, which changed its name to *Lutèce* with his encouragement, and published Verlaine's *Poètes maudits* as well as offering vocal support to the Symbolist Movement before it folded in 1886. He subsequently assisted in the foundation of the *Mercure de France*. He was better known for his essays than his poetry, but his visionary fantasy *Il est resusscité* (1911; tr. as *He is Risen Again*) and the collections *Quincaille* (Albert Mesein, 1914) and *Rideau de pourpre* (1921) are notable.

"Nabuchodonosor" and "Narcissus" both appeared in *Quincaille* but must date from much earlier, although I have not been able to identify their first appearances; the translations are original to the present volume.

Nabuchodonosor

> I will ascend into heaven,
> I will exalt my throne
> above the stars of God; I will
> sit also upon the mount of
> the congregation, in
> the sides of the north.
> *Isaiah* 14:13[1]

Arrogantly, the palace darts its towers, its hundred towers of Babel, toward the heavens, which laugh, from the depths of their impassive eternity, at the immeasurable pettiness of the hundred towers.

. . . It is in a city in the Bible and perhaps also in those times: a city of all races and all seasons, devoid of history; a city of legends such as one divines written in the grace and emphasis of monuments, with lyrical steeples everywhere, darted at the clouds; but none of the many gigantic architectures dares to rival the House of the King. It is situated at the center, a sublime spider, and the streets emerge like threads from the hundred doors that the hundred towers design.

Everything protects her and she governs everything, the true queen. And for forgotten centuries she has been the reliquary of strength and virtue, glory and grandeur; and for centuries, welcoming and sumptuous, she testified even more generosity, the beloved, than she excited amour; and for centuries she has been installed there like a great testimony to human greatness . . .

But what is being said? What has abruptly altered the color of the sky above the arrogant towers? It is said that the Palace has

---

1 The speech is credited in the A.V. to "Lucifer, son of the morning," apparently meaning the king of Babylon doomed by the (somewhat gnomic) prophecy contained in the relevant chapter. The protagonist of the story is more familiarly known as Nebuchadnezzar II, king of Babylon from c605 B.C. to c562 B.C., who is said to have behaved irrationally in his later years, and whose death was the prelude to Babylon's conquest by the Persian king Cyrus the Great.

swollen with the pride of its strength and its virtue, its glory and its grandeur. An *excessively* enlightened monarch has taken his place on the old throne for five years, during which, day by day, the sky has darkened above the arrogant towers, and the people are forgetting, day by day, to laugh softly as they were once accustomed to do, in the times of kings infatuated with bellicose glory, proud of loving, good servants of beauty, joyful in reigning and living.

However, the present crown-bearer surpasses in wisdom, it is certain, the purest heads with which his lineage is illuminated. Why does his venerable name weigh upon all the people like a condemnation, and why do gazes not dare to address themselves to the doors of the Palace without sacred horror?

✵

The Palace darts its hundred towers arrogantly . . .

In the surrounding area, the squares and crossroads are black with people, black with innumerable people who are clamoring, clashing swords, excited, agitating banners, who are crying, as if for help: "The King! The King!" and hammering on the doors of the Palace with their fists.

The Palace is deaf and blind, the agitation of all of that crowd has no echo in the disdainful towers. Except that, from time to time, a valet opens the servants' door to make imploring gestures of appeasement at the mutinous mob.

For a thousand days now the King has refused the adoration of his people. The King is neglecting his royal duties, abandoning his people to the knavery or indolence of irresponsible ministers.

✵

Oh, the populace can appeal and become irritated; its demands occupy the King as much as the murmurs of the sea and the ordinary tumults of life . . .

It is said that for a thousand days he has been enclosed in the most profound of the vast chambers of his palace; it is said in whispers that for a thousand days, he has been face to face with a phantom of God. Since his youth he has been infatuated with the tenebrous promises of the Kabbalah, and Sages summoned from far away marveled at one greater than Solomon.

Gradually, he has sequestered himself in the solitary honor of being a Seer. Now, disinterested in his ancestors' dreams of glory and blood, having lost his taste for loving, surfeited with living, weary of reigning, he has become some inhuman heap of thoughts. Legendary in his own lifetime in the mystery that shelters him from curiosity, he appears to mortals as something unnamable, august and redoubtable, the form of which, being sacred, remains vague.

And the Palace, which had waited a long time for such a guest, is like the natural habitat of the omnipotent silence: a sumptuous edifice, as if fictitious in always being closed; a massive and inexhaustible receptacle of the shadow that it projects afar, like a reflection of its depths, a monumental vestment of a formidable being.

※

However, that vestment of granite, bronze, marble and precious stones, an entire people drunk on abandon has sworn to tear apart. The City, the City-Without-End, is also weary, and also surfeited with the hideous consolations that it has sought in all its debaucheries: a monstrous Sodom, already in haste to mirror its ruinous grandeur in the mirages of Asphaltite, because it has no longer had the joy, for a thousand days, of listening to the song of its living blood that one flowed delightfully from the Palace, as from a vast heart.

In order to extract the King from his criminal apathy, the City has imagined declaring war on the nearest Gomorrah, and already the dangerous enemies have agitated the inflamed banners in the country . . .

Let the King show himself! It is time!

"The King! The King!"

If not under amorous hands, you will fall, O Palace, under infamous and victorious hands! Open up! The people are powerful in number and desire, and have not found a goal in the pleasures into which the royal treason has precipitated them, and, since the King sees God, the people are jealous to participate in the vision of God. The people are great; it is from the God himself, from the God who seems to have abandoned them, that they want

100

to steal the glory of the divine vision, and of the Thrones and the Dominations, and the deaf Heavens: the Heavens that laugh from the depths of their impassive eternity, at the immeasurable pettiness of the people.

The battle howls and fumes at the gates of the City. Men without arms and children flee, their hands spread in horror, and cast trouble into the battalions that have formed. But why? Victory is certain, since the King is the divine elect. Only let him show himself, the royal deserter!

The army of Amazons, a lascivious and beautiful multitude, bellicose, pitiless and invulnerable, it is said—for wounds exasperate and do not stop those demons, a multitude like a stormy rain of lances—the well-led army rolls through the City the frightful din of machines of war. Can it be that the racket is not audible in the Hundred Towers? And the people, desperate, fall almost without defending themselves any longer, under the rhythmic thrusts of the furious women.

"The Enemy!"

"The King!"

Those two cries mingle, and are they not the same cry? Is not the same one, also, that immense cry of agony that fills the proud city, the city traversed and swept in all directions by the vast flood of carnage?

And the Heavens laugh, from the depths of their impassive eternity, at the immeasurable pettiness of the massacre.

The Killers have stopped and gathered at the foot of the Palace that darts its hundred towers of Babel toward the heavens. And laughter, enormous laughter, diabolical laughter, dishonors the echoes of the ancient dwelling; the laughter of victory from below, the laughter of mud thrown in the face of statues. And the doors, once obstinate in silence, groan under the formidable effort of catapults and battering rams.

The immemorial doors! The doors sculpted and painted by centuries of genius! The holy doors whose hinges rendered a harmonious sound as they rotated: what a plaint today! Oh, what sinister gasp inhabits and suddenly awakens in the profaned bronze!

And it is not the adoring violence of a faithful people that rushes and spreads through the House. The courtyards, the stairways of honor, the corridors and the halls reverberate dolorously the clamor of the triumphant, and the humiliated flagstones weep beneath the feet that insult them.

✸

Outraging hands soil celebrated portraits: old monarchs and old sages, ancient individuals consecrated by glory. Tiaras are astonished by the long and bloody tresses that they decorate. The reserve of treasures delivers like hiccups to ferocious and naïve eyes, things of which the dream alone intoxicates the imagination of the dreamer. And the most outrageous hands of all, maleficent but ignorant, take pleasure in lacerating the riches of a library unique in the world. The manuscripts of Sanchuniathon, those of Berossus, the poems of Pentaour and the hymns of Orpheus, the lessons of the Magi, the authentic texts of the Books of Thoth Trismegistus, the Revelations of Li and Ki, the Dramas of Kalidasa, the Wars of Iaveh, the Prophetic Enunciations, the Vedas, the Avesta . . . in sum, all the most illustrious testimonies of our genius—and the Heavens laugh, from the depths of their impassive eternity, at the immeasurable pettiness of those lost testimonies.

✸

"The King! The King!"

It is the enemy that is vociferating that appeal—an order!—while searching the labyrinth for the designated victim, and the vaults and the walls, with a confession of ultimate treason, repeated in a commanding tone: "The King! The King!"

That door, is it not the one that opens to the most profound of vast chambers? That door, on which mystic emblems are sculpted, dominated by the menacing visage of a gorgon? It is there that he has been, for a thousand days, face to face with a phantom of God.

The murderers hesitate, and their gazes are concerted, and their voices excited—and the door collapses.

102

And the women who launched themselves forward with bloody syllables stop, immobilized, mute, trembling and tottering with vertigo.

Alone, in the solitude of an atmosphere smoky with unknown essences, a being is standing, charged with a royal mantle whose pleated flaps trail on the ground to attest that the being was once taller. Stooped, head bowed—an enormous head, a monstrous head from which the crown has slipped—alone, a being is standing there, gazing toward the threshold and seeming not to see anything. He does not move. They do not know whether he is alive.

For a long time the intruders stay there, trembling and tottering, more tempted to flight than the assassination anticipated as a celebration.

But one bold woman finally approaches and leans over to consider the face that remains in shadow—and cries out, and falls inanimate, on seeing that the entire visage has been devoured by the forehead.

The eyes are weeping beneath, bestial and sad, like those of a bison; the eyes are weeping and filled with darkness, and about to be extinguished, while the nose and the mouth are two derisory streaks beneath the limitless forehead of Nabuchodonosor; and the Heavens laugh, from the depths of their impassive eternity, at the immeasurable pettiness of that forehead.

Narcissus

The child grew up under the gaze of the grandmother in the ancient dwelling in which, by a prodigy of prudence and fidelity, everything save for him was ancient. In the sumptuous halls, on the historic flagstones, between the ornate tapestries in which the family history was perpetuated from the dusks of the past to the dawns of the future; in the silent park, among the domesticated deer and the old white and black swans with the slow, gentle lines; in the austere Gothic chapel where the late Baron, his father, in the costumes of war, and his dead mother, in a festival gown, knelt before the venerable images of their blessed patrons; in the forest of dense darkness, between his ferocious greyhounds and his rapacious birds of prey, with the savage perspective of the Pyrenees far beyond, the child grew up, various, long motionless, taciturn, abruptly carried away by the hazard of vagabond courses, to the dithyrambs of inexhaustible soliloquies: as various as the instants of an April day, capricious and grave, and he was always ignorant of the gaiety of games in which the turbulences of assembled children expand in pleasant follies.

Sometimes, he considered with an innocent, serious and questioning gaze the lady of unknown age who reigned in that empire of prudence and fidelity, the immemorial soul of that narrow world closed to new vanities.

And as he grew up, she summoned, in order to lighten the heavy concern of the education of a man, priests with hair like falling snow. Doubtless without haste, those patriarchs enclosed the thoughts of their noble pupil within the limits of the wisdom of the early days, as well as communicating to him a little of their decrepitude. First they informed him of all that is imprescriptible in the precious prejudices of Tradition to the hazardous awakening of a very ardent mind. Scarcely was that coat of mail well-fitted than he was launched into the melee of human knowledge. His vivacious anxieties converged avidly on that multiple shadow of the unique prey. He pored over theologies, philosophies, histories and geometries; even his dreams were learned; a despotic curiosity was all of his passion, and his masters trembled, foreseeing that one day soon he would leave them far behind in that vertiginous hunt for the truth, on the ultimate edge where the beaten paths cease.

Now, the white-haired lady, in delivering the mind of her grandson and that tremulous precocity to exceedingly old magi, had reserved for herself the protection of his heart and scarcely opened senses. She awaited, with the experience of a woman and the divination of a mother, the frisson of the dawn of nascent desire that troubles and does not dare. Perhaps instructed, in some distant past, of the perils of living too rapidly, she was a jealous guardian of that adolescent candor. Mirrors in which the young man's beauty might have smiled were proscribed.

Life in the château was rude, all long toil and harsh exercise. Early on, with the fire of scruple and religious commandments, a disdain was ignited in the child for his corporeal graces, with the result that his gaze was never tempted to take pleasure in the masculine mildness of his forms, of a young hero. But the grandmother could not forbid herself the pleasure of combing his long blond hair, like the freshness of a bright summer night around the radiant midday of his visage. And while the hands lingered, besotted, in the rich curls, he dreamed.

Was that grandmotherly tenderness hiding some lure of pride? Was it to human astonishment that the marvel of such a beautiful being was dedicated? Or perhaps—and once and for all before the end of mankind!—to the accomplishment of human perfection? But, to good, wicked or indifferent Nature, did she also want to add the collaboration of the work of choice, in conferring on the elect of science and beauty the redoubtable gift of physical consciousness?

After he had exhausted on many hills the grapes of the vines of Science, the young man closed his books and left the insulting dust to powder them with forgetfulness in his study. He went into the forest, with the dusk, with the darkness; with his head bowed he walked for a long time. He dreamed.

From the world glimpsed on the edge of all the mysteries, a veiled figure had suddenly loomed up, and that apparition had thrown back into shadow all the mysteries of the world. With a tranquil terror, as if he had always known that it was necessary that the veiled figure would loom up before him at a certain moment, the young man had recognized it as his own mystery. And because that phantom had suppressed other contingencies for him, that alone made him think. Like an angel on the threshold of paradise, the phantom standing on the threshold of the House of the World said: "Further beyond are the sweet secrets; but in order to reach them it is necessary to lift or tear my veil."

And the strange words awakened a thousand voices in his opening soul, which said: "For the key to the great House is *you,* and without it you will roam its surroundings in vain, *without you*. The Questions are consonant and resolved in you. You, in your tangible reality, are the crossroads of the World. Seek the Answer in the beating of your heart, in the dreams of your life, in the eloquence of your gestures. Before pursuing risky pilgrimages to distant shores, to inhospitable shores, obtain advice of yourself."

Thus commenced to appear in the young man's will, like a torch of increasing light on the horizon of the desires of puberty, the project of learning his soul and knowing his body: his body, that interesting spectacle, that sanctuary of intimate verities.

Everyday things, not inspected before, touched him tenderly. He enjoyed, as a novelty, the elasticity of his stride, the caress of his hair. His hands loved one another, clutching one another. The habitude of chastity lent to frail details a price of rare charm. From the ease of his movement the intoxication of health rose to his brain. His feet took possession of the earth in walking thereon, his gaze took possession of landscapes. He breathed the air sensually, a conquest of the sky. Yes, what a joy it was to see in his entire self the illumination of revelation!

And much more ardently than in the days of childhood, his questioning eyes scrutinized the savant and challenging eyes of the grandmother, seeking a living mirror therein. But she, tremulous, and fearful of understanding, closed her pallid eyelids.

She had frequent conversations with the old men, in which she sometimes raised an accusatory voice, reproaching them for having betrayed her design. For why had he wearied of study? Was it not because the masters lacked knowledge or devotion? The old men humbly raised the objection of the fatal fever of a youth perhaps too long suppressed, and a warm blood rendered impatient by constraints.

And those saddened men and that heartbroken woman, kneeling in the chapel, implored the Very Merciful to remove the menacing probabilities.

One day, the one that cost so many dreads and prayers, one glorious summer day, the young man traversed the park singing. Seeing him cheerful, everything became cheerful. His greyhounds bounded; the swans on the lake rippled the water more rapidly, where the willows were no longer able to distinguish their tearful branches. He traversed the forest at a run, all the way to the limits where the sheer mountains were revealed.

A marsh was dormant in the profound forest. Huge elms cradled it with interlacements. It was a deserted place unknown to furtive hinds and flocks of sparrows. In the depths of the water there was a glaze of mud, the soft natural silvering of a liquid mirror, a calm and fresh mirror in which the floating phantom of the trees was reflected.

It was a deserted place, secret and religious, a place predestined for the accomplishment of some redoubtable amorous ritual. The light filtered through the foliage, over the dead water, the smiles of life.

Without turning his head, freed from the tranquil terror once emanated by the veiled figure, delivered henceforth to the victories of desire, now that the delightful specter promised to allow itself to be seen, Narcissus, his forehead rosy with the emotion of his voluptuous enterprise, undressed himself slowly, his gaze lost in the distance of a joyful dream.

Slowly, he came to the edge of the marsh where destiny awaited him; slowly, and as he had once pored over bleak books, he leaned over his image. Could he not adore you, image of his youth? And adoring you, too abruptly and without initiation, O murderer, O shattering revelation, could he not exhale, in his last and first sigh of amour, his entire soul?

GEORGE-ALBERT AURIER
(1865-1892)

George-Albert Aurier (1865-1892) was an ardent member of the Symbolist Movement prior to his premature death from typhus. He was a regular contributor to Le Décadent before launching his own periodical, Le Moderniste illustré in 1889. He also assisted in the founding of the Mercure de France, whose associated press published his collected *Oeuvres posthumes* in 1893. He is now best remembered as an art critic, especially as a vociferous advocate of the work of Vincent van Gogh and Paul Gauguin.

"Festin de Balthazar" first appeared in *Le Moderniste illustré*, 27 avril 1889—the first issue—under the heading *Fantaisie*, and "L'Amante" in the second issue, 4 mai 1889. "Belshazzar's Feast" and "The Lover" are original to the present volume.

Belshazzar's Feast: A Fantasia

Well, yes! Well, yes, by the pure ivory of your impeccable calf, this tale, Madame, and very indubitably, exquisite lectrice, this tale, which was narrated to me once long ago—oh, very long ago—in some nebulous desert, by my friend Chonchinette—you know, Chonchinette, that little indecent Chonchinette who speaks like she loves—this tale, then, is not very moral, and is very scabrous to relate . . . so immoral and so scabrous, truly, that I hesitate to repeat it to you . . .

Aren't you going to blush? blush with virtuous shame? blush all the way to the pretty dimples in your knees? I can already hear you excommunicating me with a terrible: "Oh, fie! The vile writer!"

But bah! Let's see. For once . . . just for this once, be indulgent! Listen to the peppery badinage of Chonchinette without pinching your charming pert madder-red lips, listen, deign to listen with a smile, since no one is looking at you. No?

In the time of la Lavallière and la Pompadour, the great ladies of the court, your ancestresses were hardly accustomed to affect grim prudishness in similar circumstances. And yet, no one is surely unaware that the good La Fontaine did not spare, for them, pimento or red pepper in the stew of his amorous anecdotes. Did that, I ask you, prevent him from being esteemed by Madame de La Sablière, becoming classic and absolutely usual in all young ladies' boarding schools?

And what about Monsieur Pavillon? You don't know Monsieur Pavillon? Monsieur Pavillon of the Académie Française? Monsieur

Pavillon was a worthy man who had composed a poem—only one poem, but a sublime poem, an indescribable and hilarious poem entitled *The Metamorphosis of Iris's Backside into a Star*.[1]

"Oh, fie! The vile word . . ."

"Your amiable grandmothers, Madame, your witty grandmothers, were not annoyed by it, did not blush at it. Oh, far from it! They laughed instead, they laughed, the little rascals, until they wet the satins and brocades of their lovely panel skirts. But that's not all. They ended up finding the lewd joke so good that they plotted to seat its witty author in the first vacant armchair under Mazarin's cupola. And, as you can well imagine, in such dainty handcuffs, the affair was quickly settled!

Certainly, I have no ambition to be, any day soon, like La Fontaine, the favorite classic of boarding-school demoiselles, and I have no hope that these pages, inspired in me by that little blonde devil Chonchinette, will open the forbidding gates of the Institut to me tomorrow. Today, a poem, no matter how hyperamazing it might be, on *The Metamorphosis of Iris's Backside into a Star* is no longer sufficient for that; it's necessary to write a history in fifty volumes of the Ducs de Castelnaudry, to have pierced a number of isthmuses, translated Greenlandish novels, to be a bishop, an admiral, or at least a veterinarian.

My ambition is not so high . . . oh, triple idiot that I am! My ambition is a thousand times higher, since it goes so far as begging your generosity, Madame, for the alms of a quarter of an hour of indulgent attention and the signal favor of a quarter of a smile on your lips!

And then, thinking about it, what's the point of all this? What's the point of all these absurd prolegomena, which are doubtless boring you? Will people not say, truly, that my story is quite terrible? As terrible as the things that are, as you know, said between men at the end of dinners?

---

1 Étienne Pavillon (1632-1705), was, indeed, credited posthumously, but doubtless apocryphally, with writing a story in verse entitled "*Métamorphose du cul d'Iris changé en astre*." His published works, which actually served as a (very slender) qualification for admission to the Académie, include "*Le Portrait du pur amour*" [The Portrait of Pure Love] dedicated to "*à l'insensible Iris*" (1687), which presumably inspired the satirical attribution.

Not at all. It isn't a matter of such horrors. When this lewd story was told to me, we were not, I swear to you, between men, since it is Chonchinette herself who narrated it. It's true that little Chonchinette is quite a lad, and wears socks—yes, socks, and short hair—like a man, but I swear to you that she doesn't put on trousers. In any case, all that's unimportant, isn't it? One more word, however, a word that will tranquilize you definitively. Let your modesty sleep in peace, Madame. All these oratory precautions are merely futile games to amuse me with your untimely emotion. Let your modesty sleep in peace, for I have bought, a long time ago, in order to draw a veil, as they say, over the overly cynical verbiage of this accursed tale, several meters of tarlatan, and I swear to you, I swear to you by all that I hold sacred, on Chonchinette's snowy tits, that I shall dress the most scandalous item in this story chastely, in the most prudish of tutus . . .

So here it is.

The scene is happening in New York, at about two o'clock in the morning, in a private room in a restaurant.

The debris of victuals is strewn on the table-cloth, and champagne bottles are lined up, desperately empty.

The apples of his cheeks carmine, he is sitting with his head tilted back and the nape of his neck on the back of the armchair, full of a slightly drunken amorous bliss.

Astride his knees, laughing, with her eyes unusually shiny, She is amusing herself pinching his cheeks, tugging his moustache and blowing in his nostrils. From the skirts tucked up by the mischievous straddling of the female—whom, you will have divined, is none other than Chonchinette herself—emerges the end of a leg, the end of a leg clad in a sock, a bright blue sock, the end of a leg that is swinging, back and forth, back and forth . . . He, stimulated, places an avid caressing hand on the pale nudity of the calf. The hand climbs . . . The knee . . .

Here, I make it a duty to keep my solemn engagements by placing a few meters of tarlatan, prudish tarlatan!

The gesture was brief. But, seizing that rascal Chonchinette in his arms, who struggled—for form's sake, and not very much—and who laughed, and laughed, the laugh of a tickled woman, he, quivering with desire, carried her to the divan, the large divan of nacarat velvet.

Then, as he was meticulous, he bounded to the door with the evident intention of shooting the bolt.

But then, O stupor, scarcely has he put his fingers on the handle of the bolt when, moved by an ingenious mechanism—oh, these Americans!—a placard surges forth from the wall, like the prophetic hand at Belshazzar's Feast, a black notice, on which these words are traced in flamboyant golden letters:

Do not employ table linen; there are napkins in the chest of the divan.

For a long time, oh, a very long time, Chonchinette laughs at that!

What? You're not laughing? Madame is indubitably an exquisite lectrice, you're not laughing? You're grimacing, a little moue of disillusion? Oh, I get it! You haven't understood? You don't speak English? No?

Well, neither do I.

The Lover

When I returned from the Hindu lands, where I had loved the daughters and wives of rajahs as beautiful as simulacra of new bronze or cornelian in fabulous palaces with golden roofs, walls of jasper, paving stones of ruby, amethyst and chalcedony . . .

When I returned from the mysterious provinces of China, where, for a long time, I had caressed by moonlight, in a fantastic garden full of polycephalous statues, blue eucalypti, painted porcelain turrets and peach-blossom, the little princess with the turned-up eyes, the minuscule feet of a doll, the little princess who was none other than the precious and dear child of the Celestial Emperor . . .

When I had returned from Cytherean azures where, on a bed of pink roses, the divine Aphrodite, more dazzling than the genius of Praxiteles sculpted her, had offered herself to my kisses many times . . .

When I had returned to these sunless climes, obedient to the most bizarre of crazy fantasies, I wanted to choose, among all the women who are for sale, my mistress: very thin, very small, with big blue eyes bitten by the acid of old tears.

I wanted my mistress with big blue eyes bitten by the acid of old tears, because such eyes are exceedingly diaphanous and I like to contemplate, in the depths of the limpid lake of my beloved's gaze, her soul, her woman's soul, a cloaca of all malevolence and all corruption.

I have chosen my very small mistress in order to give me the childish illusion of a more intimate and more entire possession, in order to be able to enfold her more completely in a single embrace, and to say to myself, infatuated with mad pride: Your arms are vast enough to embrace a universe of felony and egotism.

I have chosen my very thin mistress in order to feel, in the midst of our ardent kisses, the nails of her vertebrae and the trellis of her ribs, and thus to remind myself, in accomplishing the work of life, that the grimacing skeleton of death is lying in wait and watching, eternally hidden beneath our skin.

Thus I wanted to choose my lover, when I returned from the Hindu lands, where I had loved the daughters and wives of rajahs as beautiful as simulacra of new bronze or cornelian in fabulous palaces with golden roofs, walls of jasper, paving stones of ruby, amethyst and chalcedony.

PAUL ADAM
(1862-1920)

Paul Adam shared the distinction with Catulle Mendès of being fined and imprisoned when his first novel, *Chair molle* (1885), was prosecuted for obscenity, and like Mendès he went on to a successful and prolific career. After his early association with Jean Moréas and Gustave Kahn, he devoted himself primarily to writing novels, deliberately attempting to fuse and hybridize Symbolist and Naturalist techniques; he is now best known for historical novels set during the Napoleonic Wars. His novels often include interludes of utopian speculation, and he wrote one of the most important utopian texts of the *fin-de-siècle* in *Lettres de Malaisie* (1897 in *La Revue Blanche*; reprinted by the periodical's own press in 1898), which makes extravagant use of graphic symbolism.

"Amen" first appeared in *La Revue Blanche* mars 1892; the translation is original to the present volume.

The item translated as "Mercury" first appeared in *La Revue Blanche* 15 avril 1897 as "Dixième letter de Malaisie," but became Lettre VIII of the book version. The translation was originally published in the version of that text contained in *The Humanisphere and Other Utopian Fantasies* (Black Coat Press, 2016).

Amen

During last winter, circumstances—and a powerful sympathy of ideas even more so—determined that I encountered the English painter W., whose work is well-known. In spite of the simplicity of his subjects, he enlarges the real, he fixes the spiritual ambience of things.

One evening when he, the musician F., and I were talking about rather elevated matters of metaphysics, a being of integral beauty was detached from the tableau that our words were tracing. It happened that our minds took on a sudden consistency; and the appearance under which they decided to manifest themselves made us proud.

The young woman had been dreamed of before, as regards her smile and gaze, by Leonardo da Vinci when he painted the Gioconda and Saint John the Baptist. For the allure of her body and the svelte hieratic gesture, she also expressed the gaze of Sandro Botticelli, a little like the maiden running in the background in the left-hand fresco in the Louvre.

Her imagination dazzled ours. She said that she was seventeen years old.

For a few weeks she ornamented our conversations with her grave and elevated chatter. Then, one day, the illusion dissipated, doubtless because she wearied of the narrowness of the circle in which our dialogue turned.

In England the illustrious William Crookes once evoked a figure of the suprasensible world. He baptized that presence with a simple vocable.[1] We gave ours the name of Amen; and here are a few overheated phrases written during her appearance. At least they might serve to denote the current state of our wishes at the moment when they were objectivized in her.

Amen!
Would that everything were like You!
in time.
eternal initiatrice,
You
for the Peace of whoever paints the unconscious souls of races.

Once
you were known near the shores of lakes
and in mountains at dawn.
Rare amber rang at your heels, when,
Violent huntress,
you uttered such cries of glory
at the corners of gorges,
at the summit of cascades.
The horde of males followed your course,
for a supple pack.
They bayed softly,
and lay down in a circle
under the green moon
around
your repose.

Later you were the priestess,
whose hands of pearl
announced the god from the height of terraces.

---

1 Katie [King]; or KT—hence Amen, or MN.

Gardens flourished at your cantilena;
and your veil appeared,
stopping in the distance
the chariots rolling over the flagstones of military roads.

That Queen
with-the-Eyes-of-Crime
Who astonished the future
with her galleys,
her melancholies,
and her great days . . .
You were her.
The harbor where your banners were inflated
was drowned
in the blood of battles fought.

Amen!
Would that everything were like You!

Brother, Sister
Amour and Death
Emanate
from your form; and of your
mute gesture
Harmony
is the Mother.

Your tread
marks the center of cycles
and the wind
that touches your hair
no longer knows
its direction.

You walk:
the waters swell;
the sky rises;

plants are exalted;
the air cries.

Your gaze
causes to bloom
architectures,
cities,
republics,
art strives to imitate you alone.
The world
seeks to become . . .
What?
Your reflection.

Before your vestige
the joyous fury of humankind
embraces freely
death,
your Future
Threshold.

For toward the Unknowable God
You are
the Route.
Would that everything were like You
Amen!

After we had traveled the City and its crowd, Amen showed pity for the agitation, for all that poor luxury, for the monumental lairs in which our rejoicing instinct groans. That moved us considerably. How could she be good, to the point of feeling pity, since—as we told her many a time—that sentiment only exists by virtue of the dread we have of suffering the misfortunes that afflict the poor? She, being of hyperphysical essence, ought not to experience that dread, nor, in consequence, pity. We proposed that objection to her.

Amen developed a remark familiar to theologians refuting heresies on the beauty of sacrifice for the sake of sacrifice, without utility. "Christ rose again toward the Father because he suffered all the Passion knowing full well that the martyrdom in question was insufficient to redeem humans from their shame. He really inaugurated the worship of Dolor for Dolor's sake. And in that, above all, God is manifest."

There was an adolescent among us oppressed by the folly of loving Amen and desiring her. Since discourses maddened him, he wrote this note:

> *The curls of your hair—and also those of seas—inundate our*
>   *tempted soul.*
> *Water, like force, brightens or effaces.*
> *The crests of your hands—and also those of reefs—shine for*
>   *our temeritous heart.*
> *A reef, like a battle, is surmounted or wrecks.*
> *The whips of your gaze—and also those of the north wind—*
>   *sting our dismantled prudence.*
> *The north wind, like amour, vivifies or disperses.*
> *The influences of your voice—and also those of vertigo—*
>   *move our Central passion.*
> *Vertigo, like thought, attracts into the End.*
> *For You,*
> *Beauty itself.*
> *Like the Aphrodite of Hellas.*
> *You are the Double Sign,*
> *With the face that is named Urania*
> *Mirror of intelligible worlds*
> *And that other Face*
> *By which the Goddess*
> *Troubles the Sea.*
> *Ah, shall we ever be those gods*
> *Whose Empyrean arms*
> *Embrace your Double Form,*
> *Universe of Universes?*
> *Or must we too*

Perish before the Peril of your Beauty
Exhaling our life-desire,
Arms open
Like the wings of murdered birds?

Amen did not want to show the slightest compassion. She spent an entire sunlight alone with him . . .

When evening came she undid her hair and uncovered her neck . . .

He told us subsequently that he advanced toward her, arms open; but as he drew nearer, such anguish appeared on the young woman's face, and her smile curved in such a cruel, suffering form that the adolescent fainted at the anticipation of the dolor stimulated by his desire.

At that time, Amen's presence dissipated.

I cannot translate precisely the impression of the attractive gulf that her splendor evoked. I could scarcely succeed by saying that her eyelids, and the blue-tinted skin or her temples emitted, at times, a kind of infinite cloud, behind which her eyes shone like gods.

Sometimes, she was able to offer all the gaiety of youth, and she thus played the part of a flame, while our dry hearts crackled.

She also had imperious, ageless moments.

It was extraordinary.

Mercury

The most recent cities of the Dictatorship are, like this one, planted in the middle of forests. Lively waters whisper around the buildings. Swans swim on the shade. Pink ibises meditate standing on one foot. The electric trams bear graceful sculpted figureheads on the prow, projecting like those of antique ships, which hold the headlight in their hands. Automobiles with the form of attenuated hippogriffs run on the roads covered by vaults of verdure furnished by the foliage of tropical trees; the half-closed wings enclose the hood while the monster's swollen neck and bulging breast terminate the anterior trunk. Crowning the hippogriff's head, six ornaments are electric bulbs; and when night falls, those beautiful beasts of dark lacquered wood are seen gliding vertiginously, crowned with light.

In one of those vehicles we have gone along the masonry dyke that sustains and elevates the monstrous telescope three kilometers long and proportionately stout. We have circled the lakes of reagents in which the scientists study the warfare of substances; we have circulated for hours between the glass domes in which, vacuums having been created, odic currents and the moist subtle fluids undulate and float, alive, revealed by diaphanous shimmers and sometimes by brief blue flashes; we have scaled the crystal paths of the magnetic hill from which a spray of glaucous essence darts on certain evenings, toward which innumerable drops of yellow, green and blue light flow through space, and lightning zigzags continually.

This is the region of scientific miracles. As soon as the sun sets, the people light up, because of a phosphorescent preparation that dyes their garments. Then the brightness of pedestrians illuminates the streets in a soft and charming fashion. The shadows fill with brilliant phantoms who talk as they glide two by two or three by three. The hidden organs sing. One perceives a close relationship with the hypothetical beings inhabiting the myriads of planets in suspension in the profundities.

In truth, enthusiasm has conquered me this time. How can I explain the secret of the wellbeing I sensed? Does it relate to the speech of the scientists who explain the composition of worlds with mystical voices? Does it come from the air impregnated with suave effluvia, or the faces embellished by an honest adoration of the Harmony of Forces that all of them name God? Here, no pain is legible in any gaze. One does not encounter anyone who laughs, but one does not encounter anyone who is sad.

"Listen," Pythie sings to me. "Listen, if your ears are capable of it. Can't you hear the sound of the invisible life of Ideas around our limbs? Don't you feel as if the vigor of Great Beings is fortifying you, in this place? Can't you taste the delightful confidence of knowing minuscule organs of the Planetary Person? I don't know whether you can perceive, as I can, the sweetness of losing oneself in a form more total than our human individualities. I don't know whether the sense of being diluted in the immense current of the Gnosis transports you outside your carnal sheath as it transports me. Everything flows out of me that isn't thought. A magnetism discorporates mentality here. Doesn't it seem to you to be easy to conceive what each of these strollers hopes, glimpses and contemplates in the mind? Oh, you talk to me about love, souls in communion, distinct beings reassembled into a single being; you recommend the fusion of our two sentiments into a single passionate ardor . . . this is what fulfills your desire. All the inhabitants of the city live in the same soul, which strives to know more of the secret of worlds, and the rest is abolished before their desire to seek the veritable God . . ."

Certainly, the atmosphere of the city is special. One enjoys a calm intoxication in the magnificently colored gardens.

Have you not, my dear friend, on certain days, been subject to the driving force of the crowd in the streets of a capital? Doesn't the indignation or mockery that animates it before spectacles of brutality or disgrace grip you, in spite of the advice of reason? Mingled with the popular crowd, have you not acclaimed the sovereign who passes by, jeered at the quarrelsome drunkard, applauded the heroine of a stupid vaudeville or pursued the thief who has just stolen something from a shop's display?

At least, if you have not gone as far as action, you needed, at such times, a victory over the inclination, a resistance to the appeal of the multitude. The contagion of the example is maddening, when the crowd is numerous. The preoccupation with the incident suppresses the sum of other concerns in the members of the crowd. The entire will of each is concentrated in participation in the general emotion, playing a part therein. Angers, mockeries, furies, hopes of victory and bestial desires unite above the human residues and compose a single omnipotent force whose effluvia intoxicate. Instincts are excited to paroxysm; they flood bodies, and their external mixture creates a collective being of which individuals become the servile limbs.

That anger or joy of the street can give an approximate impression of what I feel in the environment of this city. I have become a docile member of a collective idea of existence. The fury of scientific pursuit is drawing me away with the crowd of people frenetically avid to participate in it. My attention is augmented in a phenomenal manner. Without knowing anything about physics, chemistry, mathematics or cosmography except the rudiments learned at school, I see the evidence of phenomena, laws, formulae, calculations and solutions revealing itself. Between others and myself there is a continuous endosmosis of knowledge. In gazes and smiles, as much as in speech, I read the certainty that it is appropriate to acquire, as I run with the crowd to the hunt for the truth. Nothing can resist that driving force.

"That's it, that's it . . . I love you," Pythie said to me this morning. "You've just clarified the rationale of the rhythms that regulate the formation of substance in the imponderable ether, and my mind espouses yours, adores it in admiration . . . O dear lover, dear lover, who makes the force of your intelligence manifest; you've understood the emotions of the world, the motives of its genesis, and creation is palpitating on your eloquent lips. Take my body, and, for good measure, my hands, my breasts and my mouth, and the rest of me . . ."

We had a divine embrace . . .

Théa has not accompanied us to the city of Mercury. She has gone back to Jupiter, to which her office summoned her. We are walking alone, Pythie and I, through the miracles of the scientific city.

Pythie is full of charm. Light and magnificent, in her blue costume, above her light brown gaiters, she goes forth. The mat gold of her visage radiates around her profound and ironic eyes; but her smile has gained ineffable indulgences.

The palaces smile with their colored ceramics at the end of arbors united in the air by roofs of lianas and wild vines. Clad in blue, people walk with the allure of a grave happiness. There are paths of scarlet sand; fountains of violet, crimson, orange and mauve water; grouped statues of noble individuals gazing at the stars with passionate eyes, or whose gesture in marveling before the minerals hatched in the transparency of a retort. An exceedingly fine metallic mesh encloses in the sylvan perspectives the running of red deer, fallow deer and roe deer. The beautiful animals wander between the trees. Pheasants peck at the ground. Peacocks spread their tails, perched on the edges of fountains. After the dark verdure of the thickets, pink flamingoes are bathing their filigree feet in a pool constellated by enormous flowers.

The strangest place in the city is a hollow like a gigantic Byzantine Hippodrome. In that valley, negroes and Malays live in solitary fashion, each in the shelter of an arcade closed by grilles. Many artificial cascades impregnate the streets that give access to the facades with freshness. Bushes and blinds propagate shade.

Those prisons form a kind of triangular avenue, the base of which is a stage of a vast theater. The right-hand line on the angle is inhabited by women, the left-hand line by young men. Odorous flowers ornament the hair of both. Their bodies emit a heavy perfume. One sees them incessantly in the hands of masseurs. Voluptuous music visibly enervates the languor of their eyes. Within the reach of their arms, tables are laden with fruits, beverages, certain succulent and spiced preserves and singular sauces drowning ruddy purées.

In melodious voices, phonographs recite certain Malay rhapsodies that seem to interest the reptilian allures of domestic jaguars, cats and panthers brushing the rose-bushes. Those animals stretch, creep and then yawn. They rub along the bars or mewl at the sky, which sparkles, ringed on the circular crest of the valley by the quivering of the forest.

There are times when the theater is populated by Javanese dancers. Their copper tiaras shine above black tresses. Their erotic hands agitate and cleave the air left the fins of fish cleaving the water. Often, a horde of howling negresses imitates the obscenities of amour. It is the habitual representation of the theaters of this land, but with something more bestial, with savage music, alternately frenetic and lugubriously slow.

It makes the jaguars wail. They pursue one another. They mewl. The tomcats also become nervous and fight. Claws are bloodied. Their anger coughs. Lying on their backs, showing their white bellies and their rows of pink nipples, female panthers appeal to the males, which, in order to surge forth, cut through the bushes, where the petals of mature flowers fall like snow. Then, frantically, the animals bite one another and couple. A warm odor of wild beasts corrupts the air.

Bands of somber silk unfurling along masts swell up softly in the breath of artificial winds.

One perceives the solitaries stirring behind their silvered grilles. Eyes and teeth illuminate the brown physiognomies beaten by the thick fringes of eyelashes.

The narrowness of the angular avenue only maintains a minimal distance between the men and the women. They consider one another, stretching themselves. Gazes declare the mutual covetousness of flesh. Pensive, the young women press against the bars of their arcade and contemplate the lust of the jaguars and cats. Nervous frissons shake their shoulders and their breasts while the spectacle and the music go on. The flowers shine in colors against the blue-tinted hair of the captives. The perfumes of bodies emanate more powerfully. One begins to groan. Other plaints respond. All the faces are plastered against the silver bars; the brown hands clench. Staccato hysterical laughter unites with the frenzies of the orchestra. The men also yawn dolorously and twist their arms in the grilles.

"They're suffering," I said to Pythie, the first time.

"Yes," she replied, "they're suffering. Those foodstuffs, the fruits, the sauces, the preserves, of which you've tasted samples, are powerful aphrodisiacs that stimulate their desire or their instinct to paroxysm. Soon they'll be leaping on the spot, spurred by the delirium of the flesh that the music and the dances are still exciting. And yet, no one will open the silver grilles between whose bars they're passing their arms, thighs and dolorous mouths."

"And why this torture?"

"Aha! You understand! This is the reason. These two hundred barbarians in the flower of strength and youth, thus saturated with desire, are in the state in which their nerves disengage the greatest force of will. They're projecting their fluids, their souls, their psychic vigor, outside themselves. They're trying to spring forth from their bodies to join the forms of the opposite sex, just as electricities of different denominations project themselves from the tips of spikes in order to unite in the brief joy of a blue spark. Our scientists estimate that something similar is occurring with regard to these savages. Their voluntary fluids spring from the points of their bodies—hands, legs, mouths—to attempt to join up and fuse.

"If the hypothesis is justifiable, that narrow angular avenue contains a quantity of psychic force, human fluid, that is accumulating invisibly. One can thus infer that a healthy person momentarily bathed in that flow will attract a part of the static force, and, being neutral, will be charged with fluids of contrary denominations. The deneutralization, as it occurs, will occasion a state such that, for a moment, at least, the bather will be able to contain the paroxysm of the psychic force emitted by those two hundred savages.

"Imagine a scientist, penetrated with the importance of a capital problem, who suddenly senses that the solution is imminent. He enters this avenue. He walks, eyes closed, through that accumulation of fluids. Fasting, a bath, and preliminary copulations have prepared him in such a manner as not to be sexually stimulated. His mental power will thus be increased by a considerable fluid sum borrowed from the special atmosphere. It will be concentrated more vigorously; it will expend, more forcefully, an effort multiplied a hundredfold. There are a thousand chances to one that our thinker will find the result of his problem in that immersion.

"Look: a glass ceiling in two parts is lowering progressively over the avenue. The fluids are going to be condensed by the pressure of a gas recently created for that purpose. How the air is thickening before the grilles—can you see it turning blue? At the extremities of the hands and legs, minuscule sparks are emerging. That's how one distinguishes the psychic waves. Currents are acting in layers, in opposite directions. Ah! The cats and the jaguars are beginning to moan. Good, all the hysterical laughter is bursting forth. What a racket!

"Look how the poor brutes are pressing against the bars . . . and that one, tearing her robe, pushing her flesh into the interstices of the grille . . . and her rictus, and her hair standing up between the crimson flowers. So many male and female odors emerging from the epidermis in sweat are suffocating. Notice also the safety belts that preserve the captives from any artificial relief. For another hour the desires and deliria will be exasperated in their bodies. Oh, how high that panther leaps! One's beginning to feel ill at ease. The phosphorescences are dangerous to look at. My torso's twisting on my hips and my breasts are hurting. Let's go out for a while. We'll come back in an hour."

When we returned, the spectacle was repulsive. Like lianas and ivy wrapped around trees, the bodies of the captives were still knotted around the silver bars. Almost all of them were voiceless from howling. Tongues were twitching in their open white mouths. Several, in pressing against the bars, had left their flesh bruised and bloodied. There were young women who were writhing on the ground, weeping, men who were lying on their bellies, panting. The jaguars, cats and panthers, huddled in corners, among the bushes, no longer moving, were mewling faintly.

In the middle of the angle, sitting on a throne, was a motionless veiled figure. We saw that the veins were swollen in the old man's hands. The dense air had red, violet, mauve and blue zones, and the currents were acting in rapid waves in its phosphorescent thickness. The frenzy of the music had fallen silent. Shadow filled the theater. The closed glass ceiling trapped a colorless mass of gas in an atmosphere under pressure. At the silver bars the solitaries were still extending hands and lips, banging their foreheads, with their raucous sighs and their fiery eyes.

The form of the scientist did not move at all for an hour, insensitive to the plaints of the tortured. Suddenly, he uttered a cry of triumph, and quit the throne in order to run to the exit.

"He's found it," said Pythie.

At the same moment all the grilles turned on their hinges, opening outwards, and the solitaries surged toward the open arms of the women, toward the quivering bodies and the bruised breasts. Scarcely had they stood up, however, then they tottered. Neither the women nor the men could cross the narrow avenue. Bodies sank on to the rose-bushes, from which the jaguars fled. A great sob resounded once more. Desire had abolished the strength to realize the embrace.

Gently, the ceiling was divided. The two glass sections were re-raised. The air escaped through the fissure, whistling. We left.

Outside, the phonographs were proclaiming the miraculous discovery obtained by the patient of the twelfth mathematics group. A celebratory cortege was forming at the crossroads of the gardens.

FRANCIS POICTEVIN
(1854-1904)

Francis Poictevin (1854-1904) was known as a Naturalist and member of Edmond de Goncourt's salon, but he also befriended Jules Barbey d'Aurevilly and Léon Bloy, and began frequenting Le Chat Noir. His collection of dream stories *Songes* (1884) had obvious affinities with Symbolism, and his novel *Seuls* (1886) was hailed as an important exemplar by the early Symbolist periodicals, where several extracts from it appeared. His subsequent novels, like Paul Adam's, consciously fused Symbolist and Naturalist techniques, but he fell silent after 1895, when he moved to the Midi to shield himself from the encroachments of tuberculosis and was suspected of a descent into madness.

"Loners" is a translation, original to the present volume, of the excerpt from *Seuls* published under that title in the first issue of *Le Symboliste*, 7-14 octobre 1886.

Loners

Across an area of heath closer to the sea Édouard went in the matinal light, which brushed the flocculated and dropletted branches almost horizontally. He followed the clouds dappling with a ruddy gray the uniform light whiteness of the sky, as if about to dissolve into it in the course of their slow passage.

From a hillock in the heath, the dunes to the south-west, crowned with pines, were tightly packed, gleaming here and there under the clouds, seemingly ready in their vast semicircle to collapse into the waves bathing their feet. One might have thought that others, on the contrary, were at risk of being swallowed by the sand, the polished concave wall of which took on by contrast an illusion of immobility. The expanse plunged, undulating and glaucous, toward one corner of the horizon, as if between the distant pines.

On sunny days they went to eat the morning meal at the top of the large dune, a few meters lower down, in the shade of a pine. Graciously, whoever had brought the basket became ecstatic and fearful on the incessantly shifting sand. To the west, the sky, a great window, cut the waves with its blinding line. They were shiny, but, behind the sandy point of the lighthouse, they ran in bands, displaying a creamy surf. To the east, the forest deployed its swell, diminished by the misty perspective. And the sunlight, falling perpendicularly on the smooth summit of the dune, made the silence almost sonorous.

One day, far advanced in the forest, they asked a stout resin-collector for directions. In her cabin, in the midst of her chickens, she articulated a few words in her dialect. They believed that they were in an unexplored corner. Pines, one of them forked, rose up high, strong and scaly, extending their inflexible branches, almost devoid of twigs, in hesitant curved, communicating a power to the place. The undergrowth formed bushes, and even more than on them, somewhat closed, the eye strayed along the giant branches. Then, Lucienne and Édouard came back, and sat down above a little valley. Slender pines descended along the slope, as if to fill in the solitude.

One afternoon, she had put on her white flannel dress, garnished with blonde. They went up as far as the long winding road. She sat down on the ground there. In those days of the end of February, one might have thought the atmosphere velveted, especially after hours of rain, through which distances filtered. They remained sitting close together, without talking, in the silence of the surroundings. The balsamic effluvia penetrated them. And she replied to his delicate, as if indirect question regarding her contentment or displeasure in those minutes by means of a prettily directed glance around her, not at all fixed this time, lost in the yellow-green of the broom clustered around the ruddy trunks, toward the searching, sniffing lap-dog, and replied that she felt out of place . . . She did not recall anything, did not suppose anything else . . . Between such indefinite remarks, they drew closer together and plunged more deeply into the fusing life of the forest.

✳

In winter, in the Pension Mooser in Montreux, their previous room was occupied. They had one on the second floor with a balcony. The two windows overlooked the lake.

This time, they had a young Russian Baron for a neighbor, who was in the final phase of consumption. While she served meals in the room, the maid talked about the invalid. She was astonished that, when his mother had come, he had positively refused to see her; he had the idea, according to his domestic, that as she received her share of his annuity income as the orphan son of an officer, she was motivated in her solicitude by the interest she had in his not dying. In the corridor, she was encountered handkerchief in hand. He threatened that if she persisted, he would disappear in the Valais. He only went out rarely in a carriage; he spent the sunlit hours on a chaise longue on his balcony, his domestic shielding him with an umbrella. Always dressed irreproachably, he turned the rings of his fingers with a scrupulous slowness.

Their distraction was the lake, each in a boat. He took to the open water; she, not wanting to lose sight of the bottom with its large rounded stones, remained close to the edge. Each of them had the lapdog in turn, but she always wanted to leap overboard and swim to the other. And they let their oars float in the shadow of the mossy, cracked wall of Chillon, beneath a sapling growing in a hollow.

Or, at the foot, they stopped shortly before the old castle, beside the railway: to their left the walled embankment of the road winding between the rocks, hidden by its parapet; to their right a line of thickets behind which the lake hid, lower down. It was difficult to get through there. They found themselves in a sort of corridor, with a ceiling of sky. Lucienne sat down on a block of stone strayed into the short grass. Édouard became restive as soon as the reflection of Chillon, bathed by soft daylight on green and jasper water, could no longer be seen. Above the castle, and ivy-clad wall which could be seen obliquely, and whose turrets massed their angles, the summit of the Dent de Midi loomed up, implausibly heightened, apart, in a giant crystallization. And they seemed, almost involuntarily, to be in an unvisited land, in front of a mountain different and more curious from the one known.

At the end of winter, they picked narcissi on the slope west of Glion. The cup-like corolla, was according to Lucienne, as white as Indian muslin, a slightly yellow-white, according to Édouard, as if steeped in a wave. Those nuances, they said, had no odor.

On the way back, they dawdled, sitting or walking on the terrace of the church. No longer seeing it by night, they found it lessened and protestant in the sunlight. The sound of its bells was sad. But behind the choir, windowed by an indecisive shadow, there was a find: a large tilting walnut tree, embraced by ivy, clenching the tips of its branches, and next to it, a little stream draining into the meadow. Below the grotto, the spring was signaled by the threads of grass, constantly dripping.

What remained, always new, were the dusks, in which each strove to affirm a hue. At those times, the ultimate mountain of the Savoy became imposing, like a promontory; beyond, the band of the Jura plunged into the sky, or, to the right, clouds were disseminated eccentrically on the green and azure whitening in crystal. Beneath, blondnesses darkened, on the edge of the concluding conflagration. Further down, the gray of the lake, so softly ashen there, was green-tinted and broken. On the mountains of the Savoy, in a high jagged rampart, with a slight semicircular curve, the snow had a torpid whiteness.

One afternoon, in the sloping street of a village in the vicinity, Lucienne thought that saw herself at eleven years of age in a little girl sitting on the external sill of a window, with the shutters closed upon her, and nothing but her legs dangling outside. There was the pleasure of warmth in a lonely place, where she could hear other people coming and going, enjoying immobility.

Having arrived in Menton before mid-November they did not want the hubbub of a hotel. They preferred a little boarding house in a garden in the Avenue de Carrei; they were given a sunny room with a view over the country; in the dining room they chose a separate table. The host's table only had three guests: a young English consumptive, a German about twenty-five years old who put on French airs, and an engineer in his forties, string, not fat, his curly hair receding. Installed in the region for a long time he had lost large sums of money in Monaco. He liked teasing, his gestures muted, his eyes smiling.

The first week, they took a carriage to Castillon. From the terrace of the village perched on a rock and accumulating loophole windows on the high walls of its seemingly undivided buildings, they saw the shadow of the mountain, behind which the sun was setting, crawling over the opposite slope, truly capturing it, an evil, oppressive shadow. Directly above it, a horizontal line of sulfur light endured, regretfully giving ground to the slowly rising shadow.

The autumn rains came, abundantly. Through them, the landscape seduced Édouard. He marveled, in the aqueous atmosphere, at the concentrated violet hue of the mountains, like an immense curtain that stirred in the slightest breeze. Lucienne thought that the gray rocks plunging down at the last French customs-post resembled a large crumpled sheet of Genoese velvet—blanched with snow, Édouard added.

The twists of the old olive branches were blackened, oozing and desperate under the thinner, almost magical foliage. Through the less silvery green of the olive trees, the tender green of the pines and the violet backcloth of the valleys, thus perceived, rendered a magnificence.

The crowns of the plane trees, not entirely defoliated, played upon the soft background, deepening a tapestry whose weave seemed worn, no longer having any but withered yellow-pink flowers.

The Mediterranean appeared, not blue, deeper, nor green, not so irritating, but the shade that is beyond desire, but unexhausted. The waves made a coarse and curt sound on the shore. Édouard was wearied by them, because they lacked the rhythm of oceanic waves.

One evening, above the sea, around the moon, clouds had assembled, some black, others pale, living unnamed forms on the alert, held in respect and imminent. The moon had marked, uncertainly, a burnt yellow circle; clouds were passing by limply, of a blue that was almost too bright. Others, however, extinct, were filing past, suspending the scene. Over the sea, nothing could any longer be seen then but a distant radiance, shining without dazzling. And the diamantine moon revealed herself, sniggering. Along the shingle, the edge of the water simulated a shroud in its slow unfurling. From the lighthouse, an insignificant fire fell upon the water in a column, drowned with its coppery light.

❋

From their window, at five o'clock in the evening, they watched the edge of the day, like a fire lost, so to speak, between the fading apricot-tinted sky and the treetops in the process of darkening. The lamp had not been brought yet. Without looking at Édouard, Lucienne caressed his face. She had just taken her quinine sulfate, her hands were intermittently cold and hot, the irises of her eyes marked with a tawny clarity. She felt shriveled, her skin drying out on her . . .

She went to bed early. Between midnight and one o'clock in the morning, she asked Édouard, who was pacing in the room or reading, if he could hear "the gossip," as she had baptized the Comte, because his voice resembled that of a toothless old woman. It was, in fact, the Hungarian, who had succeeded in retaining the carter or the engineer in the lounge, to play cards and drink. Drink had no effect on him. In the next room, the Russian was singing, speaking as if in a dream. Was he asleep?

Chatting at night inconvenienced Lucienne. And then, it seemed that voices changed at night . . . they spoke with less assurance, became boastful. Whereas, in the silence, she felt well, especially in the friendly presence of the moon, which gave her, she said, the sensation of Salammbô. The moon was a goddess, of whom one asked where she was going. And the battle of the noon with the sunlight in the morning, she added, preoccupied her: that veiled yellow light gradually giving way to the white light of day. The sun, afterwards, seemed to her to be a brute.

REMY DE GOURMONT
(1858-1915)

Remy de Gourmont was the most important literary critic of his era, and his studies of authors involved in the Symbolist Movement, many of them collected in *Le Livre des masques* (1896) and *Le Deuxième Livre des Masques* (1898), provided an invaluable map of its extent and a commentary on its ambitions. He became the principal theorist of Symbolism and Decadence, which he regarded as identical. He was one of the founders of the *Mercure de France* and its most prolific contributor, developing his distinctively mannered short fiction in its pages. He collaborated with Alfred Jarry in 1893-94 on *L'Ymagier*, a periodical devoted to Symbolist art extensively trailed in the *Mercure*, which developed a theory of archetypes similar in many respect to Carl Jung's. Disfigured by lupus, he became a recluse before the century ended, and his health deteriorated steadily thereafter, although he kept on writing relentlessly while he could.

"Le Magnolia" was reprinted in *Histoires magiques* (1894). The translation was originally published in the translation of that volume, as "Studies in Fascination," in *The Angels of Perversity* (Dedalus, 1992)

"Hamadryas" was reprinted in *D'un pays lointain* (1898). The translation was originally published in the first issue of the periodical *Weirdly Supernatural* in 2001.

The Magnolia

The two sisters, Arabella the beautiful and Bibiane the plain, came out of the house together. Arabella's beauty emphasized her youthfulness, while Bibiane seemed older by virtue of her plainness, so they seemed more like daughter and mother than orphan sisters.

They came out of the house that had been touched by grief and paused beneath the magnolia: the magical tree, which had been planted by no one, and which bloomed so magnificently even in the grounds of the desolate mansion.

The magnolia came to life twice in every year, after the fashion of its kind: first in the spring, when it pushed forth the green spears which would become its leaves; then again in early autumn, before the tired leaves began to wither. In autumn, as in spring, the proud display of the enchanted tree put forth huge flowers, which were like those of the sacred lotus, each snow-white corolla cradling a tiny red spot, as if it were a shroud marked with a single drop of life's blood.

While she leaned upon the maternal arm of Bibiane, who was always tolerant of her weaknesses, Arabella looked up at the magnolia's branches, dazedly.

"He is dying, like the autumn flowers of the magnolia, which have withered on the branches. The one who should have nourished the flower that I am with the drops of his vital fluid is dying, and now I am destined to remain eternally pale!"

"There is still one flower left," said Bibiane.

It was a flower that had not yet opened fully: a bud that stood out among the complacent leaves by virtue of its virginal purity.

"The last one!" Arabella complained. "It will be my bridal ornament. But is it really the last? No—see, Bibiane, there is one more yet, faded and nearly withered. They are like us—the two of us! Oh, it is a sign! It frightens me . . . I am all a-tremble . . . there we are, he and I, our fates mirrored in these two flowers. I will pluck myself, Bibiane—see, here I am! Shall I also have to die, like him?"

Mutely, Bibiane lovingly embraced her trembling sister. She was afraid herself, but she led Arabella from the sad and sorry garden, away from the magnolia, which had now been stripped of the last relic of its former glory.

❋

They went into the sad house, from which the prospect of happiness had so unexpectedly fled, leaving grief to reign in its stead.

"How is he?" asked Bibiane, while she lifted from Arabella's shoulders the mantle that marked her as a bride.

While Arabella sat down, as timidly as a child, to contemplate the unopened flower that she was clutching between her fingers, the mother of the dying man replied: "There is no time to lose. He is dying, and his greatest desire is still to be realized. Come with me, my daughter Arabella—I must call you that although your husband-to-be lies dying—and let the presence of your beauty bring forth a final flourish of love amid the last round of prayers. Death awaits you, my darling—would that it might be otherwise! The kiss that his lips will place upon the forehead of his bride is the kiss of one bound for the tomb—but his last smile will defy the invincible shadows with its radiance, a glimmer of light echoing in the darkness that lies beyond the reach of your own beautiful eyes. The son I bore is going to die; he is dying, and I am deeply sorry that you must be given in marriage to a dead man. To you, alas, who are so full of the joys of life, who was born to lie in a bed of fragrant flowers, I can offer nothing but the putrefaction of the tomb—oh, would that it might be otherwise!"

They wept together while they waited for the arrival of the men who were to witness the last rites, which would unite Death with Life. The priest came with them, not quite sure whether he had been brought here to tie the indestructible knot or merely to anoint the forehead, the breast, the feet and the hands of the moribund son.

They all went upstairs together, in silence, stepping as leadenly as a troop of pall-bearers. "He might as well be in his coffin as in his bed," whispered one of the men, "prepared for a burial instead of a wedding."

They hesitated at the top of the stairway, but the mother urged them on, repeating what she had said before: "There is no time to lose. He is dying, and his greatest desire is still to be realized."

※

In the bedroom, they all sank to their knees, save for Arabella, who took her place beside the nuptial bed, wearing her bridal gown like a shroud. When she too knelt down in her turn, touching her forehead to the edge of the pillow, the hearts of all those present went out to her, sharing her anguish. It almost seemed, as she lowered her pretty head to rest it on the pillow, that she was dying too. The bride-to-be laid her right hand upon the thin and wasted hand that lay on top of the coverlet, while her left hand pressed to her lips the unopened magnolia flower, the emblem of her virginity.

The priest began to pronounce the solemn words of the marriage service. All eyes were fixed upon the bed where the son was propped up, supported by his mother. His face was tormented by knowledge of the impending catastrophe, his expression so despairing as to seem satanic; it was bitter with envy of those who possessed the life that was deserting him, angrily resentful of the love that had to be left behind. The nearness of the young and beautiful Arabella served only to ignite a fervent but impotent flame of hatred in his hollow eyes. *How terrible his suffering must be!* thought the onlookers.

The dying man managed to raise himself up a little further. From purple lips that had already been touched by the cold hand of death, he spoke, while the men made a final effort to smile and the frightened women sobbed like mourners:

"Goodbye, Arabella—you belong to me! I must go, but you must follow me I will be there every night, I will wait for you beneath the magnolia, for you must never know any other love but mine. None but mine, Arabella! Ah, what a proof you shall have of my love! What a proof! What a proof! Your soul must be reserved for me."

And with a smile that wrought a diabolical transfiguration of the shadows that lay upon his wasted face, he continued to repeat himself. His voice struggled against its imminent extinction, perhaps devoid of any sense, but perhaps mysteriously infused with some unholy wisdom drawn from beyond the grave, saying: "Beneath the magnolia, Arabella, beneath the magnolia!"

❋

For many days and many nights thereafter Arabella could not sleep. Her spirit was sorely troubled, and her heart was heavy. At night, when the wind rattled the dying leaves of the deflowered tree, and when the moon stood high in the sky, bathing its magical crown with bright rays cast down between the October clouds, Arabella frequently trembled with fear, and threw herself into her sister's arms, crying: "He is there!"

He was indeed there, beneath the magnolia: a shadow amid the fallen leaves that were swirling in the wind.

One night, Arabella said to Bibiane: "We loved one another, so why should he seek to harm me? He is there. I must go to him!"

"When the dead call out to us," Bibiane replied, "the living must obey. Go, and do not be afraid. I will leave the door open, and I will come out to you if you call me. Go: he is there."

He was indeed there, among the fallen leaves that were swirling in the wind. When Arabella came out to him beneath the magnolia, the shadow extended its arms to her—sinuous and serpentine arms, which fell upon her shoulders, writhing and hissing like hellish vipers.

Bibiane heard a stifled scream. She ran out.

Arabella was stretched out on the ground. Bibiane picked her up and carried her back into the house.

There were two marks on Arabella's neck, like the imprints of two thin and bony fingers. Her once-beautiful eyes were glazed, transfixed by horror—and, tightly clasped in the clenched fingers of her hand, Bibiane found the second flower that they had seen on the day of her sister's wedding: the sad, withered flower that they had compassionately left upon the tree; the flower that was the Other; the flower that flourished beyond the grave.

Hamadryas

The Marquise Fioravanti received the elegant mythological nickname of Hamadryas upon her entry into the Academy of Asolans, where Cardinal Bembo[1] delighted beautiful and noble ladies and learned gentlemen with amorous casuistries. Meetings of the Academy were held at the cardinal's villa, situated beneath pines and oaks. There, all the cases of conscience that might

---

1 The Venetian scholar Pietro Bembo (1470-1547).

concern lovers whose mastery of sensation was no less than their mastery of feeling were discussed after the fashion of the peripatetic philosophers.

Bembo, smiling gravely, usually had the last word—at which time he would lift his head with satisfaction, shaking the red tassels that hung from his white felt hat. Sometimes, however, the assembled gentlemen would discover serious questions while recalling their adventures—and the princesses and marquises, although ever-inclined to irony, would often find ingenious resolutions to questions of principle which perplexed the cardinal and caused the priests to become thoughtful.

For instance, the question might be posed:

"If a woman is loved by a timid admirer, how far may she encourage the admirer in question by giving him unequivocal evidence of her solicitude? For example, might she openly seek out his company? Might she ask for his hand to assist her in descending a staircase? Might she compliment him on his figure? Might she even go so far as to kiss him?"

The controversy aroused by that particular question eventually settled on the matter of the kiss, and extended at some length. The women, who were refined and committed egotists, waxed lyrical upon the delight of being loved by a man so discreet that he spoke with his eyes alone. There was, they said, an exquisite pleasure to be derived from the mute adoration and painful constraint of a creature so devoted as to be enslaved. The kiss would spoil everything, because it would transform timidity into audacity, and it would soon become necessary to surrender on all fronts at once, abandoning to the victor all the redoubts, and the castle itself, which he should have conquered for himself.

"The Castel Sant'Angelo!" ventured one cavalier, whose manner of speaking was light but bold.

That description brought a smile from the cardinal, and then a merry laugh. Encouraged by that condescension, the princesses and marquises repeated the pretty metaphor in a slightly scandalized tone.

"Sir," said Hamadryas—who had not yet said anything that evening—"your description is one of the most beautiful to have emerged from our Academy. Together with the fame that will be attached in future centuries to the name of our cardinal, if I am not mistaken, it will surely secure our eternal renown. The Castel Sant'Angelo is the key to Rome, to the extent that whoever holds that fortress is master of the city. It is the same with a woman: once master of the gateway, you are master of the entire palace: all the pleasures, thoughts, desires and dreams that bestir the little world of her pleasant form. Whether you take it by consent, trickery or force the result is always the same and her submission is absolute."

"You are going too fast, Madame," said the cardinal. "You are settling questions of the utmost subtlety with too much violence."

The marquises and the princesses said, ingenuously: "Madame, you have betrayed us."

✳

Hamadryas never returned to the shadow of the pines and the oaks to dispute with the Asolans. She found them puerile and rather hypocritical. She had joined their company having believed that frank and honest discussions would help her to revive, stylishly, the pleasures of love to which she had wearily bid adieu, in spite of the fact that she had scarcely turned thirty. Alas, the refinements of their cold intellects, light hearts and fashionably perverted spirits exasperated her, and she also found them humiliating. She had lived so much and loved so abundantly that their discreet and cerebral debauches seemed to her to be the dreams of sick children, and the cardinal, whom she held nevertheless in some esteem, appeared to her to be like a vain and bland schoolteacher, as naive as he was complicated, probably impotent and a trifle ridiculous.

Having thus abandoned the Asolans, she wished to purify herself in action, and to wash away the Platonic blue whose cold tint she felt upon her skin with kisses that were not at all metaphorical. So she abandoned herself to love for the hundredth time, with all the pagan sentiment she could muster, thus putting to the final proof all that remained of her faith and unselfishness.

But the viol had lost its music.

Then, she considered her beauty and the immortal will.

Her beauty, her body, her figure—when all was said and done, she had never loved anything else. What joy she had felt, on returning from each of her voyages of discovery and love, to be possessed of herself again! It was as if her beloved flesh had received a long-awaited free pardon!

Michelangelo had sculpted his own glorious Hamadryas in marble, and the Marquise Fioravanti exhibited in her palace, among the fountains of agate and gods of bronze in the gallery of the festivals, the unparalleled masterpiece of her own beauty. Her pedestal bore the inscription of her one and only name, Hamadryas, in order that posterity might revere like a goddess the woman who desired nothing but the anonymous glory of having been beautiful.

And the cardinals, the priests, the cavaliers, the princesses and the marquises passed through the gallery of the Palazzo Fioravanti, admiring the work of the sculptor even as they deplored the shamelessness of Hamadryas.

She was there to hear their envious remarks, but she remained pleasant and proud, dedicating herself to her supreme moment, intent on leaving behind the memory of a uniquely imperious grace. Then, when everyone had departed to the accompaniment of violins and harps, she lifted to her lips a poison-bearing ring, a gift from the late Pope—and her servants carried her away.

❋

The next day, Giacinto Carrera, disgraced cardinal and Bishop of Foligno, received this letter:

Most Faithful Friend,

The Emperor has slept in my bed. I have been the delight of a Pope and I have excited cardinals with passion. I have numbered among my lovers young men astonished by their happiness and old ones respectful of my caprices, artists who forgot to please me because my beauty intoxicated them, devotees who adored me wholeheartedly, poets who had wonderful dreams in my arms and poets who had none, Castilians as stupid as goats and melancholy Teutons—men of all kinds, even those whose sterile love required the special spice of obscenity. I have been loved sufficiently to be the envy of my peers and I have disarmed their jealousy.

(Ah, most faithful friend, what a confession that is—if that is what it is!)

What remains?

The unexpected?

I can scarcely believe that there is anything un-expected by a woman of my beauty, my age and my liberty. All risks have confronted me and I have taken them all, even if they had naught with which to seduce me but the baton of Harlequin or the costume of Pantaloon.

Love? And yet more love?

I have loved far too often to believe in it any more, and I have been loved far too often for to-morrow's love to have the power to make me forget yesterday's.

Remember, most faithful friend, that Cristoforo the Neapolitan—whose genius troubled Michel-angelo while he was only twenty-three years old—was killed for me, and that I adored him, and that I have wept for him, and that I have forgotten him, so completely that I can no longer recall the color of his eyes: the eyes of Cristoforo, once my joy, my Heaven, my Lake of Nemi, my Gulf of Naples!

No, most faithful friend, there is no hope left to me but the determination to die beautiful; that will be the last self-indulgence of my sensuality.

ANDRÉ-FERDINAND HEROLD
(1865-1940)

André-Ferdinand Herold was a regular at Mallarmé's *mardis* before publishing *Les Paeans et les Thrènes* (1890). He formed close friendships with Henri de Régnier and Pierre Louÿs, and became a key contributor to the *Mercure de France*. Although best known for his non-fiction, poetry and dramatic work—he wrote plays in collaboration with Ephraim Mikhaël and Jean Lorrain—he also published novels and one exceedingly scarce collection of short stories, *Les Contes du vampire* (1902).

"L'Ascension des Pandavas" was first published in *Le Centaure* volume 1 (1896). "The Ascension of the Pandavas" is original to the present volume.

The Ascension of the Pandavas

I

When Yudhishthira,[1] the magnanimous hero, went into the hall of justice, his eyes were radiant with joy and his mouth was illuminated by a divine smile. Brahmins and warriors, merchants and laborers, those of the city as well as those of the country, were waiting for him to appear; he was the one who was about to settle differences, punish and recompense. And all of them, as soon as the King had crossed the threshold, sensed gladness in their hearts, and a unanimous cry rose toward the vaults: "Glory to the Master of the earth, glory to the one who protects the castes, glory to the son of Pandu, glory to Yudhishthira."

And they saw that the handsome King was shining that day with a superhuman beauty.

---

1 Yudhishthira is a character in the Hindu epic *Mahabharata*; he is the eldest of the Pandavas, the five acknowledged sons of King Pandu, who fought and won a great war against the Kauravas, and who were all married to the same woman, Draupadi.

Yudhishthira, as was his custom, ordered every individual to expose his complaint or his defense without fear, and he judged in accordance with equity. And yet, he did not look at those who advanced toward the throne; it might even have been thought that he did not hear their words. His eyes remained fixed on the marvelous vision of some distant world; his ears were listening to voices that were not of the earth, and it was doubtless an invisible God, sitting beside him, who was dictating his replies.

All the cases were judged, and the King's subjects went out. A few favorite courtiers remained in the hall with the royal dreamer, and he fell silent.

His divine silence lasted for a long time. Finally, however, he bowed his head, shivered slightly, and his gaze was humanized; he quit the world to which his dream had taken him for the earth. He made a sign to the Guardian of the Door to dismiss the court; the Guardian obeyed, and when he was alone with her, Yudhishthira spoke to her.

"Call my four brothers, O Guardian, and tell them that I am waiting for them here. Also call the one who is the common joy of my brothers and myself, the one who was the faithful wife of Pandavas for many years: Draupadi, the woman with the long nocturnal hair."

II

As soon as they were apprised of Yudhishthira's order, the four brothers came to the hall of justice. They were Arjuna the magnanimous and the grave Bhimasena, with the twins Nakula and Sahadeva; and at the same time as them, their beloved came in, the one who had once shared their perils and who was now their companion in glory, the beautiful Krishna Draupadi.

"Why have you summoned us, brother?" cried Aruna from the threshold.

"Does your wisdom have need of advice?" asked Bhima.

"Or must we console you for some unexpected and mysterious dolor?" asked Draupadi.

142

The King looked at Draupadi tenderly.

"Dear woman, you will not have to console me for any dolor; I am happy today, and it seems to me that we shall now be happy forever."

And he replied to Bhima: "Brother, I shall not interrogate your wisdom, and I shall not ask the valiant Arjuna to aid me with his courage. The time is coming, I believe, when we shall no longer live on the earth; the time is approaching when we shall no longer hear the sorrowful voices of men; the days are shining when we shall no longer see the pale rivers of this world. O my brothers, O beloved Draupadi, I had a dream last night; I dreamed divinely."

He fell silent momentarily, and his mouth had a smile of light.

He continued: "Where was I? In what world? And who had taken me there? I do not know; but suddenly, I saw myself in a marvelous meadow. Everywhere, there were flowers, oh, flowers such as do not grow in any land on earth, huge flowers whose perfumes cured ills and troubles. From a melodious forest that bordered the meadow the voices of birds unknown to humans escaped, and groups of young women were dancing here and there. Brothers, in that beautiful meadow, I felt completely happy; I was delivered from human dolor. I understood that I had reached the land of the Gods: the Apsaras were welcoming me with their dances, and soon, I heard the Gandharvas, who were singing their songs for me. And then Indra himself appeared, and made me a sign to follow him to his immortal dwelling."

Yudhishthira's eyes seemed once again to be contemplating the nocturnal dream, and one might have thought that his voice was distant.

"I have followed Indra into the victorious dwelling; I have seen his divine companions, I have seen the Heroes and the Sages; and I am still full of the joy of the great dream that was sent to me. I cannot forget the splendor of my slumber."

"Certainly," said Arjuna, "the dream was beautiful, and it is just that you are still gloriously moved by it. Doubtless it presages some imminent happiness."

"Arjuna, there will be no more happiness for me on earth. I know the warning that there was in the dream. Indra is summoning me to him. I must quit the kingdom of Hastinapura."

"Brother, brother," cried Nakura, "we have been faithful to you, in the past, in misfortune; when you had lost everything, and you were wandering through the forest of exile, we did not abandon you. And now that we have vanquished our enemies, now that we can forget the chagrin and we can rejoice, you want to leave us, cruel brother."

"Do not leave us alone, Yudhishthira," cried the brothers and the spouse, and they all extended their imploring arms toward the King.

In a grave voice, Yudhishthira replied: "Have I said that I would leave you in Hastinapura? Oh, if I had said such a thing, I would not be worthy of the glory that Indra has sent me. O Brothers, and you, cherished wife, I have sworn never to abandon you, and in the great voyage that I must make in order to obey the Gods, my brothers, and you, Draupadi, shall be my companions. Tomorrow, the five Pandavas and their wife will quit the royal palace; pilgrims toward the abode of the Gods, they will emerge from the walls of Hastinapura, and we shall march over the earth, seeking the foot of the mountain of gold, on the celestial summit of which the immortal Indra dwells."

And they all had eyes illuminated by joy.

III

The people of Hastinapura groaned when they knew that they would not see the Pandavas again. They had left the kingdom to their relatives and the wisest of the Brahmins, and, clad in sacred bark, they had left the city at daybreak.

At first they marched eastwards.

They were still not far from the city when they heard a dog running breathlessly behind them. Yudhishthira turned round, and he recognized Virajna, the faithful beast that had guarded the palace reliably for a long time.

He said to his brothers: "Stop. Virajna has followed us, and he wants to join us. It is necessary that we do not chase him away; he was the humblest of our servants, but often the most devoted. Now, without knowing where we are going, he is attaching himself to us, ready to suffer, he might perhaps believe, the cruelest of woes. Our duty, brothers, is to wait for him. Let him accompany us on our fine voyage."

And they allowed the dog Virajna to join them, who marched eastwards with them.

For three days they went along roads bordered by fields and meadows. Sometimes they crossed a river at a ford, and said the usual prayers. Finally, on the evening of the third day, they arrived at the entrance to a grave forest, and there, suddenly, they saw a being of gigantic stature who loomed up in front of them.

"You shall go no further," cried the being that had appeared, and his voice was loud and terrible.

The giant had, in every respect, the face and body of a man, but around his head there were seven burning flames, and by that sign, Yudhishthira knew that it was the god Agni who had spoken to him.

"Agni, Agni," he cried, "why are you stopping the Pandavas on their route? We are seeking the mountain of gold, the holy mountain crowned by Indra's dwelling. We are seeking it as humble pilgrims, clad in bark, and at the hours and in the places prescribed, we say the ritual prayers. Indra, by means of a dream, has summoned me to him. Why, Agni, are you forbidding us to go any further?"

"Sage King," replied the God, "I am not unaware of any of what you think you are informing me. You will arrive, Yudhishthira, at the summit of the pious mountain, but in order to find the route, it is necessary to quit all pride."

"Our souls are not proud, Agni."

"In the hands of your brother Arjuna I see the indomitable bow, the sound of which alone once dispersed enemies, and to keep such a weapon is scarcely a sign of humility."

"Arjuna," said Yudhishthira to his brother, "you have heard the God's words. Throw away your bow, O warrior; it is not a time for grim battles."

Arjuna looked at the bow for a long time. He thought about the countless battles in which he had launched victorious arrows against his enemies.

"Agni," he begged, "may I not enter Indra's dwelling bow in hand? Oh, I have abandoned my riches with joy, but permit me to keep the weapon, thanks to which I have vanquished cruel enemies. I shall have no more use for it, I know, and I no longer want to make use of it; however, I take pleasure in seeing it. It reminds me of great memories; I have a kind of amity for it, and it seems to me that in throwing it away, I would be throwing away something of myself."

"Throw away the bow, Arjuna," the God Agni ordered.

Arjuna hesitated momentarily. In the end, he kissed the invincible bow, and then threw it on the ground. And he wept.

"O Pandavas, go into the forest," said the God. "When you have traversed it, take the road that leads northwards. It is by following it that you will reach the holy mountain."

He disappeared. The Pandavas advanced through the forest; and with them marched Draupadi, the beauty with the lotus eyes; and the dog Virajna also marched with them.

IV

The route to the mountain was long. The Pandavas skirted many meadows, they passed over many fords, they wandered in many forests. The sun crushed them and the rain weighed them down; but they kept on marching; they did not feel fatigue, and they were joyful.

One night, they went to sleep at the foot of a mountain, which, in the darkness, they divined to be very high. They had marched all day and all evening too, and they did not stop until it was pitch dark. When they woke up at dawn, they all cried out unanimously in surprise and joy; the mountain, in the sunlight, had a golden gleam, and the summit was lost in the heavens.

"Glory to Indra," said Yudhishthira. "This is the holy mountain. Be courageous, brothers, be strong, Draupadi, and we will reach, at the summit, the land of glory and felicity."

And the Pandavas, with Draupadi, commenced climbing the sacred mountain, and the dog still followed them.

Yudhishthira marched in the lead; then came Bhimasena, and then Arjuna; then there were the twins Nakula and Sahadeva; and lastly went the woman with the beautiful hips, Krishna Draupadi, and her long night-dark hair floated in the breeze.

They climbed slowly. The ground beneath their feet was gilded, and there were perfumes in the air that filled them with joy. Yudhishthira smiled, the same luminous smile that had appeared in his eyes and mouth when he entered the hall of justice after the dream in which Indra had appeared to him. Sometimes he looked at his brothers, who were following him, and encouraged them with a smile. And they all climbed the mountain, gradually.

They arrived at a meadow, an immense emerald encrusted in the golden earth. Here and there, diamonds and rubies, sapphires and topazes, figured as flowers, and droplets of pearls had fallen there as dew.

The Pandavas and their companion, and also the dog, set about traversing the meadow. They often slipped.

Suddenly, Yudhishthira heard Draupadi cry out; he turned round and saw her lying on the ground.

"Yudhishthira, Yudhishthira, I have fallen and cannot get up, and I sense that an invincible force is overwhelming my will. I am being drawn to the foot of the mountain. Alas, alas, shall I not climb it? Yudhishthira, have I ever been at fault? Am I being punished for some ancient sin?"

"O Draupadi, poor beloved," said the King, "this, I believe, was your sin. You were the common wife of the five Pandavas; you swore to love the five brothers with the same amour. And yet, to the other four of us you always preferred the valiant Arjuna; in truth, you only love him. Perhaps you dare not admit that amour to yourself, but you have never been able to vanquish it, and your eyes shine with desire when they contemplate Arjuna. That, O Draupadi, is doubtless the sin for which the Gods are punishing you."

And he recommenced climbing; and his four brothers, and also the dog, climbed behind him.

The meadow seemed increasingly slippery, and the anxious voice of Sahaveda came to the King's ears.

"Yudhishthira, brother, I have slipped, and no matter what effort I make, I cannot get up. Reply to me, you who can divine everything: have I sinned, even once?"

"Incessantly you boast of your knowledge, Sahadeva; no one, you think, can equal you in wisdom. And I do not believe that the Gods are punishing you for any other sin."

And Yudhishthira continued climbing; and three of his brothers, and also the dog, climbed behind him.

Another plaint made them shudder.

"Brothers," lamented Nakula, "I have fallen; I cannot get up; am I a sinner, then?"

"Alas, brother, do you not think yourself the most handsome of men? And is it not that vanity for which the Gods are punishing you?"

And the King climbed the slippery meadow, and now only had two of his brothers with him; and the dog was still following them.

A wild cry troubled the King's reverie.

"Brother, brother, it is now me, Arjuna, who has been felled by a mysterious force. I want to get up, but alas, I cannot. I am dragged down regardless. What sin have I committed, then?"

"Did you not say once: 'In a single night I will kill all the enemies,' and that you did not do? You only had scorn for other archers. You judged yourself invincible. When some warrior was mentioned in your presence, you mocked and laughed loudly. Such was your sin, Arjuna, and the Gods, alas, have not forgiven you."

Now with Bhimasena alone of the Pandavas, the King climbed toward the celestial abode, and the dog had not quit him.

Soon, they had emerged from the meadow, the edge of which touched the sky. Beyond was the dreamed land, the realm of Indra.

A somber moan broke the contemplation in which Yudhishthira was already immersed.

"Look, O King. Alas, I, Bhima, who is so dear to you, have fallen too. Why have I fallen? Why will I not see the splendor of Indra?"

"Brother, you have sometimes abused your strength, you have glorified your courage and your prudence too loudly, and the Gods are punishing you cruelly."

The hero marched on toward the sky, and the dog was alone in following him.

V

Beyond the sky, the King reached the summit of the mountain. And there, it really was the enchanted land that he had seen in the dream. The laughing Apsaras welcomed him with their dances, and he heard the Gandharvas singing. But he did not experience the great happiness for which he had hoped; his brothers had not reached the divine country, nor had the dear Draupadi.

He advanced into the marvelous gardens; he scarcely glanced at the joyful flowers that blossomed for him; he was thinking about his brothers' disgrace. Now the God Indra came to meet him.

"Be welcome in my dwelling, Yudhishthira," said the God. "I have been waiting for you for a long time. Come and enjoy the same glory as Indra."

Indra was guiding the King. Suddenly, he stopped.

"Pandava, what unworthy companion have you brought with you? Chase that vile animal away. It is necessary that a dog does not sully the celestial gardens with its presence."

"Indra," replied Yudhishthira, "I will not abandon this dog, which has always been devoted to me, and which has had the strength to climb the mountain."

"You are now immortal, O King. Now, your condition is mine. You have absolute felicity. Abandon your dog."

"I do not want a felicity that I would gain by abandoning a faithful servant."

"A dog is an impure beast, which steals offerings and troubles sacrifices."

"Killing a Brahmin is not a graver sin than abandoning a faithful servant. This is a being that has always been gentle and devoted; he has grown old now, he has grown weak; in guarding my palace he has become thin; he wanted to follow me, and when I have the supreme glory within my grasp, shall I be ingrate toward this humble friend? No, Indra, I shall only stay in your abode with this dog."

Indra was smiling.

"Let the dog accompany you, O King, faithful to your friends and your servants," he said, in the end.

And he ordered that his chariot be brought. He climbed into it, and invited Yudhishthira to climb into it, and the God and the King traveled through the garden of the sky.

VI

"Indra," said the King, getting down from the chariot, "you have shown me divine marvels. I have heard songs that charmed me and seen dances that dazzled my eyes. I have scented living perfumes, I have drunk from joyful springs, and yet, O Indra, I am sad."

"You are sad?"

"Yes. Nowhere, here, have I seen my brothers; nowhere have I seen Draupadi."

"Do you not know that they fell while climbing the mountain?"

"I hoped, O Indra, that you had wanted to spare them fatigue, that you had removed them to your abode by more rapid routes, and that they would be here to welcome me."

"The weight of their sins has dragged them down toward subterranean realms."

"Without my brothers, without my beloved, I cannot be happy, Indra."

"Look at the inhabitants of the heavens, Yudhishthira, look at the Siddhas and the Devarshis, look at the Gandharvas and the Apsaras, more beautiful than your Draupadi."

"No, without my brothers, Indra, there cannot be any happiness for me; without my brothers, I cannot stay here. I want to go where my brothers have gone, where my wife with the long hair has gone, the wife with the victorious eyes, the best of women, my Draupadi."

And Yudhishthira went down the holy mountain, and searched the world for the entrance to the subterranean abodes.

ADOLPHE RETTÉ
(1863-1930)

Adolphe Retté was on the editorial staff of *La Vogue*, and published his first collection of poems, *Cloches en la nuit*, in 1889. That was followed by the remarkable *Thulé des Brumes* (Bibliothèque Artistique et Littéraire, 1891), a portmanteau of dream-like prose poems. He experienced something of an ideological conversion in 1893 when he became a committed anarchist and gave his allegiance to an esthetic theory that preached the necessity of a return to nature and a celebration of everyday life. In 1906 he underwent another conversion, this time to Catholicism, and his subsequent literary work was doctrinaire.

"La Fin du rêve" is one of the sections of *Thulé des Brumes*. "The End of the Dream" is original to the present collection.

The End of the Dream

I

Silence, like an accumulation of cloud on the violet horizon.
Silence, the martyrs in tunics like albs
And a thousand clematis blossoms float in the silence.
Silence, like a very ancient god . . .
✳

A young woman with pale hair and lunar eyes is sitting in the russet grass where orioles are hopping; she smiles strangely, very amused, dispersing swan-feathers in the lactescent air . . .

A spring sleeps, swathed in sweet marjoram . . .

The city, in the distance, is a dragon sheeted in gray and mounted by a knight in an emerald helm.

The sun so bright and devoid of warmth at the zenith . . .

Bells, great silver lilies, and their clapper a golden pistil, emit scents of benzoin.

A cemetery quivers, strewn with violets . . .

The Prince, leaning his forehead on the knees—so cold—of the young woman—who is death—contemplates an ebony coffin in which a child queen reposes, descending into the depths within himself; but he is bored.

He senses the obsession of a white weeping willow . . .

The Prince gets up; he shields his eyes with his hand and looks toward the Orient, set ablaze by a furious wyvern
A swaying caravan, orange and blue, snakes and tinkles out there, toward a port at which the Mage Kings will embark.
The Prince sets forth and catches up with the caravan. The young woman meditates; one might think that she was praying; the swan-feathers settle.

And the silence darkens . . .

Silence, like an antique carpet, woven with faded figures shiny with wear
Silence, like wings toward elsewhere.

II

The prelude to *Lohengrin* disperses in icy spirals toward the heights. A white daylight reigns, dotted with blue sparks that soar from the tautly-threaded strings of thin harps.

One might think them undulating tresses . . .

A river surges, rolling fire, gold and blood, and draws—with what rapidity!—the funereal gondola that is carrying the Prince.

The Prince says: "That is me, the Poor Man of lost roads; that is me, the effigy on forgotten medallions . . . but what does it matter? I am weary of being, and that is why I'm taking pleasure, in the leisure of the hour, in stretching my limbs a little on the silky cushion that this gondola offers me; and then too, the landscape is agreeable."

And he empties the cup that the Mage-Kings hold out to him.

The banks of the river are fans of coral, from which a red dew falls, drop by drop. Here and there, plaintive madwomen are leaning on the crenellations of towers of jasper. The waves are whispering a melancholy *complainte* as they die away.

One might think that the dwarf Tidogolain is singing his lovesickness in the florid pathways, and that the Lady is moved to pity . . .[1]

The horses of the sun are snorting in the torpid sky: the labarum sun of the Unreal, before which the Prince, suddenly kneeling down, makes the sign of the cross devoutly.

Meanwhile, the faint music congeals in filigrees of ice toward the heights . . .

And the river covers itself with foam, broadly, soundlessly and majestically.

One might think it the slumber of an old man . . .

---

1 Tidogolain is a character from Arthurian legend. More pertinently to his citation here, he is the titular character in one of Jean Moréas' early poems.

III

The Night, pale and proud like a royal nun. A river of flowing milk brushed by flocks of pink flamingos. The slender ivory gondola speeds toward the enormous arches of a marble bridge, where mutilated knights, in armor corroded by rust, are leaning over the cool rumor of the waves.

Low in the sky, a half-moon, cherry red and violet.
And the Night seems a cloister in which golden nuns are kneeling.

The Prince extends himself in the bottom of the gondola, facing the stars. "Such soft velvet ramps this Night for the ascension, with groping hands, of my blind soul! An infancy within me is astonished by so much shadow and charitable gold; I sense new eyes blossoming within me, better to reflect the poppies and periwinkles in flower up there . . .

"Oh, I would like a little of this Night to enter into my heart!"

The gondola passes under the bridge; and antique thunder awakens; dusty flags are waved; bats circle.

The knights cry: "Take us with you; we were in your retinue when, quitting the Unfortunate Isles where you reigned, you attempted the conquest of the Princess of Pearls . . ."

The Prince sings: "*The knights are dead in the crusade . . .*"

Then they all throw their shields into the river.

But the gondola has passed by.

IV

"Let's disembark! Let's disembark! The air is vibrant with the wings of delight; the verdure bursts forth cruelly; a swell of flowers undulates, swollen with good sap; a red vapor trepidates in the distance; and the Summer bounds like a young tiger through the countryside."

It is the harvest, the harvest of poppies.

"What red intoxication rises to our brains here? My Prince, you are tottering, and your hands are clenched."

"Oh! Look, here comes the jubilee with the redness of dreams. Oh! look at all that red, resounding with triumphal marches . . ."

The poppies are crowded together, rubescent expectation; the poppies are strutting, heavy and somber; the poppies are swollen, an infernal paradise, a sunlit debauchery of red slumber. And long arrows of fire hail down on the exultant earth; terrible perfumes, as impetuous as stallions, sonorous perfumes, like red trumpets of conflagration.

It is the harvest, the harvest of poppies.

Large golden insects with ruby stripes and adamantine wings circle and dispute their opiate juices, and then fly away to deposit their booty in crystal hives dazzling in the distance, on the edge of a tawny wood.

The Prince rolls over among the poppies: streaming blood, an imperial couch, a crimson cloak of pensive dreams, a glory of orgy and oblivion that drowns him with furious kisses.

And the Prince falls asleep. Red petals bleed over his lips; red opium lees tint his fingernails; red sweat glistens on his forehead of a Christ of Illusion haloed by the irritated swarm of golden insects.

It is the harvest, the harvest of poppies.

V

Beneath the starry night, the exceedingly somber road snakes across a plain, yesterday's battlefield, covered in corpses. Wounded horses, abandoned, whinny dolorously; the winter wind stings the wounds that shine in the dark, like the flowers of aloes. The dead sleep, quite tranquil, with the astonished expression of no longer being alive; their eyes congealed by horror reflect the stars.

All alone—his Argonauts have remained, inebriated, in the poppies—the Prince marches with a long stride, toward where? He does not know; he goes on. Sometimes, rarely, people whom he encounters salute him and fix him with long, sad gazes. Judging by the wrinkles that slash their faces, one suspects that they have suffered a great deal; none are limping. Some whisper to one another, reflect, and then come to the Prince as if they want to give him some advice, but they stop, and back away. *What's the point?* they seem to be thinking. And they pass on, after having bowed very low, not without a certain irony.

The Prince also stops, and turns round; he thinks, confusedly, that perhaps he would have made them some reply if they had spoken, but what? He has forgotten. And he passes on.

Silence, like attentive eyes.

Meanwhile, a rumor is born at the extremity of the horizon; fleeting lightning flashes puncture the night, setting the country-side ablaze for the time of a thought, and then disappear.

And the Prince arrives on the seashore.

VI

The rotating beam of a solitary lighthouse is radiating its desert light in swarming prisms over the waves, as far as the eye can see. The sea crumples its seething waves at the foot of the lighthouse, where enormous white cetaceans spout phosphorescent geysers. A fringe of foliage bloodies the ashen horizon faintly, which closes on the traveled route close by. Night closes its golden lashes.

The Prince climbs up inside the lighthouse; an iron staircase rings under his footsteps; at the summit, in the multicolored cage, there are three watchmen in mourning. The Prince goes to speak to them, but with fingers over their lips they enjoin him to be silent. Then they draw him toward a window open over the sea and point into the distance, where a blue radiance is visible . . .

There—O unknown Dream!—somber fir-forests are moaning, undulating; fields of broom are ringing a million little golden bells in the wind. A roseate marmoreal palace rises up; on the threshold, an old man . . .

The three watchmen precipitate the Prince into space.

VII

Riding a blue ray of light on which Ariel is dancing, the Prince flies, at lightning speed, into the distance. The theme of the Holy Grail trembles in the darkness, and Astolfo's hippogriff circles.

Sudden daylight: the warm light of a summer day; pale mists like a brown espoused by the morning. And the sea becomes exasperated, and brandishes algal standards toward the nacreous cliffs.

O familiar Dream: it is the Island.

The Prince follows the florid meandering paths—all legend acclaims him—and arrives before the palace, so pink in the somber enlacements of ivy. On the perron, an exceedingly old King is waiting for him, among the twelve peers of Dream and dainty illusory fays; and buccinas of gold and bronze roar, frightening flocks of doves, feathered snow among the firs. The King descends a few steps to meet the Prince; he takes him in his arms and kisses him on the mouth.

"My son, you have suffered life and the dream; you were the Poor Man of the lost roads and your feet are still bleeding because of the pebbles that lacerated them during your pilgrimages in the land of Consciousness. Listen: your ordeals are over, you have donned the alb-like tunic of silence; your recompense is due. Come, the slumber with no tomorrow is open to you; your soul will breathe in Nothingness. Come and sleep with us, my son."

VIII

Thule of Mists sways on the waves, like the flower of the lotus in which the three gods meditate. And so many essences of unusual souls—the Prince and the Poor Man, the King and his twelve peers, the genteel fays; all of legend—repose forever, delighted, in the Afterlife.

Silence hangs over Thule of Mists.

Silence, like a virgin, with lunar eyes,
dispersing swan-feathers in the pale air.
Silence, like a cemetery strewn with violets,
silence, like our mother: Death.

BERNARD LAZARE
(1865-1903)

"Bernard Lazare" was the pseudonym of Lazare Bernard, who was born and raised in Nîmes, but came to Paris in 1886 at the insistence of his friend Éphraïm Mikhaël, who introduced him to Mallarmé's *mardis* and José Maria Heredia's salon. He became one of the principal exponents of Symbolist short fiction, reprinting his periodical fiction in *Le Miroir des légendes* (1892; tr. as *The Mirror of Legends*) and *La Porte d'ivoire* (dated 1897 but actually 1898; tr. as *The Gate of Ivory*), the latter published shortly after the curious portmanteau *Les Porteurs de torches* (1897; tr. as *The Torch-Bearers*), which explores the question of whether and how Symbolist "parables" can be adapted to the political cause of Anarchism, a philosophy that Lazare had embraced even more earnestly than Adolphe Retté. His productivity was interrupted when he became one of the chief instigators of the Dreyfus Affair, and then terminated when he died following a surgical operation to remove a cancerous tumor.

"Le Triomphe de l'amour" was reprinted in *La Porte d'ivoire*, in the English translation of which, published by Snuggly Books, "The Triumph of Love" was originally published.

"Les Fleurs" was reprinted in *Le Miroir des légendes*, in the English translation of which, published by Snuggly Books in 2017, "The Flowers" was originally published.

The Triumph Of Love

In accordance with his custom, after the dinner that brought them together every week, Anselme spoke:

"I once knew an old professor of philosophy," he said, "a very straight-thinking man, above all very logical, who seemed to take pleasure in contradicting his thoughts by means of his actions. He had no peer in debates; he knew how to depart from reliable principles and to deduce irrefutable consequences therefrom; and people derived great profit from his speech, if they consented not to examine his actions. He preached an austere morality and his existence was the most profligate in the world; he was able to expose all the dangers of drunkenness, but he was never as persuasive as when wine had gone to his head; similarly, he spoke perfectly about the deadly influence of women, but he found his most convincing theorems and his most seductive axioms in places of debauchery, when he had clearly demonstrated the fragility of his senses.

"He explained his contradictions by denying human liberty and, nourished on the marrow of Spinoza and fortified by the spirit of Schopenhauer, he had no shortage of good reasons to explain his weaknesses and those of humanity. He had undertaken a great work against free will, in which he showed that a man is the plaything of the most infimal causes and accidents, independent of his vain will. In that work he studied the most characteristic and the most notorious individuals, those he called the voluntarists, and he took them above all at their debut, wanting to prove that their vocation had always been determined by the god Hazard, all-powerful in directing souls while leaving them the illusion of guiding themselves.

"He had allowed me to leaf through his unfinished manuscript. It was enriched by numerous and curious anecdotes, all very ancient, since the most recent was that of Saint Paul on the road to Damascus, and I obtained an extreme childish pleasure in that reading.

"The professor of philosophy died a long time ago, of indigestion, some said, of a congestion caused by drunkenness or the abuse of women, affirmed others. He left me his work, not to publish, but in order to extract the most touching stories and entertain my friends with them. I shall follow his desire and tell you the first this evening. In reporting it I shall scrupulously conserve the style and manner of my dead friend."

✳

Before the ascetic Candilya astonished India, and later the world, with his unusual austerities—it is said that he remained without any nourishment for six months, standing on the heel of his right foot with his left foot lodged in his loins—he was one of the most joyful princes that the divine Ganges had ever seen. He took pleasure in the society of courtesans, did not detest fermented beverages, gorged himself on meats, perhaps forbidden, and indulged in gambling, in spite of the remonstrances of the Brahmins who had watched over his childhood. In spite of the license of his mores, Candilya had a cultivated mind, he loved learning, and he held science in great esteem, considering her as the only goddess capable of giving happiness, by making the truth known.

After a few years of an idle life, wearied by futile pleasures and eager to develop his intellect, he decided to travel, in order to listen to the lessons of the best philosophers, the most savant mathematicians and the most illustrious moralists. He remained absent for more than ten years, he visited all the countries in the world, and legend says that he went as far as the blessed isles that are in the north, the isles veiled with mist and circles by ice, in which people know happiness.

It is scarcely possible today for us to admit such an assertion, the most recent works having demonstrated irrefutably that those islands only ever existed in a few eccentric minds, but we can suppose that Candilya perceived one day in the mists, the shores of the isles of the Cassiterides,[1] now Great Britain, and that he

---

1 The Cassiterides ["Tin islands" in Greek], were mentioned by Herodotus

160

listened to the lying tales of some Phoenician. We do not have the same reasons for denying the arrival of Candilya at the Pillars of Hercules, which are doubtless our modern Gibraltar.

At any rate, Candilya profited intelligently from his voyages. He visited the most celebrated schools, followed the most renowned lessons, and did not even disdain to listen to the opinions of a few strange black men dominant in distant tribes, in which it is permissible for us to recognize fetishist sorcerers, and perhaps Dahomeyans.

When Candilya returned to India, an immense reputation had preceded him. It was said that he was learned in all things, that he had penetrated the most mysterious arcana and that he could pronounce the name of the supreme essence in twenty languages, which demonstrated to the most incredulous that he knew it perfectly. So, in the towns through which he passed, everyone gathered around him in order to hear him speak.

With great benevolence, he narrated his adventures, described the countries that he had visited and delighted in details and anecdotes about the mores of the inhabitants. Doubtless he lied a little, for he affirmed that he had climbed a pretended mountain of solid gold guarded by a centenarian old man, which we have been obliged to relegate to the domain of fable, in view of the impossibility of localizing it geographically. However, as no one could check his boasts, so natural for a traveler, Candilya was accompanied everywhere by an attentive cortege, and poets sang his praises, carried away by their enthusiasm, and also the hope of being attached to Candilya's house—for that was the time when princes nourished poets, albeit frugally, and were paid in smoke and sound.

He was received in his native city as a hero, which caused the warriors—a race even more jealous than bards—to murmur. Those paltry sentiments did not stop anyone, and all the young men desirous of contemplating Prince Candilya and listening to his discourse invited him to a respectful feast. Candilya accepted, and the following day, on the bank of the river, he presided over the feast offered to him by his admirers and friends.

---

and various other classical writers, most of whom were uncertain as to whether or not they were imaginary.

When the most tenacious appetites were appeased, Candilya was asked to speak. He did so with a good grace, although it put him in the obligation of telling again stories that he had already told a hundred times over. The guests paid the greatest attention to his marvelous stories; as they had credulous minds they did not doubt for a moment the mountains of gold, the sea of milk, the ape-men, the giants and the pygmies. They similarly admired the emerald ocean where the marine herds grazed, and they were not wrong, for the most positive of our navigators have seen the Sargasso Sea.

Nevertheless, those fables, which had enchanted the people, did not satisfy the most subtle of those who were fêting Candilya. They asked him at what philosophy he had arrived after that long absence and those long days of study. Candilya reflected momentarily, and then, summarizing his beliefs and his metaphysics, he declared that what he had retained most clearly from the lessons heard was that desire is at the origin of things, that Kama is both the first and most powerful of the gods, and that it is him alone that gives and sustains life.

People approved of Candilya and praised him for having arrived at such a beautiful conception; only one young man, the youngest of those who were there, shook his head disdainfully. Candilya perceived that, and interrogated him softly: "Why do you seem to be scornful of me?"

"Listen to this story," replied the young man. "It will be my response. The merchant Matanga had a daughter, Saranya, as beautiful as the dawn. He had promised her in marriage to Sambadar, who loved her, and whom she loved, and they both rejoiced at the thought of soon living together. But the devas take pleasure in testing humans. Sambadar departed for a long voyage, and his lover, desperate, paraded her chagrin through the gardens and the woods.

"One morning, when she was picking flowers and thinking about her beloved, she was bitten by a snake, and died pronouncing Sambadar's name. Matanga had her beautiful body burned, conserved the precious ashes in a jade vase, and presented them to Sambadar when he returned to look for his fiancée. Sambadar did not weep; he pressed the urn to his breast, and then he composed in honor of Kama a song of supplication and praise, and, when he finished, Saranya was resuscitated.

"That tale was told to me by an old woman who hunts the outskirts of the city," the young man concluded. "It made me understand that love is the highest of the gods, that it was the creator, and I had no need, in order to know that truth, to quit the banks of the Ganges . . ."

Then, Canilya was humiliated. He confessed the vanity of science and the futility of quitting the land where one has been born and nourished, in order to find the truth. He spent the night in prayer and, after being purified, the next day, he took off his garments and withdrew to the nearby forest in order to meditate on the truth.

✳

"'Thus,' my philosopher concluded, 'Candilya owed his sanctity to the words of an old woman, repeated by a child.'

"He also owed it to the circumstance that he was, in sum, a poor intelligence, for imbecility is the indispensable condition of sanctity.

"If Candilya had had a more open mind he would have been able to reply to his young interlocutor that he had not heard mention of the egotistical and particular love celebrated by the old woman of the outlying district, but of the vast, profound, subtle an intelligent love that permits the knowledge, comprehension and service of humankind. But voyages could not teach Candilya anything, because Candilya was a simpleton, and he was born to believe that wisdom resides in the squealing of simple minds interpreted by sophists and mild skeptics, the philosophers of uncertainty—which is to say, the most vain and stupid of human beings.

"That is why the sole effort of which that prince found himself capable, after years of reflection, was that of sticking his left foot in his crotch."

The Flowers

And I gazed into the depths of the placid lake.
Shelley.

For weeks, months and years, the enemy army had invested the
city that the valor of intrepid captains defended. Then, one morning, the besieged troops were defeated, decimated by multiplied
assaults and fruitless sorties and weakened by privations. In spite
of the fabulous heroisms, devotions and superhuman sacrifices,
the walls had fallen under the shock of irresistible battering-
rams, and, the breach having been made, the hostile cohorts had
invaded the ramparts. The wielders of slings and the archers,
henceforth masters of the towers, had rained their stones and
arrows upon the crowds, and the following day, the hoplites and
pikemen had spread out through the streets of the city, shaken by
the horses of heavy cataphractarii.

Rendered impatient by their long wait, the invaders rushed
forward with furious cries in the exasperated desire for gold,
murder and palpitating women. To preserve their familiar gods,
which the priests removed far from the carnage, the virgins had
descended on to the thresholds, and, pale in long white bridal
garments, they had offered the agonizing lilies of their flesh to
the lust of soldiers maddened by long continence. Soon, in the
blood of defunct maidenheads, the young women were gasping,
mingling their terrors with dominating spasms; soon they died
on the thresholds, chosen altars, and even death did not liberate
them from inexorable embraces.

Night put a stop to the evil work; the sky was covered by a
silent pack of black clouds, and the peace of darkness prostrated
the sated males on the ground.

The bloody dawn of battles extended its simarre over the
bleak palaces and over the city reminiscent of a garden mourning the death of candid rose-bushes. The scattering of flowered
bodies made the pavements of crossroads and squares pale, and
the priests who followed the conquerors cried in horror at the
sacrilege. Their purifying processions moved through the streets

and the porticos, and the harsh militiamen mingled their repentant voices with the chants of the hierodules who were warding off avenging calamities by means of their incantations.

Pyres of sandalwood impregnated with propitious balms burned all day, penetrating the air with lustral emanations, preparing for the expiatory rites, and the vigil for the dead was made by the most valiant leaders, who, wreathed by their weapons, remained prostrated all night, while the cavaliers of the sacred lesions sounded in bronze buccinas the glory of the immolated and the remorse of the murderers.

The next day, the virgins were placed on stretchers florid with scabious; they had been decorated with necklaces of amethysts, and each of them bore on the forehead an opal whose cold ocellus was open. They were carried between the cinerary braziers outside the ramparts, and the cortege headed toward a consecrated lake that the priests had chosen. There the cadavers were laden with heavy gold chains, and then the benevolent hands of eunuchs buried them in the waters, which opened up with mysterious welcoming sounds.

In the evening, the devastators burned the city, and, by the light of the colossal torch that launched hectic flames toward the stars, they drew away, carrying with them the sumptuous booty that was heaped upon the carts.

When only the last standards were perceptible in the distance, fluttering on the horizon like birds with sparkling plumage, the vanquished came down from the hills where, hidden among the oaks, they had witnessed the rapes and the supreme conflagration. On the blackened columns and the broken battens of bronze doors, they sat down in groaning despair, and the tacit dolor of abolished marble harmonized with their anguish.

They wept over the insulted gods, the powerful reduced to flight, like helpless children carried away by their nurses; they wept over the looted hearths, deprived of their cherished jewels and atavistic riches, of which destiny had frustrated the heirs; but when they thought about the beautiful virgins who had made the offering of their first fruits, dying without knowing chosen amour, the clamor of their sobs spread the mourning of their souls over the plain, all the way to the nearby woods.

The memory of evenings when tender conversations and furtive confessions had been scattered along the paths penetrated the ephebes with an irreparable sadness, and their hearts, empty henceforth, clamored with futile appeals.

O amicable woods populated by attentive couples, only the violet mists of twilight will come now to recall the former presences; only the faithful echoes will repeat the syllables once heard; but the mirrors of springs will no longer reflect beloved faces, and the deflowered garlands hung from rustic cippi devoted to the goddess will perpetuate the regrets by their testimony.

Now, a venerated ascetic who had accompanied the funerals came to the young men and offered to take them to those buried in the tomb of the waters by the repentant violators. They followed him along the roads scarred by the wheels of the war-carts.

Here and there, in the hollows of ruts, lay precious objects dropped by the predators, whom the heaped-up spoils had doubtless rendered inattentive; there were gem-studded monstrances, caskets with emerald stria, amulets ornamented with inestimable jewels. But the feet of the widowed lovers collided indifferently with the caskets, the monstrances and the amulets, and none of them could be gladdened by the abandonment of things, for the flood of salty tears drowned their eyes, and the claw of coughing fits clutched their breasts.

On a mound overlooking the lake the guide stopped, while the desolate descended toward the shores denuded of reeds. They lay down on the ground and, their foreheads leaning over, they brushed the cold metal of the waters. Some, immobile, their eyelids closed, appeared to be listening to illusory voices; others dilated their haggard eyes, trying to pierce the glaucous densities that detained the polluted and ravaged bodies; some implored the dead, speaking to them as before, pausing to hear the responses that resonated within them and then resuming the imaginary dialogue; and some, less modest, heaped the heavens with insults and threats, exhausting their chagrin in convulsive movements.

Standing on the hill, the noble ascetic clad in his woolen robe extended his hands over the funerary waters, spreading benedictions, invoking the gods that the devotees had preserved from insults.

"Very great," he said, "let your power be manifest in honor of the pure maidservants devoted to your temples. When frightened, in the arms of our priests, you requested protective shelter, they went toward the assailing hordes, and their frail breasts were preservative for you, more than the outdated ramparts. Fearless, you knew the fear of insults that were spared you by the meek loins offered; manifest your glory and your clemency; resurrect the chaste who died to save you."

With the ascetic's prayers, the ephebes mingled the chorus of their supplications. Suddenly, on the surface of the lake, like a thousand jetting springs, drops of blood surged forth. They spread out, crimson leaves issued from invisible plants, and those leaves were streaked with veins; they grew, and from them, flowers were born, illuminating the air with their strange splendors: calices whose nacre evoked the absent flesh, hyaline corollas whose perfume was reminiscent of the vanished balms.

They were alive, the supernatural flowers; their pistils capped with gold rose up and their stems, proud or softly flexible, agitated like lovers' arms. They reminded the supplicants of the attitudes and gestures of yore, for their new plasticity had kept the reflection of departed forms. In the carmine of petals, the young men rediscovered the smiles of old, and even the droplets that trembled on the flesh of calices and on the green tunics seemed to them to be the tears that the lovers had wept before the profaning warriors.

Then, still kneeling, they called to them, uttering insistently the cherished names of the resuscitated, and the flowers moved in response to the words heard. Slowly, modestly, lowering their stems like the necks of swans, they advanced, undulating and supple, toward the ecstatic adorers.

Many, driven by their impatient tenderness, went into the water, and those the flowers seized, dragging them swooning and enraptured into the depths of the nuptial lake; others extended their hands, which the flowers came to join, they implored them, and on their bosoms they grew, multiplying, intoxicating them with ineffable odors, filling their heads with vibrations of amour; but in the fingers of some, the flowers withered, morose and desiccated, and all of those fled into the countryside, keeping the treasure acquired or lamenting the hope deceived.

Alone, beside the newly impassive waters, the solitary individual remained, nobly clad in his woolen robe, distributing his benedictions, thanking the gods whom the pure and the chaste devotees, who had died to save them, had preserved from insult.

JEAN LORRAIN
(1855-1906)

"Jean Lorrain" was the pseudonym of Paul Duval, adopted at the insistence of his father, a Norman ship-owner, who wanted to protect the family name from the disgrace of employment by a poet. A flamboyant homosexual dandy, when forced to make a living from his pen after his father died ruined, he became one of the most prolific and highest-paid journalists of the *fin-de-siècle*, and the personification, in his lifestyle as well as his writing, of the Decadent Movement. *Monsieur de Phocas. Astarté* (1901; tr. as *Monsieur de Phocas*), compounded out of numerous short stories, is a kind of retrospective summary of the Decadent world-view, written after he was forced to leave Paris because of health problems occasioned by his use of ether as a stimulant, which did not take long to kill him thereafter. English translations of some of his short stories are contained in *Nightmares of an Ether-Drinker* (Tartarus Press, 2002; reprinted by Snuggly Books, 2016), *The Soul-Drinker and Other Decadent Fantasies* (Snuggly Books, 2016) and *Masks in the Tapestry* (Snuggly Books, 2017).

"Conte du Bohémien" first appeared in *Gil Blas* 26 janvier 1896, and was reprinted in *Princesses d'Ivoire at d'Ivresse* (Ollendorf, 1902); "A Bohemian Tale" originally appeared in *The Soul-Drinker and Other Decadent Fantasies*.

"Le Crapaud" appeared in *Sensations et souvenirs* (Fasquelle, 1895). "The Toad" was originally published in *Nightmares of an Ether-Drinker*.

A Bohemian Tale

As April approached, the rumor spread throughout the land that a strange singer, an invisible and mysterious musician, had established himself in the forest of Ardennes. He lived there in the densest thickets with the birds and beasts of the woods, and since his arrival, among the ravines, the clearings and the green shade of the paths, there had been an effervescence of lilies of the valley and primroses, a frenzy of unslaked lust and such a joy in living that from dawn to dusk, there was an audible delirium in the nests in the branches, and the red deer were belling every night by the light of the moon.

As a rising tide of sap and desire unfurled henceforth in the leafy forest, exasperated gasps agonized in the air that covered the region. In the heavy and storm-laden atmosphere, the guitar and voice of the strange musician could be heard. His song rose up in the coolness of mauve and roseate dawns, and in the blazing sadness of evenings, infinitely sweet and pure, and also infinitely sad, while trills and pizzicati sparkled, fused and spilled, scintillating and pearly, under the guitarist's fingers.

The accompaniment was all mocking, scornful and satirical gaiety, while the ardent tenderness of the voice was imploring and tearful, and the mockery of the loquacious guitar over that passionate and poignant appeal was one melancholy more.

In the suddenly-invaded forest, clumps of asphodels and digitalis surged forth, beside pathways that became impenetrable for weeks beneath an unprecedented growth of vines and creepers; there was an overflowing of life, hectic grass and blooming flowers in the midst of an enamored concern of reckless nightingales. The thirty leagues of forest sang, laughed and loved, suddenly enchanted; the voice of the musician was always lamenting there.

A fever took hold of the entire land. By night, especially, the voice of the invisible singer took on unexpected, delightful, intoxicating sonorities. One could no longer take a step in the countryside without falling upon tax-gatherers and good-for-nothings lying in furrows or roadside ditches; they came in bands to surround the forest and lay in wait until dawn, attentive and charmed. Young women ran away from villages and cowherds from farms to come and listen at closer range; young soldiers deserted; the tocsin sounded until daybreak in the convents to recall souls in peril to God, and aged monks blanched by fasting and prayer suddenly stopped by night in the depths of cloisters in order to dissolve in tears, thinking about the past.

A great trouble agitated all hearts. A surge of stupor and adultery was unleashed in all the towns. Women abandoned their homes to go with travelers; one no longer found anything along the hedgerows but entwined couples; agricultural laborers prey to vague sadness left the fields fallow; artisans from the towns spent days wandering through the countryside; and the roads were no longer safe because there were so many vagabonds scattered around the province.

That damnable musician had bewitched the whole region, sowing laxity and sloth among the rabble, distress and mourning among the nobility and the bourgeois—so much and so thoroughly that the Duc de Lorraine, in his good city of Metz, was upset, and made the decision to rid his people of the accused singing sorcerer. No one had ever seen him. He was, it was said, a very young bohemian estranged from his tribe, and who, during the last passage of the Lords of Egypt through the marches of Lorraine, had settled in the Ardennes, and was singing there despairingly day and night. Perhaps his nostalgic appeal would be heard one day by one of his own people. As feral as a wild beast, however, and surely a past master in the art of spell-casting, he had thus far hidden from all gazes. Besides which, a superstitious dread protected his retreat and, since he had been singing in the florid forest, no one any longer dared to go into it.

That went on for months.

One beautiful night in May, the Duc de Lorraine set forth on a campaign with a large party of cavaliers. He brought with him the Bishop of Nancy and twelve members of the chapter, in case there were charms to break and exorcisms to perform. They marched for two days, and reached the edge of the forest on the second day.

Since dawn they had encountered no one on the road but pilgrims in procession and foolish young women wandering along the hedgerows with amorous gazes. Then, in the dusk, a soft and pure voice sang, and the Duc and his companions bowed their heads and lowered their lances involuntarily over the necks of their horses, which had stopped suddenly. One might have thought that the marrow was melting in their bones, and a delightful chill gripped their hearts.

But the Bishop of Nancy recited the prayer of Saint Bonaventure and, having made the sign of the cross, the Duc and his men-at-arms entered the forest. They wandered all night beneath a rising moon, distracted and charmed by the voice that sometimes sang to the left, and then resumed to the right, and seemed to wander hither and yon; the blossoms of the wild apple trees embalmed the air, nocturnal vapors floated before their eyes like robes; sometimes bare feet appeared on the moss; sometimes silky contacts touched them; but they were illusions that the prelate of Nancy soon scotched.

The sad and pure voice of the unknown singer was still mourning and imploring, but now more distinctly and closer at hand; and through the thickets, bathed in quicksilver, through the suddenly enlarged forest they marched, bizarrely disturbed, beneath an odorous shroud of petals, with the precautions and gestures of mounted falconers.

Suddenly, the voice broke into a kind of laughter, as limpid as water, and the stupefied cortege came to a halt.

The bohemian was there!

Standing on the edge of a spring, he was leaning over foolishly under a cold ray of moonlight, and, his guitar in his hand, was looking at his reflection in the water, intoxicated by his own image, as if drawn forward and bent over the water by the weight of his hair, a chimerically long flow of yellow silk, and the joyous arpeggios sparkling beneath his fingers.

The Duc's cavaliers fell upon him as if on a prey, tied him up before he had uttered a cry, and threw him, bound hand and foot, over the rump of a horse. The Bishop of Nancy had picked up the guitar.

At daybreak, the Duc and his retinue emerged from the forest and returned to Metz by way of side-roads. During the three days of the journey, the captured bohemian did not say a word. From time to time, a gourd was raised to his lips and he was made to drink, and as his prestigious beauty might have intrigued passers-by, he was covered by a mantle. At the third dawn, the little troop reached Metz and the ducal palace.

The strange musician lived there for two months, immured in a grim silence, almost free under the surveillance of three guards, his gaze bleak and absent, deflecting all conjectures and troubling men and women alike with his quasi-divine beauty.

He was a slim youth, seventeen years old at the most, with slender arms and muscular legs, imposing with his supple stride and agile movements the idea of a proud and dangerous animal; long blond hair hung down to his waist, and a kind of rictus drew back his lips at times in a slightly bestial fashion; but the abyss of his eyes was astonishing.

The Duc, simultaneously alarmed and charmed, had conceived an amity for him; he was one more work of art in the ducal castle. The bohemian wandered from room to room all day long, his arms folded without unclenching his teeth; sometimes he stopped before an open window and gazed at the clouds for a long time, and then resumed his restless march, observed from a distance by the eyes of the courtiers.

He had been dressed in the richest garments, and his guitar had been returned to him, but he scarcely seemed to recognize it, and the mute instrument was trailed through all the rooms, within the reach of his hand, without him deigning to honor it with a glance; so the Duc wasted his effort and the courtiers their trouble. The intoxicating song that he had once sung recklessly for the vagabonds of the roads and the poor, the accursed bohemian refused his master and the grandees of the court. The sad and pure voice had fallen silent forever, and the Duc's daughter, who was consumed by the desire to hear it, became melancholy, and fell into a languor.

In a towering rage, the Duc had the diabolical musician thrown into a dungeon along with his guitar, and then left Metz for his château in the woods, for the summer was advancing and it was very hot.

Some time after that, on a stormy night in August, one of the jailers in the city prison heard an infinitely soft and sad voice rising up from the dungeon. A tumultuous music accompanied it, quivering, strident and also joyful; it was like a melodious tide rising in the tower and beating the walls: a poignant music, in truth, made of bursts of laughter and tears, and the jailer, who had never heard it, recognized the voice of the bohemian.

He went down the stairs at a gallop and, shoving aside the sentinels, who had all come running to hear the voice and were sobbing with anguish, sitting on the steps, he ran toward the barred judas-hole of the damnable musician's cell.

The prisoner, standing up in his cell, was singing recklessly, his hands clutching his guitar. An enormous, strange golden yellow moon was shining through the barred window of the cell, cutting out a kind of mirror of water in a large bowl placed on the ground, and, leaning over the reflection of the star, the bohemian was mirroring himself therein, and singing wholeheartedly, enveloped from head to toe in the yellow sheet of his hair.

He sang all night before the eyes of his guardians, who were heaped up, shivering, at the judas-hole in the door; and in the square at the foot of the prison walls, a mob of poor people waved their fists at the sentinels, tore out their hair and fainted amorously.

The bohemian sang all day, and toward evening a great rumor went up in the surrounding region, and the governor of the citadel, having climbed up to the watchtower, saw that the fields were black with crowds, processing slowly toward the city; one might have thought them an army on the march.

They were coming from all points of the horizon. They were the vagabonds of the roads and barefoot peasants, the entire legion of the poor, running to the appeal of their singer. They had finally found him, and had been traveling since dawn, drunk with anger and joy, and the dusk was full of terrible threats; pikes and scythes were brandished under the pink sky. A breath of panic swept over the countryside, and the city-dwellers, gathered on the ramparts, listened fearfully as the clamor grew and came closer.

The bohemian was still singing.

The Duc, hastily warned, reached the rebel camp at the gates of the city in two days; the garrison made a sortie and the ill-clad and poorly armed vagabonds were easily crushed.

It was an atrocious, pitiless slaughter; more than thirty thousand dead remained on the terrain, women and children among them, for the unfortunates had come in couples and in families, as if on a pilgrimage, and the countryside around Metz was red with blood.

The Duc slept in his city that same night, where the mob was still grumbling, but when someone went to fetch the bohemian in order to torture him and hang him, his cell was empty. He had disappeared.

A few days later, however, as the superior of the Brothers of Mercy was wandering over the battlefield with some of his followers in order to gather together and bury the dead, a captious music suddenly burst forth above the charnel-house, and, having raised his head, the monk perceived a young and slender boy who was singing and laughing, his guitar in his hands, standing on a mound encumbered with cadavers.

A blazing golden sky was bloody at the horizon. Draped to the waist in flaming hair, the musician mingled vibrant bursts of laughter with his song, and, leaning over a pool of blood, looked at his reflection.

And the gravedigger monk recognized the bohemian, the bohemian Amour who sings in the woods for the disinherited and the vagabonds, falls silent in palaces, mirrors himself in Death, and loves no one but himself: Amour, as free and wild as solitude.

The Toad

It must have been one of the most frightful sensations of my childhood and it remains the most tenacious of all my early memories. Twenty-five years have gone by since that little misadventure of the school holidays, and I still cannot think of it without feeling my head reel and the bile of horror and disgust rising into my mouth.

I had attained my tenth year, and with it the two-month-long vacation of a schoolboy recently elevated from a humble village school to one of the best in Paris. I spent it at the house of one of my uncles, whose surrounding acreage was a parkland of deep shadows and sleepy ponds, at the foot of a hill whose sides were covered by a beech wood. It was a charming landscape with an even more charming name: Valmont. I was to rediscover those two Romanesque syllables in an evil book, the cruelest and most dangerous of the eighteenth century.[1] Valmont: whose tender and melancholy image, compounded out of tall trees, spring water, long and silent walks along covered lanes, is still mingled in my memory with the chromo-lithographs of Tony Johannot, Scottish lakes surrounded by forests, castle-dominated valleys beyond the Rhine and musical fragments drawn from my mother's piano twenty years before!

My uncle Jacques owned a considerable property in that part of the country. It had once been the estate of an abbot, in whose convent—now converted into a country house—he lived. The former cells had become so many neat and narrow rooms, the refectory a dining-room, and the parlor a drawing-room. There were more than a dozen family members resident there that summer, including various male and female cousins and their parents, and parties went out every day for the amusement of the children.

---

1 Valmont is a village near Fécamp, the town where Lorrain was born. The "evil book" in which the narrator rediscovered the name is *Les Liaisons dangereuses* (1782; tr. as *Dangerous Liaisons*) by Pierre Choderlos de Laclos, whose viciously cynical male lead is named Valmont.

These expeditions pleased my little cousins—there was much excited hand-clapping and joyful capering—but I always took care to avoid them. I was already enamored, even as a child, of solitude and daydreaming, and I had an instinctive distaste for the noisy games the boys played and the newly-coquettish teasing of the girls. To noisy parties on the beach, picnics on the grass or in the woods, fishing for crayfish and all similarly delightful amusements, I much preferred wandering randomly in the great park, with no company but my own.

The lawns and meadows seemed mysterious to me, bathed by a dreamlike clarity between the tall crowns of poplars, beeches and birches. Some of the gilded aspens beside the ponds were trained into spindle-shapes and I loved their eternally unquiet foliage, although I could not watch it without a certain fluttering of the heart. I was equally attracted and fascinated by a summer-house with tinted windows, half-hidden among the osiers of a little artificial island surrounded by tranquil water. There I dreamed the long hours away, stretched out on my back in a little boat secured to the bank, with my arms folded behind my head and my eyes following the clouds as they fled across the clear blue sky.

Oh, the somnolent torpor of warm July days that I spent in that corner of the shadowed park, when all the gentlefolk of the estate retired to their cool rooms, listening to the quiet hum of insects, interrupted from time to time by the monotonous noise of a rake scraping on the sand of the pathways! Then, when the first rusty tints of September showed through, the leaves would fall from the plane-trees to form translucent amber-yellow plaques on clotted ponds the color of tin!

How far away it all seems now. And yet, it is present within me even to this day—and how I wish that all those yesterdays were tomorrows!

When I sneaked off on expeditions of my own during the somnolent siesta hours of summer and the afternoons of autumn, I embarked on veritable voyages of discovery across the unexplored hinterlands of the estate, whose mysteriously alternating light and shade so intrigued me. There were long pauses by ant-hills, enraptured contemplations of frogs sitting stock-still on lily-pads, prudent inspections of beehives: all the pleasures, in sum, that children take in the study of creatures who do not know that they are under observation. Finally—perhaps strangely, given my age—there was a particular sensuality to be obtained from the rapt contemplation of water.

Water has always attracted, seduced, captured and enchanted me. It bewitches me still, and God knows that I was served according to my desires on that estate, where a succession of islets, rustic bridges and ponds were laid out in a chocolate-box landscape. It was the first English park to be created in the entire country when the romances of Rousseau became fashionable. All these marvelous water-features were fed by a lazy river, which was swelled in its turn by four or five little springs, which the original owner's vanity had provided with as many chapels. They were spread out along the length of the park, like so many paved and cemented bathing-pools set beneath slate roofs, each with four or five steps descending into the transparency of the cold green-tinted water produced by the wellspring.

These, I admit, were the principal objects of my elective pilgrimages. One of them, sometimes called "the ferruginous," pleased me most of all. Situated on the edge of the park, at the foot of a stand of pines whose blue shadow drenched it with a lunar twilight, it was quite still and deliciously cold, like a block of ice embedded in a quadrilateral of walls. The limpid spring welled up in such a leisurely manner that it scarcely seemed to be moving, although a few bubbles of quicksilver continually burst upon its surface. Surrounded as it was by wallflowers, ground-ivy and slender ferns, the spring no longer seemed to be water at all, but a mass of molten rock-crystal set at the bottom of a reservoir.

One of my pleasures—I already preferred those that carried a slight edge of guilt, refined by the attraction of forbidden things—was to slip swiftly away after the mid-day meal and run straight across the park in order to arrive hot and sweating, completely out of breath, at that favorite spring. Once there, I would drink madly and deeply of the blue and glacial water: the water that was never allowed to us at table, although our eyes drank in the mystery of the carafes misted by condensation.

I rolled my sleeves up to my shoulders in order to plunge my two shivering hands into the water, scooping it up by the handful, filling my mouth and gullet with sensual gurgling, I poked my tongue into it as if into an ice-cream, and I felt a sharp coldness descend into my being, penetrative and yet as gentle as a flavor. It was a kind of frenzy, utterly sensuous, tripled by the consciousness of my disobedience and by the scorn I had for others who did not dare to do likewise.

And afterwards, it felt so good to be in that retreat, in the calm and seemingly eternal shadow of the great conifers, resting my eyes on the velvet of mosses!

Oh, the ferruginous well of the old park at Valmont! I believe that I loved it just as passionately, and possessed it just as sensuously, as the most adored mistress—at least until the day came when, by virtue of a cruel revenge of circumstance, I discovered the most degrading of punishments there.

One day, when I came, as was my habit, to drink slowly and deeply of the intoxicatingly cold water, supporting myself on the palms of my hands—that day, indulging my gourmet sensibility, I was lying on my stomach in order to lap at the spring like a puppy—I noticed on the tiles of the surround, crouched in a corner, a motionless black form that was watching me.

There were two round eyes with membranous lids horribly fixed upon mine, and the figure was flabby, as if collapsed into itself. The mere idea of touching something as nearly-black and limp emasculated me. Its immobility, too—the immobility of a monster or a ghost—filled me with anger and terror as I gazed across the transparency of the well into the toothy shadows of the ferns.

Then the gelatinous brown mass stretched its limbs slowly, and two palmate and miserably thin feet took a tentative step towards me,

The toad moved—for that was what it was: a filthy toad, pustulous and grizzled. It had come out of its corner now, and the light filtered by the conifers fell on its back, displaying its entire form. It dragged its milky white belly between its feet, enormous and inflated, like a boil about to burst. It moved painfully, each crude forward movement full of effort. The heaviness of its low-slung hindquarters was loathsome.

It was, moreover, a monstrously large toad, whose like I have never seen since: a magician toad, at least a hundred years old, half-gnome, half-beast of the Sabbat; one of those gold-crowned toads that one hears of in folktales, set to watch over hidden treasures in ruined cities with a deadly nightshade flower beneath its left foot, nourishing itself on human blood.

The toad moved, and I had drunk the water where that monster lived and swam!

And I felt in my mouth, in my gullet, in my entire being, a taste like dead flesh, an odor of corruption.

And to heap horror upon horror, I saw that the pupils of the toad's eyes, which had seemed at first to fix themselves upon me, had burst, tinting its eyelids with blood.

I understood then that it had taken refuge in the spring, tortured and breathless, in order that it might die there.

Oh, that blind toad! The agony of that mutilated beast, in that clear water with the taste of blood!

PIERRE LOUŸS
(1870-1925)

Pierre Louÿs adopted the variant spelling of his surname—originally Louis—in 1890, when he launched himself into the Symbolist Movement as its principal exponent of erotic themes, commencing with the poems making up "Astarte," which he published himself in 1891 in the short-lived periodical *La Conque*, and continuing with *Les Chansons de Bilitis* (1894; tr. as *Songs of Bilitis*), celebrating a fictitious contemporary of Sappho. His first novel, the best-selling *Aphrodite: moeurs antiques* (1896; tr. as *Aphrodite*), set in ancient Alexandria, is one of the masterpieces of the Movement; it was followed by the Rabelaisian *Les Aventures du roi Pausole* (1901; tr. as *The Adventures of King Pausole*).

"Leda, ou la louange des bienheureuses ténèbres" first appeared as a booklet from Libraire de l'Art Indépendant in 1893, and was subsequently reprinted in *Le Crépuscule des nymphes* (1925; tr. as *The Twilight of the Nymphs*). "Leda; or, The Praise of Blissful Darkness" is original to the present volume.

Leda; or, The Praise of Blissful Darkness

It was almost too dark to see.

An invisible Artemis was hunting under the inclined crescent, behind the black branches that pullulated with stars. The four young Corinthian women were lying in the grass near the three young men, and they did not know whether the last would dare to speak after the others, so silent was the hour.

Tales ought only to be told in broad daylight. As soon as the shadow has entered somewhere, one does not listen any longer to fabulous voices, because the fugitive spirit settles, and speaks to itself delightedly.

Each of the reclining women already had a secret companion, the charm of which she created in the real image of her childlike desire. However, they all opened their eyes in the darkness when the grave Melandryon spoke these first words:

"I will tell you the story of the Swan and the little nymph who lived on the bank of the river Eurotas. It is in praise of blissful darkness."

He raised himself up, but only partly, and supported himself with one hand in the grass, and this is what he said:

I

In those days, there were no tombs along the roads, nor any temples on the hills.

Humans scarcely existed; there was no mention of them. The earth was delivered to the joy of the gods, and favored the birth of monstrous divinities. It was the time when the Echidna gave birth to the Chimera, and Pasiphae the Minotaur. Little children went pale with fear in the woods under the flight of dragons.

Now, on the humid banks of the river Eurotas, where the woods are so dense that one never sees the light therein, there lived an extraordinary young woman who was as blue-tinted as the night, as mysterious as a thin crescent moon, and as gentle as the Milky Way. That was why she was named Leda.

She really was almost blue, for the blood of irises ran in her veins, and not the blood of roses, as in yours. Her fingernails were bluer than her hands, her nipples bluer than her breasts, her elbows and her knees entirely azure. Her lips shone with the color of her eyes, which were as blue as deep water. As for her loose hair, it was as dark and blue as the nocturnal sky and extended so vividly along her arms that she seemed winged.

She only loved water and the night.

Her pleasure was to walk over the spongy meadows of the river banks, where one felt the water without seeing it, and her bare feet had frissons of pleasure in being obscurely moistened. For she did not bathe in the river, for fear of jealous naiads; besides which, she did not want to deliver herself to the water entirely. But she liked being damp!

She mingled the extreme curls of her tresses with the rapid current, and stuck them to her pale skin with slowly curved designs. Or else she took a little of the river's freshness in the hollow of her hand and let it trickle between her young breasts all the way to the pleat of her round legs, where it was lost. Or she lay face down on the damp moss in order to drink slowly from the surface of the water, like a silent hind.

Such was her life—that and thinking about satyrs. One of them sometimes surprised her, but quickly fled in alarm, for they mistook her for Phoebe, severe to those who saw her naked. She would have liked to speak to them, if they had stopped nearby. The detail of their appearance filled her with astonishment.

One night, when she had taken a few steps into the forest, because rain had fallen and the ground was torrential, she had seen one of those demigods at close range, asleep; but she had been frightened in her turn and had suddenly turned back. Since then, she had passed them occasionally, and was troubled by things she did not understand.

She also began to look at herself. She found herself mysterious. That was the epoch when she became very sentimental and wept into her hair.

When the nights were bright, she looked at herself in the water. Once she thought that it would be better to gather all her hair together in order to expose the nape of her neck, which felt pretty in her caressant hand. She chose a supple rush to secure her blue chignon and made herself a falling crown with five large aquatic leaves and a languid nenuphar.

At first she took pleasure in going forth thus; but no one looked at her because she was alone. Then she became unhappy, and ceased to play with herself.

Her mind was unaware of it, but her body was already awaiting the beating wings of the Swan.

II

One evening, when she was scarcely awake and thought of resuming her dream because a long river of yellow daylight was still shining behind the night of the forest, her attention was attracted by the sound of reeds close by, and she saw the apparition of a Swan.

The beautiful bird was as white as a woman, as splendid and rosy as light, and as radiant as a cloud. It seemed like the very idea of the midday sky, its form and its winged essence. That is why she named it Dzeus.

Leda was able to consider it, as it flew slightly in walking. It circled the nymph at a distance, looking at her obliquely. When it was very close, it drew even closer and, hoisting itself up on its long red legs, it extended the undulating grace of its neck as high as it could before the young blue-tinted thighs, all the way to the soft pleat on her hip.

Leda's astonished hands took the little head carefully and enveloped it with caresses. The bird quivered in every feather. With its profound and soft wings it squeezed her naked legs and caused them to buckle. Leda let herself fall to the ground.

She put her hands over her eyes. She was neither afraid not ashamed, but she experienced an inexplicable joy, and her beating heart lifted up her breasts.

She could not guess what was about to happen. She did not know what might happen. She did not understand anything, not even why she was happy. She felt the suppleness of the Swan's neck along her arms.

Why had it come? What had she done in order for it to come? Why did it not flee like the other swans of the river or the satyrs of the forest? Since her earliest memories she had always lived alone. Thus, she did not have many words with which to think and that night's event was so disconcerting . . .

The Swan . . . the Swan . . .

She had not called to it; she had not even seen it; she had been asleep; but it had come.

She no longer dared look at it, and did not move for fear of making it fly away. She felt the coolness of its wing-beats on her burning cheeks.

Soon, it seemed to retreat, and it caresses deteriorated. Leda opened to it like a blue river flower. She sensed the warmth of the bird's body between her cold knees. Suddenly, she cried: "Ah . . . ! Ah . . . !" and her arms trembled like pale branches. The beak had penetrated her frightfully, and the head of the swan moved within her furiously, as if it were eating her entrails, deliciously.

Then there was a long sob of abundant felicity. She let her feverish head fall backwards, eyes closed, tore up grass which her fingers and clenched her small feet, which expanded in the silence, convulsively, on empty air.

From a long time she remained motionless. At the first gesture she made, her hand encountered above her the bloody beak of the Swan.

She sat up, and saw the great white bird before the bright frisson of the river.

She tried to get up; the bird prevented her from doing so.

She tried to take a little water in the palm of her hand and cool her joyful dolor; the bird stopped her with its wing.

Then she took it in her arms and covered the bushy plumage with kisses, which bristled under her mouth. Then she lay down on the bank and slept profoundly.

The next morning, as the day commenced, a new sensation awoke her abruptly, and it seemed to her that something was detached from her body. It was a great blue egg that had rolled before her, as bright as a sapphire stone.

She wanted to pick it up and play with it, or even to cook it in warm ash, as she had seen the satyrs do, but the Swan seized it in its beak and went to deposit it in a clump of slanting reeds. It extended its deployed wings over it and gazed fixedly at Leda, and, flying straight up into the sky, rose so high and so slowly that it disappeared into the growing dawn with the last white star.

III

Leda hoped that at the next star-rise, the Swan would come back to her, and she waited in the reeds of the bank, near the blue egg that had been born of their miraculous union.

The Eurotas was populated by swans, but that one was no longer there. She would have recognized it among a thousand, and even with her eyes closed, she would have sensed its approach. But it was no longer there; she was quite sure of that.

Then she took off her crown of water-leaves, dropped it into the current, undid her blue hair and wept.

When she wiped her eyes and looked, a satyr was there, whom she had not heard walking.

For she was no longer similar to Phoebe. She had lost her virginity. The satyrs would no longer be afraid of her.

With one bound she was on her feet, and recoiled fearfully.

The aegipan said to her, softly: "Who are you?"

"I'm Leda," she replied.

He was silent for a moment, and then said: "Why are you not like the other nymphs? Why are you blue, like the water and the night?"

"I don't know."

He looked at her, quite astonished.

"What are you doing here, all alone?"

"I'm waiting for the Swan." And she looked toward the river.

"What Swan?" he asked.

"*The* Swan. I hadn't summoned it, and I hadn't seen it, but it came. I'm so astonished. I'll tell you."

And she told him what had happened, and parted the reeds to show him the egg as blue as the morning.

The satyr understood. He started laughing, and gave her coarse explanations, which she interrupted continually by putting her hand over his mouth, and she cried: "I don't want to know. I don't want to. Oh! Oh, you've told me! Oh, is it possible? Now, I can no longer love him, and I shall be mortally unhappy."

He seized her by the arm, passionately.

"Don't touch me!" she said, weeping. "Oh, how happy I was this morning! I didn't understand how happy I was. Now, if he comes back, I won't love him any longer. Now you've told me! Oh, how wicked you are!"

He put his arms around her, and caressed her hair.

"Oh! No, no, no . . . ! No!" she cried, again. "Oh, not you! Oh, not that! Oh, the Swan! What if he came back . . . ? Alas, alas! Everything is finished, everything is finished."

She had her eyes open, without weeping, and her mouth open, and her hands were trembling with fear.

"I'd like to die, I don't even know whether I'm mortal. I'd like to die in the water, but I'm afraid of the naiads, that they might take me with them. Oh, what have I done?"

And she sobbed noisily over her arm.

But a grave voice spoke in front of her, and when she opened her eyes she saw the god of the river, crowned with green herbs, who had emerged partly from the water, leaning on a tiller of bright wood.

"You are the night," he said, "and you have loved the symbol of all that is light and glory, and you are united with him.

"From symbol is born symbol, and from symbol is born Beauty. It is in the blue egg that emerged from you. Since the beginning of the world it has been known that she would be called Helen; and the man who will be the last man will know that she existed.

"You have been full of love because you did not know anything. That is to the praise of blissful darkness.

"But you are also a woman, and in the evening of the same day, the man has also fecundated you.

"You bear within you the obscure being who will be nothing but himself, whom his father has not foreseen, and whom his son will not know. I will take the seed of him into my waters. He will remain in nothingness.

"You have been full of hatred because you have learned everything; but I will enable you to forget everything. That is to the praise of blissful darkness."

She did not understand fully what he had said, but she thanked him, weeping.

She went into the river bed in order to purify herself of the satyr, and when she came back to the bank, she had lost all memory of her dolor and her joy.

※

Melandryon was no longer speaking. The women remained silent. Eventually, however, Rhea said: "What about Castor and Polydeuces. You haven't mentioned them. They were Helen's brothers."

"No, that's a false legend. They aren't interesting. Only Helen was born of the Swan."

"How do you know?"

" . . ."

"And why do you say that the Swan wounded her with his beak? That isn't in the legend, and isn't plausible. And why do you say that Leda was as blue as water in the night? You must have a reason for saying that."

"Didn't you hear the words of the River? It's necessary never to explain symbols. It's necessary never to penetrate them. Have confidence. Oh, don't doubt. The person who has imagined the symbol has hidden a truth therein, but it's necessary that he not make it manifest, or why symbolize?

186

"It's necessary not to rip the Forms, for they only hide the Invisible. We know that there are adorable nymphs enclosed in those trees, and yet, when the woodcutter opens them, the hamadryad is already dead. We know that there are dancing satyrs and divine nudities behind us, but it's necessary not to turn round; everything will already have disappeared.

"It's the undulating reflection of springs that is the truth of the naiad. It's the he-goat standing in the middle of the she-goats that is the truth of the satyr. It's one or other of you who is the truth of Aphrodite. But it's necessary not to say it; it's necessary not to know it; it's necessary not to seek to learn it. Such is the condition of amour and joy. That is to the praise of blissful darkness."

CAMILLE MAUCLAIR
(1872-1945)

"Camille Mauclair" was the pseudonym of Séverin Faust (1872-1945), whose *roman à clef Le Soleil des morts* (1898) is an affectionate memoir of Mallarmé's *mardis*, featuring many of the writers still in attendance in the 1890s. He was more prolific as an art critic and music critic than a poet or writer of fiction, and eventually became a specialist in non-fiction, but *Les Clefs d'or* (Ollendorf 1897; contents translated in *The Virgin Orient and Other Stories*, Black Coat Press, 2016; and *The Frail Soul and Other Stories*, Snuggly 2017) is one of the most significant Symbolist prose collections of the *fin-de-siècle* and he later added *Les Danaïdes* (1903) and the remarkable novelette *Le Poison des pierreries* (1903; tr. as "The Poison of Precious Stones").

"Le Regard dans l'infini" first appeared in *Les Clefs d'or*. "The Gaze into Infinity" was originally published in *The Virgin Orient and Other Stories*.

"Tristesse de la pourpre" first appeared in *La Revue Blanche*, avril 1892; "The Sorrow of the Purple" is original to the present volume.

The Gaze into Infinity

The house where we came to savor autumn and solitude was situated on the edge of a great forest, he said to me, one evening, and
it was Nora that had desired it thus. From the wooden balcony
our gazes lost themselves in the half-light of foliage or floated
toward the violet plain, according to whether we were leaning on
the sill of the eastern window or the western, in such a way that
a verdant obscurity filled the rooms turned toward the east and
those lit from the west were bathed in a bright light. That disposition pleased our souls; following their joy or their penchant
for sadness, we reposed in the light appropriate to our thoughts.
The windows were their confidants and sufficed to signify the
extreme dissimilarities of our passions and our dreams.

You have never come to that house, he continued, and I am
almost unsure as to whether I ever really lived in it. But it is
such a vain fatigue to want to be sure of what is real! One knows
nothing. At times, I believe that the house did not exist; at other
times, I hesitate; but I always see it with clarity.

In the grounds, the old woman who served us walked with
precaution; bent over, she slipped between the flower-beds,
along the paths, skirting the hedge. The pulley of the well was
mute; the espaliers were heavy, seemingly full of lassitude, and
the flies danced, quivering, against the windows. The masses of
red and golden fruits no longer attracted them; one might have
thought that they had ended up loving something other than
the light. The crystals in the penumbra lit up their little braziers
of tremulous enchantment, and scintillated like eyes devoid of
thought; the designs of the carpet led our dreams into sinuous
forgetfulness, in incessant complications endlessly curling back
upon themselves and repeated in restricted ornaments.

At the hour when the eastern rooms were dark, and those
of the west allowed the long horizontal rays of the ailing sun to
enter through their bays, the lamp, with its luminously tender

gauze, brought more joy. It was the moment when Nora's ashen hair commenced to be admirable. She let it fall freely over her shoulders, in such a way that when she picked up a book, all I saw of the dear inclined fringe was a stream of pink gold.

We very rarely went outside; the view of the plain sufficed for us, and the violent vitality of the forest troubled us a little.

Nora was strange, disposed to philosophy with a rare and subtle power, such as one never encounters among women—and you know that I have always had a taste for what is hidden. Thus we lived, edifying our happiness on inconceivable affinities that the amour sufficient to fill ordinary hearts does not provide. Our conversations were astonishing. I loved Nora in those moments of exaltation when the gaze alone reveals the upheaval of the soul, when the course of the dialogue, aiding with its mutual replies the elucidation of something difficult, leads to the glimpse, in a flash, if a truth that words can never sketch. Her eyes, supported by mine, penetrated beyond me, while gazing at me, the shadow of another being, which one might have thought concealed by my self.

She had the double vision of veritable mystics, the gaze that seems to live between two pupils, one of which considers clearly the visage of life, while the other, the more remote, contemplates, through the first, with an unknown disturbance, the immaterial visage of pure ideas. Nora also mingled within her, like the mystics, voluptuousness and dreams. She could not separate them; in her, the most violent physical enjoyment was entirely mental, just as she brought to the sensuality of the mind an intuition aided by extraordinarily keen senses. She was one of those for whom the physical and the mental are two indiscernible elements dissolved in a single harmony, and our conversations were terminated by love-making in which nothing appeared to us to be shocking or discontinuous.

I believe that we went too far, he said to me, in a whisper. I believe that we went further than is permitted to happiness, and that is the cause of what happened. Solitude left our minds too free; there is no durable peace without some banality and some disturbance. I had certainly thought about that during the first weeks, after certain evenings when the union of our thoughts was pursued in our kisses with such force that we were left exhausted, as vibrant as violins that are about to break. But Nora was simultaneously so ardent in those emotions and so normally equilibrated in her mind and her body, that my presentiments faded away.

If only there had been a rupture then, a discord or a malaise! Fear would have stopped us. But nothing happened, and truly, I was able to believe that it was given to us, among all beings and for ourselves alone, to touch surprising beauties. Truly, I am not responsible . . .

Listen now to how Nora died in my autumnal house, how the greatest injustice, or at least the most enigmatic will, of nature demanded that she die, he told me, dejectedly. Our constant solicitude was for the sky; we spent hours following the play of the clouds in the light or watching descend from the zenith and rise from the horizon those violet tinted mists and those gardens of gold and rose that untie in mid-air slowly to efface the declining day. The combinations of the clouds were familiar to us, and their lines, in which we had first learned to divine the next day's weather, had then revealed images to us and unknown analogies with the things of the earth, mirages and bizarre duplications of objects and material beings, of which you might perhaps be able to read the notes we made in a few albums, if I have the courage to collate them in order to publish them someday.

But it was, above all, the empty nocturnal sky, with its brilliant fires and its lakes of sapphirine obscurity that impassioned us. We considered it long into the night, and often got up again in order to look at it. She, above all, awoke with a start, as if the stars were summoning her, wanting to be seen.

I perceived increasingly that Nora had the malady of infinity. I don't know whether the words I've just pronounced are intelligible, but I can't speak any more clearly. It was a hyperphysical illness that left no trace, and which was not madness, but which wore her away internally. I divined a perpetual, mute, unconscious and immense effort of that soul to escape the body and touch the universal object of its thought. It was a hidden struggle that rendered her, in appearance, more calm, and on those days her beauty attained heights of serenity that I had never seen in her. At times, I doubted that I had before me a being made of the same particles as us, even though she was very much alive. But that impression mingled within me with an increasing dolor and admiration, and I resolved to be sparing with amour in order to conserve it.

The most dangerous precaution of all! We never know what it is necessary to do in the presence of the soul, and Nora's spiritual malady was only augmented. I could not prevent her from dreaming and attaching herself to the spectacle of the sky and the night. She arrived at living exclusively through her eyes, of acting mechanically in all the rest. But all that was extremely dissimulated, ungraspable; it brushed my ideas without precision, for you might be astonished that I didn't take her away, and deliver her, for her salvation, to the beneficent contact of the vulgar. I only saw all that later . . .

That evening, the evening when it happened, there had been nothing extraordinary, until everything was suddenly accomplished. She was standing on the balcony, and I was sitting next to her, holding her hands, while she was gazing at the stars. The weather was very clear, and it must have been a long time that had been absorbed in the rotation of the infinite, when, not daring to break the silence or make her any reproach, I kissed her hands and kept them on my lips. But she didn't move, and, after a moment, I raised my head. She was stiff, and her forehead was turned upwards, and she was so motionless that I was afraid.

Finally, I said: "Can't you look at me, Nora?"

Then I sensed against me, coming from her entire body, a strange, violent, mortal interior tremor, as powerful as the stirring of a world. And it seemed to me that her voice came from millions of leagues away, her unknown voice, which replied in a whisper:

"I can't, any longer."

Oh, what a terror there was in that voice, and yet, mingled with I know not what inexplicable ecstasy! My lips returned to her hands, and I remained leaning over thus, still listening to the uncanny tremor that was passing from her flesh into mine. My tears flowed over Nora's fingers.

"Can't you feel that I'm weeping over your hands?" I said to her. "Look at me."

"Why won't you come yourself, my love?" she said. "I want so much to kiss your eyes, but I can't, any longer. I know that your tears are wetting my fingers, but I can't not look up there! I believe I'll never be able to—they'll never come down again, my eyes. My gaze has been stolen . . . *and it's in the process of being taken.*"

Penetrated to the depths of my soul by an icy horror, I surrounded my beloved with my two arms, and I leaned over the balustrade in order to look up at her eyes. They were staring and immense, and all the stars were reflected therein, as in polar lakes, but there was no longer anything in their gaze known to humanity.

Then I stood up before that insensible statue, in order to put my presence between her and the thief of the infinite, but, at the instant when the opaque show of my visage covered her luminous face, and when my gaze placed itself on hers, I sensed a fracture . . . yes, I had just broken the double golden thread of life and dream that linked my Nora's eyes to the heart of the eternal sky!

And between my futile hands, at that very second, she dissolved into death.

The Sorrow of the Purple

They dared not be poets, because many had told them that that was not good, and they could not discover any evidence within themselves that it would be good. They dared not be poets, because many had told them that the time for that was past, and that everything had become gray, as if enclosed in rooms, and that all dusks resembled all other dusks, and that all the Purple that they thought good was tarnished, and that all the terrible forces of the earth and the ether were listed in manuals of education; and they could not convince themselves that all the terrible forces had not run down in that fashion. They began to envy politicians making speeches under porticos and shouting persuasive words that they did not believe; and those who dared not be poets thought that they too ought to say persuasive words, but, not believing any of them, they could not pronounce them. Thus, they were very miserable because they dared not be conscious of their conscience, as cowardly, in truth, as women.

One of them, however, got up and said: We are cowards, and we have not become conscious of our conscience; all the things of the color purple that we say are good we have covered with ash. Why do we not look into ourselves?

Then each of them went toward the widow lamp, and toiled beneath the lamp of that pensive spouse, and on a bloody evening they all came, from times past, to assemble in a crowd; their eyes darted like épées, their fists were brandished like clubs, and there was not one among them who gazed at the horizon with the serenity of a just man.

When they were assembled, someone said:

Let the one who cried to us to be conscious of our conscience summon us, not at hazard, but in a perfect and sequential order, in order that no one is forgotten, and ask each one what it is necessary to do in order to take pleasure in all things Purple, which are the color of good amid the grayness of evil; and let each one reply, not at hazard, but in a perfect and sequential order, in order that none should be forgotten.

Then the first one summoned got up and said:

I have researched the Purple things that are good for poets, and I have been toward the crowd, repeating that it is the Purple that is the mantle of good, and of which Ideas are the fringes; I have exalted with the ends of my arms, all the nobility of my soul, and all the vibrations of my voice, all the beautiful things spread around. But the people of the crowd looked on like cattle, and they did not even smile with joy; they were not even afraid, and yet I was conscious of my conscience in acting in accordance with what it was equitable to do.

The response was made: It was necessary not to say to the crowd that the Purple was the Purple, for it is that which cannot be designated, and for which my eyes, which do not hesitate to love it and smile at it, are made. And it is just that the crowd did not believe you when you said: This is the Purple that is the color of good for poets, for it ceases as soon as it is spoken to be the indubitable Purple, and your word loses all virtue, and you have not been conscious of your conscience if you do not believe that you lied.

The second one summoned got up and said:

I have researched all that it was good to research in accordance with the truth, and I have praised the resplendent oriflamme while keeping my lips sealed, like the mute angel that extends the sunlight toward human eyes, and I have traversed life with my taciturn glare, thinking that everyone would follow me and finally know the Purple. But they did not follow, and I have seen that unless their eyes are extracted from their orbits, in order for other eyes to ignite there, and flay their souls and their senses alive, in order to endow them with a sensibility to veridical things, they would not see, and I was unable to make them understand that the Purple was undeniably exultant around me, and they did not come toward me.

The response was made: It was necessary that the Purple you bore was so absolutely and uniquely the Purple that the eyes of all would fall from their orbits in order to allow other eyes to be born; and of that you were not sure.

The third one summoned got up and said:

I gathered sages with profound minds, and I said to them things that have given their souls wrinkles. And I said to them things that had white hair, and they knew from me the formulae that render their possessors mute. Then they enclosed in urns the verities than I had taught them, and they sealed them in order that the profane would never respire them, and in order that they should preserve their balm throughout the ages. Thus I became conscious of my conscience, and I acted in accordance with what it was equitable to do for the Purple that is the color of good.

The response was made: Were they, then, dead verities of which you furtively collected the ashes in sealed urns? Perhaps that ash, spread over the foreheads that you call profane, would have revived a flame within it to gild them with the desired blazon. But of that you were not certain. What, then, permitted you to extinguish the light before whoever entered?

The fourth one summoned got up and said:

I considered that I was alone and I ornamented by mind like a beautiful temple, and I marched without discipline and without persuasive gestures, allowing a subtle ether to evaporate from myself, in order that it would impregnate the shadows and the light, and that people would thus be able to respire the beauty that emanated from me.

And the response was made: You have only served yourself, not understanding that you were only thinking for yourself and enticing yourself; for it was necessary that the Purple become so evident in your mind that it was dissolved therein and that it alone remained real there. Thus, it did not survive you, and you have not been conscious of your conscience.

Then the others summoned said nothing; but, raising their arms, they pointed at one or the other of those who had spoken, confessing that they had thought the same.

And no one saw any longer the one who had replied to them all, by which they knew that it was the Purple Itself that had lamented, with long denials.

And as all the things of the earth and the heavens remained the same, and the dusk remained similar to other dusks, and they raised themselves up in vain without seeing anyone on the horizon, and no form or absence of form was manifest, and all the terrible and latent forms did not want to become tangible and terrible, they all sighed after gray and bland things; and they all went away, indolent and null, feeling very cold, grotesque laggards going back in great disorder with cries in the throat and a broken blade in the hand, furtively, without perceiving that no future rendezvous had been fixed by the One that had spoken, while above them, the splendid uncomprehended Purple wept copious bloody tears.

STUART MERRILL
(1863-1915)

Stuart Merrill, American by birth, lived in Paris from 1866 to 1885, where he had initially been taken by his father, a diplomat. He was taught at school by Stéphane Mallarmé, and two of his classmates, Pierre Quillard and René Ghil, subsequently joined him in regular attendance at the *mardis*. He published his first volume of poems in French, *Les Gammes*, in 1887; his only book in English was his collection of translations of French prose poetry, *Pastels in Prose* (1890). He returned to Europe to live in 1890, having been disinherited by his father for his espousal of Anarchism. He published three more collections of poetry before his death, but, like Mallarmé before him, he attracted a group of loyal acolytes to the café near the Panthéon where he held forth.

"Le Jour des jours," "Un Roi pleure" and "Ma Douleur . . ." appeared as "Trois poèmes en prose" in *Vers et prose* July 1905. The translations are original to the present volume.

The Day of Days

Before that day of days, my friend's life was comparable to that of a peaceful village whose inhabitants depart sagely every dawn, to work in the fields and the gardens, and come back every dusk to dance and sing in the black room of the tavern or the green square of the church. Throughout the year one sees there, rising from the hearths of thatched cottages toward the sky full of swallows or crows, the light smoke that announces to mendicants the family supper. And one hears there, at the hour when the lamps are extinguished, the low and humble murmur of prayers in which the voices of little children mingle with those of old people.

Since that day of days, my friend's life has been comparable to that of a village sacked by barbarians. The trumpets of war howl there at dawn, the red light of which seems to be prolonged until that of dusk; heavy horses caparisoned in gold trample the wheat in the fields and the roses in the gardens; the flame of conflagrations launched toward the sky amid the lances that challenge God and the standards on which strange monsters are painted. The prayers I have forgotten. I can no longer do anything but howl in the din of crumbling houses and the gasps of old people and children who are being killed.

A King Weeps

I am the king of a tenebrous valley. I am seated on an iron throne. My cloak is only a rag, my sword has rusted in the rain and I have thrown my scepter into a river in a distant country.

I no longer possess a palace in which to shelter my old age. The wind of the eternal night blows in my hair, and I only have the strength to sing the appeal to the dead. Inexhaustible tears flow between my fingers.

I have forgotten the name of the queen who consoled me and I have driven away the little child who asked me why I hid my eyes. I can hear nothing in the distance but the howl of my dog-pack pursuing phantoms.

I await Death on my iron throne, untiringly. But she does not come, for I am as immortal as my dolor, and I can only weep forever, my head in my hands, in the tenebrous valley of which I am the king.

My Dolor . . .

My Dolor will not put on a heavy cloak of mourning, and will not cover her head with ashes and dust. My Dolor will put on her most beautiful festival robe and will crown itself with roses and violets.

My Dolor will not be preceded through public squares by a procession of weepers and wailers. My Dolor will go through the streets surrounded by singers and musicians playing joyful tunes.

My Dolor will not be the prostitute who begs, her hand extended and eyelids red, for the pity of passers-by. My Dolor will be the queen who smiles at the people and who sometimes closes her eyes in order that no one will see that she is weeping.

EPHRAÏM MIKHAËL
(1866-1890)

Ephraïm Mikhaël was the form of his name adopted by Georges Michel, who attended Mallarmé's *mardis*, and started a splinter group of his own, "Les Moineaux francs" [The House-Sparrows] in collaboration with his friend Bernard Lazare, whose members included Pierre Quillard and Saint-Pol-Roux. He published a small collection of poems, *L'Automne* in 1886 and wrote three plays, one in collaboration with Lazare and one with Catulle Mendès, before dying young of tuberculosis.

"Le Solitaire" was reprinted in a posthumous collection of Mikhaël's *Oeuvres* (Lemerre, 1890). "The Solitary" is original to the present volume.

The Solitary

Anywhere out of the World.

In order to carry out the orders of a distant king, servants exposed the child in a place of forests and rocks. The abandoned infant was placed on a stone amid monstrous grass; harsh flowers around him opened their hostile red corollas like maws. But that night the jubilee commenced, and the priests gathered in the forest perceived the child.

One of the hierophants, leaning over toward the stone, prophesied. "This one," he said, "is of noble race. He will be delivered from malevolent approaches."

The priests sang the customary hymns; then they all went together to confide the child to the king's pastors. A sounder of the conch preceded the procession; they were in mourning and, turning toward the plain, they made tumultuous and desperate plaints resound. But from the depths of the forests the buccina players in white robes responded with rich fanfares and the haughty straight clarions were seen rising in the dawn like golden lilies.

In the shepherds' village the child was named Stellus. He grew up wild and disdainful, and yet there was a tenebrous tenderness in him. He opened his arms to children. He ran to mothers and hugged them filially. But he suddenly stopped, as if wounded by an unknown evil; he lowered his head and fled toward shadowed corners, toward the broad deserted highways. Other children threw stones at him and beat him with branches. The old men said: "They're right; you ought to play with your brothers."

Meekly, he then tried to follow those of his age when they went into gardens to steal fruit and pillage the beehives. But suddenly, without understanding, he had a desire to weep and to hide.

Often, he fled away from roads and villages, into the forest where he had once been found. A vast peace descended upon him; the friendly branches brushed him with welcome freshness, and it seemed to him that healing hands were being placed on his forehead. Silently, he sat down in a sunlit place, on the edge of a lake so profoundly impregnated with ancient light that it seemed to retain within its shores a marvelous liquid of cinnabar and gold.

Stellus stayed there, without a dream, without desire, intoxicating himself by listening to the wind. At first he heard nothing but a monotonous and confused noise spread over the entire country. Soon, he was able to distinguish the frisson of each wood, of every branch. Then he discerned unusual, supernatural sounds reminiscent of the songs of magical spinners and the sighs of celestial flutes.

And that rumor of the wind had a miraculous power. As he listened to it, Stellus sensed new thoughts surging within him. He understood, he knew and he saw the forest living; he saw the ineffable soul of the trees, the grass and the waters; and sounds fallen from the stars taught him divine things. He was not astonished, however. That revelation only seemed to him to be a recovered memory, and every idea that entered into him was like a returning exile. He listened placidly, and it seemed to him to be quite simple that the information was brought to him by the wind, like flowers plucked from the orchards of the night.

But when the breezes finally fell silent, an immense sadness grew in the child's soul. After the revelatory words that the wind brought him, he felt more prodigiously that he was a stranger.

An imperious desire sometimes came to him to repeat to others what he had learned from the forest, but he divined that he would speak in vain, and he remained dolorously silent. When he returned to his companions, a strange malaise oppressed him. Every day he lingered for longer in the forest, in its unexplored sectors.

For one entire summer, he lived among the trees. He stayed there, loving and savage, regretting his companions but nor daring to return to them. Mist soiled the dusks; a long, sad quivering agitated the branches; the trees leaned over backwards, frightened and tremulous, as if baulking fearfully before the approaching winter; the flocks in the short grass grew thin and bleated lamentably at the moon.

A man came from the village to enquire about the belated pastor. Stellus confided his dolor to him; he begged him to leave him in the forest. The man listened with an appearance of understanding.

"I can see what you desire," he said, finally. "The priests have told you that you were of a noble race. That doubtless signifies that you are not made to be a herdsman. Go forth into the world in quest of glorious hazards. Be a soldier."

Stellus believed that man. *Yes*, he thought, *perhaps I will be better among soldiers.*

Having climbed a rock, he saw the troubled fires of a camp in the distance. He left the flocks and followed bitter paths toward battles. The calls of the sentinels on the hills guided his progress; trumpets sounded in the distance, as if to welcome the man that was coming.

His helmet crested by a bronze bird, his armor bristling with nails, Stellus fought with the ax and the sword. He served a conquering king whose army advanced triumphantly, odious to the nations. Such a hatred growled behind the invaders that they killed the wounded in order to spare them the expiatory tortures that the enemy would doubtless have inflicted upon them. And in order that no one would be captured alive, the soldiers were linked together in battle by chains. But a mysterious force pushed Stellus to fight alone.

He tried in vain to get closer to his brothers in arms; an invisible power moved him away. On nights of alarm, he galloped alone toward perilous positions; he was the solitary torch-bearer who explored the barbaric woods; he was the unique defender of rearguards who was left behind like a martial offering to the gods of war during the flight of kings and captains. And yet, how he would have liked to mingle with his companions, to drink pillaged wine with them in stolen cups and sing with them around the bivouacs! How he envied those who, on the eve of massacres, slept together fraternally under flapping tents! But he never had companions.

In the days of the first battles he thought: *Doubtless, being of a noble race, I cannot please myself among mercenaries; I would be happy if I were marching with the leaders.* He accomplished such exploits that the kings saluted him as their equal. He received the golden lance and banner, and had his place among the princes of the army. But in the ardent cortege of young sovereigns, the ancient dolor surprised him again; in the squares of conquered capitals that he was given as a privilege, he sensed, as in the shepherd village, that he was a passing stranger.

As he was afflicted, an old captain who admired him said to him: "I know what you desire. What you lack, Stellus, is amour. Go forth into the world in quest of some white princess. Be a lover."

Stellus believed the captain. He put ample branches of lilac into his saddle-bag; he rolled vine-branches and foliage around his lance and departed toward amour. Magical birds, dazzling the air with bright wings, fluttered around the cavalier; nuptial perfumes floated over the rivers and fields.

In a land of sunlight and fresh waters, Stellus found the white princess. She was standing beside a spring, drawing water in a silver pitcher; her pale and supple arms were leaning on the rim. The young woman began to laugh because the magical birds settled upon her abruptly, and sprayed bright droplets over her face as they folded their wings. When Stellus approached, she fled.

She ran into the country, and while she ran she laughed. At times she stopped, hastily picked red roses and white roses, and threw them at the cavalier, ironically. Her tawny hair was undone and spread over her shoulders like the mantle of a huntress fabricated from the pelt of a young lioness.

In the end Stellus overtook her, put his arms around her and pulled her up on to his horse. She was still laughing.

"Drop the reins," she said.

Gently, with caressant words, she guided the tamed charger. She conducted it along a pathway strewn with blue powder to her palace, and that night the sistra and tymbals announced a royal wedding.

The nuptial garlands had not yet faded on the palace balconies when Stellus came to sit down in the gardens, sobbing. He raised his plaintive arms toward the sky and murmured: "Who, then, will come to my aid? Who will advise me?"

Then he saw a tall old sacerdotal man who was listening to him. "Father," said Stellus, "if you are the savior sent to me, if you know hidden things, tell me why I am forever solitary. Tell me why, as a child, I was unable to play with the other children, why I was unable to reveal to young men the words of the wind, nor laugh with the soldiers, nor sleep voluptuously beside my wife?"

And in a supernatural voice, the old man replied: "Stellus, Stellus, since the enchantments of the kiss have not vanquished you, since your incurably noble heart cannot be intoxicated by banal sensualities, I will speak. You are suffering, Stellus, because you are not similar to other men, because you cannot know their joys, nor their hopes, because you have obscure dreams within you, unnamed passions that you cannot express in words. But it is necessary that you know now that all men are, like you, solitary monsters.

"Do you remember, Stellus, when you were a small child, you could not distinguish he-goats from rams and ewes from she-goats. And when you heard bleating in the distance, you said: 'It's the livestock moaning.' As the he-goat differs from the ram, one man differs from another. What is called humankind is only a disorderly flock of unknown and disparate beings.

"Stellus, the clairvoyant eyes of initiates perceive differences where vulgar eyes only see evident similarities. But men, ignoring the horrible, divine truth, believe themselves to be similar to one another. They speak to one another, the insensates, as if words could go from one soul to another. They look at one another as if they were not separated by insurmountable walls of darkness.

"You, Stellus, have understood obscurely that you are the only one of your race. It is for that reason, Stellus, that you have suffered. You appear to yourself to be different from other men, and you cannot resign yourself to your nobility. You fled into the forest because your companions were strangers to you, and you suffered in the forest because you no longer had companions. You loved solitude in the country because you suffered from being alone in crowds, and you have not been able to seek the deliverance promised by prophesies.

"Yes, the priests told the truth. You are of a noble race. But madly, like the others, you have searched for others of your race on earth. You have searched for them among soldiers and kings, and you thought you would find an equal when you encountered one. I have revealed secrets to you. Meditate, in order that you might one day, as has been predicted, be delivered from the maleficent approaches of those you cannot believe to be your brothers."

Outside the gardens, outside the palace where his wife was asleep, Stellus drew away. He marched in stony plains; he climbed arid slopes; he followed the banks of funereal rivers. He came eventually into a land overhung by harsh mountains with sheer and smooth walls.

The inhabitants of the country that Stellus had entered were in affliction, because, from the heights of the mountains, a monstrous winged horse vomiting flames had fallen upon their houses. The hippogriff with diamond hooves shook the walls of the ancient houses with its resounding wings. It pawed the ground, tore up the sown grain, felled the oxen during the plowing; it abducted virgins, carrying them beyond the clouds. Then they were seen falling to earth, naked and bloody, like red and white flowers falling from the opening sky.

A great clamor had resounded at the advent of the monster, as imperious and loud as the voice of a herald, and prophetic words had been perceived. The victorious hippogriff would devastate the country until a man would voluntarily sit down between the scintillating wings and consent to go with the monster toward the stars.

Stellus arrived among those frightened people. He saw the monster from afar, and a hope rose up in his heart. Radiant, he went to find the village chiefs, and proclaimed that he would mount the hippogriff. The men saluted Stellus with long cries of admiration; the women embraced his knees and spread oils and balms over his feet.

The sages harangued the people. "See," they said, "the man who will sacrifice himself for you. He is young and glorious; he could live royal years, and yet he will quit the soft dusts on which we walk with joy; he will leave the natal mud, in which we delight; he will go toward the foreign stars, toward the sky at which prudent men do not like to look. Glory to the hero! Contemplate the man who loves us enough to flee the earth, the man who will be devoured for his fellows."

While they spoke, Stellus, seizing the resplendent mane with both hands, intoned a song of delight:

"Hippogriff, liberator hippogriff, carry me higher than the sky. In order to obey the divine old man, we shall go, O monster, beyond the gates of the horizon. I shall ride above cities, above landscapes where I have suffered. If nothing awaits us above the worlds, let us wander forever in the desert of the constellations. You will spring from the earth through the night of joyful stars, and I shall be delivered; I shall no longer have to endure human beings, I shall no longer have to love human beings and I shall finally know, freely, among the mute stars, the voluptuousness of being born solitary. But if I have merited, O savior monster, discovering those who are of my race, carry me toward them. Winged horse, charger worthy of a noble cavalier, carry me at last to where my true brethren are. Hippogriff, liberator hippogriff, like a king returning from a battle, I shall reenter the realm of life, toward my high celestial dwelling."

Stellus caressed the colored mane of the winged horse. The astral vaults opened peacefully to their course; the breezes of the heavens murmured words of welcome; luminous blonde forms leaned over on the clouds and, through the mists of a strange dawn, the solitary finally saw burning, in the utmost distance of the skies, the light for which he had searched so long, the light of fraternal eyes.

HENRI DE RÉGNIER
(1864-1936)

Henri de Régnier (1864-1936) formed a friendship at school with Egbert Vielé, who began signing himself Francis Vielé-Griffin when the two of them became Symbolist poets, briefly associating themselves with *Lutèce* and then moving on to other periodicals, founding one of their own in collaboration with Paul Adam in 1890, *Entretiens politiques et littéraires*. Régnier was a member of José Maria de Heredia's salon and married Heredia's daughter Marie, a noted writer in her own right under the pseudonym Gérard d'Houville. The marriage upset Pierre Louÿs greatly, but Régnier smoothed things over by inviting him to join them on their honeymoon. Regnier published his own "Symbolist Manifesto" in *Le Bosquet de Psyché* (1894) and several collections of Symbolist prose, most notably *La Canne de jaspe* (Mercure de France, 1897), which reprinted most of the stories from *Contes à soi-même* (1894) and all of those from *Le Tréfoil noire* (1895). After the turn of the century, his writing, mostly in the form of novels, became more conventional, but never entirely lost its Symbolist fascinations and affectations. A sampler of his translated fiction is *A Surfeit of Mirrors* (Black Coat Press, 2012).

"Le Récit de la dame des sept miroirs" first appeared in *La Canne de Jaspe*. "Hermogène" first appeared in *La Revue Blanche* in juillet-août 1893. "The Tale of the Lady of the Seven Mirrors" and "Hermogenes" originally appeared in *A Surfeit of Mirrors*.

The Tale of the Lady of the Seven Mirrors

My father's decrepit old age went on for years. His neck oscillated. His shoulders became stooped. Gradually, he bent further over. His legs trembled. He withered away.

Every day, however, he went out alone into the gardens. His footfalls dragged over the shingle of esplanades, the tiles of terraces and the gravel of pathways. He could be seen, minuscule and shriveled, at the far end of avenues, with his thin cloth cap and his vast fur-lined silken overcoats, impaling a fallen leaf with the tip of his long walking-stick or straightening the stem of some flower as he passed alongside a flower-bed.

He slowly made a tour of the fish-ponds. There were square ones, with pink porphyry rims; circular ones, bordered with olive jasper; and oval ones rimmed with blue-tinted marble. The largest of all was surrounded with yellow breccia, and the golden gleams of tench glided therein. The others held red goldfish, carp and strange glaucous fish.

One day, my father could not go out for his accustomed walk. He was sat down in a large red leather armchair and it was dragged to the window; the castors grated on the checkered mosaics, and the old man considered the vast perspective of the gardens and water features for a long time. The sun was setting, reddening over the monumental gilt of November. The park seemed to be an edifice of water and trees, intact and fugitive. Sometimes a leaf fell into one of the ponds, on to the sand of a pathway, or the balustrade of a terrace; one, driven by a slight breeze, scratched its fleshless bird's wing against the window, at the same time as a bat scraped the darkening sky with its flight.

At dusk, the invalid sighed deeply. Footsteps were audible outside on a nearby pathway; a black swan beat the darkening water of a pool with its palmate feet; a magpie took off from a tree, chattering, and perched, hopping up and down, on the rim of a vase; a dog howled hoarsely in the kennels. Inside, a huge and taciturn item of furniture creaked dully in its skeleton of ebony and ivory, and the thong of a whip with a horn handle, set horizontally on a chair, uncoiled and hung down all the way to the parquet. No breath emerged from the old breast; the head sagged as far as the hands clasping the tortoiseshell snuffbox. My father was dead.

I spent the whole winter in the constraint of mourning. My solitude ankylosed in silence and regret. The days went by. I lived them in a scrupulous attention to that melancholy memory. The time passed without anything being able to distract me from my dolorous and funereal meditation. Only the approach of spring reawakened me to myself, and I began to observe the singularities that surrounded me, and which exceeded the reports that were given to me.

As if the paternal presence had imposed around itself, by its duration, a kind of attitude to people and things, the effects of his disappearance expanded through the surroundings. Everything came apart. Invisible joints cracked in some occult dislocation. The oldest servants died, one by one. Almost all the horses in the stables perished; the old dogs in the pack were found eternally torpid, their eyes vitreous and their muzzles buried between their furry paws. The château deteriorated; the roof became dilapidated, the sub-basement cluttered; the trees in the park fell, blocking the pathways and putting horns on the bushes; frost broke the stone of the fountains; a statue fell backwards; and I found myself, in the unusual solitude of the deserted dwelling and the disordered gardens, as if awakening from a long season in which I had slept through the hundred years of the fairy tale.

Spring arrived in gentle showers, warm and precocious, with high winds that shook the closed windows. One of them opened under the exterior pressure. The perfumes of the earth and trees entered in a suffocating gust. The window flapped like a bird's wing; on the wall, the mythological wall-hangings quivered; the jets of water in the tapestries oscillated, and a wrinkle in the fabric made the Nymphs smile unexpectedly and the woolen visages of the Satyrs snigger. I breathed in deeply and I stretched away all the lassitude of winter; my numbed youth shivered, and I went down the stairway of the terraces to visit the garden.

They were admirable in their spring sap, and every day, from one hour to the next, I witnessed the blossoming of their beauty. Foliage accumulated in the crowns of the trees; the golden fins of the tench brushed the swollen water of their ponds; the blue-tinted carp circled the green-coated bronze of the central figure that twisted in the dulcified metal the slenderness of its voluptuous curves; sturdy mosses climbed the smooth legs of statues and secretly insinuated their flesh into the marble; the split sleeve of the Hermes was garlanded; their hollow eyes became velvety with a somber gaze; birds flew from tree to tree, and the composite charm of spring was unified into the harmony of an estival beauty.

Gradually, the azure of the adolescent sky deepened and hung in suspense over the extent of the park, over the grave anxiety of the foliage and over the circumspect dream of the water features. The water of switched-off fountains became still, drop by drop, in the silence; from the beds of the ponds, growths of bright green vegetation enlaced, on the surface, around solitary floating flowers; the flower-bed overflowed into the pathways; the branches of the trees were interwoven over the avenues; green lizards crawled over the warm balustrades of the terraces; and the heavy scent of vegetation was exhaled everywhere.

A kind of superabundant life animated the disorderly park; tree-trunks twisted into near-human statures. Hares appeared;

rabbits pullulated; foxes showed their slender muzzles, their oblique march and their plume-like tails; deer took aim with their horns. The old gamekeepers, dead or disabled, were no longer destroying the inoffensive or carnivorous vermin. Winter had broken the fences that separated the gardens from the surrounding countryside, densely forested, chosen by my father because of the very solitude that safeguarded his retreat. It surrounded the grounds with an abundance of enormous trees, uncultivated fields and unknown places.

I wandered along the pathways. The summer was flamboyant; my shadow was so black in the sunlight that it seemed to hollow out before me the effigy of my stature; the grass of the avenues came up to my waist; insects buzzed; dragonflies caressed the water opalized by their reflections. There was no wind; and, in the immobility of their stupor or the posture of their expectation, things seemed to be living inside themselves. The day burned its beauty until the dull consumption of sunset; every day announced itself hotter than the last and suspended in slow dusks the end of its suffocating languor.

A malaise overtook me; I walked more slowly; I interrogated the avenue along which I was about to venture, the corner I was about to turn; an anxious round-point halted me at the center of its bifurcations, and without going any further I retraced my steps.

Once I had been wandering all day, and was sitting by a pond, gazing into the green-tinted water at the vague Medusan faces configured by the eddies and the serpentine tresses of the water-weeds: fluid gorgonian medallions divined and dissolved, bronzed by the reflections of a green-gold dusk, redoubtable and fugitive. The moment was equivocal; the statues sank back into the angles of hedges; the silence clenched mouth after mouth with a paralyzing echo.

Suddenly, in the distance, far away, a cry rang out, guttural and reduced by distance to a minuscule and almost interior perception: a scream both bestial and fabulous. It was remote and unusual, as if it came from the depths of the ages. I listened. Nothing more; a leaf stirred imperceptibly at the top of a tree; a little water trickled drop by drop through a fissure in a bowl and moistened the surrounding sand. Night fell, and it seemed to me that someone behind me laughed.

The next day, at the same time, the cry rang out again, more distinctly, and I heard it again almost every day; it was getting closer. For an entire week it had been silent when it burst forth again, directly to one side, terrible and vibrant, followed by an abrupt gallop. It was still bright, and I saw, protruding from a thicket, the naked torso of a man and the leg of a horse, scraping the soil of the pathway with its hoof. Everything vanished, and I heard in my memory the singular voice, which seemed to unite in its ambiguity laughter and whinnying . . .

The centaur walked placidly along the path. I stood aside to let it pass; it went by, whinnying. In the dusk, I made out its dappled horse's rump and its human torso; its bearded head bore a crown of ivy with red berries. In its hand it held a gnarled thyrsus terminated by a pine cone. The noise of its amble was stifled by the long grass; it turned round and disappeared. I saw it once more, drinking from a fountain. Droplets of water pearled its red mane, and that day, toward evening, I also met a faun; its yellow-haired legs were crossed; little horns protruded from its low forehead; it remained sitting on the pedestal of the statue that had fallen over during the winter, and it was tapping its goat-like hooves together, making a clicking sound.

I also saw nymphs, which lived in the fountains and the ponds. They raised their blue-tinted upper bodies out of the water and plunged in again as I approached; a few played on the edge with algae and fish. Their wet footprints were visible on the marble.

Gradually, as if the presence of the centaur had reanimated the fabulous ancient people, the park furtively filed up with singular beings. To begin with, mistrustfully, they hid from my sight. The fauns ran away briskly and I never found anything in the places where they had stood but their reed flutes, with half-eaten fruits or a split honeycomb. The water of the ponds swiftly covered the shoulders of the nymphs and I was only able to divine their presence by the ripples of their dives and their hair floating among the water-weeds. They watched me coming, their little hands shading their eyes in order to see better, their skin already dry and their long hair still dripping.

The others became bolder too; they circled around me or followed me at a distance; one morning, I even found a satyr lying on one of the steps of the terrace. Bees were buzzing over its hairy pelt; it seemed enormous, and was feigning sleep, for as I passed by it grabbed the hem of my dress with its hairy hand; I freed myself and fled.

After that, I no longer went out, and stayed in the deserted château. The excessive heat of that terrible summer was fatal to my last old servants. A few more died. The survivors wandered around like ghosts; my solitude was increased by their loss and my idleness augmented by their inertia.

The vast rooms of the palace awoke at my footsteps and I lived in them one after another. My father had assembled sumptuous marvels there; his taste delighted in rare and curious objects. Tapestries dressed the walls; chandeliers suspended their proud scintillation of crystalline flashes from the ceiling; groups in marble and bronze opposed one another on carved pedestals; the squat feet of tall golden sideboards clenched their quadruple leonine claws on the parquets; vases in opaque or transparent substances stretched the sinews of their throats or swelled the amplitudes of their paunches; precious fabrics filled cupboards with tortoiseshell or copper doors. The clutter overflowed. There were glaucous or wine-colored silks, woven algae and embroidered grape-clusters, plush velvets, wrinkled moirés, pale satins sparkling like wet skins, misty and sunlit muslins.

I soon wearied of the spectacle of the tapestries; they represented the singular guests that had invaded the park; porphyry and pewter groups also depicted Nymphs and Fauns. A centaur sculpted in a block of onyx reared up on a pedestal. With their moist grace, their grimacing bizarrerie, their Thessalian robustness, those which had troubled the tranquil waters, those which had haunted the rustic forests and grassy avenues, all of them— all of the monstrous life that was laughing, bleating or whinnying outside—were reproduced on the walls in flesh of silk and manes of wool, or lay in ambush, huddle in corners, in the solidity of metal and stone.

The scorching and furious summer had melted in rainstorms when summer arrived. My forehead pressed to the windows, I watched the gold of the park dripping in the sunlight in the intervals between downpours. The numbers of the monstrous guests seemed to increase further. The centaurs now broke cover in herds on to the pathways; they chased one another, prancing or racing. They had been joined by some that were very old, whose mossy hooves stumbled on pebbles; they wore white beards; the rain lashed their hairy rumps and hollowed out the thinness of their torsos. The satyrs, in flocks, gamboled around the pools where the nymphs swarmed in a mingling of blue-tinted flesh and russet hair; I heard the fracas of kicking, the swift trot of little capriped hooves, the whinnyings, the cries and the discordant concert of muted tambourines and shrill flutes.

In an attempt to thwart the anxious enervation that was irritating my solitude, I tried to distract it by putting on fine clothes and ornamenting myself with jewelry. The trunks contained a considerable quantity of them. I walked through the vast galleries, dragging the sumptuous weight of velvet; but its touch reminded me of the fur of hairy beasts, whose eyes seemed to be watching me through the gems that I wore; I sensed that I was fascinated by the ocular fixity of onyx, palpated by the caress of silks, clawed by clasps, and I wandered, miserable and adorned, through the solitary sequence of the long illuminated rooms.

The autumnal rain and wind grew one evening into a tempest. The old château shook. I took refuge, on my own, in a heptagonal room with walls made of seven huge mirrors, limpid in frames of bright gold. The gusts outside slid through the cracks in the windows and under the doors, causing a large adamantine chandelier to swing, amid the tinkling of its crystal pendants and the vacillation of its candles. I thought I could feel the rough tongues of the wind on my hands; I felt myself gripped by its icy invisible talons.

It seemed that, suffocating in my glaucous satin dress, I was becoming by virtue of its contact one of the fluid and fugitive nymphs that I had seen undulating beneath the green waves, in the transparency of the pools of water. Instinctively, in an interior struggle, I tore away the insinuating fabric in order to defend myself against a mysterious penetration that was making me utterly listless; I gripped handfuls of my hair; my hands drew it out it like floating algae, and I appeared to myself, standing naked in the limpid water of the mirrors. I looked around at my sudden and fabulous statue, standing around me seven times in the silence of the looking-glasses, animated by my reflection.

The wind had fallen silent. The stridor of a claw scratched the glass of one of the tall windows, through which the abruptness of a lightning-flash designed the phosphoric track of the furtive scrape and vanished. I recoiled with horror. At the windows, attracted by the light or chased by the tempest, I saw faces and muzzles stuck to the glass. The nymphs were applying their moist lips, their wet hands and their dripping hair to the crystal; the fauns were putting the lips of their mouths to it and the mud of their fleeces; the satyrs were crushing their pug-nosed faces to it frantically; they were all pressing, climbing over one another.

The vapor of nostrils was mingling with the drool of teeth; fists were clenching bloody fleeces; the grip of thighs was squeezing the breath out of flanks. The foremost, climbing on to the sub-basement windows, braced themselves under the pressure of those coming from behind and below; some were crawling and insinuating themselves through the hairy legs that were trampling them, and, in the terror of its silence and the mêlée of its effort, the host of fabulous flocks was kicking and leaping and laughing, collapsing under its own weight and reconstituting itself, only to collapse again; and that horrible bas-relief was swarming behind the fragile transparency that separated me from its sculpture of darkness and light.

Then I evoked, in the tumultuous night, the pikes of gamekeepers, the fists of valets, lashing that bewildered and muddy horde with whips, the great hounds of the pack biting the calves of fauns and the ankles of centaurs; I summoned the horns, the knives, the blood and the entrails of kills, muzzles digging into torn flesh, the measuring gestures, the fresh pelts . . .

Alas, I was naked and alone in that deserted château, beneath the furious night!

Suddenly, the windows cracked under the monstrous pressure; horns and hooves shattered the windows into shards; a bestial odor invaded the room violently and entered with the wind and the rain, and I saw, by the flickering light of the half-extinct chandelier, the unified rabble of fauns, satyrs, and centaurs hurl themselves upon the mirrors, to extinguish therein every allusion to my beauty—and, in the fracas of the smashed and bloody looking-glasses, hands extended to exorcise the horror of that terrifying dream, I fell backwards on to the parquet.

Hermogenes

As I entered the forest I turned my head, and, with my hand on the dappled rump of my horse, I paused to gaze over my shoulder through the first trees at the land I had just passed through, in order to try to catch one more glimpse of the house of my master, Hermogenes.

It should have been at the extremity of the bleak, briny and boggy plain that displayed its checkered salt-marsh, flat and far and wide, where roseate puddles reflected and crystallized the rays of the setting sun. The sun blinded me, for it was straight in front of me, and the whole of that broken ground, traversed in the dampness of an autumnal afternoon, was no more, at that hour, than an expanse of gilded mist upon a glitter. The vapor and the glare outside the forest were reemphasized by the demi-obscurity slumbering in the interior of the covert.

Tall pines loomed up from a dull and felted ground, their slender trunks sunlit to mid-height, the shadow increasing as the sun descended over the sea. I could see the sea, smooth on the horizon, beyond the bare plain checkered by the pools in which, so brackish was their lukewarm water, my horse had refused to slake its thirst. It pawed the russet ground of the underwood with its hoof, causing the pine-cones with which it was strewn to roll gently down the slope.

They reminded me of those that were burning in the hearth of my master, Hermogenes, the other evening, whose delicate scales, where tears of resin scintillated, I manipulated with my fingers, while my host, sitting beside me, told me his story, so quietly that his voice seemed to come from within myself, as if it were to the depths of my own being that he was speaking.

Oh, how often I had thought of him again while riding along the little crackling paths alongside the salty mash-waters. The dampness of the spongy air was so impregnated with salt that my tongue could taste it on my lips. Hermogenes' sadness could certainly not have been sharper or sourer. He had seemed to me to be retracing the path of his days and I told myself, as I resumed my route through the place that was already darkening; "May I be able to enter the twilight like him! May I be able to sit down at the spring, where there is a hearth for all the ashes of my dreams!"

I had arrived in a part of the forest where it appeared to me in its supreme autumnal beauty. There was a clearing between the tall trees. The foliage was red-brown and gilded, and even though the sun had disappeared, it seemed that a gleam continued in the treetops, where the illusion of its survival persisted by virtue of the tint of its presence. None of the leaves was moving and yet one of them, dull gold in color and already dry, or bright gold and still living, sometimes fell, as if the tiny melancholy sound of the spring in which their suspension was reflected had sufficed to determine, in the silent indifference of the atmosphere, the pretext for their fall.

I watched those which were falling into the pool of the spring. Two, then others, and one that I felt brush my hand. I shivered, for I was waiting, anxious in the silence, in order to continue my progress, for the cry of some bird to break the immobilizing spell. Everything fell silent, from tree to tree, to such a distance that I felt myself going pale, perhaps less because of the solitude than the caress of the leaf that had brushed my hand, lighter than a dream on the lips of memory itself.

I went closer to the water, instinctively, in order to look at my face in it, and, seeing it pale and perplexed, aged by all that a ripple can add to the nocturne of that which is mirrored within it, I thought of Hermogenes, of my master Hermogenes. I heard his voice again in the depths of my inner being, and it repeated the melancholy story that he had told me, the story that also began at a crossroads in a forest, near a spring in which he could see his face.

✻

By what mysterious ways, Hermogenes said to me, through what pitiless adventures must I have passed, only to have acquired the sentiment of a sadness so immense that it has veiled, by the excess of its bulk, the memory of its origin and the progress of its estate. It oppresses me with the total oblivion of its causes and all the weight of its consistency.

Nothing in that dark and secret past is illuminated. Golden blades among the cypresses, rings of joy and alliance lost in seductive waters, torches, on the threshold in the night-wind, smiles in the depths of twilight: nothing illuminates that invariable shadow from which I had come, by laborious paths, to the point at which, weary of a march of which fatigue alone caused me to feel the distance, lost in the forest, I sat down on the edge of a spring, as one rests next to a tomb.

All that I had suffered was dead within me, and I breathed in the odor of the ashes that my memory exhaled. It was certainly mingled with flesh, flowers and tears, for I found therein a triple perfume of regret, melancholy and bitterness. There were echoes in the depths of that interior taciturnity, but they were torpid, and that formless and mysterious past surrounded me with its dolorous darkness. Without knowing its circumstances, I still felt regret, melancholy and bitterness. I would have liked its lips to murmur the cause in my dream; I would have liked to drink from its Lethean lake a memorial youthfulness, as in the water of that spring I perceived myself coming toward me, as silence comes to solitude, each with the desire to learn from the other the secret of their accord.

Was nothing of myself going to appear in my face in the intermediary water, then? My hands reached out their wounded palms toward the reflection. *O my shadow, who appears to me thus, you seem nonetheless to have come from the depths of my past.*

You must know its ways, mysterious or ordinary, its adventures piti-
less or otherwise. Speak! Smiles in the dusk! Golden blades among the
cypresses, or perhaps the torch, or the rings . . .

A fallen stone had destroyed the mirror, and caused me to
raise my eyes. They met those of the Stranger who had thus interrupted my reverie, and who seemed to be following her own,
without perceiving my presence.

She was standing in her torn and ash-stained dress, which
surpassed the bare foot with which she had pushed the perturba-
tory stone. A singular curiosity led me to speak to the newcomer.
It seemed to me that I would only have to hear what she would
say to me to remember. Our Destinies must have touched their
lips and hands before separating for some inverse circuit in which
they were finally meeting again at a point of their duration. They
were two halves of a whole, and my sadness could only be the
understanding of her silence.

Yes, my son, Hermogenes continued, she spoke to me. She
told me why she had left the town. The life she had led there was
loquacious, bombastic and frivolous; a futile slumber. The eve
did not fructify any tomorrow therein, and the transient flowers
of every day perished. The town was immense and populous. Its
innumerable streets intercrossed in a thousand junctions, and all
of them ended, via some that opened thereon, in a vast central
square paved with marble.

Odorant trees grew here and there between disjointed paving
stones, and sculpted a delightful shade there; fresh water sprang
forth there amid the moist silence in a crystalline atmosphere.
But the square was always deserted; it was forbidden to pause
there, and even to cross it. One would have been able to dream
there under the trees, drink the water and confront the solitude,
but the crowd had to wander incessantly through the labyrinth
of dusty streets, between the tall stone houses with bronze doors,
amid the different faces and the superfluous speeches.

Oh, sad town! One wandered desperately there, in search
of oneself—those, at least, who were not satisfied with arguing on the street-corners, making speeches on the boundary-
markers, trafficking over the counters or dancing to the music of
tambourines.

The majority were content with that. They came and went without coming together save for the agreement of a bargain or the satisfaction of a desire. A few sages walked there, with mirrors in their hands. They looked at themselves obstinately, trying to be alone, but spiteful children smashed the evidential looking-glasses with thrown stones, and the crowd laughed, thus imposing the authority of its despotism . . .

As she spoke, it seemed to me that the vision she evoked with disgust was reconstituted in me. I heard it, like a distant interior buzz. It raised memorial and analogous rumors from my past, and I said again, as the Stranger had said: "Let us leave the town, let us abandon the frivolous and vain life . . ."

She had left one morning, weary of wandering amid the composite and uniform crowd, amid the dust of sandals and the sweat of faces. She passed others beneath the postern, who were coming from elsewhere to increase the number of those living there, and when she was outside the walls, she heard a bird singing in a tree. The pride of being alone exalted her, and she felt herself grow as she isolated herself further.

The hem of her dress brushed flowers, while she descended by charming roads toward the sea. Sandy shores bordered it, roseate in the dawn, which melted into gold at midday and became violet in the dusk.

Oh, dusk on that first day of dreams! Her shadow on the sand told her that she was alone, and that the residue of herself was no more than a phantom at her feet, and it was to her shadow that she sacrificed, thrown into the sea as night fell, the stones of her necklace, which tinkled more melodiously than tears. Her necklace was made up of three kinds of stones, all valuable, and the whole was inestimable. There was, all night, a star over the sea—a star over the sea, until morning!

But I paid even closer attention to what the Stranger was telling me when she told me how the satyrs and fauns stripped her and left her naked in the forest. I understood that her actions and outcomes each represented my thoughts. I understood how I had lived the emblems of her adventures internally. They were what constituted my sadness.

The satyrs had first surrounded her, dancing. The long lush grass had hid the lower halves of their bodies and their prancing bestiality, while their hands offered bunches of grapes, fruits and odorant apples—but their hands had soon become bolder.

It was afterwards that she became a wanderer, entirely devoted to some mysterious and desperate quest: a philter to create souls within the hairy flesh of prowling goat-foots. She lifted up enormous stones with her frail hands but, instead of a balm or talisman, there were toads or stagnant water sleeping there. Snakes slithered under the dry leaves, hatched from golden eggs, which she believed to be those of peacocks or doves; a seething poison, where a remedy had been promised . . .

My son, Hermogenes said to me, I finally knew the origin and the substance of my sadness by virtue of all that the Stranger had told me. It was necessary for her to come to me for me to obtain, through her, consciousness of my misery. It had seemed immense and confused before; then I found it immeasurable—but, in seeing it more clearly, I recognized that I had deserved it.

One can no longer find oneself once one is lost, and love does not return us to ourselves. Why had I not been one of those cautious sages, who walk about the town with a mirror in hand, in order to try to be alone, facing themselves because it is necessary to live in one's own presence?

✳

Such was the tale of my master Hermogenes and his encounter with the Stranger. He had taken curious lessons from it, because his mind was rational, but he loved to invigorate his reason with allegories. Perhaps he had wanted to make more impact upon me by mingling a fable with his instruction.

His apologue was ingenious and certainly had not been fruitless, for I exclaimed: "Fortunate are those who, like Hermogenes, meet themselves on the path of life through the intermediary of a dream; more fortunate still are those who have never quit themselves, and for whom their own presence has taken the place of the world!"

Night had fallen; my horse was walking over the dry leaves and stumbling over roots. I did not know how to find my way out of the forest and I searched the stars, through the trees, for the road to the dawn.

JULES RENARD
(1864-1910)

Jules Renard is now remembered for his literary celebrations of nature, and as one of the original members of the Académie Goncourt, of which his published journals provide an interesting memoir. He was, however, intimately involved with the *Mercure de France* in its early years, and was one of the four writers who produced the bulk of its contents in those years, casting his celebrations of the natural world in prose poetry possessed of a subtle and delicate Symbolism.

"L'Orage" and "Les Rainettes" both appeared in the *Mercure de France* in octobre and novembre 1891. "The Storm" and "The Frogs" are original to the present volume.

The Storm

Toward midnight, through the shutterless window and all the cracks, the house with the thatched roof filled and emptied with flashes of lightning.

The old woman stood up, lit the oil lamp, unhooked the Christ and gave him to the two children in order that, lying between them, he could protect them.

The old man was apparently still asleep, but his hand was clutching the eiderdown.

The old woman also lit a lantern, in order to be ready, in case it was necessary to run to the cowshed.

Then she sat down, her rosary between her fingers, and multiplied signs of the cross, as if she were removing cobwebs from her face.

Stories of thunderbolts came back to her, setting her memory ablaze. At every crash of thunder she thought:

"This time it's over the château!"

"Oh, this time, of course, it's over the walnut-tree opposite!"

When she dared to look into the darkness, in the direction of the meadow, a vague herd of cattle was immobilized, irregularly white, by the glare of ephemeral torches.

Suddenly, a calm. No more lightning. The residue of the storm, futile, fell silent, for up above, directly above the chimney, for sure, the great strike was in preparation.

And the old woman, her back bent, who was already sniffing the odor of sulfur, the old man, stiff in his sheets, and the children clutching the Christ in both fists, were all waiting for it to fall.

The Frogs

Sitting on the bench set in front of the door, they are exchanging their memories without remorse and telling one another stories, always the same, which might have happened at any time, in any place.

While the indefatigable frogs roll their *r*s in the distance, the oldest one quavers at first. As it is dark, every phantasmal appearance has its success of fear. The children listen, huddled between the old men and the dung-heap glistening in the moonlight.

"Do you believe in that?"

"It's been seen many a time."

"How many stars there are!"

"Shall we go to bed?"

They stay where they are. At regular intervals, a blue-tinted flame escapes from a pipe, quickly extinguished, all alone on the earth against the stars up above. A geranium leans over the rim of a broken flower-pot, and drips its odor from its crane's-beaks.

The headlights of a vehicle pass between the acacias of the road.

"What's that?"

"It's the wharf-master going home."

The vehicle draws away, and the curiosity dies away with the sound.

The frogs continue their strident appeals, so clear that they seemed to be quitting the damp bushes, the leaves as green as them, drawing nearer to the wall, and entering into the cracks in the stone, noisily.

It is necessary, however, to go to bed. Tomorrow they are picking hemp.

The watchers yawn, finally getting up. What a pleasant evening!

They might have gone to sleep outside. In the morning, they would have been found there, numb, white with dew.

"*Bonsoir!*"

"*Bonsoi . . . soi . . . soi . . .*"

They plunge into the darkness. A few women, young ones, light a lantern, for fear of stumbling. Doors close, uttering their long cries of anguish, which cause the belated men to shiver.

And even the frogs, weary of struggling, their roulades being vain, prudently yield to the silence.

SAINT-POL-ROUX
(1861-1940)

Saint-Pol-Roux was the name eventually adopted for his writings by Paul-Pierre Roux, although his first Symbolist poems were published as Paul Roux in 1883-86. He was born in Marseille and educated in Lyon before moving to Paris and joining Mallarmé's *mardis*. Along with Remy de Gourmont, Jules Renard and Gaston Danville, he was one of the writers who supplied the *Mercure de France* with most of its prose during its early years, the stylistic flamboyance of his material forming a sharp contrast with Renard's subtlety; much of it was reprinted in the three volumes of *Les Reposoirs de la procession* (1893, 1904 and 1907). He quit Paris in 1898, however, apparently feeling that his genius had not been sufficiently acclaimed, and disappeared from view after

1907, although a brief flurry of work appeared shortly before he was murdered during the Nazi occupation.

"Sur une Roche, dans le vent robuste et pur de la mer" first appeared as part of "Tablettes de voyage" in *La Revue Blanche* octobre 1892. "On a Rock, in the Pure Strong Wind from the Sea" is original to the present volume.

"Le pèlerinage de Sainte-Anne" first appeared in the *Mercure de France* mars 1891 and "L'Autopsie de la Vielle Fille" in novembre 1891; "The Pilgrimage of Saint-Anne" and "The Old Girl's Autopsy" are original to the present volume.

On a Rock,
in the Pure Strong Wind from the Sea

Vigorous memory of a frail sail once torn in the Temple, or sickly hypothesis of the enormous trumpet to come of the Last Judgment!

Many aerial crosiers on pilgrimage in my skull and the rapacious wolves grazing in my brain take fright with the howls of black martyrs . . .

Vigorous memory of a frail sail once torn in the Temple, or sickly hypothesis of the enormous trumpet to come of the Last Judgment!

And through the drain of my disgust, all the nightmares of poisonous dusks escape, tattooed as if by the whip of The-One-who-betrays-the-Caress . . .

Vigorous memory of a frail sail once torn in the Temple, or sickly hypothesis of the enormous trumpet to come of the Last Judgment!

Now here come the active washerwomen of legend to appropriate the guardian wing of my soul so that my reason might be regenerated baptismally . . .

Vigorous memory of a frail sail once torn in the Temple, or sickly hypothesis of the enormous trumpet to come of the Last Judgment!

The meadow of my ideas will no longer see again, therefore, malevolent teeth falling upon the shoots of hope like intolerable butterflies . . .

Vigorous memory of a frail sail once torn in the Temple, or sickly hypothesis of the enormous trumpet to come of the Last Judgment!

A band of invisible freshness around my temples and my forehead decorated with mistletoe, I finally come, like a lapidary druid, to harangue the enthusiasm of the sea . . .

Vigorous memory of a frail sail once torn in the Temple, or sickly hypothesis of the enormous trumpet to come of the Last Judgment!

The Pilgrimage of Saint Anne

The five Lads of faience, with the skin of a cliff and eyes the color of a calm ocean, are going, arms on top, toward the painted chapel where the good Saint, agedly lovely, is smiling.

In their Sunday clothes, perfumed with sweet marjoram, arms underneath, the five Promises of porcelain accompany them, as dainty as dolls and whose cheeks are as radiant as a lady-apple—for they are coming back from the whales, the lugubrious whales with villainous mouths, the salubrious mariners destined for their beds.

So, the juvenile garland is walking toward Saint Anne, across the puerile heath, through the linen and the windmills, the bee-hives, the buckwheat, the mills, the manors, the bells of brown bread, the cows, the ewes and the goats bleating like ancestors.

And, souls alive, they arrive at the painted chapel where the good Saint, agedly lovely, is smiling.

They have come, the sons of the waves, to offer their tribute to the Godmother with the delicate algal eyes, to the Godmother of mariners, who, saving them from the gluttonous wolves of the north-westerly wind, guided their great wooden sheep toward the fold of Cornouailles.

224

And here they are, searching the depths of their pockets, under the welcome of the bells, and here they are, seeking the golden or silver Heart promised before the reef that gaudily paints in mourning the women of fustian going to weep at the fountain . . .

And here they are, searching for the golden or silver Heart, while all the sweet fiancées with the long hair in sheaves, wearied by the route, lie down in the grass and the moss.

But in their pockets, under the welcome of the bells, they only find copper coins, coral, tinder and medallions, no golden or silver Hearts at all.

Surprised, and paler than surplices, they immediately understand that they have forgotten the village ex-voto.

Then the mariners weep, docile pilgrims who have no wish to deprive of gifts the Saint with the delicate algal eyes, sending rafts on fragile voyages—one becomes so pious going over the blue sea beneath the superb cross of the mast and the yard-arm!

In the soft breeze, the Promises of porcelain perfumed with sweet marjoram are already asleep.

✳

Suddenly, straightening their necks, the five Lads of faience take from their belts five knives shinier than five Lorient sardines, and they head, on tiptoe, toward the five sleeping virgins.

The ears of the latter, mingled with blonde tresses, resemble shells in the sands of the seashore.

As if to perpetrate follies, the five Lads kneel down beside the Lovelies dreaming in the grass, as green as a frog is green.

When each young man has undone the neckline of the corselet in which two Quimperlé apples are laughing, with prompt gestures, with eyes like stanchions, they plunge the steel sardines into the living breasts.

Spurting suddenly, rose sprinkles the face of the ancient moss. One might think that a fire of a forge is adorning them with a reflection, and that they had been eating, from the cleavage to the throat, mulberries and strawberries.

Their hands finally plunge into the beautiful breasts and bring forth five hearts, five fluttering hearts.

In the breeze, the Promises of porcelain perfumed with sweet marjoram are still asleep.

Then, having sewn up the flesh—with the thread of a dear kiss in the needle of teeth—and reclosed the necklines of the corselets where two Quimperlé apples are laughing, the five Lads of faience enter the painted chapel to offer the hearts, the fluttering hearts, to the Saint with the delicate algal eyes who, saving them from the gluttonous wolves of the north-westerly wind, guided their great wooden sheep to the fold of Cournouailles.

✳

Alas, when they emerge toward the moss and the grass, their Lovelies with the long hair in sheaves are no longer to be seen.

All of them have gone away, gone along the white road that goes all the way to the village where they bill and coo.

They call them by their names: Yvonne, Marthe, Marion, Naïc and Madeleine.

But the beauties, Yvonne, Marthe, Marion, Naïc and Madeleine, do not turn round, and they keep going, far away.

So far that their headscarves, at first gull wings, become butterfly wings, and then snowflakes, melted by the horizon . . .

The five Lads of faience fall down then, limply, while the five Promises of porcelain perfumed by sweet marjoram disappear.

✳

No longer having hearts, Yvonne, Marthe, Marion, Naïc and Madeleine can no longer love.

The Old Girl's Autopsy

On the marble, the old waxen body lay; one might have thought it a solid, perceptible soul.

Around it, three medical students were joking, pipes clenched in their teeth, giving the impression of a final and decisive tribunal.

"Oh, a neighbor of the Church, with fingers gardening the missal . . . !"

"Oh, a goat-girl with the underwear of a nun and the headgear of the valley . . . !"

"Oh, a voice like dead leaves in the breeze . . . !"

"Oh, a virgin without a chemise . . . !"

They were going to see whether that was true.

And the impious individuals part the needles of a compass, wanting to take account, parting the two legs of the old and waxen body . . .

The bird had not flown the nest.

Disappointed, the medical students utter this cock-crow:

"That proves nothing, except the fear of a paunch and then a sin-that-sucks, or that, prudently and sagaciously gluttonous, the old hypocrite haunted Minervan Desire behind closed blinds! But we'll find out!"

They have now decided on a subtler autopsy: of the Senses, in a sense.

Scattering a buzz of crepuscular insects, invisible blades—fine viper's tongues—immediately converge on the cadaver.

Incredulous waltzes take flight in spirals from pipes: smoke mocking in the manner of turned-up moustaches.

Her Feet revealed pilgrimages to the naïve hill where the Firmamental inspired, under the seal of its fugitive heel, a consoling bouquet of water. The frequent and capricious caress of a rosary and various contacts with blessed objects emanated from the Hands.

From her nostrils were taken the reeks of incense, hawthorn, candles, sepulchral herbs and precious bones buried in glass coffins.

Behind her pure Teeth were found the savor of hosts, fish with white flesh and eggs, as well as abstinence from wine and sweetmeats.

The two Eyes produced, in the form of diaphanous steamers, gazes expressing the ceremonies of rainbow chasubles, processions with laudatory banners, and merciful visions in which a Virgin with lilies flourished, a Saint Peter with keys, and a grandiose Doll swaddled in the primitive breath of a donkey.

The Ears delivered sonorous ingots of the angelus, precepts in flesh, organs and praises. But also, distantly, as if scarcely audible, words fifty years old, weary, futile words of a proud, nubile pastor who passed under the innocent and candid window one morning: "Madelon-Madeleine, humbly I love you; take the pastor and his sheep, if you love me as I love you!"

In order to go as far as the Heart it was necessary to open the breast, nibbled by the incisors of a cilice.

A perfume of the presbytery gushed forth.

Then the Heart appeared, transpierced by seven blades like that of the Dolorosa.

Then they knelt down, reverently, amid the pipes that had fallen from the mouths; and three signs of the cross, made by three red hands on the three white aprons of the medical students vaguely resuscitated three Knights of Malta . . .

GABRIEL DE LAUTREC
(1867-1938)

Gabriel de Lautrec arrived in Paris from the Midi in 1889 and found employment as a schoolteacher while frequenting Le Chat Noir and other literary cafés in the evening. He contributed to various periodicals before publishing a notable collection of *Poems en prose* (Léon Vanier, 1898). Resident in Passy, he established a salon there where his guests included Jean Lorrain—briefly a neighbor—the ubiquitous Verlaine, Alfred Jarry and Oscar Wilde. As the Symbolist Movement faded out, Lautrec rebranded himself, after a brief flirtation with Occultism, as a humorist, and became very successful, developing a quirky quasi-surrealist kind of comedy far ahead of its time. A sampler of his translated short fiction is *The Vengeance of the Oval Portrait and Other Stories* (Black Coat Press, 2011).

"Les Funèbres" first appeared in *L'Écho de Paris*, 18 décembre 1892, and was reprinted, along with "Le Fait glorieux" in *Poems en prose*. "The Mourners" and "Glorious Action" were originally published in *The Vengeance of the Oval Portrait and Other Stories*.

The Mourners

They were living on a solitary island on the far side of the great Sea. And they lived there, separated from other men by fear. They were called the Mourners, and whenever they chanced to descend toward a town, with their long beards and their heads partly shaven, as if in mourning, as they passed by, the people traced the cabalistic signs that were used to chase away evil spirits.

The people of that distant epoch lived on Death. When one of them was about to expire, the body, placed on a deep raft, was sent to the isle of the Mourners, to the accompaniment of violas, violins and drums, and yellow candles burned with pale flames beneath the sun and on the sea.

For it was the Mourners to whom the lugubrious care of the dead had been consigned. They were the priests of a melancholy and definitive Cythera, save for the fact that, unlike that other embarkation by Watteau,[1] the passengers bound for the happy isle were not heading for Love but for Death. In great sumptuous palaces with profound mirrors, the bodies were laid out and subjected, from then on, to the ceremonial ritual. Before transforming the human remains, the priests wanted to ensure the absolute freedom therefrom of the delicate soul, still anxious at the gates of the body, and their religion was primarily composed of powerful chanted formulae that disengaged the immaterial. Then there were aromatic pyres on which the bodies were burned—and the ashes were reserved for the communion of the living.

They actually ate the ashes of the dead, and their lives were perpetuated thus, in a sad and lofty symbolism, by which the souls of their ancestors found a definitive transformation in them. They were ignorant of any other nourishment, and their souls of any other poetry. Love did not exist yet, and humans reproduced without joy. Their only mystery, perhaps of a grandeur that they did not suspect, was that of a human race living on the problem

---

1 Jean-Antoine Watteau's *Embarquement pour Cythère* was the inspiration for a famous poem by Baudelaire, in which the embarkation for the island in question, famous for the worship of Aphrodite, symbolized the initiation of an erotic adventure.

of its own death. And their soul, haunted by the fear of, and also the desire for, the Mourners, was like a lunar landscape in which there would have been no forms, no music and no perfumes.

✳

One day, among the bodies transported on a daily basis to the island, that of a little child was found, so melancholy and so delicate that the Mourners wept, in an emotion never felt before. His white wings, soiled by every kind of mud, were those of a vagabond, but his dead eyes had a gaze whose malicious and arrogant pride was that of a god.

The body was dispersed according to custom, and soon the fragile lines from which that subtle flower of beauty were born were broken and lost forever. And the people ate the bitter and unsuspected ashes that were to give them an endless regret for the Beauty that was real for a single moment of the past. Oh, what white-clad seraphim would recover the lost lines of the Form too dolorously beloved!

For, as soon as the unknown child was dead and his ashes dispersed, I believe that Fear in its most charming and palest form descended into that universe. A terrible sickness fell upon the cities. Those who ate the divine ashes were poisoned forever. Their eyes lit up. Prey to an intense fever, they ran into the country, the daylight dying on the fragile stems of flowers and the night mingling the mystery of alcoves with the voluptuousness of blue stars. They conceived mysterious affections for the trees, the clouds and motionless nature; then, like the Chaldean shepherds of ancient times, they saw the midnight sun of Love rising in the eyes of women.

And for the first time, they knew that eternal thing, love, and that painful and nostalgically personal thing, the frisson of beloved flesh.

Their dull eyes, their burning lips, and their halting respiration permitted them to recognize themselves in one another; with love, too, came forms, music and perfumes.

✳

Now, those who ate the eyes of the Child would have love in their eyes for all eternity; those who ate his lips would have it in their lips; those who drank his blood would have the blood of a god

230

eternally in their veins. And they were beloved for their lips, their blood or their eyes.

Others would have his harmonious voice, and would know the secret of making people weep by means of music and words.

They were seen going along the streets, isolated from everyone else, fearful of their strange appearance and seemingly-immeasurable dolor. Disdained and disdainful, they lived in one of those worlds parallel to the real one, which are the worlds of dreams, mirrors or madness. They invented measure and rhythm, according to the new intonations that their words had taken since the coming of the Child.

With the vague memory of the divine reality that had once existed, they knew their role as mysterious reflections. Sometimes, on contemplating the dolorous face of beloved individuals who loved them for the tender frisson of their eyes, they saw a line appear there, a smile, a gaze, a lost fragment of the Form, and fixed in their poems, like a streak of luminous gold, that sparse laughter of the Absolute.

They were men of genius, those who made manifest by means of the pen, the word or the brush.

And the remembrance of the strange event slowly disappeared from memories. And the lovesick lived on, forever incurable; to console them, they had the delicate caresses of the stars, of wings, of pupils, and in one supreme moment, in every life, the suffering and advent of the Kiss. For the kiss was born after Love, a thing more amorous than Amour.

The children descended from them, sadder and more beautiful than humans, sang beneath balconies for their daughters. And more mournful than the Mourners themselves, they bore on their foreheads from then on the mysterious sign that drives women mad, and also makes them afraid of love. And it is since then that the incurable suffering of immortal poems has been born.

That happened in a very distant epoch. The funeral organs of eternity had scarcely fallen silent, in order to listen to the tremulous prayer of the first new-born world.

Thus was born the race that suffers from lovesickness.

Glorious Action

It was a happy city; in the streets bordered by low houses with polished walls, air and sunlight circulated freely. The rare strollers who ventured out during the hottest hour paused on the thresholds of doorways, overtaken by a sudden nonchalance, to listen to the monotonous song that some idle poet was singing beneath a pale-leaved fig-tree; and through their vibrant souls passed, everlastingly, the thrill of musical harmony that takes flight but never dies, being the very respiration of the gods. Through the wide open porticoes, horizons like those painted by Leonardo da Vinci could be glimpsed, where blond adolescents struck artistic poses beneath foliage and beside marble statues, while others caused grave music in the Dorian style to resonate on their musical instruments—and all the streets, paved with lava, descended in gentle slopes toward the marketplace on the edge of the sea.

The glorious sea, younger sister of eternity, breathed in silken waves beneath the subtle caress of the air. Slow ships could be seen gliding smoothly over its surface to the sway of lateen sails. From a green transparency at the foot of the coast, the sapphire infinity of the waves became bluer with distance, in successive water-color shades, and far away, on the distant shore formed by the crease of the gulf, the waves extended immutably in a sheet of profound indigo.

Sometimes, in the sultry afternoons, the young ephebes descending rhythmically to the beach, as far as the eye could see, took off their clothes with calm and beautiful gestures, worthy of causing the desire of a troubled soul to die; naked, arrogantly proud of the cadenced movements of their subtle movements, they impregnated the lukewarm air with their perfumed youth. Philosophers, lovers of souls, expatiated on the good and the beautiful, while courtesans with firm breasts and algal gazes let their purple garments fall about their ankles with gestures like the flutter of wings, in order to prove the divinity of the gods, and stood up straight beneath the sun, haloed by their russet hair.

These people adored only one god, leisure, and one goddess, beauty. They knew, thanks to fabulous travelers' tales, that other peoples lived beyond the hills, and other gods than their luminous and gilded demons, but their souls had been open since their dawn to the intelligence of all supplicant attitudes to the ideal, and in their temples they had dedicated, albeit while smiling, temples to the unknown gods. At the very least, they did not want a religion that was not a joy. Sometimes, at solemn festivals, they gathered in vast enclosures, where skillful performers made representations of an even more intense and harmonious life quiver before their eyes.

The chimerical imagination sang in beautiful lines, before their eyes and lips, of the misfortunes and gigantic works of demigods, and the legends of which their ancestors had formed the brazen pages of their golden book. Passionate for the sober and living crease that a movement of the soul imprints on the floating peplum of the performer, they did not permit clownish gestures and grotesque spectacles, and sent rope-dancers and bear-handlers back to the barbarian lands. They lived thus, searching with solicitude for beauty in all things, and profoundly ignorant of everything that was not the inutility of life—but all the porticoes were painted with frescoes, and white marble statues stood in the streets, launching marble arrows toward the sky!

One day, in the public plaza, a bizarre individual presented himself, dressed in a somber garment that made a sinister stain on the gilded brightness of the surroundings. They thought at first that he had come from the fabulous land of legend where darkness reigns uninterruptedly; it is there that the larvae of indeterminate form roam, which come to suck the blood of children by night and drag themselves over their shadowy soil as they return, blinking their eyes at the yellow light of the moon.

On the head of the unknown was a strange hat, black in color and extraordinarily tall, like an Asiatic tiara with a broad brim. His black peplum, like the dresses of female mourners at a funeral, extended from his shoulders to his waist and then, bizarrely cut short in front, was elongated at the back as far as his knees in the form of a bird's wings. A narrow and rigid double tunic was wrapped around his legs, his feet disappearing into two supple and shiny black animal-skin caskets. And his beard, far from imitating those of the majestic philosophers, was separated on the two sides of his shaven skin, like the acroteria on the fronton on the temple. An old fig-merchant who was sleeping on the hot pavement rose nonchalantly to his feet and came toward him, while the children playing knucklebones on the threshold of a theater fled in fear.

But the people flocked from all directions, amused by the craziness of his appearance, and by the hoarse and muffled intonations with which he pronounced their language. A passing courtesan took off her saffron cloak and threw it over the unknown's shoulders to veil that ugliness, more obscene than nudity. He told them that he had come from a distant country, different from theirs, whose more advanced civilization had realized prodigies that they could scarcely imagine. There were immense cities there, with tall houses sheltering thousands of citizens; all the industries and all the sciences were ruthlessly and desperately cultivated, having given new forms and new words to life. By night, gigantic light-sources insolently replaced the light of day. Powerful machines multiplied labor and human strength tenfold. It was a grandiose civilization, disdainful of ideas and dreams, hostile to philosophers, poets and jugglers of words— and the unknown man found inspired tones to paint for that naïve and credulous people the beauty of the gospel that he was preaching to them.

The people listened; some of them, leaning on columns, put their heads in their hands pensively. Others extended their words and gestures toward him, interrogatively. He told them that their idle existence was unworthy of free human beings, and that their facile happiness was not the only dream in a world of avid competition and hostile efforts. They were frightened by these ideas; the unknown man appeared less grotesque in his appearance and the ugliness of his clothing, and they understood confusedly that they had, until that day, forgotten to live, while gigantic forms and mirages of feverish activity appeared to them on a misty dream-horizon, in the midst of a forest of chimneys, ships' masts and tall houses, beneath a fuliginous sky that the divine light of the sun no longer penetrated.

Months went by. The unknown man had not left the city, but a gradual and inexorable metamorphosis had transformed everything, and nothing remained of the smiling and calm life of earlier days but a memory. There was a new décor and new mores.

After having laughed, in their esthetic arrogance, at the stranger's bizarre garments, the people had adopted them. They had discarded the long, brightly-colored tunics, the gilded sandals so well-adapted to treading on shifting sand or the large flagstones of streets and the loose peplums adapted to the majestic gestures of orators. One might have thought that the obscurity that extended over the sun was composed to the wing-beats of their old chimeras, flying away from their eternally dreamy eyes.

Tall houses of desolate appearance, with dark windows, had emerged from the ground as if by the power of magical evocation. The polished ground had been covered with a layer of mud, as black as the preoccupations that haunted their hearts. New crimes had become manifest. Hands armed with daggers were seen emerging from obscure coverts, and men were learning to take human life by means of iron, fire, poison and vibrations of the ether.

A devouring activity having replaced the former nonchalance, labor now extended from one dawn to the next, even for those tormented by no anxieties. The odors of coal, oil and filth had stifled the delicate aromas of oleanders and the mysterious warmth of female bodies that had once brushed the soul. And the city offered an aspect of unspeakable horror, even though gigantic sewers had been constructed with the marmoreal ruins of the temple of beauty, feverish veins through which the corrupt blood of the city ran.

From then on, instead of ancient leisure pursuits, it was practical action that ruled. In the violet hour of evening, tradesmen, bankers and travelers came together in the marketplace and formed a circle, gesticulating with barbaric and unknown words.

There were people who lived and grew old behind grilles, sitting in exactly the same place, eternally covering sheets of paper with complicated and incomprehensible symbols, without anyone thinking they were mad. Networks of metal wire criss-crossed the city at an extraordinary height, in order to transmit thought, for which slow and harmonious language fallen from the lips of gods was no longer sufficient.

By night, heavy vehicles of massive form, deprived of harness, ran noisily through the streets, sowing sparks and fear as they went. And one day, after a terrible riot in which all the people took part, a company of actors, the last remaining priests of the mysterious religion of art remaining in the city, were shamefully expelled. They went along the lugubrious boulevards, insouciantly sad, with their tambourines and charming masks, on to highways fringed with gorse, heading for the rosy horizon of the ideal.

The beautiful blond ephebes who had spent their lives in the sunlight, and in the shade of plane-trees, put their supple limbs at the service of useful tasks. Forgetful of the dawns of olden times, they no longer went along pathways at the belated hour of confessions, humming tremulous songs of love with brightly-laughing girls who drank fresh spring-water between two kisses. Their joy was extinguished in nights of fabrication, and their bodies took on the rigid and complicated forms of the machines in the midst of which they lived. Slowly, their blue eyes became dull. The buzz of their trades made them forget the refrains that they had once circulated in their sonorous cups when drunkenness in bacchanal dress, the folly of divine nights, had knocked at the door of feasting. Fever made their teeth chatter and their skin crawl.

Even those who died—and how numerous they were!—did not escape the triumph of practical action. Their calcined bones were reduced into chemical substances; their tanned skin was exposed to the sun like that of animals; ropes were made from their viscera for the rigging of vessels that set forth to search for unknown treasures, and small works of art from their teeth, displayed in the showcases of the noisy city under the wan glow of artificial light.

But when that vigorous and esthetic race was dead, and the sparse semen of men no longer gave rise in the wombs of sterilized women to any but paltry and sickly children, prepared by their birth for that new life, the work of civilization was complete—and the sun, which was had still been shining, went out.

The divine demon that is naked humankind disappeared forever beneath the grotesque burden of clothing. In their narrow breasts, no longer lifted by the sob of lost things, the blood, beating in isochronic movements, imitated the monotonous coming-and-going of crank-shafts and pistons, and a powerful and terrible voice was heard in the dismal night, proclaiming the eternal death of ideas, dreams and beauty, while the triumph of modern horror—and unlimited action—extended like a shroud over the filthy streets, the black houses and the lividly-gleaming sea, mocked by the moon.

PIERRE QUILLARD
(1864-1912)

Pierre Quillard studied at the Lycée Fontanes with Éphraïm Mikhaël, Stuart Merrill, René Ghil and Jean Ajalbert. With Saint-Pol-Roux and Mikahël he founded the short-lived periodical *La Pléiade*. His first collection of poems, *La Gloire du verb*, appeared in 1890, and he became a regular contributor to the *Mercure de France* thereafter. An Anarchist and a Dreyfusard, like his close friend Bernard Lazare, he also became a campaigner on behalf of the Armenians, who were in the process of being wiped out by the Ottoman Turks, and spent four years teaching in an Armenian school in Constantinople from 1893-97. A skilled linguist, he published numerous translations from the Greek; most of his later work was political.

"Les Trois femmes en deuil" first appeared in the *Mercure de France*, octobre 1891. "Three Women in Mourning" is original to the present volume.

Three Women in Mourning

The three women in mourning are walking along the grassy roadway.

The river is glistening in the sunlight, reminiscent of a princess clad in changing silk, holding on her pale hand, instead of a hunting-hawk, a tame dove; in her luminous robe, in her robe of silk and joy, the river is hastening toward the nearby sea.

The three women in mourning are walking along the grassy roadway.

But on the other side of the road, the marsh is dormant in its steely cope; an old, silent king, he darts the gaze of his white pupils; the sad opals that are weeping on his mute breast are burned by obscure flames; war, murder and rape are haunting his slumber.

The three women in mourning are walking along the grassy roadway.

Mysteriously, they are going; their monotonous footsteps are muffled, and they glide as in a room in which a beloved dead man is lying, a dead man whose hands are still warm; they are going toward the country, far from the sea and far from the surf, mysteriously, without looking back.

The three women in mourning are walking along the grassy roadway.

Two of them are old, or aged by tears, by the swords of the seven dolors; their shoulders are weary of having buckled under the burden of the sufferings of life; and narrow black headscarves enclose their resigned black hair, while their mantles hang down in funereal folds.

The three women in mourning are walking along the grassy roadway.

The third is blossoming and smiling; her hair is radiant as the dawn over her neck, and, her ears, straining toward the song of the joyful river, toward the merriment of the sea, are awaiting the boat of amour, the boat of amour and daylight, which will carry her far away from forgotten tears.

The three women in mourning are walking along the grassy roadway.

MARCEL SCHWOB
(1867-1905)

Marcel Schwob was sent to Paris in 1881 to study at the Lycée Louis-le-Grand, where he met the future writers Léon Daudet and Paul Claudel; he lived with his uncle, the novelist Léon Cahun. He became a professional journalist in 1888, working on both *L'Évenement* and *L'Écho de Paris*. His great admiration for Edgar Poe is very obvious in his story collections *Coeur double* (Ollendorf 1891) and *Le Roi au masque d'or* (1892), translations from which can be found in the sampler *The King in the Golden Mask* (Carcanet, 1985). Other works exhibiting a strong Symbolist influence include the quasi-autobiographical *Le Livre de Monelle* (1894) and a book of fictitious biographies, *Vies imaginaires* (1896), but his health deteriorated catastrophically as a result of an undiagnosable chronic condition, which eventually killed him.

"L'Homme double" first appeared in *L'Écho de Paris*, 20 janvier 1890 and was reprinted along with "La Terreur future," which first appeared in the same periodical in 7 décembre 1890, in *Coeur double*. "The Double Man" is original to this volume; "The Future Terror" was originally published in *The Germans on Venus and Other French Scientific Romances* (Black Coat Pres, 2007).

The Double Man

Footsteps sounded in the tiled corridor, and the examining magistrate saw a white-faced young man enter the room. He had glossy hair, with side-whiskers stuck to his cheeks, and his eyes were perpetually wandering or searching. He had the bewildered air of a man who did not understand what was happening to him. The municipal guards left him at the door, with a glance of commiseration. The gleaming and restless eyes seemed to be the only living elements in his ashen face; they had the luster and the impenetrability of glazed black pottery. He was clad in a frock-coat and baggy trousers, which hung about his body as if suspended from a coat-hanger. His tall hat had been crushed by low ceilings. The collective impression, with the telling detail of the side-whiskers, was that of a wretched lawyer pursued by his colleagues.

The judge, seated beneath a lamp whose light fell upon the face of the accused, studied the pale gray flatness of that leaden visage, whose lines were traced by vague shadows. And while he thumbed mechanically through the documents that lay scattered on his table, the apparent respectability radiated by the man gave him—like one of those momentary explosions which illuminate the blame—the strange impression that he had before him another examining magistrate, with a frock-coat and trimmed side-whiskers, impenetrable and piercing eyes: a sort of unfortunate caricature, awkwardly sketched out in the charcoal-gray of the evening.

That indescribable respectability, which was certainly inferred from the cut of the beard and the clothes, nevertheless confused the magistrate, and made him hesitate over the case before him. The crime had appeared banal at first: one of those murders that had become frequent in recent years. A woman of easy virtue, who lived in a little apartment in the Rue de Mauberge, had been found in her bed with her throat cut. The cut, just below the thyroid gland, had seemingly been made by a hand accustomed to butchery; the carotid artery had been neatly severed and the neck laid half-open. Death had been almost instantaneous, since the blood had gushed out in a series of three or four liberal jets. The bedclothes, slightly disordered, were marked with extensive bloodstains, disposed in opaque patches, thick at the center and fading gradually towards the edges to brown-flecked pink. The mirrored wardrobe had been smashed and wooden splinters scattered across the floor; the mattress had been torn apart and disemboweled.

The murdered woman, already of a certain age, was not unknown on the party circuit. She was out every evening at various theatres and restaurants. Her stolen jewelry had been valued, and when the goldsmiths and silversmiths recognized her distinctive rings and carefully-wrought necklaces, their testimony had been sufficient to direct the chief of police to the guilty party. The individual who stood before the judge had been unanimously identified. He was not in hiding; the second-hand dealers of the Marais and the petty shopkeepers of Saint-Germain knew his address. He had come to sell the jewelry with the same air of respectability that he had now: the air of a man who is inconvenienced and wants to liquidate his assets.

When the magistrate interrogated him, he could not help employing polite expressions and sympathetic attenuations. The man's responses were manifestly mealy-mouthed and evasive, but they were as respectable as his exterior appearance. He was, he said, a solicitor's clerk. He gave the name and address of his employer. A word from the judge almost immediately brought back the reply: *unknown*. The man made a gesture of astonishment and murmured: "I know no more."

Files containing deeds and transcripts had been found in his room in a lodging-house in the Rue Saint-Jacques. When they were shown to him, he said that he did not recognize them. The magistrate, thinking that the files had been planted as evidence, was surprised. On pressing the interrogation, he ran into inexplicable contradictions. The man had the external appearance of a lawyer, but had no knowledge of legal terminology. He knew nothing about the solicitor who was said to be his employer except his name and address—and yet he persisted in his affirmations.

The jewels, he said, had come from an inheritance, and they had been entrusted to him to sell, to realize a sum of money. To the traditional question as to how he had spent his time on the night of the crime he replied: "I was asleep in my bed." When the landlord, called to give evidence, testified that the man had not returned home that night, only arriving the following morning, his face pale and in some distress, the accused looked at him in surprise and said: "No, no. Look here, I know perfectly well—I was in my bed."

The magistrate, nonplussed, summoned three shopkeepers, who recognized the man. They admitted without the slightest hesitation that he had sold them the jewelry.

"Look, monsieur," he said to the judge, "I've already told you that all that was entrusted to me by a person I met in the solicitor's office, to sell and then to take the proceeds to my employer."

"What person?" asked the judge.

The man reflected for a moment, then said: "Well—listen—I can't quite bring it to mind . . . but it will come back to me."

Then the magistrate began to speak, showing him the inconsistencies in his story while maintaining a sort of respect for the external appearance that the man presented, as if taking pity on his crestfallen attitude and his idiotic reasoning. He called him "my friend" while gently pointing out his contradictions. He explained the crime the man had committed, since he seemed to be unable to understand it. He attempted to make clear its gravity and abominable nature, stressing the overwhelming sum of the evidence, and finished up with an eloquent peroration in which he said that the President often chose to exercise his supreme right to grant mercy to those who confessed their guilt.

The man appeared to appreciate the indulgence of the magistrate, and took his turn to speak when the judge had finished.

Until that moment the man's voice had been dull, monotonous and impersonal: utterly devoid of all nuances, as uniformly gray as his ashen face. The magistrate could not remember ever having heard one like it. But when the man replied to the judge's exhortation, he became exhortatory in his turn. The tones of his voice became accusatory, a pale imitation of the tones which the magistrate had employed in addressing him. The words that emerged from his lips were copies of the words that he had heard.

His discourse was negative; he limited himself simply to rejecting the contradictions and denying the evidence. He could not count on the clemency of the President, since he knew nothing of the crime.

When he came to this point, the judge had to stop him. The clerk of the court smiled as he wrote it down, in spite of the seriousness of the man and the horror of the crime. Standing before the examining magistrate's table was a singular being who mimicked the magistrate with a real talent, who colored his monotonous voice with the judge's tones, who impressed upon his own dull features the same expressive lines as those in the face of the man sitting opposite, who seemed to inflate his loose clothing with exactly the same borrowed gestures. He did it so well that the vague impression that had struck the examining magistrate as the accused made his entrance had now become the precise and distinct image of a man of law in conference with a colleague. It was as if the outlines of a gray, soft and blurred sketch had been reinforced to the point at which they attained the sharpness of an etching, or a white line set against a black background.

The judge went to the heart of the matter, authoritatively. He no longer talked of possibilities, but of facts. The victim's throat had been cut by a practiced hand; the instrument in question had been found. The judge placed before the man's eyes a knife—a sharp butcher's knife—stained with blood, which had been discovered under his bed. The back of the blade was half as thick as a finger. This was the first evident connection established between the man and the crime. The effect was prodigious.

A tremor shook the accused from top to toe and his features convulsed. His eyes rolled, and became bright. His hair stood on end, as did the side-whiskers which seemed to be an extension thereof. His brow was furrowed and his mouth tightened. The man's figure now took on a painful rigidity, and with a strange gesture, as if he were waking up, he rubbed the skin beneath his nose two or three times with his index-finger. Then he began talking again, in a drawling fashion, his hands no longer stiff but following his words with gestures. These words were evidently addressed to people who were not there. The judge felt obliged to ask where he thought he was. At that question the man shuddered; his mouth opened without any effort on his part, as if it were overflowing.

"Where'm I at? Where'm I at? Why, at 'ome, o'course! This is what c'n 'appen t'yer, where I'm at!" He took up a pen from the table. "'Ere's *a dip-your-stick-in-the-blackstuff*[1], I allus help m'self. It makes a mess of yer bib, mind. They were good. I've gone afore the Red—'twas a merry dance, that. It's swallered what I writ wi' that there instrument. A good score! I'm a real showman when it comes t'jewels. Oh, they ain't cotton—see how they run!—like velvet. I've stuffed t'other pie, I've 'obbled'n'nobbled what 'e 'ad squirreled away. I've fooled 'im good'n'proper wi'a nice sham, summat beat. An' I don't fear macs what turn their coats, me. I work alone—an' I go t'sleep in me *gimme-yer-wood*."

The man lurched towards the judge's chair. The frightened judge got up, surrendering his position to the other.

Scarcely was the man seated when the reaction set in; his face became bloodless, his head lolled back and his eyes closed. His entire body collapsed into inertia.

And the judge, standing before the other in his turn, felt that he was faced with a terrible problem. Of the two semi-simulated persons that he had had before him, one was guilty and the other was not. This man had two personalities, but the two were united in one: which was the real one? One of them had done the deed—but was that one the fundamental being? In the double man who had revealed himself, where was *the man*?

The Future Terror

The organizers of the Revolution had pale faces and eyes of steel. Their vestments were black and close-fitted, their speech curt and arid. They had become this way, having once been different—for they had preached to crowds, invoking the names of love and

---

1 A literal transcription of this portmanteau word would be "dip-your-two-arms-in-the-black-vessel". The French "vase" has a double meaning, so "vase noire"—literally translatable as "black vessel" or "inkwell"—also implies "black mud", but the whole expression is obviously intended to carry at least two meanings—perhaps three if (as seems likely) there is a sexual innuendo as well as the obvious analogy between the clerk's pen and the butcher's knife. The problems of translation posed by the portmanteau expression extend even more acutely throughout the remainder of this colloquially slurred and delirious speech; I have tried to capture the gist of it as best I can.

pity. They had traveled the streets of capitals with belief in their mouths, proclaiming the union of populations and universal liberty. They had inundated dwellings with proclamations full of charity; they had announced the new religion that would conquer the world; they had gathered initiates enthusiastic for the nascent faith.

Then, in the dusk of the night of its execution, their manner changed. They disappeared into a town hall where their secret headquarters were. Bands of shadows ran along the streets, overseen by strict inspectors. A murmur was heard, full of deathly presentiments. The environs of banks and rich houses trembled with new, subterranean life. Sudden outbursts of clattering voices were heard in distant quarters. A buzz of machines in motion, a trepidation of the ground, terrible sounds of ripping cloth; then a stifling silence, similar to the calm before a storm—and all of a sudden, the tempest was unleashed, bloody and enflamed.

It burst in response to the signal of a flamboyant rocket launched into the black sky from the Town Hall. A general cry was released from the breasts of the rebels, and there was a surge that shook the city. Large buildings were trembling, broken from beneath; a rumble that had never been heard before passed over the earth in a single wave. Flames rose up like bloody pitchforks along the instantly-darkened streets, with furious projections of girders, gables, slates, chimneys, iron T-beams and ashlars. Window-glass flew everywhere, multicolored by firework sprays. Jets of steam burst out of pipes, gushing out from various floors. Balconies exploded, twisted out of shape. Bed-linen reddened capriciously, like dying furnaces, behind distended windows. Everything was full of horrid light, trails of sparks, black smoke and clamor.

Buildings, falling apart, were reduced to jagged fragments, their shadows covered with a red cloth; behind the buildings that collapsed on every side the fireballs spread. The crumbling masses seemed to be enormous heaps of red-hot iron. The city was nothing but a curtain of flames, bright in places, somber blue in others, with points of profound intensity, in which passing black shapes could be seen gesticulating.

The portals of churches were inflated by the terrified crowd, which flowed everywhere in long black ribbons. Faces were turned, anxiously, towards the sky, mute with fear, eyes staring in horror. There were eyes that were wide open, by dint of stupid astonishment, and eyes hardened by the black rays they shot forth, and eyes red with fury, mirroring the reflections of the conflagration, and eyes shining and pleading with anguish, and eyes that were wanly resigned, whose tears had ceased to flow, and eyes tremulously agitated, whose pupils roamed incessantly over every part of the scene, and eyes that were looking inwards. In the procession of livid faces, the only visible differences were in the eyes—and the streets, amid the shafts of sinister light hollowed out in the gutters, seemed braided by moving eyes.

Enveloped by a continual fusillade, human hedgerows retreated into the squares, pursued by other human hedgerows that advanced implacably, the fleeing company agitating its strangely-illuminated arms tumultuously, while the company on the march was tightly-packed, dense, orderly and resolute, its members moving in step, without hesitation, following silent orders. The barrels of rifles formed single rows of murderous mouths, from which extended long, thin lines of fire, irradiating the night with their mortal stenography. Above the continuous roar, amid the frightful pauses, a singular and uninterrupted crackling sound was audible.

There were also knots of people, grouped in threes, fours and fives, interlinked and obscure, above which whirled the flash of straight cavalry sabers and sharpened axes stolen from the arsenals. Thin individuals were brandishing these weapons, furiously cleaving heads, joyfully puncturing breasts, sensuously slashing bellies and trampling the viscera.

And through the avenues, like scintillating meteors, long cylinders of polished steel rolled at high speed, drawn by fearful galloping horses with flowing manes. They looked like cannons whose barrel and breech were the same diameter: at the back, there was a sheet-metal cage manned by two busy men tending a furnace, with a boiler and a pipe from which smoke emerged; at the front, there was a large, shiny and trenchant indented disk

246

mounted at an angle, rotating vertiginously in front of the muzzle of the central tube.[1] Every time an indentation encountered the black hole, a clicking sound was heard.

These galloping machines paused outside the door of each house; vague forms were detached from them, and went in. They came out two by two, charged with bound and moaning parcels. The stokers fed these long human bundles into each steel tube, regularly and methodically. For a second, jutting out to shoulder-level, a discolored and contorted face was visible; then the indentation of the eccentrically-turning disk threw out a head in the course of its revolution. The steel plate remained immutably polished, the rapidity of its movement launching a circle of blood which marked the vacillating walls with geometric figures. A body fell on the roadway, between the machine's large wheels; its bonds broke in the fall and, as a reflex movement of the elbows propped it up on the flagstones, the still-living cadaver ejaculated a red jet.

Then the rearing horses, their flanks pitilessly lashed by a whip, drew the steel tubes onwards. There was a metallic shriek, a profoundly shrill note in the sonority of the tube, two lines of flame reflected in their periphery, and an abrupt halt in front of a new door.

Save for the lunatics killing in isolation, with naked blades, there was no evident hate or fury—nothing but destruction and orderly massacre, a progressive annihilation, like a continuously rising tide of death, inexorable and inevitable. The men who were giving the orders, proud of their work, surveyed the action with rigid faces, perfectly fixed.

At the corner of one dark street, the clattering hooves of horses encountered a barricade of headless corpses, a heap of trunks. The battery of steel tubes paused amid the flesh; above confusedly contracted arms a forest of fingers was raised towards

---

1 The word I have translated here as "central tube" is *âme*, which is used here in a specific sense to refer to the central element, or axis, of a mechanical assembly, but has the more general meaning of "soul" or "heart". The resultant wordplay is sometimes carried over into English references to "the soul of a machine", but does not translate.

the sky, pointing in every direction, like the colored spearheads of a future revolt.

Stopping the guillotine-guns, the whinnying horses refused to mount an assault, their nostrils steaming, crushing the backwash of green entrails beneath their iron-shod hooves. Amid the palpitating flesh, between the branch-work of inanimate hands, desperately stiffened, there were spurts of flowing blood.

The priests of the massacre climbed up on the human barricade, into which their feet sank, taking the horses by the head, dragging them by the bridle, while they snorted, and forced the wheels to pass over the scattered limbs whose bones cracked. Standing in the midst of their butchery, faces lit up from within by the Idea and from without by the conflagration, the apostles of annihilation gazed attentively into the depths of the darkness, at the horizon, as if they were expecting to see an unknown star.

Before them they saw an accumulation of broken facades, randomly distributed stone steps and smoking rafters, with bricks, splinters of wood, pieces of paper, scraps of cloth and sandstone paving-blocks in vast numbers, jumbled up in heaps as if hurled by some prodigious hand.

There was also a half-ruined poor-house, in which the chimneys, cut vertically, had released a long band of soot, with branches at different heights. The lower part of the wooden staircase had collapsed, broken half-way on the first floor, with the result that the shaky steps led nowhere in particular, towards rampant flames and contorted cadavers, like a frail footbridge descending from the heavens.

All the interior life of these wretched rooms was visible, exposed to the light of day: the grate of a coal fire; a patched-up peat-burning stove; a brown clay fire-pot; dented black saucepans; rags heaped in corners; a rusty cage from which a few green sprigs still protruded, in which a little gray bird was lying on its back, its feet withdrawn into its belly plumage; scattered medicine-bottles; a camp-bed stood against a wall; torn mattresses from which tufts of seaweed were protruding; pots of withered flowers, mingled with soil and plant debris—and, sitting amid polished floor-tiles, torn away from the gray cement, was a little boy face to face with a little girl, triumphantly showing her the brass spindle of a rocket that had fallen there.

The little girl had a spoon stuck in her mouth and was looking at him with a curious expression. The little boy clenched his fingers, whose tender skin was already wrinkled, about a movable lock-nut and, rotating the screw, lost himself in contemplation of the device. They stamped their thin feet in turn, taking their shoes off, profoundly absorbed, not in the least astonished by the air that was coming in or the horrible light that was flooding them—until the little girl, drawing out the spoon that was swelling her cheek, said in a whisper: "That's funny—mama and papa have gone, along with their room. There are big red lights in the streets, and the staircase has fallen."

All this the organizers of the Revolution saw, and the new sun whose dawn they awaited did not rise—but the idea that they had in their heads suddenly flared up, they experienced a sort of glimmer; they vaguely understood a life superior to universal death; the children's smiles broadened, and brought about a revelation; pity descended upon them.

And, with their hands over their eyes, so as not to see all the terrified eyes of the dead—all the eyes that eyelids could no longer cover—they staggered down from the rampart of slaughtered human beings that surrounded the new city, and fled recklessly into the red shadows, amid the racket of galloping machines.

FRÉDÉRIC BOUTET
(1874-1941)

Frédéric Boutet arrived a little late on the Parisian literary scene, but in time to hang out at Le Chat Noir and to encounter Oscar Wilde, whom he helped out of an awkward situation and befriended. His first collection of stories, *Contes de la nuit* (Chamuel, 1898; second ed. 1903) was set very solidly in the Decadent and Symbolist tradition, as were two collections of stories cast as horrific and melodramatic dialogues, *Drames baroques et melancholiques* (1899) and *Les Victims grimacent* (1900). The two novellas *L'Homme Savage et Julius Pingouin* (1902; tr. as the title stories of the two samplers of his work *The Antisocial Man and Other Strange Stories* and *The Voyage of Julius Pingouin and Other Strange Stories*, both Borgo Press, 2013) are also striking exercises in Symbolist fiction, but as the pressure of making a living forced his work to become more commercial, the baroque aspects of his style and subject matter gradually faded away.

"La Victoire veritable" first appeared in *Contes de la nuit*. "The Veritable Victory" was originally published in *The Antisocial Man and Other Strange Stories*.

The Veritable Victory

> And I fought desperately with
> the frightful Azrael . . .
> Edgar Poe, *Ligeia*.

In the darkness, the man, hidden by his black cloak, marched along the deserted quay beside the river.

To the right, at the bottom of the riverside walls, the water ran, as deep and tranquil as that of a canal. In places, oblique staircases descended. Red beacon lights blazed on moored boats. The opposite bank was only indicated by the distant patches of yellow lanterns and the illuminated windows of invisible houses.

Bordering the broad quay to the left, the old houses loomed up, with their gray facades, their iron-barred doors and their long, narrow windows mostly dark or shuttered. On the shadow of the ensemble, a faint light filtered through thick curtains or cracks in Venetian blinds. At intervals, the dimly-lit corner of a solemn room could be glimpsed, with its large severe portraits and its fretted oak furniture.

Sometimes, separating the old houses, there were long dilapidated garden walls, above which the grimacing branches of trees seemed to be gazing curiously at the passers-by. Here and there, set back in an obscure side-street, a hanging lantern projected its moving light over the top of a wall; here and there, at the top of a flight of steps, a bronze door surmounted by a motto or a title carved on a coat of arms, marked, along with the morose grandeur of the edifice, the hereditary palace of one of the noble families of the old city.

Dusk had not long fallen: a foggy November dusk in which livid clouds ran across the moonless sky, pursued by gusts of wind, like large fantastic flocks emigrating precipitately.

And beneath the clouds and the nocturnal wind, in the barely-troubled silence, the city of ancient splendors rested in its mysterious and venerable antiquity.

The man, however, contemplating all of that as something familiar, increased his rapid pace. He passed a bridge and soon, stopping on the threshold of a narrow house, opened a low door with steel bolts.

The vestibule was vast, illuminated by a ruddy lamp suspended from the vault. At the back, a stairway extended its flat banisters and its broad steps. He went up to the third floor, which was the uppermost. Approaching the arched door beneath the lamp and the sculpted lintel, he knocked three times. A moment went by. He knocked again and, as a dull sliding sound was heard inside, he threw back his cloak and took off his hat. His features were visible in the faint light. His face was pale, but his eyes, eyebrows and beard were entirely black.

A judas-hole opened, and then the door, with the numerous sounds of locks and chains.

He went in. In front of him was an old woman wearing a nun's head-dress and habit. As she took his cloak, the newcomer appeared, clad in black; on his white hands, from which he removed his gloves, rings sparkled with the various gleams of their stones.

He pushed back the long hair covering his forehead and looked at the old woman.

"Yes," the woman said, "she's waiting for you. She's waiting for you in her shroud. But why must I repeat that every time? Don't you know, then, that she's waiting for you, in her shroud, alas?

That she's always ready, and that it's me, a poor old woman, who always prepares her, and who will burn with you for centuries in hell because of it? But who can resist you, and why do I bother to say that? You're not listening to me! Take care, though—there might come a night when it's true!"

Paying no heed, as if to vain words heard every day, the visitor went past. In a small dressing-room, lit by long candles between mirrored panels, he got undressed, put on a long robe of black silk, perfumed himself, and quit the place.

A violent emotion agitated him. He seemed paler; his lips were taut and his hands tremulous. And the opium he had taken before coming began to invade his brain with a dreamlike and concentrated ardor.

Now he found himself in a square room garnished with broad divans and ebony furniture. Pale, brocaded with silver corollas, the violet silk of the wall-hangings dressed the ceiling, hung down in curtains over the windows and hid the door. To the right, there was a vast draped mirror; to the left, a silent clock; sheaves of roses inclined in bronze vases; the carpet reproduced the ornamentation of the drapes. A lamp on a side-table spread a vaporous light through a globe tinted with pink and mauve.

Going to the back of the room, the man moved one of the wall-hangings aside, uncovering a deep alcove draped with white velvet attached by silver cords. It was occupied by an ivory bed, completely white, with lace pillows and satin sheets, its curtains made of immaculate batiste.

A young woman of great beauty was lying there, motionless. The snowy quilt rose to the undersides of her beasts, whose firm roundness stood out beneath the silver silk tunic tightened and wrinkled around the bosom. The delicate neck was surrounded by a triple row of pearls; a silk headband framed the translucent pallor of the face and veiled the hair.

She remained motionless, her hands folded beneath the throat that did not appear to be agitated by any breath. White roses were scattered on the bedclothes; an ivory crucifix had been placed between the breasts. A silver night-light illuminated her beauty softly. Perfumes saturated the warmth.

The visitor contemplated the woman, and an immense grief was born within him, and the violent disturbance of sensual emotions, for she was desirable beyond all expression, and offered the perfect image of death. It seemed that those long eyes would never raise their translucent lids again, that those pink lips, so slightly parted over the gleam of teeth, would never open again to kisses. It seemed that the bare arms, circled with pearls and silver, would never uncross their delicate hands in order to embrace the man she loved . . . that she had loved . . .

Under that lamp, had her life not yielded its last sighs? Were the flowers that covered her not the flowers of death, the crucifix the one that would go with her into her coffin, and her adornment that which would prepare her for the eternal marriage with the Angel of Death?

Gradually, he submitted to the illusion. Kneeling beside the bed, looking at her passionately, he lost consciousness of the reality. The opium and the perfumes in the warmth of that closed alcove enveloped him like vertigo. Despair descended upon his heart, and also a sensual desire that grew with every passing second . . . he wept; he had seized one of the woman's hands and was caressing her bare arm. And in his soul, lust and despair, love and death, intermingled . . .

He had undone the headband over the black curls. He contemplated the beautiful visage and, within the illusion to which he had surrendered complete credulity, a vehement hope rose up, redoubling the irresistible desire—the sacrilegious desire, now. He was beside her, kissing her slightly parted lips, recklessly embracing the supple and slender body. And the hair spread out like a flood over the lace, and the parted tunic uncovered all the secret beauties.

He thought: *What does tomorrow matter? She is beautiful tonight; she is all mine; and I shall love her until I vanquish death!*

He possessed her in a voluptuous delirium multiplied tenfold by opium. Now the lips parted further to render kisses and moan with love; the supple arms reached out for reckless embraces; the translucent eyelids allowed the blue of the large eyes to pass through, and voluptuous tears to flow. And from her entire being, a divine perfume of love rose up . . .

For him, hallucinated by powerful sensations, sensing life born beneath his kiss, he swooned, in a boundless voluptuousness, in an extraordinary pride, and thought:

My love has been torn from the tomb! Once again she is alive! Once again . . . and I am the master of death!

※

What the man was doing that night he had done on many previous nights, always drunk on opium, in that white alcove, with that woman waiting for his kiss in the languorous ambiguity of her beauty, ornamented for the tomb like a virgin who had died before her first taste of love. And in truth, he must have accomplished it several more times, since it was not until the last evening of the present year that he had come for the last time.

A mystical snow was falling over the old city in the darkness. The flakes were dressing everything in virginal robes; their fluttering fall was engulfed in the black waters of the river, as tranquil as a canal—and the old city was utterly mute.

Through the snow he walked, already invaded by the opium, whose strange visions populated the moving curtain gliding around him.

He went into the house beyond the bridge and climbed the stairs. He knocked and, as usual, the old woman opened the door. She seemed agitated by terror and more troubled than usual, but the visitor, occupied with his thoughts, did not notice anything.

She said: "What, it's you! I hoped that you wouldn't come . . . but I don't know why I hoped that, for I knew full well that tonight she was to wait for you, and I know full well that you always come . . . but it's necessary that you not go to her. She's in her shroud, she's ready for the tomb, and this evening, it's the truth . . . It happened a short while ago. My God, a very short while ago. Alas, it's me, poor woman, who has laid her out, and who'll rejoin her in eternity where she'll burn, if I let you in. But you will go in, for I'm talking in vain; you're not listening to me at all, and who would dare resist you? But know this: tonight, it's the truth."

He did not hear and had already gone past. She was left to her lamentations.

He was in the violet room, then the alcove. Everything was exactly as it always was.

The woman who was still lying in chaste whiteness, under the nebulous lamp, looked like a statue lying on a tomb. She had the same pallor, the same immobility. She was what she was every time. If her lips were less rosy, her eyelids whiter, her bare arms colder in spite of the perfumed heat, her lover did not realize it. So he did what he always did; he sought and found a limitless despair—a despair that he succeeded in rendering veritable. Desire gripped him . . .

She was in his arms and beneath his kiss . . .

But he exhausted himself in vain in gluing his lips to the pale mouth; she did not part her own any more. In vain, he caressed the voluptuous body passionately, but she did not quiver and her arms did not return the embrace. The translucent eyelids remained closed over the large blue eyes, the little feet were icy, the limbs became ever colder, ever heavier. And the veridical power that she had formerly simulated for the man's pleasure reigned over her beauty irremediably.

Perhaps it was because, that night, in spite of the voluptuousness of his caresses, he was unable to love her enough. Perhaps, instead, it was because she, who, had played dead so many times, was finally curious to know it in reality; or even because, plunged in the horror and terror of her game, she wanted to make it a reality by way of expiation . . .

At any rate, the visitor was obliged to recognize that the old woman, in the words that he had misunderstood, was not mistaken, and that it was the truth. Then, without illusion, he permitted himself to experience the heart-rending distress of that which is irreparable. And the desire was dead, slaked.

Thus were abolished the last links that retained that man to life. He opened one of his rings and took the poison that he kept in it like a faithful hope. He embraced the one who was no longer lying. He kissed the lips that he had loved so much . . . and his weary head fell upon the bare breasts, in the final vertigo, the final intoxication . . .

And for his definitive and veritable victory, the Angel came . . .

PIERRE VEBER
(1869-1942)

Pierre Veber began his journalistic career at *Gil Blas* before turning up at the offices of *La Revue Blanche* with his brother-in-law, Tristan Bernard, touting for work; he became one of the periodical's regular contributors throughout its Symbolist period before going on to a highly successful career as writer of vaudevilles, librettos for operettas and other dramatic works, including numerous movie scripts, as well as dozens of novels. Several of his comedies were adapted for production on Broadway.

"Barbe-Bleue" first appeared in *La Revue Blanche* juillet-août 1893, and was reprinted as "L'Histoire veritable de Barbe-Bleue" in the story collection *L'Innocente du logis* (1895). "The True Story of Bluebeard" is original to the present volume.

The True Story Of Bluebeard

Here it is, as it is appropriate to tell it to little girls in order to protect them from irreparable curiosity. It does not contain any towers, sword-thrusts in the back, bloody corpses, or Sister Anne playing lookout; but, simple as it is, it is no less sad, for there is more mystery in a scantly noble soul than all the romantic novels in the world.

You have never heard mention of young Sir Max Bluebeard. The echoes of the daily newspapers have never mentioned the length of the ribbon of his monocle; no reporter has ever been reflected in the convex mirrors of his varnished shoes. He is a young lord extremely discreet in his private life, who does not keep letters or signed photographs, any more than locks of hair. He makes use of his fortune—oh, colossal—uniquely to put the opinions formed about him on the wrong track. He also has straw men whom he passes off as his friends, in order to avoid impetuous people from offering him their importunate amity.

His entresol was so exquisitely finished that it would have inconvenient consequences if it were described; people would only copy it. In any case, no one had visited it, but everyone was in agreement in declaring that no similar entresol had ever been seen in living memory. Perhaps it was in the heart of the Champs-Élysées—who knew?

Young Lord Bluebeard had a beautiful beard, black to the point where blackness become blue. Ordinarily, he trimmed it into a point. His eyes and face were handsome—but what point is there in these vain commentaries? He had great success with women, from streetwalkers to Le Bourget's American women. What had he done to have so much success? He had taken the trouble to be born, and that was all. If people knew in advance the difficulties of being born, and then of having been born, no one would volunteer.

The young man had been in love with several women, not all together—it is unnecessary, the proverb says, to suffer two fevers at the same time—but in succession; he had had what are popularly believed to be the dolors that are commonly called "happiness" six times over. Nevertheless, although his passions were very sturdy, they had not all been built by the Romans. A moment came when . . . alas, alas, alas!

He met a young woman—somewhere in the world, wherever you like, it doesn't matter—and immediately thought: "That's her!" and stopped.

Well, no, it didn't happen like that. Fraudulent psychologists have invented that convenient means of overcoming difficulties; as soon as furniture no longer serves for the description of the state of the soul they say: "It was like a flash of lightning," and move the furniture back, imagining that the game is over.

There were suddenly profound and yet complex reflections when Sir Max's blue beard was introduced to the young woman's blonde hair. He had a description of the woman who would be Her, significant features of states of soul, complementary to his own, anticipated, as if Masonic, anticipated gestures, as if

Masonic, as if shaped by the same elite, the appearance of being an exile of sorts among the vulgarities of the people around her.

It would not have taken much for him to say: "Why, it's you! I haven't seen you for a long time, since some reverie in which I evoked you as predestined." But he did not overstep the politeness that foreigners desire, at least in appearance.

They pretended, albeit reluctantly, to be meeting for the first time, in spite of the centuries spent waiting. They chatted for a few isolated minutes: a conversation that was, of course, perfectly banal, if one does not read behind the lines.

What were they? Relations they had in common.

"My Aunt Peinedecoeur knew your mother intimately."

"My cousin Noirsouci married your childhood friend."

"I adore mauve."

"Me too, but I especially like dark green."

"Oh, music! And also elevated reading, as you can see."

And other inconsequential remarks, passwords exchanged between citizens of the Absolute. The eyes are telling the truth, while the lips are agitating vainly.

"Anyway, bell skirts are taking us back toward the crinoline." (I'm ready to love you; the time has come.)

"Undoubtedly, minus the whalebone." (I shall not resist; I know that it is fated.)

No one suspects the tacit engagement; the eyes rapidly calm down, reflections of the pointless things arranged to their left and right. They separate. Meanwhile, two amorous roses come together at the same time.

Then there are the officious requests for information, awkwardly sought. Amiable competences open their registers. "Mademoiselle ***? Yes, I know who you mean. A young woman producing a good yield, marriageable, in possession of a heap of distinguished talents, linked on one side to the Richbadern family and connected on the other with the Nobleveaux; to make an offer address oneself to Madame X*** or her parents."

Chats at balls; conversations here and there; decisive words; final confession and submission to the necessity of loving one another and telling one another so; the indiscretion of the indifferent and the hostility of those predisposed to malevolence intervene; stations at the various customary ceremonies, encounter in some Comic Opera to the musical gallop of de Villars' dragoons—what a pity! Horrible formalities delay their union further. Here comes the pomp of the promised Day, on which it is necessary to tolerate the assault of the annoying one last time . . .

In the evening, before getting into the sleeping-car on the honeymoon voyage, amid the sensual finalities, he says to her very, very softly: "You know that I'm yours forever, *such as I am.*"

And she says a solemn: "Yes, me too."

And the train takes them away.

Oh, the admirable, radiant and perfect honeymoon voyage! They stopped in a corner of the Norman strand where, much later, the memory of their famous amours and the piety of misunderstood lovers will create a fashionable beach.

For the moment, they were alone, or almost, as if in an Eden to which the Celestial Vaucanson had added to the other animals anthropoids with cotton bonnets and faces of the ruddiness of placid digestion.

There, he gave her a guided tour of his especially precious soul, so carefully planted with the most beautiful orchids, which do not grow in just anybody's brain: greenhouse imaginings. Then too, he had read so many misunderstood and ignored books . . .

She listened, genuinely delighted; never, even in the course of her most emphatic flirtations, had she been taken into such a fabulous soul. What had she to exhibit in exchange? Her poor little Cinderella soul, furnished by education with faded chromo-lithographs that she hastened to throw out. She had a desire to weep, because she did not feel herself to be "at the right height."

She knew that he was ornamented by the qualities of a Master of lifelong amour: how vulgar those of the heroes of her novels, seemed thereafter! And he, proud and smiling, certainly, was glad to have conserved himself, thus far, worthy of that exquisite ad-mirer. He did not tell her that, and that was his initial stupidity; should he have given her leverage on himself? No, but rather than leave her with the anxiety of not having "made an impression" and only replying "Thank you," when she said to him: "I will love what you love, for love of you, dear heart!"

Once, she interrogated him about his past. "My love," he said, suddenly serious. "Do you remember: *such as I am*. I date from our first kiss; I shall die in our last." She did not insist.

Winter came and they agreed to go home. He wanted his beloved to reflect for his lover other aspects of the world, in order to perfect her, the estimable stock-breeder; there were further initiations in various Fine Arts, in which she showed her self to be increasingly subtle.

They were obliged to see people, against whom they put themselves on guard; any happiness suspected of being of noble essence is an insult and a theft committed against the public, for it is forbidden to be happy apart.

So, what had to happen happened, because what has to happen always does, as philosophers have observed. A former friend, visiting, said to her: "And . . . you're happy?"

"Better than that." Her ecstatic eyes were gazing at the horizon.

"Bah! Is your husband faithful?"

"Am I not myself?"

"Good, good. I thought . . . with preparations like his . . . ? For you must know details of . . . you know . . . his anterior life?"

"Not at all. I love him *as he is*, and don't know anything beyond that."

"Well, that's strange! All wives ask their husband to tell them the story of his life, it's expected."

"Oh?" (Already she was sad.) "You think he had one of those youths that speak for themselves?"

"So it's said. Anyway, no one has precise details or names. So . . . *au revoir*, my little confidante."

The friend departed with that, the abominable woman. You can understand that if she had persisted, Lady Bluebeard would have risen to her feet with a fine gesture of indignation.

That evening, Sir Max found her anxious and distracted. She waited for nightfall, which lends itself to confidences, and sighed, in a low voice: "My beloved, do you love me a great deal?"

"Yes, I love you more than anything."

"And . . . you've only ever loved me?"

"I love you more than anything."

"And . . . you've only ever loved me?"

"I love you more than anything."

"Oh, you don't want to understand, wicked man. You haven't loved other women as much as me?"

"Imprudent child, you're in the process of waltzing amid porcelain vases; be careful you don't break something."

"Oh! You're scaring me. Tell me immediately, I insist. Have you loved other women?"

He sealed her eyelids with two definitive kisses. "My adored wife, there is a surprising adventure of an apple in the Bible. Think about it, I beg you, and go to sleep, for it's time."

A first attempt, so be it. She returned to the charge two days later.

"If you could see how inconsiderate you're being! Be thankful to me for keeping quiet. The past, when one opens it up, blows a deadly wind that would chill our dear amorous plant. I don't want to talk about it."

"Yes, yes! Speak. I'm unhappy to the point of moving a confessor to pity. The desire to know is pinching the marrow of my bones. I can no longer enjoy pleasures and life; I'm like a poor thirsty dog lingering at a dried-up well."

"Don't you trust me any longer? If I keep quiet it's because I need to keep quiet. Don't you know, darling, that it's even more dangerous to be jealous of the past than it is to be jealous of the present. Don't interrogate me."

For days and months she was obsessive. She searched antique writing desks, distressed because she discovered nothing there; the drawers ought to have contained packets of letters tied up with ribbons. She sniffed them, trying to rediscover the extinct perfume of the flowers that had faded there. Henceforth, existence seemed dolorous to her, so much did her desire torture her, and no joy was able to render her completely free.

He observed it, but her will was no longer in his control; he had given her an order: "I don't want you to worry any longer," but she had continued; he became more irritated as she ceased to contain herself. There were chills, almost quarrels. And when she did not speak, her eyes, tenacious eyes of curiosity, implored and threatened him. She took interminable detours in order to end abruptly with the question: "What and who were the women that you loved before?" Their amour was irredeemably attained.

Then, seeing her deteriorate, go pale and wither under the ardor of her anxiety, he was seized by an immense, melancholy commiseration. One evening, when she no longer had the strength to harass him—apart from her eyes, which never gave up—he said to her: "My beloved darling, I implore you by our amour and your promises. We are within a hair's breadth of the greatest of catastrophes."

She shook her head. "Go, I no longer love you."

He became irritated. "Shall I be the eternal Lohengrin, then! You, I've chosen you, having scarcely reflected, without a formed passion. I have fashioned you in my image and now you too have been attained by the rust of jealousy. So be it; interrogate me; I will respond. Now, I will talk."

"No, I'm afraid. I no longer want it now. Dear heart, keep your secret."

"Tomorrow the serpent will return, and there will be new struggles, of which I'm weary. You've worn away the hard shell. You wanted to open the cabinet in which the dead of the past sleep. Go in, then, and take the spectacle for your happiness, for that is the price that it will cost you. I have loved six women . . ."

And he listed them all. The first, Pandora, so pale and so frail that he did not even possess her, suddenly vanished rather than died. She was nevertheless the first, the guardian of years of suffering. She could not imagine that she had inaugurated his heart, and died of the desire to know that which was not.

The second, Eva, he loved for a long time; then the desire seized her in her turn; from then on she was dead to his heart.

The third, Elsa, discovered the secret at the price of her body. He repudiated her, ashamed of himself and her.

The fourth, Psyche, stole a forgotten portrait from him while he was asleep. On awakening, he perceived the crime and fled in order not to strangle her.

The fifth, Delilah, almost killed him; she exasperated him and her contralto could be heard in the street. He told her the secret, and that was it.

The sixth, Ophelia, also wanted to know it, and went mad.

"Now," he said, "there's no longer any remedy. In your turn, you're entering the Cabinet of the Dead, the Cabinet of the Past; and since you have failed—you, the most perfect, the elect of the ultimate amour—it must be the case there is no love that curiosity does not kill. If I had kept the secret you would be dead in life, not in my heart; I have not had the strength to save you from life.

"Now, having had a union of absolute confidence, it is stained by mistrust, and dolor will not befit us. There is no Sister Anne to discover the cavaliers of hope from the top of the tower; all is finished. Adieu."

He kissed her lips for a long time, while she wept, and having laid her out on her bed with her hands joined like a dead bride, he left, never to return.

Since then, Bluebeard's seventh wife has wandered through the world, searching for her husband. Clad in the lilac of widows, she weeps for her deadly weakness, and if she pauses, she relates her story for the edification of little girls, the deplorable story of Perdita.

TRISTAN BERNARD
(1866-1947)

Tristan Bernard was born Paul Bernard; he does not seem to have been related to Lazare Bernard, alias Bernard Lazare. He studied law and then embarked on a career managing velodromes, but became involved in journalism and writing vaudevilles along with his brother-in-law, Pierre Veber, similarly writing for *La Revue Blanche* during its Symbolist phase. He was arrested and interned during the Nazi occupation, but—unusually—released rather than being transported to a concentration camp.

"Avatars" first appeared in *La Revue Blanche* octobre 1892; the translation is original to the present volume.

Avatars

And the one who made the manna fall
rejoiced in his heart
Judges II: 27.[1]

Reality, the murderer of possibilities . . .
Harpagon.

A feminine but very honest voice, one of those voices that seeks not so much to seduce as to convince, was reading on the other side of the wall.

I had dragged my wicker armchair all the way to the corner of the familiar garden, and I was exerting great efforts on the first chapter of a consecrated book. My hunger for reading had been sated by a sixty-five-page introduction, and my snobbery was not spurring me on sufficiently to continue.

"The *Figaro* now," said the voice from the neighboring garden.

"Yesterday, the Comédie-Française had one of the most prestigious evenings in the history of the theater. The interpretation was perfect. But all the honor of the performance and the greater part of the success revert to the author, Monsieur Gabriel Munroe, unknown yesterday, famous today . . ."

I listened until the end of the dithyrambic article. At the end, the author threw a handful of praise to Mademoiselle Bartet, another to Lebargy, a pinch of mixed grain to Proudhon, and emptied the crumbs of his sack over the likes of Garraud, Baillet and Laroche, who ran avidly to peck at them. Having read all the week's newspapers regularly, and that morning's very attentively, I was very surprised, for I had not seen any trace anywhere of that performance; no journalist had made any mention of it recently.

---

1 This reference is fictitious. So is the other.

Interview with Glabre, the gardener: "Can you, who know the entire neighborhood, tell me who lives in the little cottage next door?"

Leaning over a pot of flowers, Glabre does not move immediately. An obscure mastication is taking place between his jaws. Then he raises his head, pleased, all things considered, to be interrogated, and smiles with ease between his unequal cheekbones.

"It's Mademoiselle Munroe who lives there with her brother, a poor devil of a paralytic, who's blind into the bargain!"

"Aha! Thank you." I return to my armchair and Glabre to his glebe.

✳

Fatally, the next day, Sunday, I met Mademoiselle Mouneraud— not Munroe. She was a spinster about thirty years old, rather robust. I noticed her dark eyes, very kind, in which a spark of mockery glinted at times, her complexion of an insufficiently womanly woman, which the probable exclusive abuse of fresh water must have jaundiced slightly. We were introduced to one another, we chatted, and we left together. I asked her point-blank why she read imaginary reviews in her garden. She blushed and told me the whole story.

Père Mouneraud had been a solicitor in Reims, in the Rue des Marteaux-Chantants. The premature death of her mother and the care required by her brother, four years younger than her, had developed in the young woman a precocious maternal instinct (cf. Coppée, *Contes* and Daudet, *passim.*).

When her father died, she was twenty-five years old. She came to join her brother in Paris, who was sagely following his studies in law and literature there. It was shortly thereafter that the consequences of a chill developed a whole series of hereditary maladies in the young man: paralysis, visual troubles, etc. (See specialist works.)

Mademoiselle Mouneraud installed her brother in the country and, as he had become completely blind, she completed to his dictation a drama in verse that she had to submit to the readers of the Théâtre Française. The drama was refused.

"But, you understand, I couldn't tell him that. I preferred to lie and to carry my lie through to the end. I read him the official letters, the readers' opinions, the summons to rehearsals, all the way to the requests for rewrites, for the sake of plausibility. Thee days ago, I fabricated the first articles, and that same night, I wrote Monsieur Sarcey's review from beginning to end.[1]

"If you knew how happy he is—but something still astonished him and upset him. He was expecting a visit from Monsieur Claretie . . ."[2]

She stopped, seemingly hesitating over a request . . .

✳

Well, it's done. Henceforth, my name is Claretie, my forename Jules. It's understood that I've just rented a sumptuous villa in a neighboring village. In order not to compromise the drama in question, which Mademoiselle Mouneraud gave me this morning, I've read it. It is, it seemed to me, a possible and plausible Bornier,[3] which the Comédie might have been able to put on without peril. This evening, I was introduced to the author.

Assuredly, my heart had already revealed my generosity to me many a time. Had I not sometimes felt ready to sacrifice my life to cheer up a sad beautiful woman, to gather under my solicitude some pretty baby, not too shrill, and blonde. The pity that I experienced in Mouneraud's presence was certainly less comfortable, but more hygienic for my moral health.

His deformity is only moving on reflection. In spite of his already-gray hair, he gives the impression of a child of sixteen, with his tapering skull, his beardless chin and his seemingly

---

1 The notoriously conservative theater critic Francisque Sarcey (1827-1899) became a particular object of hatred for the Symbolists and Naturalists alike. The humorist Alphonse Allais published a series of fake articles bearing his signature, which subjected him to merciless abuse and ridicule.

2 Jules Claretie (1840-1913) was the director of the Théâtre Français from 1885 until his death, and was elected to the Académie in 1888 (even Immortals sometimes find it politic to suck up to those who have jurisdiction over their careers). His fiction—although not the titles cited below—is now most interesting for its pioneering dramatizations of various state of abnormal psychology.

3 The French word *bornier* now refers to a kind of electrical connection, but Bernard's capitalization implies that what his metaphor is intended to suggest is a then-popular brand of mustard.

hammered-in nose. He would be ugly if he didn't have closed eyes. So I didn't struggle against the learned aversion that a brother devoid of apparent genius always inspires in me.

Such is the individual in which we are cultivating, like fervent botanists, a marvelous flower of joy.

※

Sometimes, little alerts shake us. Dining with the Mounerauds yesterday evening, Claretie heard mention of his works, of which he only knew the titles. Without the clever assistance of Mademoiselle Mouneraud, Claretie would have been sunk. That same evening, I procured from the reading room *Les Amours d'un Interne, Prince Zilah, Monsieur le Ministre*, etc., which I devoured with the delight of martyrs, and—shall I confess it?—with an inestimable benevolence. For, I must admit, I sense myself becoming favorable to Monsieur Claretie. This morning, an article that defamed him vexed me. That imaginary self, annexed scarcely a week ago, is already under the protectorate of my vanity.

※

What have we done to merit the rare sensuality of being able to create happiness easily and cheerfully? Isolated from the world by the providential veil of his eyes, Mouneraud is stupidly living a special lie, made to measure, of which we are the benevolent artisans.

Yesterday we talked about the red ribbon. He wouldn't refuse it, but he doesn't covet it, he affirms; we'll decorate him with it next July fourteenth, and, if he still affirms his disdain, who knows whether we might not bring the date forward slightly and have him favored by a special appointment.

One of my relatives, duly primed, has come on behalf of the editor of the *Éclair* to ask him his opinion about a passionate drama. Has not the *Revue des Deux Mondes* just written asking for a new one? He was photographed this week for *L'Illustration*.

He has a desire, born of his eighteen years, to enter into communication with his favorite writers.

"Who are they?" Monsieur Claretie asked. And Mouneraud, in a tone that is usually nasal, but which became emotional for the occasion, confessed that they were Cherbuliez and Sully Prudhomme, not to mention Pailleron.[1]

Tomorrow I shall see two of my friends, one of whom will imitate, at my desire, the poet and the other the vaudevillist. It is impossible to find a Cherbuliez. After a conference, we afflicted the Genevan novelist with an arthritis that confined him to his home.

✳

We would have acted sagely in also leaving Sully Prudhomme in Paris. He had been very obliging at first, exaggerating in accordance with vague reports the delicacy and fragility of his person, saying in a soft murmurous voice things that seemed quite appropriate in consequence. Then, retained to dinner, he unleashed dirty jokes at us over dessert and assured us that his works are stuffed full of obscene double meanings, which those in the know have no difficulty perceiving. I was obliged to say to him:

"Master, my desire is to keep you, but our duty is to warn you that you only have fifteen minutes to catch the train." Supported by a somewhat shy but sufficiently worthy Pailleron, he finally reached the platform.

✳

All jokes have a punch-line. The Grim Reaper, suitably equipped, was summoned to the Mouneraud house last night; his soul was carried away, by virtue of which only his illnesses were known. The envoy of God offered a broad range of excuses.

Mademoiselle Mouneraud and I kept vigil over the body, without daring to give ourselves away—for what if we had been overheard?

This morning, behind the bier, there were no delegations, no guard of honor, and nor crowned heads, only a few women from the village, the sister of the deceased, two uncles from Reims and the administrator of the Comédie Française, removed from office by virtue of an irrevocable decree.

---

1 The prolific novelist Victor Cherbuliez (1829-1899), the Parnassian poet Sully Prudhomme (1839-1907) and the dramatist Édouard Pailleron (1834-1899), all Academicians, would have been regarded as somewhat old-hat by the *avant garde* of the *Revue Blanche*; Sully Prudhomme had not yet been awarded the Nobel Prize for literature when Bernard wrote the story.

JUDITH GAUTIER
(1845-1917)

Judith Gautier was the daughter of Théophile Gautier and, briefly, the wife of Catulle Mendès. Her work frequently employs Oriental settings, often using the symbols of Chinese or Japanese culture as a means of organizing story-arcs, and routinely adopts a distanced narrative tone typical of a good deal of Symbolist writing, while lending itself to a *conte cruel* seasoning. Her most relevant collections include *Les Princesses d'Amours* (1900), *Le Collier des jours* (1902) and *Le Paravent de soie et d'or* (Fasquelle 1904).

"Une Descente aux enfers" and "L'Impératrice Zin-Gou" both appeared in *Le Paravent de soie et d'or*. "Descent into Hell" and "The Empress Zin-Gou" were originally published in the sampler *Isoline and the Serpent-Flower* (Black Coat Press, 2013).

A Descent into Hell

One day, the beautiful Miou-Chen awoke from a long sleep. She was in a wild forest, lying on lotus flowers; a tiger the color of jade was asleep at her feet.

While she scanned her surroundings with a surprised gaze, she saw a young boy with shiny brown skin coming through the trees, who was carrying a flag that was flapping in the air and brushing the foliage.

The child approached and, setting the flagpole on the ground, bowed to her.

"I have come to you by command of the Lord of the Hells," he said. "The great Jade King admires your wisdom, and if your courage is unfailing he will consent to let you pass through the gate of the terrible city of Fou-Tou-Tchan and visit his realm."

Miou-Chen rose to her feet without trembling, and gazed at the narrow strips of blue sky through the dark foliage.

"Wherever I am, so long as my virtue does not weaken," she said, "the Master of Heaven will protect me."

"Come, then," said the boy, lifting up his bloody banner. "The King of the Ten Hells is waiting for you at the golden bridge of Pou-Tien."

He cleared a path through the branches noisily, and Miou-Chen followed him.

They emerged from the forest and entered a solitary valley. After having walked for some time, Miou-Chen perceived a man sitting on the ground at the entrance to a cave, and stopped in surprise, for the man was surrounded by a band of demons who were attacking him, while scorpions scaled his body. To his left were beings with the bodies of leopards and frightful faces, stirring red-hot chains and shaking furious serpents. A frightful she-devil, her breasts pendulous, her head shaven and her muscles stripped of flesh, was holding a frog by the foot, and was jiggling it in front of the victim's eyes, laughing stupidly and toothlessly. To his right, two young women of superhuman beauty, magnificently ornamented, but allowing foxes' tails and deformed feet to be glimpsed beneath their robes, were displaying the gleam of their beautiful smiles and seductive gazes, while their rosy lips murmured soft words.

Miou-Chen said to the King of the Hells' envoy: "Who is that unfortunate man?"

"That man is the sage Ma-Min. The great Jade King has sent his devils to tempt him."

Then Miou-Chen drew nearer to the sage. "O Ma-Min," she said, "I see your immaculate thought rising from your forehead like a vapor and forming a glorious cloud that will raise you up to the realm of the immortals."

Then the young woman continued on the route toward the Hells. She arrived in the province of Sée-Tchoen, and reached the golden bridge that ends at the Gate of Hell. As she was about to cross it, she was forced to retreat by a tumultuous host of men and beasts, which was running from the other end of the bridge.

As she stood there, astonished, her young guide said to her: "You see here those who are returning to life in a new form. These superb kings were once poor and virtuous; these deformed beggars were once full of pride; these reptiles crawling and hissing have been envious and crafty men; these birds were young fools with light and careless hearts; as for that herd of donkeys rushing and braying, they're mostly former functionaries devoid of probity."

When the noisy troop had drawn away, Miou-Chen went over the bridge and found herself in front of the arched gate—yellow, like an imperial gate—of Fou-Tou-Tchan, the Severe City. To either side of the entrance two demons, one with the head of an ox, the other with the head of a horse, were posted as sentinels; a third being, the color of soot, whose head was made of iron, was sweeping the threshold. As the young woman approached, it drew aside and the gates opened. She went in; the two heavy battens closed behind her, with a plaintive clang.

She went along the broad streets of the City of Justice, following the crowd of the newly dead, whom soldiers were driving toward the Palace of Supreme Judgment. At the corners of the crossroads she saw, along with heaps of useless debris, old torn-up account-books and instruments of torture worn out by overuse and no longer good for anything. Further on, however, active blacksmiths were hammering their anvils and twisting iron.

The boy who was guiding Miou-Chen went into the hall of a vast palace, and the young woman followed him. Then she perceived the Jade King on his throne. She admired his head-dress fringed with pearls and his face, the color of a ripe orange, exhaling honesty and equity. Facing him, on a platform, stood the ultimate tribunal, where the great judge Loun-Yo was seated, beneath two banners flamboyant with stars, assisted by numerous servants riffling through and setting in order the dossiers of the summoned dead. All around the hall were the mandarins of Hell: Fou-Chou, the bearer of the three-pronged lance; Pen-Tchan, the gourmand, the pou-sah of good cheer; Ti-Tsan, the priest of the infernal cult; and Ta-Tcha, the nocturnal spy who records insomnias and criminal dreams.

The Jade King bowed to Miou-Chen and said to her: "Would you care, young woman, to descend with me the seventy-two stairs of Hell?"

She made an affirmative gesture and the King got up from his throne. Then Miou-Chen saw a yawning gulf in the middle of the hall, and the first steps of a stone stairway. The King began to descend; she followed him, pale and trembling, and plunged into the heavy darkness of Hell.

Soon, howling and sobbing rose up like a bitter wind. The young woman saw a precipice beneath her, populated with serpents, dragons and furious monsters; a narrow bridge traversed it, guarded by the demon of that hell, assisted by a warrior with the head of an ox, bearing a placard on which was written: *Good and Evil*. The damned were driven toward that bridge and, stumbling, full of terror, they fell, with cries of horror, into the gaping and avid mouths.

"This is the first region of penitence," said the King. "You can see the ambitious, the cruel and those swollen with pride."

And he continued the descent.

She then saw a pale and motionless demon sitting on a throne of ice, its body covered in snow, and, as if caught in crystal shackles, the reddened heads of condemned individuals, whose teeth were chattering with a sinister sound, passing at regular intervals over the hard surface of the pool.

Miou-Chen wept, and her tears froze on her lashes.

"These men are the avaricious and the implacable rich, who allowed supplicant mendicants to die at the doors of their palaces," said the Jade King.

They reached the third hell, where women attached to stakes were being tortured. Several demons with bloody bodies were tearing out their entrails and replacing them with hot coals, then sewing up the skin again.

"Those are adulterous wives. Let their guilty entrails be subjected to burning remorse."

And the King plunged on toward the fourth region. There was a vast sea of blood therein, in which a host of men and women were fighting, while the gondola of that hell's devil sailed its thick waves. That devil was entirely clad in white and wore an immense conical hat on its head. When the damned approached to climb into the boat, it gouged out their eyes, ripped out their tongues, and writhed with laughter as it repelled them with kicks.

"You're witnessing the torment of debauchees and women of loose morals," said the King. "That white devil is Ti-Fan, who presides over storms."

Miou-Chen went down a few more steps and saw the fifth hell, the floor of which was paved with trenchant blades, over which the demons cause iniquitous judges and calumniators to run incessantly.

The sixth hell was the most terrible. The devil that ruled it, with his one-eyed face the color of ebony, bristling with red hairs, was the most redoubtable of devils. Under his orders, the damned, imprisoned in wooden troughs are slowly and methodically sawed by toothed implements.

On penetrating into that region, Miou-Chen sighed, and put her hand over her eyes, but the Jade King said to her: "Don't groan like that, young woman, for these men are parricides."

They went rapidly down the lugubrious stairway and reached the seventh hell, where the victims were howling in boiling oil. They were poisoners.

The young woman, her heart full of sadness, shedding floods of tears, arrived in the eighth circle, and saw that an enormous cutlass, rising and falling, was slicing the bodies of thieves and murderers into a thousand pieces.

In the ninth infernal region iron mills were crushing arsonists, while furious dogs were licking up the blood and tearing shreds of flesh from the victims.

She finally reached the last of the ten hells, where the teeth are broken in the mouths of liars and their tongues are torn out with red-hot pincers. There, she threw herself to her knees and, wringing her arms, cried: "A-Mi-To-Fo!"[1]

Then, lost in ardent prayer, she remained motionless for a long time.

---

1 "O Great Buddha!" [Author]

Then, slowly, a rain of lotus-blossoms descended to the ground; from circle to circle, the demons' cries of rage were heard, and the sound of instruments of torture breaking; the damned, delivered from their suffering, intoned songs of joy, the sound of which flew toward the western sky.

✳

Miou-Chen is venerated today in China and Japan, under the name Kouanine or Kouan-Chi-In. She is the Goddess of Mercy.

The Empress Zin-Gou

It is evening; the imperial palace is asleep; the guards are on watch; all is tranquil.

Invisibly, however, a man has climbed over the wall, slipped through the courtyards and the gardens, and now, abruptly, he is penetrating into the apartment of the Empress, who is already asleep.

In the bedroom, perfumed like a temple, the lamps are burning, veiled with silk. The man advances without hesitation; the parquet creaks beneath his feet and the Empress wakes up with a start, but does not cry out.

She looks at the man, and recognizes him. It is the handsome general Také-Outsi-No-Soukouné. He is clad in battle-armor, all stained with dust and blood imperfectly wiped away.

With a feverish gesture, she tears apart the gauze mosquito-net and leaps toward him, tall, beautiful and graceful in her long, pale nocturnal garments.

"You, here," she exclaims, "far from the combat! What has happened? Defeat?"

Také-Outsi prostrates himself. "No, Princess," he says, "but worse than that."

"What? What, then?"

"The descendant of the gods, the sublime Emperor, your husband, is dead. He was fighting at the head of his warriors, leading them to victory. A Korean arrow struck him. He has returned to the celestial abode."

"Ah! My presentiments!" cried the Empress, clenching her fingers in her long, scattered tresses. "The supernatural advice that was given to me that the master of Japan ought not to march in person against that people. Tisou-Ai-Teno did not want to believe me, and he is no more! He has quit the earth, the heroic spouse the son of the Prince of Warriors, who, out of filial piety, assembled more than a thousand white birds, his father's soul having taken refuge in the body of a *sira-tori*, the heron with large wings! Where, in its turn, is the soul of the tender son? Alas, alas, where is it?"

Suddenly, however, the Empress calmed down, shook her proud head and made a sign to the general bidding him to get up.

"Then all is lost," she said. "Victory has escaped us."

"Nothing is lost, my sovereign," said Také-Outsi, who remained on his knees. "Everything is merely suspended. I brought the body of the Mikado back in my arms, and laid him in his tent, saying that he was merely wounded, that he would be healed. Then, confident in the guards, who would pay with their lives for the slightest indiscretion, I left in secret and, sowing my route with dead horses, arrived at your feet.

The handsome warrior raised his eyes toward the charming queen, who, her head inclined, was also looking at him. She read in that ardent soul heroism, genius, devotion, perhaps affection. And she, simultaneously omnipotent and weak, understood that, with the support of such a heart, she might become redoubtable, invincible. A strange and entirely new sentiment quivered within her, made of ambition and courage. As if the soul of her spouse had come to reinforce her own, she felt ready to confront any danger—her, the nonchalant coquette who trembled at the slightest anticipation!

"Thank you, illustrious leader," she said to Také-Outsi. "You have done what needed to be done. The Mikado still lives; he is only wounded. Tomorrow, we will go to join him in the camp. I shall replace him. We shall march to victory. You, Také-Outsi, shall be the support of the Empire; I give you the title of Nai-Dai-Tsin."

✳

For several days, the illustrious Empress Zin-Gou has been *en route*. Také-Outsi accompanies her, and a new troop, which she is taking to reinforce the army, follows her.

The lancers march at the head, armored, with visored helmets extended over the nape and ornamented in front with a sort of copper crescent, lance in hand and a little flag planted behind the left ear. Then come the archers, their foreheads encircled by a strip of white cloth, the ends of which float behind, backs bristling with long arrows, each holding a great lacquered bow in his hand. A new corps of archers has joined that one, and the soldiers composing it carrying bows of singular form, with the aid of which one launches stones, and which is of recent invention.

The foot soldiers advance after them, armed with halberds, two-handed swords and axes; their faces are covered by grimacing black masks, bristling with moustaches and red eyebrows; their helmets are ornamented with copper antennae or large deer-horns; others hide behind hoods of mail, which only allow their eyes to be seen.

And above these marching troops floats a whole host of banners and insignia of the most various forms.

The Empress, on a fine horse whose plaited mane forms a sort of crest, her feet in large sculpted stirrups, marches in the lead, and they arrive thus at the edge of a river called Matsoura-Gawa.

Then the beautiful Zin-Gou orders a halt. She is still a woman, and a singular idea has occurred to her. She wishes to fish with a hook in that river.

Standing on a little mound, she casts the line and says in a loud voice: "If I am to succeed in my enterprise, the bait will be taken; if not it will remain intact."

A great silence reigns; all gazes are fixed on the light buoy floating on the water. There it is, oscillating and dancing; with a swift gesture, the sovereign lifts the line, at the end of which a smelt is wriggling, shining like a dagger.

Joyful acclamations burst forth.

"Forward!" cries Zin-Gou. "The fleet awaits us, and victory is certain."

They arrive at the harbor of Kaifi-No-Oura. The fleet appears magnificent and formidable; the great junks resemble monsters, and their sails are like wings. The mariners cheer the imperial army, which responds with a long cry.

The sovereign dismounts; she advances to the edge of the waves and, taking off her golden helmet, lets down her long hair. To efface its perfumes, she bathes in the sea, then winds her tresses and puts them up again in the form of a single chignon, such as the men wear. Then she seizes a battle-ax, and embarks on the most beautiful of the junks.

There, to everyone, the warrior Empress appears as on a pedestal. She has put on armor of black horn, whose plates, joined by threads of crimson silk, hang down below her knees, over the ample trousers of white brocade with cloudy designs, tightened at the ankles. She has black velvet shoulder-pads and enormous, exceedingly majestic sleeves that hang down to the ground, forming a kind of cloak. They are made of a cloth sown with gold florets disposed in diamonds, and uniformly lined with satin.

A golden chrysanthemum shines on the breastplate of the armor; the tall conical helmet is retained by a silken braid knotted beneath the chin; the battle-ax is passed through the belt beside two sabers, and the warrior woman leans on a staff of ivory and gold as long as a pike.

The sails stretch in the wind, and the waves rock the ships, while Zin-Gou, her gaze lost in space, cries: "Look! Look! The sea-god Foumi-Yori-Mio-Zin will be our guide and march before us!"

She is alone in perceiving the god of the sea, but no one doubts her word.

The king of Korea trembles and weeps in the depths of his palace. His Estates are invaded, his soldiers defeated. Before the invincible Japanese army, no resistance is possible, and before going into combat he feels vanquished.

Already the conquerors have taken the city. The warrior Empress is at the palace gates. She is truly animated by the soul of a hero. She it is who, through tempests and obstacles, has led her army to so many victories.

She is the first to launch the assault, crossing the ditch and hammering at the royal door, crying in a ringing voice: "The king of Korea is the dog of Japan!"

The battens burst and collapse, and the conquerors pass over the debris.

Above the entrance she has her ivory and gold pike suspended, which will remain there for centuries.

It is the hour of carnage and pillage; the soldiers finally want payment for the blood they have spilled; they are only waiting for the sovereign's order.

But here comes the king of Korea, his head bowed, his hands tied behind his back, advancing through his court of honor, strewn with the dead and the wounded. He has chained himself like a prisoner, and he is coming to humiliate himself, to submit, to surrender . . .

"I am your slave!" he cries, with a sob, falling at the feet of the beautiful warrior woman.

Then, beneath the rude breastplate, the woman's heart awakes and is moved. Zin-Gou lifts the poor King to his feet, unties his bonds.

"You are not my slave," she says. "You shall remain king of Korea, but you will be my vassal."

And she forbids the pillage of the city. They will only take possession of the King's treasures, reserving for her the paintings and the works of art, all the beautiful things created by China that Japan cannot make as yet.

Despair is succeeded by joy; the conqueror is acclaimed as magnanimous, who seeks her personal recompense in the eyes of the handsome Také-Outsi, increasingly troubled by admiration and affection.

❋

Today it is more than thirteen centuries since the glorious Zin-Gou-Gvo-Gou returned triumphantly to her capital, gave birth to a son, and followed the course of a long and happy reign. And can one not say that in the modern Japan, so avid for progress, so different from the old, nothing has nevertheless changed?

The soldiers no longer wear the black helmet decorated with shiny horns; instead of the bow "of recent invention" that hurls stones, they have the most up-to-date cannon and rifles—but they are still the same intrepid heroes, disdainful of life.

The Mikado who reigns today, Mitsou-Hito, the Conciliatory Man, of the divine dynasty that, according to the official formula, reigns over Japan "since the beginning of time and forever," is the direct descendant of the illustrious Empress Zin-Gou. The cycle inaugurated by her accession to the throne is named Mé-Dgi, "the luminous reign," and it does, indeed, shine in a brilliant fashion. The present sovereign, whose victories astonish Europe, is certainly worthy of his forebears, and the Sun Goddess Tien-Sio-Dai-Tsin, his radiant ancestor, can recognize in him the son of her sons, and smile upon him from the heights of Heaven.

HUGUES REBELL
(1867-1905)

"Hugues Rebell" was the best-known pseudonym of Georges Grassal de Choffat, now remembered primarily for his erotic novels, but his collection of poems and prose poems *Les Chants de la pluie et du soleil* (Librairc Charles, 1894) is stylistically innovative, showing a very strong Symbolist influence. Prolific while his career lasted, but always struggling, he died penniless, in wretched circumstances, of peritonitis.

"À une Locomotive" and "Le Mauvais Christ" both appeared in *Les Chants de la pluie et du soleil*; "To a Locomotive" and "The Rotten Christ" are original to the present volume.

To a Locomotive

In the mist, in the smoke, among the stars of blood, the stars of gold, the moons of blue snow, it is you, then, who is whinnying and roaring and spitting flame. Monster of the Infinite!

In the palace of iron where everything is shadow, where everything is something, there are adieux of handkerchiefs and

279

little speeches mingled with other little speeches, and then you go away, lightened of the burden of these strange existences, prolonging your great vanquishing cry over the voiceless plains.

O man, you have created a God to torture you and crush you! How many poor beings have been thrown into torrents, broken in the night of caverns, treated like martyrs, whose very cadavers have disappeared?

What does it matter? That sublime creation was necessary in order to proclaim once again the nullity of your being and the divinity of your thought. That monster was necessary in order that the genius of every people and the richness of the entire earth should be revealed.

How, once again, inexhaustible human genius is preparing to create! Dreams that repose and caress our mind, dragons with vertiginous speed to carry our activity.

O locomotive, you represent well the human soul of this century, which I see bounding and precipitating itself toward the Unknown.

O locomotive, your cry summons me to knowledge, to amour.

Go on, carry me to the end of the world; you know that I have not lost my taste, and my desire has no bounds.

I want to see the sunlit cities where every face has its smile, where the eyes of all the women invite you to the charming embrace;

The somber cities, the cities of the North where existence is a merciless battle, where everyone has his desire for an enemy;

I want to see the blue mountains, and the peaks that evening tints with rose;

The sea with its calms and its angers, its drunken evening song, when all its waves are nothing more than a great hymn of glory or when they are a fury of surf against the rocks;

The intimacy of fields of gold and glaucous pallor in which thyme mingles with Chinese asters;

The little domes of wool of sheep huddled together, so fraternal, so fearful of the immensity;

The wild bulls scattered in the plain;

And the fresh mystery of the forest;

And everything and everyone.

Go, then, traverse the dormant woods, the tumultuous cities, plunge into those caverns that you have had hollowed out, over the rivers, the streams and the torrents.

Go, divinity. Let one beauty more be revealed to us, one new thought come to enrich us.

The Rotten Christ

I have seen him at a bend in the stony path, above the torn hedge, as if trying to raise himself toward the sea, which can be heard in the distance rumbling against the rocks, I have seen him, the rotten Christ!

He was looming up, ugly and ridiculous in the shade of the path, between two muddy pools, on his excessively high cross; I had never surprised any other rustic Christ so pitiful, so paltry in appearance.

All the birds avoided him, like a scarecrow; lovers, when they went past him, stopped laughing and released their embrace.

He had no friends except for old ladies with heads like roasted chestnuts, trembling cripples whom he was able to cause to grimace, and whose tearful eyes amused him in his solitude.

But once I found a gracious young woman in mourning, the widow of some mariner, who was praying in a flood of tears, kneeling before that humiliated body of a slave. She was lamenting, and suddenly, convulsively: "Lord, have pity on me! Lord, have pity on me! I'm suffering so much; how, without your grace, can I bear this unhappiness?"

The poor woman continued praying; then, after a long orison, she went away tranquil, more courageous.

Then, with my cane, I struck the hypocritical consoler, the ignoble gibbet that clodhoppers conserve like a talisman.

"May you be knocked down by the tempest," I said, "emblem of cowardice, you who stole the energy from people and their faculty of enjoyment, and then left them disarmed and miserable. That unhappy woman has hope in you, alas; you reassure her, you lull her with vain promises, but when she abandons herself to the tenderness of weeping, when her eyes have no more tears, she will sense her solitude and her distress, and it will be too late, because she will no longer be able to struggle against life, she will only have the strength to blaspheme. Oh, deceiver, your agony on the cross was not long enough; have, you, then, expiated the sin and the dolor of centuries, all the tortures ordered in your name and so many groans that History has not heard? You have hidden the sun from us, you have hidden the odorous flowers and the sexual flesh—so soft!—and the smile of Nature that acclaims us. Oh, infamous wretch, it is because of you that our youth was sad, that our eyes, sick with tears, cannot see the beauty of things; it is because of you that our terrified imagination can no longer know virile and heroic dreams!"

Thus I became indignant in the evening, while, as if to mock me, the shadow of the cross was magnified.

But that malediction was not vain; stormy nights came, dark administrators of justice that broke the grotesque wood, and, one day, passing along that road again, I perceived him overturned and soiled with mud, barring my path.

And when, after having contemplated that ruin, I went down toward the strand, I saw the sky resplendent with gold, from which armies of clouds and giants of fire were advancing, with light choirs of nymphs and multitudes of hyacinths.

The sea was a seething mass of stones and surf, from which a song as grave as a hymn rose up.

And from the harmonious waves, Venus emerged, in a splendid resurrection, immense, magnificent in youth and beauty, as if joyful in the caress of the wave that furled around her hips of a fecund goddess, and joyful too in the sunlight that inundated her shoulders and set her hair ablaze.

At that moment, from every direction, voices celebrated the joyous rebirth, while an unknown summer blossomed within me.

GASTON DANVILLE
(1870-1933)

"Gaston Danville" was the pseudonym of Armand Blocq. He was the brother of the psychologist Paul Blocq, and declared that in his writings he was trying to develop a new kind of Naturalism based on contemporary psychological theories, especially those of Théodule Ribot. He was, however, one of the authors who supplied the *Mercure de France* with much of its prose during its first few years of existence, including a series of *Contes d'au-delà*, collected under that title in 1893, in which the "beyond" is not the afterlife but the unconscious, and almost all of his short work has a strong Symbolist flavor.

"Des Remembrances (état d'âme)" first appeared in the *Mercure de France* février 1891, and "Les illusoire caresses" in août 1891. "Remembrance" and "Illusory Caresses" were both originally published in the sampler *The Anatomy of Love and Murder* (Borgo Press, 2013).

Remembrance
(A State of Mind)

Pale withered violets, whose white petals have closed again, sadly.

And before the faded bouquet she becomes pensive.

They had picked them together. Memories return to her of that spring day.

Beneath the nascent foliage they had gone forth. A perfumed warmth filled the forest with moist and soft caresses. The tall trees with mossy trunks were enveloped by sunlight, and bees were buzzing there. They had followed a path that opened before them, where verdant arches interlaced above their heads. They walked straight ahead over the moist tender grass, toward distant golden mists. And there were flocks of little birds fleeing with a flutter of wings, flowering bushes that they brushed as they passed, ballets of midges humming in the warm air, and also carpets of anemones and lilies of the valley, undulating and quivering.

All those things made them happy, and they wandered, arm in arm, as if in a dream of love. He did not speak to her for fear of breaking the spell, but his eyes sometimes plunged into hers, informing her of ineffable adorations and extraordinary felicities. Her emotion was delightfully stirred by that exchange of glances, in which their souls sank into the infinity of contemplation. She would have liked to remain like that forever, lulled by the indistinct murmur, the continuous vibration, lost with her beloved in that isolation, in the heart of the protective forest. A vague languor invaded her entire being; she felt surges of confused desire burning her temples.

At the foot of an oak tree, garlanded with ivy, they sat down, and their lips met in a long kiss. Nearby, violets as white as lilies were bowing gracefully on their frail stems, and from florets with partly-opened corollas rose a fresh mist of odorous scents . . .

Oh, the pale withered violets, whose white petals have closed again, sadly.

Now the azure of the skies lights up again, and embalmed breaths of wind come through the open window. But the vision, radiant for her, darkens, because it renders the memories of the past more poignant.

She alone was in love, for her love is so strong that it forgives the ingrate the cowardice of the abandonment. But her wounded heart is still bleeding, and she cannot yet believe the hideous reality. Her suffering is renewed by the dolorous return of those moments, which she had believed to be eternal.

Daisies enamel the meadows; she will not interrogate them any more, the lying flowers that reply deceptively. Birds are singing, which seem to be mocking. Why has this spring come back, so similar to the other—and how odious it is! And further new springs will be reborn, without bringing back her vanished happiness!

Tears trickle from her lowered eyelids.

She allows those tears to flow, whose crystal prismatizes the horror of the at-present, and gradually, the dolor that is their cause vanishes. Her soul becomes serene again and recovers a benevolent calm. The oppression that gripped her with all its force of a clearly irreparable consciousness dissipates.

And, her eyelashes still moist, but with tranquil eyes, forgetful of the past, unconscious of the present, and perhaps confident in the future, she gazes at all that remains to her of a love into which she had put her life—the faded bouquet—and smiles at the pale withered violets, whose white petals have closed again, sadly.

Illusory Caresses

"Poor advisers are the hours of solitude and darkness, when the black moths come to burn their wings of darkness in the flames of Dream! I'm weary, oh, very weary, of stirring vainly, incessantly, the incoherent broth of memories that simmers within me, surging forth at the whim of unexpected, undesired associations, like some villainous fellow, of whose presence you had been unaware, emerging from the fog in front of you.

"Life? An exceedingly monotonous and sad succession of gray things, when not lit up by the blaze of sensual or ambitious desires. And then, even then, it's the forcible, brutal grip of reality, the cruel hand-to-hand battle with the enemy sensation that quickly wearies the initial impulse, avid for better and colliding with the insurmountable barrier of rapid, fatal disgust, against which it dies.

"The arms, extended with faith, with force, toward suspected unknowns, ideals, fall back even more discouraged, limp once again, incapable of recommencement, as soon as they have perceived the interminable withdrawal of the goal, which they take to be a chimera.

"Why, then, continue the series of necessary but futile actions, perpetuating the quest for the unrealizable, and knowing it—why? And suffering the contradictions of its nature, the inevitable impacts, losing oneself in rebellions that have no result? When it would be perfectly simple to descend without shocks, eyes closed, into the soothing calm of the only possible Nirvana: Nothingness! Because, resident in the soul, bruised but lucid, rational and fully conscious, is a minuscule and perfidious leaven of unhealthy curiosity, disappointed in advance, but which nevertheless persists: a need to see whether tomorrow will be similar to yesterday, to today, to every day. Everything tells me that it will be . . . perhaps.

"How often will the problem be posed, without arriving at a solution, and who will compromise in seeking the marvelous, the undiscoverable Edens, the radiant horizons of pure light and voluptuousness, never experienced? Edens fertile in enchantments, infinitely renewed in searching for them in fortuitous, temporary intoxications—immensely attractive, to be sure—whose only flaw is procuring too painful an awakening, too heavy a disillusionment, once they have dissipated.

"These voluntary hallucinations are, therefore, insufficient and injurious, for they favor the intrusion of melancholy and disgust, which await you at every exit—as if existence alone, without that, is insufficient.

"I'm not a skeptic, however, and would like to believe. Believe . . . in what? Experience, acquired with birth, is an ancestral legacy that I cannot reject. Oh, to make a new skin, to revert to the primitive existence that does not lack the essential bases of belief, because the centuries have not destroyed them!

"For the sky is very bleak where the eternally drifting stars shine, the same ones at which the people of thirty centuries ago, or more, gazed . . . how do I know? And what I just said was proffered for the first time a long time ago—a very long time ago. Did it even exist that first time? A risible murmur is that of human speech, the infidel translator of thought . . .

"Here comes the livid light of day, and I haven't slept a wink!"

. . . A diffuse gleam fills the room with a vague clarity. With a few last flickers, the candle-flame goes out; for a moment longer, the fuliginous wick remains red; then it is carbonized, and all light vanishes from the lamp.

His forehead slumped over the books that have distracted his insomnia, an extinct cigarette between his fingers, Jean, his eyes now closed, is drowsy. Only his frowning eyebrows, and a few feverish shifts of position, testify to the continuity of his obsessive preoccupation.

Now, it seems to him that he is far, far away, lost in the depths of an infinite obscurity. The faint chimes of a bell ring feebly in his ears, and also the sound of whispering voices, too low for him to grasp the meaning of the words he can hardly hear. That sound draws nearer, is magnified; it is the formidable buzz of a vast vibrating bronze; then, without any apparent transition, it retreats to the limits of perception, becoming a faint, indistinct, very soft susurrus.

He tries to move; his limbs are flaccid, numb and disobedient. Resigning himself, he takes pleasure in making that condition last, which suspends him between unconsciousness and reason.

"Constraining oneself to the adoration of virtual images, evoked by oneself, without caring whether their presence is real—what's the point? With the acquired sum of sensations, it's sufficient to combine them cleverly; those sheaves of things once glimpsed, grouped in a variable fashion, at the whim of the inclinations of the moment, will take on an adequate appearance of truth, a projection of the will producing almost all their initial intensity. I could thus attain a maximum which, by itself, would confer tangibility, but the limit that separates me from them would be very uncertain and very thin. In sum, that's the ultimate experiment to be attempted; why not risk myself in that adventure, virginal of all exploration . . . ?

"Boletta!"

In response to that appeal, a door opens, and in a flood of light that makes Jean's partly-raised eyebrows blink, a smiling brown-eyed, black-haired child appears on the threshold. The unusual dullness of her pale complexion is tempered by a transparent amber glaze, which, by heightening the flesh-tint, makes her large shadowy eyes seem gentler and more profound, the blood-red of her lips brighter and more attractive, and the nacreous gleam of her teeth, almost entirely uncovered, iridescent. Raising up her torso slightly, she advances, with an extreme grace, and her hands, whose pink fingernails are glistening, form two bright patches at her hips, against the dark cloth in which she is clad.

Like funereal drapery, a heavy, mute and crease-free curtain, silence has fallen again behind her. But soon, at a sign from Jean that she has understood, beneath those little fingers, which become animated—and with what life!—the cello strikes up.

The harmonies, evocative of the hallucinations so greatly desired, weep and sing, growl and sigh, flying around the gloomy room like a long—very long, interminable—procession of phantoms, ungraspable and rapidly disappearing.

"Those notes that are strung out so slowly, seem to me to emanate from the invisible, from exceedingly frail hands . . . and to stroke my brain . . .

"Yes, within my skull I perceive their rapid friction, as gentle as two flower-petals falling. And with them, I fall too, myself . . .

"An anguishing and delectable fall, into blackness, luminous blackness, perhaps roseate. I feel that a single movement—less than that—would stop me . . .

"'I don't want to do that . . . do you hear, Jean? It's necessary not to do that . . .'

"I know that very well, very well . . . no, a veil prevents me from distinguishing . . . oh! That phrase, in which the flats bleed; repeat it again, Boletta . . .

"Now I can see more clearly . . .

"Yes, I know perfectly well where I've heard it before . . .

"Oleanders and lentisks trembling over the violet water . . . so calm . . . with amethyst flamboyances . . . sunlight . . . a white swan . . . marble balustrades . . . and then, too, clumps of hyacinths and daisies . . . exhaling the warm, penetrating odor of swooning corollas . . .

"On the terrace, she's singing in a soft voice . . .

"The yellow and red stripes of the cloth . . .

"Her adorable smile, and the promises of her black velvet eyes . . .

"Always, always, Boletta . . . oh, remain thus, remain forever thus, trembling evocation of what has been, imprecise and troubling apparition! Don't go! What would become of happiness then? And I passed by, so close to her that I might have touched her, but I passed by . . .

"Now . . . now . . ."

He did not finish.

Boletta was on her knees in front of him, sobbing. Abruptly awakened, at first he had a surly expression, and imprecations rose to his lips—but before the little girl's tears, his anger melted away, and, picking her up, he kissed her on the forehead.

"*Cara mia*, it must be time for your lessons. Go and get ready; I'll go with you this morning . . ."

The girl went out, smiling, her eyelashes still moist.

Left alone, Jean folded his arms, and an enigmatic grin creased his mouth.

MAY ARMAND BLANC
(1874-?)

May Armand Blanc wrote four novels, including *Bibelor* (1899), *Mila, roman nouveau* (1900) and *Le Maison des roses* (1901), and published in such periodicals as *La Plume* and *La Fronde*, but seems to have vanished without trace after 1902, presumably having fallen victim either to death or marriage.

"Hamlet," "Medée" and "Lorenzaccio" first appeared in *La Vogue*, juin 1899. The translations are original to the present volume.

Hamlet

Hamlet—you who were asleep in the divine shroud of immortal pages, now liberated, before us, you live, animating our soul with your soul—terrible in being so various . . .

. . . Oh, but what a strange shade yours is—more real than our dream of the real? Your shade, mysterious sister, seems to have obtained, from long slumber, the secret of fear and a voluptuous tender grace . . . your shade, as delicate as youth—and ardent among its puerile songs—totters on the edge of dolor, but it is upright, and a hundred cubits magnified in hatred . . .

You roll your childlike body in wild gestures at the feet of the child you love, and, because you love her and horror embitters your heart, you reject her, and wound her, and kill her . . . were you ever more beautiful, shade of Hamlet, mysterious sister, than in the beautiful rage of no longer being able to love?

. . . Or again, the movement of your arms in a cross above crimes and maternal terrors, immeasurable movement in the shadow, was that—revealing all vengeful glory in a gesture of forgiveness—more beautiful?

But when, ceasing your frightful pursuit, your pursuit of damnation, in which you mingled the appearances of the most sublime unreason, you stop suddenly, and for an instant, on the edge of the tomb that yawns in the slippery earth—the well-rotted earth!—here you are more admirable, O Shade, sister of Hamlet, superior to him. You who recreate him in the magnificent form of a living genius . . . stop, with that skull of one you knew and loved between your delicate hands: that skull in which everything that was animate and sensible is no longer revealed except by one thing—a frightful thing—odor . . . something that still persists after everything . . .

. . . Halted, vacillating between the life that is crumbling around you, within you, and—repose? death?—*words . . . words . . . words* . . . for what name names the unknown?

Is it then that we adore you more for being so beautiful? so human in your terror—and eternal in your thought? Where do you come from, if not from having fathomed the unfathomable that dominates genius—august mystery—the unfathomable—whence comes that level, slow voice, that voice which already seems no longer to be sounding in the free air? and that sadness, so calm—even sadder perhaps than the clamor of your approaching despair?

But, after so many agitations, and such a prodigious movement in which your prodigious soul—in combat with the one who was almost your brother—your soul trembles and writhes, as if, unchained from the chains of the flesh, it is about to spring forth from your pure body, your supernatural eyes, like a great bird of prey . . .

. . . Here you are standing in death, as if in a last and immortal victory . . . finally, your body, Hamlet, lying in the hollows of walls, is borne away—and it seems that everything is finished of your tragic history . . .

But no, from the crowd, and above the crowd, your head appears and is visible again, so young, so blond, so beautiful, tilted back, facing the sky, O Hamlet! And thus, magnificent, you finally live, you who were asleep in the divine shroud of immortal pages . . .

Medea

Imperious and terrifying, she draws her robe woven of moonlight and shadow . . . a dazzling veil, an obscure veil, which, on her body, seems to be a magnificent shroud of joys that cannot die . . .

And, all embroidered with emblems, wrapped around her svelte legs, lifted around her narrow feet, it loosens and tightens like coiling serpents submissive to enchantments.

And from her neck to her cleavage, and sliding from her cleavage to her loins, and flowing from her loins to the ground, there is the bright and rattling splendor of gemstones the color of water and the color of the sky—a blue river, a softly noisy river that sobs and sings to the movement of her—Medea's—howling march amid the rocks.

But in her face haloed by metal in frozen flames, her eyes are murderous and her mouth voluptuous.

O hatred, so supple, insinuated between the amorous teeth that grip the Kiss . . . O tender folly gasping the breath of caresses until drawing blood . . . her eyes and her mouth desire all crime and all amour.

And now, here is all the blood of Hecate upon her, Medea,

and now, again, here is also all the gold of Helios . . . here she is bathed and burned by light on the threshold of the temple, which she bars with her arms in a cross . . . her arms imaging terror . . . charm . . . and, the flowers of gold in your golden hair, witch, are not such flowers as your frail hands, your blonde hands, borne by the marvelous stems of your arms . . . your arms from which spring forth—horrible dew!—the pink blood of your murdered sons . . .

Lorenzaccio

Adolescent, feminine soul . . . almost no soul . . . frail and devouring soul in which the universe is held: and the monster and the apostle in the body of an ephebe . . . an asexual silhouette: visage so pale, figure so somber, sensuality ignites in his abyssal gaze, anxiety clings—a very human rag—to your androgynous feline allure . . . Here you are alone . . .

Here you are also, at the lunar hour, before dormant Florence, between yesterday, which was all debauchery in royal company, and tomorrow, which will be the dawn . . .

Death.

You lean over the window-sill toward the sumptuous City, obscure at the base of its palaces, brightened by its steeples, where the pale sea of stars, as it flows—so slowly—unfurls in a surf of light . . . the city sated—for the hour is nearer to morning than dusk—on the bloody ferment of embraces and murders.

Your hands, Lorenzaccio—ardent, sinuous name, full of languor and strength, like you!—lean on the broad stone where a few handfuls of gilded barley have been thrown for domesticated pigeons . . .

. . . But, because you are also leaning on your soul, your soul, which is approaching its moment of spasm and horrible joy— because all that unslaked soul, Lorenzaccio, is not asleep—for that, and because its horizon is vaster, darker and purer than the

292

horizon of the sky and Florence, for that, your hands now clench mortally on the light seeds, the golden seeds spread here for the doves; and, those hands so pale, those caressant hands, after the gesture that enfevers, exasperates, claws, strangles and murders—in dream!—rise up, appealing to the gods, to the clouds . . . to everything that is not, floating and disappearing . . . and as in a similar interior movement your crushed heart opens, intoxicated by energy, now, around you, all the seeds of golden barley escape from your gaping palms, stream and scatter with a sound of hail . . .

Gesture of your flesh, admirable, triumphant . . . exact gesture of your soul—almost no soul . . . frail and devouring soul in which the universe is held: and the monster and the apostle . . . destructive gesture . . . and liberating . . .

RENÉE VIVIEN
(1877-1909)

"Renée Vivien" (Pauline Mary Tarn, 1877-1909) was introduced into Symbolist circles by one of her lovers, Natalie Barney, but produced the bulk of her work while in a relationship with Hélène de Zuylen de Nyevelt, with whom she collaborated on a number of books under the pseudonym Paule Riversdale. Under her usual pseudonym she published two volumes of prose poems and two further volumes of prose as well as the numerous volumes of poetry that helped to make her notorious as a kind of tragic symbolic embodiment of the Belle Époque: a neurotic, anorexic, alcoholic, suicidal, lesbian doomed to self-destruction.

"Lilith," "Le Foret" and "Le Chant des Sirènes" all appeared in *Du Vert au violet* (1903); "Lilith," "The Forest" and "The Song of the Sirens" are original to the present volume.

Lilith

Fundamentally, believe me, woman has only ever loved the serpent.
Villiers de l'Isle Adam.

Lilith was created before Eve.

She was more beautiful than the Mother of the human race. She was not drawn from the flesh of the man but born from a breath of the dawn.

Her crimson hair set the dusk ablaze and her eyes reflected the beauty of the universe.

When he created Lilith, God destined her to smile at the man. But she considered the man and found him coarse in essence and inferior to herself.

And she turned her eyes away from Adam.

One evening, while she was wandering in the triumphal gardens of Eden, she saw the ineffably dolorous gaze of Satan posed upon her.

He had put on the undulating and supple form of the Serpent, and his eyes were sparkling like pale emeralds.

He said to the woman: "You do not know the mystery of Amour.

"You are wrong to scorn your disgraceful companion, for you can teach him and learn from him unknown joys."

Lilith contemplated the strange eyes, like two pale emeralds.

And she replied to him: "You're lying, and you're tempting me with the vulgar bait of pleasures devoid of beauty.

"You also know the secrets of subtle sensuality that resemble the Infinite.

"You, who are tempting me with amorous words, be my mystical lover.

"I shall not conceive and I shall not give birth under the ardor of your embrace.

"But our dreams will populate the earth, and our chimeras will be incarnate in the Future."

There was a vibrant silence between them.

And from the intercourse of Lilith and the Serpent were born the perverse dreams, the maleficent perfumes and the poisons of revolt and lust that haunt the human spirit and render the human soul similar to the sad and dangerous souls of Angels of Evil.

The Forest

Come into the forest, come into the fraternal darkness. Come, I shall collect for you the flowers that resemble you, the nocturnal flowers that harbor subtle poisons.

I shall ornament your lunar tresses with aconite, foxglove and belladonna . . .

Are you not frightened to be alone with me, in the nocturnal forest that loves me and which hates you?

I should like to flee from your bright eyes, as penetrating as mortal steel; I should like to flee from you and draw you to me.

The branches of the trees incline toward you like long menacing arms that stifle in an embrace of hateful amour.

They might strangle you, but they are impotent against me, because I am the being of silence and solitude.

The entire nocturnal forest menaces you and hates you; it has seen the lie in your eyes, and the peril of your voice, and the cruelty of your caress.

But I love you, while wanting to flee from you, and I will protect you against the forest and against myself.

Tender and true things are begging me to abandon you and flee—the foliage and the ivy, and the moss and the beloved violets.

Only the fervent serpents and the moon rejoice and encourage our amour.

Oh, how sinister the voice of the owls is!

The owls are advising me to abandon you and to flee.

The bats with blue wings go astray, tormented by the weight of their body and the impotence of their wings.

Their soul is similar to my soul. They collide with one another stupidly, and the desire for infinity is in their blind eyes.

I feel, cruelly, the desire to soar . . .

If I could fly, I might perhaps be able to escape you, O incarnation of my desire.

And if I dared to love you, I would kill you, in accordance with the desire of the nocturnal forest, which would bury you under the foliage and under the branches.

I would stifle your last gasp with my kisses . . . Oh, your last gasp in the night! I would stifle you with embraces and caresses, and you would die of my lips . . .

For I am the Lover who cannot love without hate, and whose covetousness is made of bitterness and melancholy.

And you, you are the Evil Mistress who exasperates fevers and intensifies the malady.

Do you not sense the danger around you?

The odor of Death is in the air and is intoxicating me strangely . . .

Oh, how sinister the voice of the owls is!

"The Moon is laughing, the Moon is laughing . . ."

The Song of the Sirens

I

"I should like," said Ione with the violet eyes, lingering on the crepuscular shore, "to hear the Song of the Sirens."

"You know very well," replied the old fisherman Meniskos, "that the Song of the Sirens is mortal to those who hear it."

"Like everything that is beautiful and sonorous," the virgin with the violet eyes interjected, imperiously. "Only things without grandeur contain no danger."

"The sage Ulysses gave his companions the advice to block their ears with wax and attach themselves to the masts of the vessel," added Meniskos.

"Ulysses was nothing but a coward," cried the very young and very imperious Ione. "And his companions were also nothing but cowards. Prudence is eternal cowardice. Oh, to prefer the tedious Penelope to the Sirens! Myself, I would give the breath of my lips, the line, undulations and colors that my avid eyes contemplate with so much anguish, the harmonies that make me suffer so divinely, the perfumes that I respire wit so much fever, everything that makes life burning and sad, to hear the Song of the Sirens for an instant . . . And the kisses of my companions, the kisses that are like harmonies, perfumes, the joy of colors, lines and graceful undulations, the kisses as bitter as the sky and as sweet as roses, I would give them all to hear the perilous Song for an instant."

"In truth, your words are not wise," said old Meniskos, calmly. "What! You would give the long years of a human existence for a lightning flash of joy?"

"You cannot understand, Meniskos," Ione replied. "Men are cowards from birth. Only two instincts make them act: pride and bestiality. No man would ever give his existence to hear the Song of the Sirens."

Meniskos shrugged his shoulders, and went away, toward the hearth and the evening meal. In the twilight, Ione detached the boat, which was lost in the mist in which Visions floated.

She wandered for three days and three nights. And the Sirens appeared to her, in a green moonlight that broke over the waves . . .

Their song was as imprecise as the song of the waves; it attracted like the mysterious appeal of the waves; it unfurled with a grave amplitude, like the sob of the Ocean; it gripped the soul of Ione, who sank voluptuously into the waves . . .

II

She awoke, the drowned child with the violet eyes, under the fluid kisses of a Siren whose hair enveloped her like networks of algae. She awoke under the ungraspable gaze of green eyes, which had the perfidious softness of the waves. She awoke under the troubled smile of the Siren, whose voice, like the distant sound of waves on crepuscular shores, said to her:

"Since you have loved us resolutely enough to give us your human existence, we will give you in our turn the fervor of our kiss. See, I have collected with my own hands, in order to ornament your hair, the pearls that are the pale flowers of the Sea, and multicolored nacre, and the infinite grace of marvelous seashells. Your repose on the velvet of the silver sand will be lulled by the rhythm of the Sea. You will play with the crabs and you will smile at the medusae that burn like the stars. In the gardens of the Sea, living anemones are blue, and in her orchards, trees of coral sway their red branches at the whim of the eddies. You will hear the Sea's song of eternally unappeased amour, the song that rises toward the Moon, her distant Lover. For Death cures all memories, and Death is very beautiful on the bed of the Sea."

ALFRED JARRY
(1873-1907)

Alfred Jarry was closely associated with the Symbolist Movement in the 1890s. Always something of an *enfant terrible*, he caused a minor scandal by turning up at Mallarmé's funeral in bicycle shorts and a pair of yellow shoes borrowed from Rachilde. A prolific journalist, he also collaborated with his close friend Remy de Gourmont on the *avant garde* art periodical *L'Ymagier* (1894-95), initially trailed in the *Mercure de France*. He achieved a spectacular *succès de scandale* with his play *Ubu roi* (1896), while his later work pioneered "pataphysical" fiction, pataphysics being a mock-science concerned with the exceptional rather than the invariable. He was an important precursor of surrealism.

"La Passion considérée comme course de côte" first appeared in *Le Canard sauvage* 11-17 avril 1903; "The Passion Considered as a Hill Race" is original to the present volume.

The Passion Considered as a Hill Race

Barabbas, due to take part, was disqualified.

The starter, Pilate, took out his water-chronometer, or clepsydra, which wet his hands—unless he had simply spat on them—and gave the signal to go.

Jesus set off at top speed. In those days, the custom, according to the good sports reporter Saint Matthew, was to flagellate the sprinter cyclists at the start, as our coachmen do to their hippomotors. The whip is both a stimulant and a hygienic massage. So Jesus, very much in form, set forth, but the accident to the tire happened almost immediately. A seedbed of thorns riddled the entire perimeter of his front wheel.

Nowadays, one sees an exact resemblance of that veritable crown of thorns in the display windows of cycle manufacturers, as an advertisement for puncture-proof tires. The one Jesus had, an ordinary single-tube racing tire, was not.

The two thieves, who were holding out their arms, as at a fairground, took the lead.

It is not true that there were nails. The three figures in images are the so-called "one minute" tire-remover.

But it is appropriate that we give a preliminary account of the spills. And first let us briefly describe the machine.

The frame is a relatively recent invention. It was in 1890 that the first framed bicycles were seen. Before then, the body of the machine consisted of two soldered tubes fitted together at a right-angle. It was known as an upright or cross bicycle. So Jesus, after the accident to the tires, went up the hill on foot, carrying his frame—or, if you prefer, his cross—over his shoulder.

Engravings of the time reproduce that scene in accordance with photographs. But it seems that the sport of cycling, after the well-known accident that terminated the race of the Passion so unfortunately, and which recently produced, almost on its anniversary, the similar accident of Comte Zborowski on the hill of La Turbie,[1] was banned for a time, by prefectorial edict. That explains why the illustrated papers reproducing the celebrated scene depict rather fanciful bicycles; they confused the cross of the body of the machine with that other cross, the straight handlebar—and let us note, in that regard, that Jesus cycled lying on his back, with the objective of reducing the air resistance.

Let us also note that the frame or the cross of the machine, like some present-day wheel-rims, was made of wood.

Some people have insinuated, mistakenly, that Jesus' machine was a rail-car, a very improbable instrument in a hill race, on the climb. According to the old cyclophilic hagiographers Saint Bridget, Gregory of Tours and Irenaeus, the cross was fitted with a mechanism they call a "suppedaneum." It is not necessary to be a great cleric to translate that as "pedal."

Justus Lipsius, Justin, Boethius and Erycius Puteanus describe another accessory that we find reported again in 1634 by Cornelius Curtius in Japanese crosses: a projection of the cross or the frame, in wood or leather which the cyclist sits astride: manifestly, his saddle.

Those descriptions, in any case, are no more unfaithful than the description that the Chinese give of the bicycle today: "A little mule that one leads by the ears and causes to advance by tormenting it with kicks."

We shall abridge the account of the race itself, recounted at full length in specialist works, and exposed by sculpture and painting in *ad hoc* monuments.

On the rather steep slope of Golgotha there are fourteen bends. It was at the third that Jesus took the first spill. His mother, in the stands, was alarmed.

The good pacemaker, Simon of Cyrene, whose function would have been, but for the accident of the thorns, to "cut the wind" for him, carried his machine.

---

1 The American racing driver Eliot Zborowski, Comte de Montsauvan, was killed when his car crashed during the La Turbie hill climb on 1 April 1903, some ten days before the present story was published, and presumably inspired it.

Jesus, although not carrying anything, was sweating; it is not certain that a spectator wiped his face, but it is true that the lady reporter Veronica, took a snapshot with her Kodak.

The second spill happened at the seventh bend, on the slippery pavement. Jesus came off for the third time, on a rail, at the eleventh.

The demi-mondaines of Israel waved their handkerchiefs at the eighth.

The deplorable accident with which everyone is familiar occurred at the twelfth bend. At that moment Jesus was in a dead heat with the two thieves. It is also well-known that he continued the race as an aviator . . . but that takes us away from our subject.

Part Three:
Fellow Travelers

FRANCIS JAMMES
(1868-1938)

Francis Jammes spent most of his life in the Midi, but he was acquainted with Mallarmé and Henri de Régnier, and once visited Algeria with André Gide; he published work in the *Mercure* and other Symbolist periodicals; he had a strong interest in nature similar to Jules Renard's, infused by a religious mysticism based in his Catholic faith.

"En Avril" first appeared in *La Vogue*, avril 1899; "In April" is original to the present volume.

In April

I

The door open, the azure, the moisture of the grass and the wallflowers, and the hyacinths, and a single birds calling, and my dogs running flat out, and the rose-bushes with stout pink stems, the verdure of the lilac, and a bell ringing, a wasp flying in a straight line and striping the meadow with its blond vibration, which stops, hesitates, starts again, falls silent and buzzes . . .

Hearts and choirs of primroses on the damp and obscure moss of the woods; long threads of pink dew floating and swaying and suspended—from what?—in the immaterial morning; frogs with gilded eyelids whose white goiters throb; rushes whose perfume of withered peach and roses, roads already torrid trailing . . .

Irises, the cries of jays, turtle-doves, mountains of blue snow that are the rocks of the azure, square green fields, stream rolling a gilded pebble in the silence; first foliage of the waters; the frisson that chills the body beside springs when the sun cooks the hands . . .

II

Slender alders; torrid marshes where, at midday, inflating the bladders of their throat, raucous gray frogs drag themselves over the rough plants, while, slowly, from the depths of the shadowy and gilded mud, a bubble rises . . .

Dry and twisted vines; swarms of pink peach-blossom in oblique flight in the azure; pear trees and Bengal roses . . .

III

Cherry-red sunsets; nocturnal snow from a fruit tree; green and transparent shade of pathways; summits of hills at seven o'clock where the trees are sponges of night that, gradually, mingle in the severity of the uniform curve that inflates and launches forth, precisely.

Night without stars; violet night in which the white sandals of a beloved peasant-woman are barely distinguishable, and the bristling of thin, stiff trees; pallor of a calcareous hill, and water, where I know not what makes two long and profound shadows . . .

Night; fire; lines of shadow mingled with the shadow of lines; fire, humid density of the fields; fire; crimsoning and rusting of clouds; poplars; whiteness that must be a village. More water, water and shadows of water . . .

A carriage passes. The lantern only illuminates the rump of the horse, the rest is darkness. When I was a child, that astonished me: that light going out, reigniting and going out again. Another carriage . . . One can only see the pink upper body of a young woman. It glides into the night . . .

J. H. ROSNY AÎNÉ
(1856-1940)

J. H. Rosny aîné was the best-known pseudonym of the Belgian-born Joseph-Henri Boëx. He made his first reputation as a Naturalist writer, having been taken under the wing of Edmond de Goncourt when he settled in Paris in the 1880s, but his early work frequently showed the simultaneous influence of the Symbolists, that published under the pseudonym "Enacryos" showing the strong influence of Pierre Louÿs. He made a highly significant contribution to the development of *roman scientifique*, especially in the subgenre of prehistoric fantasy; all of his work in that vein is translated in a six-volume set issued by Black Coat Press in 2010. Between 1891 and 1909 his younger brother Justin shared the pseudonym J. H. Rosny, although most of the work done under the name was Joseph's, and he subsequently added the suffix *aîné* to distinguish himself, while his brother became J. H. Rosny *jeune*.

La Flûte de Pan was first published as a booklet by Borel in 1897, under the pseudonym "Enacryos." "The Flute of Pan" is the title story of a 2018 Black Coat Press collection of the works originally signed Enacryos..

Pan's Flute

Dusk was already falling. The beautiful sycamores extended enormous shadows over the river and the tall reeds. The yellow sun was seen setting and the moon rising, as pale as a silver cloud.

Lycaon savored the charming moment when the daughter and son of Latone occupied the edge of the horizon simultaneously. Covered in the dust of the roads, he was carrying a lyre of blackened wood, for he was an aede, having received the education of singers and philosophers under elegant porticoes, the caresses of painted slaves on ivory beds, in the odor of aromatic plants, amid the harmony of musical instruments. He also remembered, both pleasantly and bitterly, industrious courtesans who knew the art of converting human sighs into gold.

And he was traveling through Hellas of the hundred cities in order to find his chimera. He sang as he went, on the agoras of cities and the edges of villages, and the kindly soil of Achaea gave him hospitality, clothing and amour in exchange. He knew how to relate the legends that please young women and draw the instruction therefrom that invites sensuality.

He had arrived at the Ladon of the grassy banks. In the divine half-light, he dreamed about the son of Laertes, the destroyer of ramparts, and Nausicaa with the white arms. How pleasant it would be to see her appear amid the willows of the river, with her semi-naked followers, laughing through their wet hair!

As he was thinking that, exhausted by fatigue, with his heart full of the charm of Eros, he heard silvery laughter that was prolonged amid the song of naiads. He stopped, and looked.

The red sun was about to disappear; the large moon resembled an immense mirror in which a hill was reflected. And among the slender trees, over the reeds and the lotus, he saw nymphs or mortals, scarcely clad in pure wool, who were letting their hair dry. In the crimson and white light they were as brilliant as the daughter of Antinous and her companions.

And one of them, who seemed coiffed in radiance and woven of lilies, made him think that peoples might not have been unready to suffer for her, as for Helen.

Meanwhile, he moved forward. The sparkling young women, finally perceiving him, got to their feet in order to flee across the meadows; but he raised his hands and shouted in a soft voice exercised by music and eloquence:

"Oh! Goddesses or mortals, luminous daughters of the earth, or naiads issued from the waters, have no fear of the solitary traveler. He cannot do you any harm. Rather listen to his voice . . . for I know stories of men of old and the songs of good aedes. Would you not like me to relate for you the misfortune of Syrinx, daughter of this river of the transparent gulfs: Syrinx, who could only flee the hairy god with the goat's legs by becoming a slender reed. That story is charming on summer nights, and full of secret lessons."

The young woman who seemed to be coiffed by radiance stopped, and then the others. They all approached the aede with the gestures of curious hinds with large starlit eyes, and one of them shouted:

"Tell us the story of the nymph Syrinx, stranger. We will listen to it mingle with the voice of the river. But first take a cup of dark wine, gentle on the heart."

She picked up a goatskin full of wine and poured a cupful for Lycaon. He raised the cup toward the sky, made a small libation to the river, and savored the beverage, the winged soul of which filled him with eloquence.

"Now I will tell you the story of Syrinx, issue of the river Ladon, and the terrible god who, prowling the woods and the meadows, renders the darkness more menacing."

They sat down beside him. He respired the pleasant odor of their flesh, and saw their mouths shining crimson and silver in the light of Hecate. His breast palpitated with sensuality while he tuned his sonorous lyre; the largest of the stars came to mirror themselves in the water and in the eyes of the beautiful young women, and a breath sometimes descended that seemed perfumed with the ambrosia of a god hovering in the crystalline twilight.

Lycaon first made audible the little euphonic nymphs that are captive in the strings of the lyre, and then he spoke.

❊

So, the god Pan was hiding from the gods and from men; that is why old Hesiod did not know him. He hid in the noise of tempests, in the murmur of trees, and in the sudden voices that throw panic into livestock, travelers and armies in battle. He haunted the forests that moaned, he howled with the voice of invisible wolves, the anger of equinoxes and the resonance of the sea.

Now, the nymph Syrinx lived near the river, her father, in the scintillating meadows, on the shady islands and beside tranquil coves. She was tremulous and supple, she glided happily on moonbeams; she disappeared silently into the trunks of willows; she wove her red hair with fresh herbs. There was no immortal more fearful. A leaf curved by the wind caused her to flee; she was afraid of looking at her own image, and the song of frogs in the marsh troubled her dreams.

As soon as dusk fell she took shelter among the branches; she listened to the darkness while curling herself up. And that was not without pleasure. She knew the little sensualities of the fear that gives a voice to things and brings the stones of paths to live. She did not detest the fact that the smallest insect seemed terrible.

One morning, she heard footfalls following her over the meadow. She turned round and saw nothing. But the next day, as she lay down in the shade of a sycamore, she felt a warm breath on her neck and in her hair. One evening, when she was about to go into a grotto, an invisible obstacle stopped her for some time; she saw the vapor of breath rising.

She uttered a scream, and the obstacle disappeared.

After that, she was followed incessantly. The trees sighed as she passed by, the water uttered a soft plaint in receiving her figure, and she no longer dared to look at her naked flesh, for hidden eyes were looking at it at the same time as her. In spite of her fear of the dark, she no longer bathed except in the secrecy of night.

She understood that a god was smitten with her, and was troubled, like hinds by Autumn. Was it Phoebus, king of light, or the great Zeus, perfumed with ambrosia? She lay down on the moss of the forest or on odiferous grass. She dreamed about the blue flesh of the firmament, and the clouds, the sons of Saturn. She did not know whether she was quivering with fear or desire.

It seemed to her that she would have liked to summon Eros, but that she did not dare. The breath came down; she sensed the invisible god beside her young body, palpitating for the eternal hymen, the objective of being. Sometimes, a soft arm embraced her, with the friction of a torso. She thought that she was about to see, but she saw nothing but a furtive radiance, a fleeing animal, or the sight of a black bird in the sky.

One day, she was arranging her hair with iris flowers and little lively herbs. She was mirroring her golden head in a spring. And she was smiling, vaguely, at her flexible grace, while foliage quivered beside her and began to speak. And it said, in a voice that resembled the murmur of waves:

"It is the god Pan who loves you, nymph issued from the beautiful river Ladon. He wants to create new beings with you, who have no peers on earth. You will give birth to chimerical animals: lion-men and swan-women. You will put into the woods and the meadows figures that are not accustomed to be there. And you will be glorious among the immortals, for nothing is more beautiful than to be the mother of unknown forms."

The fearful nymph only understood what it said vaguely, but she found charm in the voice that quivered in the foliage, and she said, softly: "Has the god Pan no face, then, that he always speaks by means of the trees, the waters and echoes?"

The foliage replied: "The god Pan has many faces, for he is the king of all the beasts and all the satyrs who live among the trees . . . and who are modeled in his resemblance."

But the nymph with the bright eyes still did not understand. She said in her turn: "What is the point of so many faces, if they cannot make themselves visible?"

As she spoke, the foliage started to laugh.

"Would you like to see Pan, innocent nymph?"

She trembled, but curiosity was stronger than fear.

"Yes."

"Look!"

She saw a reflection, and then a large stag with ten branches. It threw its head back and pawed the grass with its cloven hoof. Its eyes sparkled like the red stars of Ares; ardor elevated its muscular flanks. It came toward the nymph and placed its warm mouth on her shoulder. She sensed the ardor of Eros in that agile guest of the forests, and wanted to recoil. But she found herself pressed against the vast trunk of an oak; the powerful beast caressed her white breast, and her shoulders, comparable to those of silver Hebe. Thus the wild bull on the Phoenician shore mingled its breath with that of the pale Europa.

Syrinx uttered a loud scream of fear. The stag looked at her with its bright eyes, raised its branched horns and vanished like a cloud.

"You have seen one of the faces of the god Pan," murmured the foliage. "But he can also take on human form."

Syrinx was still shivering. The gaze of the stag was within her, like a fire in a hearth. Eternal life excited her to abandon herself, for the benefit of beings that were to be born in the future. She desired to see Pan in human form, and said so in a whisper to the foliage.

Then, in the blue shade, a human face appeared. It bore a forked beard, and horns on its head; his body was covered with unkempt hair, and his limbs were those of a goat. And his eyes were resplendent with the same red flame that had appeared in the stag's eyes.

"Syrinx, tremulous daughter of the waters and the meadows, your destiny will be as sweet as Echo, to whom I gave Iynx, and Aega, who conceived Aegipan. I am the great god of the future. My descendants will populate the earth when those of Zeus, Poseidon and Phoebus are hidden in sad dwellings and disdained by men. Come, nymph with the beautiful tresses, we shall be happy on the profound moss. We shall unite in order to make the forest more mysterious."

He spoke, but Syrinx disdained his hairy body and his horned head. She rose to her feet nimbly and tried to flee toward the river with the beautiful eddies; but the god barred her route. She raised her hands toward the heavens and prayed:

"Zeus, O Father who reigns from the heights of Ida, very great, very glorious, and you, Phoebus, conductor of light, and you, divine River who gave birth to me, have pity on me; do not let me fall into the hands of this brutal god."

"Your prayer is vain, Syrinx," said the god Pan, "for I am the master of nymphs born of rivers. It is insensate, for you are refusing happiness . . ."

"Change your face!" cried the nymph. "I cannot abide your goat's feet and your hairy torso . . ."

310

"It is the form in which I desire to be a father . . . there is none more beautiful."

She fled toward the hills. She bounded like a filly that has not yet known the human yoke; he followed her like a proud stallion, the king of herds. They ran over pastures, hills and plains where men live who nourish themselves on wheat. And when dusk fell, and the shadows of the trees were elongated, when they both returned toward the Ladon, whose bend they had cut across, Pan cried:

"Stop, Syrinx. Fear, in fleeing the decree of Eros, running to your doom. The River itself cannot protect you, and for having escaped destiny, you would be similar to a sterile herb."

"I would rather be similar to a reed," she replied, "than be the mother of a satyr . . ."

As she spoke, the river appeared, all red in the dusk. It appeared for a moment that Syrinx was finally about to reach it, but as she was already throwing herself into the water, Pan extended his arms and touched the fugitive nymph.

He was holding nothing but a long, flexible reed . . .

✳

The aede stopped speaking; the young women remained silent. They were moved; their breasts were rising gently.

A violet light descended through the branches. The river scintillated among the reeds; the population of frogs sang in a melancholy fashion.

Lycaon went on: "The great god Pan cut the reed and made the amorous flute that it is so sweet to hear on fine evenings. Thus, the nymph who died for not having wanted amour took on the voice of amour, and the flute sings the eternal regret of young women who, like her, die sterile. For they are dead among the dead! It is necessary to love, virgins similar to the Immortals . . . even if the lover is animal as well as divine. He has caprine feet as well as starry eyes; his body is hairy but his action is magnificent. Those who have scorned him will never be anything but plaintive reeds . . .

"It is said," he added, "that on beautiful evenings, when the air is tranquil and rivers sleep like living beings, that those who are ripe for Eros hear the sounds of the flute rising on the shores of lakes, rivers or marshes. That is the melancholy Syrinx, who is exhorting them not to be pitiless for themselves, and to savor the felicity of being conquered."

At those words, young ears were directed toward the river. Nothing could be heard but the slight movement of the waves, the noise of the batrachians and quivering foliage, but Agamede, crowned with radiance, turned her beautiful eyes toward the aede and murmured in an emotional voice:

"I can hear the voice of Syrinx . . ."

She had allowed her veil to fall, and her youthful cleavage was visible in the moonlight. She was listening, attentively, to the faint flute whose moaning she alone could hear.

Lycaon sensed the terrible soft flame for which generations of men live and perish, and which caused the black ships of the Achaeans to depart in order to recover the daughter of Leda from the Trojan horse-tamers.

He said:

"It's the voice of the god, charming young woman. Beware of resisting him . . ."

"I have no desire to resist him," she replied.

She stood up, happy to be submissive, already letting down her long hair made of light and gold. Her companions did not murmur, for they believed that they recognized the mysterious will that no more permits the disputation of the sacrifice of a young woman than the sacrifice of a dove.

And the aede prayed:

"Be propitious to us, god of the invincible arrows, who reigns ardently over Thespis, you who conducted me to these divine shores. I shall ornament your magnificent altar, in Samos or in Crete . . . but could I offer you a victim, more superb than this one, a priestess more splendid and better made to celebrate your glorious mysteries?"

The voice and the lyre fell silent. The aede carried his ravishing prey away.

While the aede united his mouth with unknown young lips, behind the willows, in the embalmed shade, where fireflies shone like little mortal stars, the Arcadian chorus sang the light hymn of Aphrodite; and the delicious soul of Hellas, which knew how to make beauty a glory and amour a virtue, floated over the silvery waters of the river, in an atmosphere so diaphanous that it seemed that the sky and all the stars were touching the crowns of the trees.

HENRI AUSTRUY
(1871-1940)

Henri Austruy was an advocate before becoming the editorial secretary of the *Nouvelle Revue* in 1901, and eventually its proprietor. Almost all of his work after that date was published in that magazine, and his short fiction shows strong Symbolist affinities, tending toward surrealism. Most of his fiction is available in English in a set of three volumes, *The Eupantophone and Other Stories*, *The Petipaon Era and Other Stories* and *The Olotelepan and Other Stories*, all published by Black Coat Press in 2014

"La Taverne" first appeared in the *L'Humanité Nouvelle* in 1899. "The Tavern" was originally published in *The Eupantophone and Other Stories*.

The Tavern

The realization of a great event, the dawn was soon to rise over the city on the day appointed for the opening of the Tavern, unknown beneath its garment of mystery, which animated the spirit of its inhabitants.

One day, a ship had entered the port; no one knew where it had come from, and no one recognized the sky-colored flag that flew upon its mast; a man had disembarked, who simply said that his homeland was a distant country on the far side of the world, which was called Humanity. It was from there that he had come to build the city a Tavern, which his promise made unique in richness and splendor.

A few merchants, fearing an inconvenient rivalry, tried to oppose the Stranger's project, but when the latter had declared that on his death the Tavern would become the property of the city, general interest was finally won over.

Ruins stood in the central quarter; only fragments of walls remained standing, which must have vanquished many years, to judge by their enormous stones, blackened as if by the flames of a volcano, in which the rain had hollowed out deep grooves. They were the vestiges of a very ancient temple to a divinity worshiped many centuries ago; a sacred statue had been preciously guarded there, the possession of which was the pledge of the existence of the city. Speaking in the name of verity against the old superstitions, however, a new God had come; his devotees had broken the henceforth-unnecessary palladium; they had constructed another dwelling to their idol and that of the defunct divinity had become a lair of nocturnal birds, whose cries were used by mothers to frighten disobedient children.

The site of the temple was the location chosen by the stranger to build the Tavern. One of the city's administrators had advocated respect for that corner of ground, where the altar to the goddess protecting the city had been raised, adding that selling the ruins was trafficking the very soul of the ancestors, but so enormous was the sum offered that the majority, for fear of discontenting the people, dared not refuse the money, which would serve to construct schools for children and barracks for soldiers.

Several ships bearing the same sky-colored flag came to drop anchor alongside the first; they brought workmen and materials. Attentive to the enormous blocks of an unusual substance, to which the oldest scholars could not put a name, but the value of which must have been very great, to judge by the care with which they were disembarked, a crowd gathered in the harbor, vaguely oppressed by the mystery. People tried to question the workmen, but they did not appear to understand the words that

314

were addressed to them; as for their master, his weary azure eyes, in which gleams floated like pale reflections of the flag of his ship, deterred the most audacious.

As the work advanced, unanimous anxiety increased, and when the solemn moment finally came, an anxious and fatal crowd, intimately moved by the new thing that was in birth, hastened toward the attractive edifice, the roof of which, as flat as the terrace of the royal palace, was higher than the tallest monuments of the city.

A peristyle with a triple row of violet columns preceded the high-ceilinged hall in which echoes vibrated as if in an immense bronze bell. In the silence of Erebus the walls rose up, high and implacable, without the slightest ornament. Sustaining the hyaline ceiling, like an immense blue cloud, through which light filtered, gigantic caryatids were standing, their arms in the arc of a circle above their heads; they were made of a kind of marble with the pale hue of the complexion of brunette women, and over their surface, which had the warmth of the human body, blue threads traced a network of veins. Beneath the weight of the ceiling, apparently as light as the air whose troubling transparency it had, the muscles of the giantresses bulged, and on the ground, their feet clenched their toes as if to dig their nails into the hard substance, of a motionless and profound black, without any gleam, which muffled the sound of footsteps.

Immaculate doves struck by sudden death and falling in the absolute darkness, came into the infinite void of the ground and the walls to bury their palpitating souls, which shivered in that funereal frame. There were sculpted cathedra of ivory and gold, the backs of which were illuminated by dazzling adamantine stones and blazing rubies. Minuscule lakes of light, turquoise tables and stellate aventurines stood out from the somber silver cradling their drowsy sparkle, like captive stars whose delicate and slender rays, having exhausted their uncertain life, sought rebirth in the flamboyant life of the cathedras. Cups of topaz and onyx, decorated with unknown gems, glistened softly. Then there were the discreet gleams of tender opals, the virginal breath of which was softly exhaled, sage amethysts advising against drunkenness, pious and placid sapphires and green heliotropes, which tinted the radiant daylight with blood.

It was a whole supreme world for which the early morning hour would come as a bright baptism of luminous glory, and even eyes accustomed to the most incomparable solemnities were dazzled, humiliated by those miraculous splendors. Probing the reality, hands advanced, fearful of killing the triumphant vision, and yet, no covetousness for the proffered riches was ignited in hearts, so monstrous and inconceivable did their personal possession seem, akin to that of the sun.

Perhaps there were a few among the inhabitants who calculated the profits they might extract from the travelers that the Tavern could not fail to attract, but the majority, ashamed under the gaze of the Stranger standing at the entrance to the Tavern, who fixed them with his pale eyes, imprinted with a vague merciful scorn, did not linger on the idea of lucre.

It also seemed to them that with that luminous palace, the soul of a previously-obscure and very distant past had emerged from the shadows, where it had been buried for a long time, surging forth into that dazzling present. They felt their being giving birth to a soul of light and life, with which they would live henceforth, and it was not without a great anguish that they thought about the imminent departure of the Stranger.

Perhaps he was quitting them to go to construct a similar Tavern in another city, and the tortuous desire obsessed them to know whether he had ever accomplished such a work before.

With an immense interior joy that not everyone could master, they saw the ship that was carrying the stranger and his workmen away sink as soon as it had left the harbor. Assuredly, it was some benevolent god who had caused that disaster, for the sea was strangely calm, and no one knew of any reef at the site of the catastrophe.

At the same instant, a mute chorus of unanimous gratitude rose up toward the heavens. Henceforth, the Tavern was theirs, and theirs alone, and they no longer feared a dispossession or any sharing of profit with allies or enemies, known or unknown.

Every day, the inhabitants came to the Tavern. While drinking and smoking their long porcelain pipes, they chatted about their affairs, and those of the city. Scholars had given names to the precious unknown substances, which had thus become less strange to them and had acquired an existence of absolute reality in their eyes.

No one seemed to be able to believe in a different state of affairs, and the quietude was general and perfect. One day, however, a young man who had studied theology and ancient philosophy, said in a loud voice, among a circle of friends, that although the Tavern was a monument of an incomparable and an inimitable beauty, the ceiling was gradually lowering, very slowly but with a regular and inexorable progress. It was, he explained the sun's rays, the breath of respiration and the smoke of pipes that, in being gradually incorporated into the substance of the ceiling, were increasing its weight and its opacity. He added that a day would come when darkness would be complete within the Tavern and the ceiling would reach the floor, forming a single solid block with it.

A shrugging of shoulders and loud laughter greeted the crazy assertion, and one of the oldest and richest merchants, constraining his smile into a pitying and mocking grimace, asked: "Is that what your philosophy teaches you, young man?"

Without another word or gesture, the young man, who perceived that no one was paying any heed to what he said, went away.

In spite of the ridicule and the insanity of what the young man had said, on the advice of the most prudent, who were able to find a reasonable motive—just as they would have summoned a physician to see themselves or someone dear to them, even in the case of an inoffensive malady—they asked the most skillful architect in the city, who had already received many honorifics and rare distinctions, to examine the Tavern.

After a mature and very conscientious examination, the architect declared that he was able to affirm the unparalleled solidity of the edifice and to offer a guarantee of its eternal duration.

Minds resumed the absolute quietude that the young man had ruffled momentarily with his folly, and all dread disappeared.

Certain of their future, as they were of their present, joyful and proud, the inhabitants came to spend their time in that world of light and life.

"Down here nothing is perfect, and all happiness has its miseries," said the most illustrious philosophers of the city, so it was only with a very limited surprise that the inhabitants of the city who came to the Tavern related the dreams with which their sleep had been haunted. They had, indeed, seen that platform of the Tavern progressively sinking, the caryatids stiffening their muscles and flexing their backs and shoulders in vain beneath the crushing burden, to fall thereafter on to their knees in a definitive defeat one after another, their vertebrae cracking with a noise like broken seashells, and brains like their own spurting from their skulls; and they were unable to escape from the tavern themselves, their breathless chests heaving, anguished by a few bubbles of air, until the enormous weight finally descended upon them for the most horrible of deaths.

The inhabitants laughed among themselves at the atrocious unreality of their dreams—which were, after all, only vain terrors, perhaps caused by an excess of drink or brought on by evil spirits—and they made fun of the unfortunate visionaries, who, bravely and skeptically, also laughed at the terrors of their nights when they beheld the comforting sight of the Tavern, which still shone, in their eyes, with the same splendid brightness.

In solitude, however, hiding it as if it were an evil action, some of them secretly trembled with fear, and the most heroic consoled themselves with the thought that the ceiling was descending so slowly that the time of danger was very distant, and that only the generations of the far future would have to suffer it.

For some, that idea was a very real consolation, for after all, once their own task was complete and their life elapsed, it was up to their descendants to accomplish their tasks and arrange their lives; perhaps for them the labor would be hard and life difficult, but with the courageous will that new generations would inherit from their ancestors, their victory was certain, and was not, in sum, a very admirable merit.

Happy and sure of their happiness and their life, the inhabitants were in the Tavern when, all of a sudden, a loud cry cut through the air.

All eyes looked upwards, and the transparency of the ceiling revealed a giant bird, whose flight had suddenly stopped above their heads. From its beak and its claws, human bones escaped: enormous femurs and tibias, perhaps whitened by some centuries-long flight through space, which fell through the ceiling, coming to smash up the whole interior and the resplendent life blossoming there. Under the impact,the fulgurance of the diamonds was abruptly extinguished, and the pale frightened souls of agonizing gemstones expired in silent dread.

Changed into bleak and motionless statues, the inhabitants stopped, nailed by terror, and on their knees, their heads lowered, they waited for death—which did not come for them all, however, at that moment . . . but forever and ever, night and silence enveloped the city like a black and lugubrious shroud, which was never lifted again.

LÉON BLOY
(1846-1917)

Léon Bloy was the son of a freethinker who converted to Catholicism and went on to exhibit an extraordinary zeal in propagandizing that faith, although it is rarely conspicuous in the *contes cruels* that he produced on a regular basis for periodicals, most notably *Gil Blas*. He is now best remembered for the eight volumes of his *Journals*, which are an important document of *fin-de-siècle* Paris and its literary community.

"Le Téléphone de Calypso" first appeared in *Gil Blas* 22 decembre 1893 and was reprinted in *Histoires désagréables* (1894); "Calypso's Telephone" was originally published in *The Tarantulas' Parlor and Other Unkind Tales* (Snuggly Books, 2016).

Calypso's Telephone

Madame Presque could not console herself for the departure of Monsieur Vertige. In the six months since the pronouncement of their divorce had brought an equitable conclusion to their conjugal tribulations, that exquisite woman had gradually allowed herself to lapse into hypochondria.

The initial surges of a perfectly natural joy had rapidly been succeeded by the anxieties of solicitude, the alarms of insomnia, the grill of continence and, finally, bitter regret.

It was not that Monsieur Vertige was by any means an adorable man. Oh God, no! He stank like a ram, had a diabolical character and did not possess a globule of enthusiasm for his wife—but there was a piquancy about him, a mysterious quality that always makes women return to that kind of animal. It is doubtless inexplicable, but all too certain.

She was able to render herself the justice of having generously done, before their divorce, everything that a good wife can do in order to dislike her husband. She had even felt completely certain of success. She had had several lovers of an uncommon distinction. One could say unhesitatingly that the first, especially—oh, the first!—a senior employee in the administration of the Catacombs, who had, unfortunately, dropped her, was an ideal specimen.

Well, those fortunate endeavors and the favorable divorce that was their consequence had not been able to take full effect on her husband. She thought about the vile man continually and could not prevent herself from doing so.

Undoubtedly, she did not go so far as to deplore the fact that she was no longer Madame Vertige, but it became clearer to her every day that the banished spouse had been the indispensable condiment of her joys. In other words, love had lost its savor since she was no longer putting horns on a legitimate leaseholder.

It would be necessary to be the least of man not to know or to feel the extent to which divorce lifts hearts—but one is, at the same time, forced to recognize that it is not exactly a creditworthy institution, and Madame Presque was, as the familiar expression puts it, in a bind. Money had disappeared at the same time as Monsieur Vertige. It had disappeared as if into a gulf, and that circumstance had to count for something in the abandoned woman's present melancholy, as any thinking person can see.

Her amorous adventures had not been profitable—that was inevitable. In her truly puerile fear of appearing to prostitute herself, she had experienced the admirable ease with which gentlemen endure being freed of the importunate weight of paying restaurant bills, and the inconstant or ingrate individuals once feasted by her were not in any haste to come to her rescue. There was no bustle on the stairway of the tenth-rate furnished house that had replaced the comfortable apartment of old, and the question of everyday subsistence was becoming problematic.

At the height of that anxiety, a refreshing idea passed over her like a perfumed breeze over an arid spot. She had just remembered the telephonic apparatus that Monsieur Vertige possessed. The apparatus had often woken her up at night, and that was one of her innumerable grievances.

She had avenged herself for that by making use of that irresponsible vehicle of turpitudes and contemporary stupidities in various deceits. On fairly numerous occasions, Monsieur Vertige had been summoned to derisory meetings that forced him to absent himself for a few hours, of which his wife audaciously took advantage. At the office, he was believed to be overworked. The jokes had even gone so far as to cause anxiety that he might decide to stop responding.

Full of mysterious intention, Madame Presque therefore raced to the nearest booth and asked for a connection.

✳

I shall open a parenthesis here, although it is completely unnecessary, to declare that the telephone is one of my pet hates. I claim that it is immoral to talk from so far away, and that the said instrument is an infernal device.

I cannot, of course, put forward any proof of the tenebrous origin of that *voice-extender*, and I am incapable of documenting my affirmation, but I appeal to the good faith and firm mind of people who have used it. Are not the ghostly noises that precede the conversation akin to a warning that one is about to penetrate into some reserved confine in which terror might perhaps be superabundant . . . if one only knew? And the horrible deformation of human sounds, which one might think drawn out by a roller-press, which only seem to have arrived at the ear after having been monstrously distended—is there not an element of panic in that too?

A few days ago, an old scientific bath-attendant, specifically appointed for the massage of useful discoveries at the hammam of an influential periodical, celebrated the glory of an English factory that is in the process of exterminating Writing. It appears that a luminous machine is about to destitute the human hand, which will no longer have any need to write—and the turncoat naturally invited people to rejoice at such progress. I imagine the telephone as a more serious crime, since it debases Speech itself.

✻

"Hello? hello? To whom do I have the honor of speaking?"

"To me, Charlotte, your former wife."

"Oh! Very good. How are you, my dear Madame?"

"Not bad, thank you—and yourself?"

"Oh, personally, I'm getting a paunch. How can I oblige you, if you please?"

"Meet me as soon as possible, to discuss an urgent matter."

"Pardon me, Madame, but I have the honor of reminding you that we were not to see one another again."

"Well, my dear Ferdinand, my little Nand-nand, it's necessary to change that. What's the use of being divorced if we can no longer see one another?"

"What do you mean? Explain yourself, if you please," said the ex-spouse, the extremity of whose voice seemed to be dancing on the plate, on which Madame Presque planted a resounding kiss that the apparatus transmitted like a dart.

"Pay attention then, you big booby, and make an effort to understand me. When we were married, we acted like children and nearly made a mess of our entire lives, because we didn't understand anything—nothing at all—of what nature demanded of us.

"Free love, that's what we needed. Marriage is made for inferior beings and we had a higher calling. We would have been perfectly happy if we had been wise enough not to get married, not to live stupidly under the same roof, but to see one another amiably from time to time, like two piglets who adore one another.

"Why not realize that beautiful dream today? Do you think it's too late? Listen to me, you depraved man, and see whether I love you: *I will deceive everyone in the world with you*, my Ferdinand . . ."

It is probable that Madame Presque knew in advance into what dung-heap of a soul that promise was to fall, for the two stumps of the serpent of adultery, severed by divorce and reconnected by the most sordid concubinage, were reintegrated.

JEAN RICHEPIN
(1849-1926)

Jean Richepin (1849-1926) was fined and imprisoned when his first collection of poems, *La Chanson des gueux* (1876) was prosecuted for obscenity. His first collection of prose, *Morts bizarres*, was published in the same year. He became one of the most flamboyant literary Bohemians of the *fin-de-siècle*, to the extent that Sarah Bernhardt—opposite whom he starred in one of his plays—declared that he was a bigger ham than she was. Amazingly, he was elected to the Académie, in a three-cornered contest against Henry de Régnier (who was elected to the next vacant chair) and Edmond Haraucourt. He was one of the most craftsmanlike mass-producers of short fiction for newspaper *feuilleton* slots; a sampler of his work in that vein in translation is *The Crazy Corner: Horrible Stories* (Black Coat Press, 2013).

"Lilith" first appeared in *Le Gaulois* 11 novembre 1895, and was reprinted in *Le Coin des fous, histoires horribles* (1921); the translation originally appeared in *The Crazy Corner*.

Lilith

The first time the two young men had witnessed the strange scene they had not suspected anything strange, and they had scarcely taken any notice of it.

After having left their poor mansard by its sole skylight, they had installed themselves in the broad guttering of the roof in order to smoke a pipe in the tranquility of the mild late autumn evening, and they were only thinking about savoring their relaxation while breathing the fresh air rising from the large trees in the solitary garden. Their legs hanging down among the highest leaves, at the very top of the bare wall, devoid of any opening, which served as the background of the garden, they did not even think of looking to see whether anything was happening beneath them. They had, therefore, seen the strange scene, that first time, almost unconsciously, and had no suspicion of anything strange therein.

It had been almost the same the second time, and that occasion had not excited them even more, although they had experienced a slight surprise on seeing exactly the same scene reproduced at exactly the same time.

So what, though? One reflection, was there anything surprising in the fact that the old man behaved for a second time in an identical fashion in identical circumstances? Undoubtedly, hazard alone was the cause of the scenes of the other evening and this one seemed to be the same one, scrupulously repeated. It was a coincidence, of course—no more.

The scene, moreover offered nothing in itself that was not quite simple and quite natural, did it? It was the banal action of an old man making a tour of his garden before going to bed, and calling to someone to come out—his wife, his servant or his dog—and calling in that particular voice because he had that particular voice, and at precisely the same time because that happened to be the time, and that was all!

But the two young men had been forced to astonishment, and to judge the scene positively strange, when, thereafter, their attention awakened and their curiosity on the alert, they were convinced that the repetition of the actions and gestures could not be attributed to hazard, that the old man's conduct was habitual and deliberate, and that the slightest details seemed to have been regulated once and for all, minutely and, one could easily believe, ritually.

Every evening, whatever the weather, even on rainy evenings when the two young men allowed themselves to be soaked in their gutter rather than not see it, the same bizarre ceremony had taken place.

Just at the moment when the last vibrations of the nearby clock were sounding a quarter to midnight, the two battens of the French windows of the pavilion opened, and the old man appeared, clad in a long overcoat, bare-headed, carrying above his head a little muted lantern with a thin and pale beam of light.

He leaned to the left, then to the right, and then forwards, with slow movements that had initially appeared to the two young men to be the attitudes of someone leaning forward in order to see better into the shadows, but which now represented themselves as manifest salutations, like those of a priest to an idol.

The old man then took three large strides forwards, and two small ones backwards—and repeated that combination of steps three times, once in each direction in which he had bowed.

Having arrived thus at the entrance to a cypress arbor, which formed a dense labyrinth in the middle of his garden, he swiftly blew out his lantern, and then, in a plaintive, whistling, emphatic voice, which was low but nevertheless carried a long way, he called into the darkness of the labyrinth: "Lilith! Lilith! Lilith!"

What did he do in the labyrinth? How long did he stay there? By what exit did he emerge to go back to his pavilion? That was what the young men were never able to determine.

The old man probably came back by means of a path that ran along the left hand wall of the garden, garnished with a bower of virgin vines, which circled around the pavilion in such a way that he could get back in through a door located on the other side—but that was only a supposition, because no furtive human footsteps were audible on the gravel of that pathway, and his extinct lantern did not permit any divination of where he went.

The only thing of which the two young men were certain was that he stayed in the labyrinth for at least a quarter of an hour. When the clock sounded the first stoke of midnight, the old man's voice could be heard there, now as if coming from underground, doubtless because of the thickness of the cypresses—and that voice was no longer appealing, but seemed thankful, and said only once, with a profound sigh of ecstasy: "Lilith!"

The two young men were "apprentice great men"—that was what they called themselves, those poor, ambitious adolescents hungry for power and glory, of the sort that reading Balzac could still create forty years ago. They had made their poverty communal in that Montrouge mansard, where they each took turns to serve the other as cook and housekeeper, and where they had both promised to be Orestes and Pylades, Nisus and Euryale, Pierre and Jaffier.[1]

They said to one another: "We'll discover the old man's secret. Perhaps it will be the commencement of our fortune."

With prudence and cunning, they asked around the neighborhood. They learned that the old man had lived there for a long time, looked after by his aged wife, his granddaughter and a maidservant. Yes, looked after—for he was, it seemed, a little crazy. The granddaughter hardly ever went out. Only the old woman was occasionally seen outside; she went to the market herself. They were *rentiers*, owners of the pavilion and the garden. The old man had been "some kind of a teacher." In spite of the fellow's craziness, they were "well-thought-of in the neighborhood."

Armed with a name and the "some kind of teacher" the two young men set out in quest of further information. They did, indeed, find traces of the old man at the Collège de France. Briefly, a long time ago, he had taught a course there on Assyriology. He had published two pamphlets on Chaldean magic. Those publications had got him sacked, as a lunatic.

---

1 The first two pairs of exemplary friends derive from Classical mythology; the third is from Thomas Otway's play *Venice Preserv'd* (1682), but the latter is surely included because of its citation by the schemer Vautrin in Honoré de Balzac's *Le Père Goriot* (1835).

At the Bibliothèque Nationale, the two young men asked for the pamphlets, tried to understand them, and were obliged to give up. The sentences therein were bristling with occult formulae and shibboleth terms, and thus written either, indeed, by a madman, or with the design of constructing an indecipherable cryptogram. They could not discern anything therein but the name of Lilith, repeated to the point of saturation.

They admitted to one another that it was necessary to seek the commencement of their fortune elsewhere than in the old man's seemingly-vain secret.

Well, they were wrong, and the absurd imagination to which their reading of Balzac had driven them was right. They learned that only a few days ago, and I saw them both become singularly pensive when they were informed of it, and go pale with bitter regret.

It was at one of those dinners whose foundation is also due to a Balzacian idea, at which people of the same generation, all of whom emerged together from the Parisian battle and all of whom have more-or-less hollowed their niche in life, meet up for years on end, three or four times every winter.

The two young men are participants in one such dinner, but only figure there, alas, in minor parts. The former apprentice great men have not become great men. One of them is simply a government official; the other, a good advocate, is the head of a legal firm that does not handle major cases. In the Parisian battle in which they hoped to play Napoléon, they are survivors, no more. They gladly put the blame on destiny, saying: "We didn't have a lucky break."

They were talking about an old comrade who had had all the luck: honorary positions, lucrative positions, renown, power, fortune, happiness—he lacked nothing, as was repeated enviously.

"One could easily believe," someone said, "that he's a sorcerer who has a talisman. I'd think so, if we weren't in the nineteenth century."

"We've hit the nail on the head," replied Z***. "I can affirm, personally, that our former comrade is indeed a sorcerer in possession of a talisman." And, as people laughed, he added: "He's the heir of the last priest of Lilith, and he possesses a fragment of black stone."

Z*** then told us the story of an old scholar, an Assyriologist and mage, who had been reputed to be mad, and whose granddaughter had been espoused by our comrade.

Everyone knows that Z*** is one of our best straight-faced humorists, and that he loves to play tricks even on his closest friends, but as he does so wittily, with inventions of the most brilliant fantasy, people listen without resentment and even thank him for putting one over on them. Everyone therefore savored his pretended revelations, his air of mystery and the rich imagination he deployed in reviving the fantastic old man, the last priest of Lilith and possessor of the fragment of black stone that is the ultimate *open sesame* of her supreme worshipers.

Among all those charmed and attentive guests, however, two drank in his words open-mouthed, wide-eyed and pale-faced, racked by dolorous tics. They were the two former apprentice great men, who were tormented by a retrospective and impotent avarice, and the certainty that it was not a fanciful tale, that the comrade who had had all the luck owed it to a real and authentic talisman, that they might have been the esteemed and triumphant Jasons, but that they had lacked the faith necessary to obtain it.

And I, who had once been the confidant of their singular and vain adventure, now saw again, in the troubled mirror of their dilated pupils, behind the veil of suppressed tears that filled them like a tragic fog, the strange scene that they had described to me forty years before, with disdainfully skeptical smiles, of the old man making his three salutes to the idol of shadow, executing his magical march toward the labyrinth and calling into the depths of ancient darkness to the ancient goddess who was thought to be abolished but perhaps lives on, still omnipotent:

"Lilith! Lilith! Lilith!"

LOUIS CODET
(1876-1914)

Louis Codet was a late recruit to the Symbolist Movement, but published much of his early poetry and prose in Symbolist periodicals before going on to publish quasi-autobiographical novels. He died of wounds sustained in battle during the early months of the Great War, and the majority of his published works appeared posthumously.

"L'Archiduchesse" first appeared in *La Vogue* avril 1899; "The Archduchess" is original to the present volume.

The Archduchess

I

Distractedly, with her delicate fingertips, the Archduchess rotated the stem of a carnation, like the tulle dress of a very tiny dancer.

The guests seemed stimulated by the galantines of witty words. The young women gave the impression of drinking wines full of smiles that flew away in touching their lips. Old ladies whose eyes seemed to have withdrawn into their crumpled orbits, inclined, and their smiles, rigged with all the ropes of their wrinkles, wandered like futile, delicate ancient ships. A thousand candles had slight sighs, and behind velvet sheets, violins mewled with infinite softness.

Distractedly, with her delicate fingertips, the Archduchess rotated the stem of a carnation, like the tulle dress of a very tiny dancer.

"Once," Monseigneur said to her, twisting the emerald on his left hand, "in the times when archers watched on these towers, our lady ancestors nibbled red peppers during feasts in the guise of delicacies, with which the foremost tablecloths of Flanders were strewn."

"Oh!" said the Archduchess, with politely vague eyes. Her intermittent breath excited a thousand gazes in her necklaces. The valets distributed among the guests, in slender golden vases, sorbets reminiscent of torches of snow, from which a perfume of alcohol and flowers emerged.

Distractedly, with her delicate fingertips, the Archduchess rotated the stem of a carnation, like the tulle dress of a very tiny dancer.

II

From the terrace, the continuous sound of an obscure fountain was audible . . .

The Grand Dukes, using the intelligence of digestion, were chatting, and their cigars wove little bonnets of ash. The motionless Archduchess, having placed her hands on a marble balustrade, quenched the thirst of her pale hands, which displayed their rings like multicolored dew. Electric flowers kept awake a few bewildered leaves in the branches.

From the terrace, the continuous sound of an obscure fountain was audible . . .

Standing apart, a young Vicomte rolled a little tobacco in paper marked with a crown. A match caught fire with a sound of wings. The young Vicomte, being a poet, gazed at the spirals of his smoke in the moonlight and thought: *That smoke is rising dreamily and carelessly. No painter could fix the movement of that blue smoke on canvas, and no poet could give a precise idea of it. Thus, the slightest things escape the scrupulous art of men.* Then he thought: *I've rolled my cigarette; and now my cigarette is unrolling me.*

From the terrace, the continuous sound of an obscure fountain was audible . . .

Two philosophers, retired into a clump of trees, were talking in a melancholy fashion.

"I wanted to know the world," said one, "and I traveled for many days and nights. Now I have succeeded in reaching the pole of Ideas, where my ardent heart always rises as bloody as a sun."

"Alas," said the other, "I wanted to know myself, and I feel my ennui like a prisoner, in the shadow, feeling with my open hands the walls of its cell! Often, for my dear suicide, I shut myself away in the sovereign chambers of my soul; but as soon as I touch my Smith and Wesson, my heart and my temples swell, and the hosts of my blood batter the doors of my free brain."

From the terrace, the continuous sound of an obscure fountain was audible . . .

The young poet, who was admiring his smoke, reflected on the fugitive nature of flames. He thought: *O beautiful changing flames, we can scarcely grasp a few of your metamorphoses. Thus, I have observed, in the hearths of winter, elegant flames in the style of Louis XIV. But, subtle nature, you only leave us fragments of fingers and we do not grasp you in verity.* Then he thought: *Poets! We're voluptuous children, kissing our hands before images* . . .

From the terrace, the continuous sound of an obscure fountain was audible . . .

The Grand Dukes, who were chatting, had assured one another that the Imperial Constitution was the most perfect on earth. And the Archduke, raising his eyes, noticed for the first time the disorder of the stars. But the Archduchess had slipped away into a silent path. She was walking rapidly, with deep sighs, spreading her arms in the diaphanous night.

In the distance, she heard the fountains increasing and decreasing.

III

And in the moonlight, in the deserted park, statues stood confusedly, pale with the immense fatigue of being beautiful.

The Archduchess, breathless, tilted her head over one or other shoulder and fled, following the perfumed clumps of bushes. She bit her arm gracefully and, somewhat calmed down, continued walking. A warm, insipid, stifling odor of linen singed by red-hot iron invaded the air of the summer night. She inhaled the sharp odor of the cantharides that populated the ash trees

Gently, she put a shiny whistle to her lips. Then, smiling, she tipped back her face toward the clarity of the sky, and put the tip of her naked tongue between her lips.

And in the moonlight, in the deserted park, statues stood confusedly, pale with the immense fatigue of being beautiful.

The whistle was modulated; two servants appeared clad in somber tunics, which they took off. The first, behind her, slid his warm and rough arms under the Archduchess's arms, enclosing her breasts in his profound hands. The second, whose slim flanks were trembling, reached her mouth. They laid her down in the grass and lay down beside her. She gasped at slow intervals, and twisted in her unfastened dress. Fragments of her silver-spangled veils scintillated on the vaporous grass.

And in the moonlight, in the deserted park, statues stood confusedly, pale with the immense fatigue of being beautiful.

LÉON DAUDET
(1867-1942)

Léon Daudet was the son of the novelist Aphonse Daudet. He studied medicine, but dropped out and became a fierce critic of the medical profession, satirized in his first novel, *Le Morticoles* (1894). He married Victor Hugo's daughter Jeanne in 1891, but after their divorce in 1895 he abandoned his liberal views and became a fervent critic of the Republic, eventually becoming a co-editor of the right-wing *Action Française*. His early literary work showed a strong Symbolist influence, which continued to show in some of his later work, especially his flamboyant contributions to the genre of *roman scientifique*.

"Le Montreur de larmes" was reprinted in the posthumous collection *Quinze contes* (Guy Boussac, 1948); although I cannot identify a prior publication, the story undoubtedly dates from the *fin-de-siècle*. "The Exhibition of Tears" is original to the present volume.

The Exhibition of Tears

The entrance to the grotto was low and we had to duck down. The labyrinth, formed by a multitude of species chambers, connected to one another by narrow passages, as hatred is to love—an immense labyrinth, according to previous visitors—received very little light, but what did filter through the interstices of the clear and trenchant fissures took on a concentration and an extreme acuity, with the consequence that one could follow its design in the penumbra, shadow upon black shadow. It was sometimes a cone, sometimes a sheet, sometimes a thread as tenuous as a knife-edge, according to the whim of the gap.

The tears, like jewels, were arranged in display-cases, various in size and gleam, and their disposition seemed to be such that the magnificent luminescence induced by the play of the sunlight struck those pearls of the soul successively.

The man guiding us said: "It was decided, out of a horror of deception, only to employ natural light. That alone makes true tears glitter. As for false ones, of which you can see sad specimens in the last room, they draw a feeble gleam from little lamps fixed beneath them. Their poor effect makes the incomparable splendor of these stand out even more."

The speaker was a short thin man simply dressed in black, with excessively regular features, which gave him a strange almost geometrical appearance. The straight narrow nose succeeded the forehead almost without an interval. The impeccable arch of the nose seemed cruel. The clean-shaven chin added a full stop to the profiled phrase: hope no more. His dry and unmoving eyes disconcerted us with their harsh gaze, adding a sentiment of necessity to his curt speech. His only gestures were extensions of a pale hand toward the display cases, and an occasional suspicion of a courteous bow.

"These are the innumerable tears of lovers."

They were displayed on a slight slope. From the rocky ceiling to a floor sprinkled with fine sand. Blinded by their scintillation, we could not distinguish anything at first. Then our gazes adapted, and I admired their cut and their limpidity.

"Lean over. Each of them reflects the image of the male or female weeper."

I examined one of the fixed droplets for a long time. Like a memory gradually rises up to consciousness from the tenebrous depths of the mind, the face of a woman, melancholy and beautiful, emerged from the crystalline water. I saw the tender oval and the blue eyes that had shed the faithful gem in question. Thus, dolor kept its form through eternal duration. By virtue of a strange sympathy, I associated myself with that distant suffering: abandonment, despair, the monotonous trickle of hours detached from the eyelids of time, moistening the heart broken by anguish.

The next was that of a young man: a proud and troubling face, his lips trembling, his chin devoid of the slightest down; something ambiguous, as in Da Vinci's portraits. Only the determined pupils and short hair revealed his sex. I could almost have believed that he was about to speak to me, so sincere was the mysterious miniature. Enclosed in a little diamantine tear, as his distress was enclosed within him, it was perhaps for one of the others who were weeping that he wept himself, so frequent is fatal scorn.

Handsome men and beautiful women, ugly men and ugly women of all the epochs throughout ages, I saw in those "weepers," as our guide called them, who inhabited the grotto. A strange regret came to me—for being wants being to be complete—of having nothing before me but the vestiges of eyes. Where are the other scraps? That which commences with a sight finishes with a clamor. At first there is a murmur, often under the stars; then, in the ardent and naked night, body speaks to body in its own language. Then, in a solitary room, it concludes with a sob.

"These are the tears of lovers."

That was a stellar swarm, which a brighter luminous jet separated like a galaxy. Veneration gripped us. We knelt down. It is internal hymns that our soul intones when words have ceased to render their power. Bathed by harmonious pity, therefore, with great respect, I leaned over the nearest pearl. Its radiant gleam extended and stretched as if, detached itself with regret, it were still adhering to white lashes.

I perceived a soft and aged face. Those daughters of maternal love shine purest of the pure, for the redemption of infinite pains.

Then we saw the tears of faith, small in number but still blinding. None bore a face; in their depths a cross was distinguishable. I noticed that, arranged in chronological order, their gleam diminished near the edge of the display-case.

"There are phases of dryness," our guide explained.

He showed us others mounted in swords and crowns. "These are pride and glory." They burned the eyes with a vivid flame, but it was immediately forgotten, as if the slaked desire no longer propagated any light.

A field of larger gems astonished us by its amplitude.

"These are all the physical dolors."

They too were faceless. With a little attention, we noticed that they did remain motionless, but joined together in various forms, outlining spikes and talons by means of the sudden splashes, and then separated from one another, dividing like a population of agitated droplets.

As we advanced further into the grotto, I distinguished a less distinct streak on the walls, the elements of which seemed rebellious against the light, scarcely translucent, or of a milky, opaline whiteness.

"Ennui, remorse, dread and terror have their damp domain here."

They enclosed sullen faces, as if ashamed.

Our attention was becoming weary. The exhibitor perceived that and said, with a pale smile: "You understand my bleak expression now, and the brevity of my speech. When I entered this grotto for the first time it was long ago, as a punishment for an excessive wisdom, which offended the divinity. When I list my treasures, I sometimes add to them, by virtue of the tears I have retained—those that all of you are beginning to know. Since then, my eyelids have dried up. You will thus understand the empty showcase at the entrance, which will always remain empty. But before you go out, to climb up again to the source of life, look over here at those I mentioned to you in the beginning."

In the depths of a fissure, where hardly any real light penetrated, under an array of dull, livid, surly lamps, we saw the false tears.

CLAUDE CÉBEL

Claude Cébel was one of the most prolific contributors of poetry, prose and criticism to the *Revue Blanche* in the early 1890s, but otherwise seems completely unknown, and might be a pseudonym.

"Les Unes et les autres" first appeared in *La Revue Blanche* mars 1892. "One or Another" is original to the present volume.

One or Another

Presentation

The sway of your hips, flexible illusory pitches beneath the handles of pure arms, reveals how much your gesture remembers, and your eyes, in which some distant and warm sky is dying; and in spite of the fact that the casinos and matrimonial operas have abolished the clear springs from which you came, in other times, barefoot but no less fresh, young woman, it seems that— disdainful of present attire and artificial adornment, clad simply in a light tunic, among young men calculating the value of your golden belt and your heavy rings, and how much fat white livestock is grazing in your father's meadows—you are advancing toward the clear springs.

Enticement and Misfortune

She really is one of the prettiest things I know; she passes in the most exquisite grace of ideal curves that I have ever traced in the pleasure of my siestas; she is more caressant than those mid-season evenings frightened by some belated breeze; more harmonious in her gesture than eurhythmic halcyons; as supple as light silk banners on festival days. What is more, her gaze seeks yours and is charged with the heaviest tenderness; there, certainly, is a charming friend who loves you.

Thus I spoke to myself and not another. And no one would have importuned me by not adding any faith to words cast in the air if I had illuminated that satisfying decor for the most unworthy as well as myself; but, weary of ennobling the choice arabesques of the primitive fresco, it was necessary for me to admit that I was playing the dual role of the enticed lover and that of the incredulous interlocutor who smiles are so many vain confidences. So, I did not hesitate to stop before the simpleton who was sanctimoniously astonished by my attitude and that solitary discourse. I thought it a sufficient palliative to put fallacious dithyrambs into the mouth of that unknown: "You're lying," I said to him, and I raised my hand and—while he bowed his head, disconcerted, and went away—I put her in my pocket with the gesture that must have been Louis XIV's when he threw his cane out of the window in order not to strike some courtier.

Madrigal

As if desirous of making that indecisive dusk even cloudier, I filled my lungs with the smoke of an odorous tobacco; it entered and—by virtue of the mysterious law that assigns that place to them for all eternity—my arms settled on the arms of my armchair. So, since it was necessary to raise my head toward her, I took advantage of that quasi-kneeling position to spin her a compliment:

"You're no more pleasing than the others," I murmured, "so why did I strive so hard to possess you? Oh, you're laughing, and believing that your eyes, your gait or your complexion would incite me to base pursuits and to brave the sickening of so many compromises and annoyances. What more? Didn't I know the stupidity of sobbing with laughter at these skirmishes, and how similar and deceptive your kisses are? Although, veil raised, you affirm your disdain for all veils, a little enigma sure of herself, I scarcely know who you are; my room is misty with dreams, and the lamp is not yet lit.

"All of you, who illuminate me for a few hours with the gleam of an eye baited by some lust or indemnity, you to whom I addressed identical phrases, and who mocked you identically, or pleased you, which is a worse mockery, hear this: It was never on your lips or the napes of your necks that my lips of my forehead leaned, and I never, never loved anything except the one you were not, the woman of yesterday or tomorrow—what do I know?—or another, or several others, or none: passing breaths, visions that you had only enabled, I assure you.

"Do you understand now why I am ready to be enervated by the same frictions, to sip the despairing insipidity of the same flirtations and to kiss the same curtains? Oh, why!"

Then she got up and said: "It would, in fact, be wiser, my friend, to run in the night, arms akimbo, howling at the moon."

And she unfastened her mantle.

The Incomplete Lover

She is languishing in the bedroom, the little lover on whom my head is posed. And because each of her gestures crumples and twists, the delicate gestures with which she caressed my dream so prettily when she prowled uncertainly in my vague adolescent frissons, she does not care, and laughs, and sings; and, mouth closed in a coronal flowers as if to say something, she is silent, or rather pronounces words that die on the windows, which some external noise is vibrating.

And we glide on the crazy ocean of that stupid alliance, without the word emerging from our salty lips—for we are sailing thus on a real and mysterious sea—and always, always, her twittering flies away in a shrill flutter, and she is saying things to me that dissolve in the lull of the waves.

May my head, heavy with dreams, roll over your breast! And may I, perhaps, take pleasure in your silence and the absence of the expected word that was hatching in your mouth, which would close, and, along with it, the door opening in my vision?

Perhaps you too are saying the words to me, but, lost in one of those sorrows that, like raindrops peppering a mute tomb with vain comforts, I cannot hear them.

The Commodity Called Illusion

At the sight of you, the lips moisten deliciously; and it would be unwelcome for some miscreant to come and sound a horn in the void, after all—after all, certainly, as it is necessary to attach an After to everything—that nonsense and, among other things, you are perhaps not the most beautiful. Display the satin of your flesh and scorn the collisions, and be proud, you whom holy illusion has swollen with the most imposing of dignities, and also of composing for yourself, in this world where abnegation nevertheless has its price, a very satisfactory attitude. Let it astonish a few unquiet minds, which you can anemiate, so that I may reserve for you in my heart a place of election alongside that little seller of quail.

She clucks, the little merchant, "Quail! Quail! Quail!" and the gaze of well-dressed old men nibbles the cherries of her alert complexion—and how could she not be fresh, a girl who runs nimbly and breathes the fresh air?—and the gaze of poor fellows is lost in the gleaming chaplet of bouncing little birds, the gaze of poor fellows, but who square up before the plumped and savory birds. What does it matter that the big brother of the laughing crier has carefully inflated the gleaming bodies of your quail with an illusory stuffing, since your cheeks are sincere, in which those old men are taking pleasure, or that the fallacious bellies of your birds, in which the poor fellows are delighting, are fattened with lard?

Hospital

Resign yourself, my friend, to never sucking the triumphant red-currant. Why inhale the crimson of those empty skins?

Let your dream fly away in those two flicks of a fan. Is not real death in that irritating abdication in which you persist obstinately? And it is fitting to rest on such vain clouds the scepter that so many others please themselves in handling?

Cease to lose yourself in the illusion of those distant fevers and that supernatural flora, and sleep on my bosom. And go to sleep to the strict rhythm of our lukewarm amours.

And while cradling my bruised wing on her obliging breast—and were she another, their breast, which provides a pillow for my quotidian convalescent—she infused the four flowers.

Denouement

And now that every brutal veil has been removed, and also the immodesty of Platonism, chastely, we commune. No vestment and no gloss, and the most complete abandonment; for it is truly necessary that in this pure evening, we shall roam the exterior crossroads of our souls, of this soul, my own, into which I never descend—the one to which you, among all the others, have the right of entry—which is frightened and sets snares for whoever vagabonds there, and your little homogeneous soul, if one can put it thus, you who perhaps attained the shore in lazy and serene siestas where I would doubtless have landed, if the wind had lifted rancor, and some agile and willful oar had not drawn me away from those sentimental beaches.

Let us strip away interpretations and garments, for only the arrangement of the latter and the mundane perversities of some such morality mask the ingenuousness of your body, which, absolute and disengaged from the grip of those evil desires and pernicious decorations, tempts the contemplation of pure and chaste beauty, in harmonious lines not softened by unhealthy games, but posed there stupidly, and divined thereby; and let us be careful to abolish all concupiscence, like some stupid dream of rape, and inflate healthy desire, also holy since it will not be tarnished by any hidden agenda, not even a thought, except that you will then cease to be an infinite dust of velvet and perfume, momentarily, in this perishable world.

JANE DE LA VAUDÈRE
(1857-1908)

Jane de La Vaudère was baptized Jeanne Scrive and was married to Camille Gaston Crapez, who began styling himself Crapez de La Vaudère after inheriting the Château de La Vaudère from his mother. Her prolific literary work is very various but she was assimilated to the Decadent Movement firstly because of two scandalously scabrous Parisian novels, *Les Demi-Sexes* (1897) and *Les Andrognyes* (1903), and, more pertinently, because of a series of accounts of *moeurs antiques*, some of which—notably *Le Mystère de Kama* (1901)—set new standards of excess in their exotic eroticism and fascination with torture.

"Volupté rouge" was first published in the weekly supplement to *La Lanterne* on 18 décembre 1902. "Red Lust" is original to the present volume.

Red Lust

The menagerie, empty of spectators, is asleep in a strong mist of respiration and the bitter odor of droppings. The sand, freshly raked, forms slight whirlwinds around crates in which the large reptiles marbled with ocher and cinnabar are torpid. It is the hour when the wild beasts, half-veiling their shining eyes, lie down nostalgically, their claws retracted into velvet gloves. One senses, however, that they are armed for defense, ready to bound at the slightest alert, and even in sleep, their fangs glisten menacingly behind their turned-back chops.

After the evening meal, the last performance will take place, the most important one, which will join to the ordinary exhibitions the emotion of the struggle, the dance of the lions in the central cage, where the tamer Stephano will deploy the whip and the revolver, making the terrible beasts pirouette like circus clowns, and redden their bellies with the fire of burning hoops.

Myrta, the black panther, always in revolt, roars dully in anticipation of the imminent visit; her paws clench feverishly and her fur bristles in voluptuous frissons; she is believed to be amorous and jealous. Twice, already, she has thrown herself upon Stephano and, standing up, dominating him with her massive head, she has rubbed her muzzle against his cheek. But the tamer has mastered her with a glance, conquered her with a caress, and, with his boot on her spine, has maintained her there, panting, under the enthusiastic bravos of the public.

It is ten o'clock. The assistants turn up the gas, bring baskets full of meat for the carnivores' meal, distribute fruit to the monkeys and wake up the parrots, living flowers brightening the monotony of the dark pelts, and erecting in the corolla of their open wings the pistils of their irritated crests.

But a young woman has come in, escorted by an ageless and sexless governess, to exchange a few words with the lads, who know her, accustomed to seeing her every evening, since the installation of the menagerie in the suburban quarter. She is Antonia, the daughter of a rich businessman from Madrid, who comes furtively to intoxicate herself on the odor of circuses, in the unacknowledged and almost morbid desire to caress her soul with a little suffering, to see blood flowing and bones breaking.

She experiences the murderous passion that leads señoras to the *plaza del toros* and puts in the puerile heart of virgins the ferocity of inquisitors and torturers. She is, however, as frail as a reed, her voice is soft and her onyx eyes, speckled with gold, crackle in the paschal wax of her skin; she seems a mystical being of grace and bounty. But she comes from the land of the matadors, where amour seems better after the red vision of an arena strewn with spilled entrails, where the troubling perfume of woman mingles with the bitter reek of abattoirs.

For the moment, her *espado* is named Stephano, the superb tamer who juggles with the great lions, and appeases the jealous fury of the black panther with caresses and seductive words.

Antonia has stopped, pensively, before the beast's cage, and her golden gaze, aimed at Myrta's fiery gaze, interrogates it for a long time.

The panther has risen to her feet, her muzzle puckered over sharp teeth, her tail thrashing; then, stretching herself along the bars, her entire body vibrating with a lascivious spasm, she yawns nervously, and is convulsed by a hoarse gasp. The regret of the desert and free amours grips her in the solitude of her prison; her flanks agitate, and her claws scratch the ground in a desire for caresses or murder.

Antonia has slipped her umbrella between the bars, and the beast, twisting the whalebone like flexible stems, is gnawing the ivory sleeve, having passed her head through the zinzoline silk, which makes for her the collar of a female clown.

"Oh, look Gertrude, see how crazy Myrta is today!"

"It's necessary not to excite her," advises the governess. "Something bad might happen to Stephano."

A strange gleam passes through the young woman's eyes. She does not reply, but her heel taps the ground impatiently and her nostrils dilate in an ardent aspiration.

Gradually, the public arrive, the habitual public of fairground marquees, composed of bourgeois, workers, idlers, good-time girls with scented hair, little vagabonds and suspect louts.

The obstinately swaying bears, the hyenas, the foxes and the torpid boas in their crates, and the consumptive or mocking monkeys captivate attention at first; then everyone groups around the central cage for the exercises of Stephano, the handsome tamer whose breast is adorned with flattering plaques and who flexes his harmonious muscles in a bright leotard.

In the front row, Antonia remains motionless, her lips dry, her hands burning. She does not know exactly what she expects, but she senses that something is going to happen, because she wants it to, and because her criminal anguish has communicated itself to the black panther, whose fur is glistening like a velvet robe as her flesh quivers.

Here comes Stephano. Proud, nervous and agile, his whip held high, he has entered the cage and, before the fixed gaze of the women, has made the lions twirl, which come to lie down at his feet, licking his hands, superb and gentle. The pistol shots, the burn of the fiery hoops and the effort of the singular tricks have not been able to irritate them. They crawl in a servile fashion, and the royal fleece of their spine makes a soft seat for the tamer.

Hands applaud furiously, while Antonia's pretty mouth sketches a disdainful moue. Stephano, charmed and surprised by the young woman's assiduity at his exercises, contemplates her with a vainglorious assurance.

She smiles, and her imperious gaze fixes upon that of the tamer, descending into him as if into a mysterious well, and causes all the fibers of his being to vibrate. He goes pale, and the anxious expression of his features reveals that he is conscious of Antonia's tragic desire. His energy is sunk in that of the unknown enemy; he loses the personality of his free and thinking self.

"Stephano," she says, "the black panther is waiting. Only her conquest is worthy of you."

Myrta is now in front of the tamer. She seems to be plunged in a rigid immobility, and, like a cat dazzled by the light, she extinguishes beneath her weary eyelids the double star of her pupils. The young woman standing up in front of the cage is a human panther far more implacable than the captive beast. She utters a scornful laugh at the hesitation of the man, whose instinct is perhaps warning him, and murmurs through clenched teeth: "Coward!"

Stephano puts his arms round the beast for the habitual games; but she resists, roaring, embraces him in her turn and knocks him down. The two bodies roll, bound and twist, in the midst of cries and gasps. Women faint, while the employees, armed with pitchforks and pikes, hasten to the bars, mastering the panther, whose muzzle is red with blood.

Antonia, her eyes capsized with ecstasy, has detached the triple row of peals that adorns her gracious neck, and she hands it to the vanquished man.

"Thank you," she says, in the slightly guttural voice of a Madrileno virgin. "That was almost as good as the *plaza del toros!*"

EDMOND HARAUCOURT
(1856-1941)

Edmond Haraucourt was the youngest son of a fervently religious family, all of whose siblings became missionaries; his uncle was appointed Bishop of Tibet. Converted to atheism, he printed off a few copies of his calculatedly scabrous collection of poems *La Légende des sexes* (1882) for circulation to friends in the Parisian literary community before breaking through to more orthodox publication in the *Revue Blanche* and the *Revue Bleue*. He published a good deal of short fiction in *Le Journal*, and several novels, all of his work showing a strong Symbolist influence, but he made his living as a museum curator.

"La Madone" appeared in the collection *L'Effort* (Académie des Beaux Livres, 1894); "The Madonna" was originally published in the sampler *Illusions of Immortality* (Black Coat Press, 2012)

The Madonna

There was once—a long time ago—a painter who possessed a great artistic soul and cherished his art above everything. He adored it and cultivated it for himself; he saw it as an end and not a means, the objective of life and not a road leading to fortune or renown. Never, moreover, had he pondered or rationalized that way of feeling; he experienced it naively and lived according to his nature. When he had imagined something beautiful he tried to realize it, and worked on it fervently, without caring whether the people around him thought that it was good or bad. He searched, he loved—which is to say that he searched himself and loved his dream.

That had quickly brought him to solitude; to live within oneself is to live at a distance. He was, therefore, adequately disdained, and his merit was so great that no one had any inclination to believe in it.

But what did that matter to him? If, by chance, he provoked a sincere emotion, he was more excited than flattered by it, simply deeming that he had encountered a mind in conformity with his own, something akin to a friend. He went through life without being very familiar with it, having never looked at it save through the lens of his thought, with the result that it seemed to him to be sweet, tender and serene, like his soul. For that dreamer, everything was transformed into the nourishment of dreams; the pleasure of others gave him pleasure in passing, their misery implanted within him a compassion fecund in sadness; noble actions seemed to him suggestive of courage; as for villainies, he never had occasion to suffer from them because he was never able to perceive them, and if anyone had demonstrated them to him they would have been wasting their time, because he would not have been able to understand them.

In his hours of leisure, he went out of the city and refreshed himself in the calm of the fields; he only liked tranquil spectacles; he contemplated sunsets, children at play, the gazes of virgins, and the pairs of oxen that paused as night fell to plunge their shiny muzzles into water-troughs, in which the pale sky was mirrored and lulled.

Now, one evening, when the livestock were returning to the barns, he arrived at a well at the gates of a town. A young girl had set her full pitchers down, and was resting on the stone rim before going home.

Above a slender torso, her sad and serious face, lit by the reflections of the setting sun, stood out against the background of a golden sky, and the low sun, hidden behind her, dispersed tremulous gleams amid the clouds. That radiance, filtered by the child's blonde hair, made her a mobile nimbus, and in that glorious light, she resembled the saints of paradise.

He drew nearer in order to examine her more easily. She did not move, and did not see him, doubtless absorbed in some meditation. She had a smooth forehead, a slender nose, frank eyes and a mouth devoid of a smile. As austere as the evening, she was in harmony with it, became part of it, completed it and, poeticized by it, poeticized it in her turn. She emitted religion. The serenity of her attitude expressed a vague mysticism, a pious and resigned astonishment, an adoration; one might have thought that she was striving to hear some enigmatic phrase, simultaneously impenetrable, divine, happy and heart-breaking.

"What are you thinking about?" he asked

"Nothing."

"Why do you seem to be lost in a dream, then?"

"It's a beautiful day."

She leaned down to her pitchers, and departed.

"Do you often come to the well?"

"Every day."

He went back too.

"Sit down, as you did yesterday," he said, "and look at the sky."

As soon as he got back to his house, on the first evening and all the following evenings, he took up his pencils and tried to reproduce on paper the face that was haunting him. Every night, he dreamed about her in his sleep, always reminiscent of the saints in the chapels, aureoled by the dusk, opening her eyes upon a mystery; she showed herself thus, even more beautiful than in reality, for thought idealizes and fecundates nature. Twenty or a hundred times a day, behind the lowered eyelids of the man who evoked it, that virginal face sketched itself, first in a mist, and then becoming more precise by degrees, taking on warmer colors, penetrated with life—so much life that, in the end, it poured out around her; and always, the virgin with the golden hair was manifest in the same fixity, with that same gaze directed straight ahead, and that anxiety which was scrutinizing infinity. For hours, she was immobilized like a statue, as unshakable as marble, and always interrogating her enigma.

With the result that, for the solitary man, she had become something other than a passer-by, and more than a tangible being.

At that moment, she incarnated her own astonishment; she was hieratical stupor; she was an idea; she was a symbol. Assuredly, God was speaking to her; she was listening to a voice from outside the world; an angel had just revealed to her a terrible glory, and her dazzled eyes were hesitating to see clearly into a future of triumphs and tortures.

Was it not thus that the Mother of Christ must have stopped in mid-gesture, when she had felt awaken within her the germ of the divine infant? The angel had said: "The Messiah will be born of you." The angel had disappeared; the Virgin Mary was still trying to hear him, not daring to doubt or to believe, overwhelmed by the prodigy, she was imploring the Lord and trembling for her son.

Oh, to fix on canvas that soul and that moment! To grasp the ungraspable, to imprison that fugitive emotion in a work of art, to erect as a pious homage the durable evocation of someone bearing her God; and to put all his artistry, all his faith, his two religions, into a page that would be a prayer!

He saw that so clearly, felt it so profoundly, that he would certainly have been able to reproduce the holy vision with which he was filled. His idea had conquered him to the point that soon, nothing any longer existed alongside it—nothing. The child of the well was no more than an element of the internal poem; she scarcely rekindled it any more, she merely represented it; and as art is a kind of love, the day came when she, like any lover, was not cherished for her merits, but by reason of what thought added to her fragile charm.

Is not loving a woman loving all the beauty and all the virtue in the world, in order to adorn the chosen one therewith? Is not loving an idea, embracing it madly and plunging oneself thereinto, imagining God and creating him in his turn?

That is why he felt himself penetrated with reverence when he went to the well now, and his knees were trembling, as if in a confession of love, when he dared one evening to say to the blonde girl:

"Would you like to come to my house, and I'll draw your image? I'll give you a mantle of roseate silk, with a blue dress. You'll

live as you wish, without doing anything; I'll look at you, and
when I've painted your portrait on a golden background, we'll
offer it to Notre-Dame; then it will be blessed in the church, and
the faithful, believing that they're looking at the Holy Mother,
will kneel down around it."

"Visit my father and talk to him."

Three days later, she came to the painter's home; he sat her
down near the window and placed himself in front of her.

For a long time he contemplated her, and they both remained
immobile. At times, the man's lips parted as if to say something;
his staring eyes were shining and his hands trembling. She
thought that he was suffering from some grief when she saw two
tears swell in the corners of his eyes and run down his cheeks.

Suddenly, he launched himself toward the easel on which the
canvas was standing. But he stopped in front of that pale surface,
on which his mind's eye saw lines and colors in advance, the
work finished, perfect, total. That virginal whiteness was like the
mirror of his soul, a screen reflecting the ideal. He was already
admiring therein the realization of the long-cradled dream, and
the fruit of future labors. What can I say? He admired it again,
and for the last time, sensing that as soon as he tried to embrace
the chimera it would fly away, and that nothing would any longer
remain of its charm or its splendor as soon as he had violated the
magical vision with his heavy hand.

The girl was looking straight ahead.

When evening came, the master put down his brushes.

"Come with me," he said, "and sit down at the well."

The next day, when he examined his sketch, he blushed at its
poverty.

He went back to work, but the next day, he pitied himself.

He took up the task again and, every morning, was invaded
by shame before the results of his effort.

Soon, shame turned to anguish.

He began again, however, sadly. Tenderly and slowly; then
fever flared up, and there were hours of joy, minutes of delirium,
paid for the next day with the same suffering and the same discouragement, endlessly followed by the same renewals of valor
and despair

Fixedly, the girl always looked straight ahead.

O mothers! You know it, the life of those who create; to conceive in folly, to gestate in pain—and how long that expectation is!

He worked until nightfall, and, returning to his oaken easel as soon as dawn broke, let his hands hang down in renunciation. He searched for the fault, thought that he had found it, and that discovery restored his courage.

He rubbed it out and began again; that was better; it was good—almost good, the dishonor of art!

"Another day lost!"

He was astonished to have been able, the evening before, to experience some satisfaction before that erroneous thing.

"Perhaps tomorrow—perhaps!"

The next day resembled the day before.

"How long have we been working?"

"It was three months yesterday."

He groaned internally; then he became enthusiastic again.

"Oh! I will!"

But the work will not. It fights, it defends itself and runs amok; it escapes and allows itself to be caught.

"I have it!"

It is further away than ever. It is the monster that slithers and scorns, the Proteus with a thousand forms, which does not want to be vanquished.

Henceforth, he has neither rights nor strength. He is the slave of an idea; he believes it to be his own, and belongs to it. He is the possessed whom no baptism can exorcize. The more his demon resists him, the more he persists; the more it is vanquished, the more it desires victory. Does he really want it? He pursues it. He runs after it dizzily. He does not want anything; he just goes. Can one say that a stone dropped into a gulf wants to fall to the bottom? It falls without being able to avoid falling, and will fall because it must, with ever-increasing rapidity, and fury, incapable of stopping; to go is to obey; obedient to something more than a desire, more even than an instinct: a law!

"How long have we been working now?"

"It will be a year tomorrow."

Was that not life, after all? But the painter was searching for a soul. So he was unable to grasp it, that impalpable gaze, and set it there forever! Folly! To make of thought a line that one marks, to put infinity into a blue patch! That the rose should be a stupor and the white should be a prayer!

"I can't, I can't!"

The soul! But is she not changing from week to week, that child devoid of gesture and voice? Unless, at this moment, exhausted by effort and killed by impotence, he can no longer study nature, since he finds in those great open eyes even more sadness than before . . .

"Why do you seem so grief-stricken?"

"Because I'm in mourning for you."

"Why are you in mourning for me?"

"Because I love you."

When she spoke, he knew that he loved her too.

After the wedding, he went back to work, and for as long as the daylight filtering through the window permitted, the two spouses remained seated facing one another, she petrified in her Madonna's pose, he with head bowed over his palette or his neck craning toward his canvas.

"Have courage," she said, softly.

One day, she uttered a small cry and put her hand to her side; the hope of being a mother was radiant in her opened eyes.

Whether he is born to be a god, a king or a vagabond, a child is never anything but a child, no more desired or beloved by the woman who bears him, and the Queen of the Angels had no other suffering or ecstasy in her gaze when the Redeemer was stirring in her entrails.

Wonderstruck, the painter straightened up.

"Don't move, please! Stay like that!"

He threw two years' work into a corner, and took up another canvas.

He could see now; he understood; he knew; he would be able!

The difficulties were forgotten, the time wasted no longer regretted. To work! He too had his empty cradle; he too, in his eyes and his heart, bore a maternal voluptuousness; in him too the sacred child was stirring anew.

Yes, he would be victorious! What does it require to be victorious? One hour in life! And to win that hour, scorn and faith are sufficient: scorn for the past, faith in the future; disdainful pity for the work accomplished, always miserable; valiant love for the future work, still adorable; do not judge that one has done well, but affirm that one will do well; observe one's impotence but retain pride in one's potency; doubt one's work but believe in oneself. Like worthy writers consoling themselves for the pages they have written with the pages they will write, worthy painters forgive the canvases completed when they salute the majesty of new ones.

He worked, feverishly, hastily, and the months went by.

As our ideas are modified with our souls, and our souls with our lives, he said one morning: "Put your child on your knee."

The hours seemed less slow to the woman thenceforth. In the evening, she smiled affectionately when she contemplated in the painting the image of the little blond figure, so frail and so dear, of baby Jesus, pink and soft, holding out his lovely bare arms.

And when the child died, she wept tenderly at still finding him there.

But she resumed her seat next to the window, her seat and her pose, and looked straight ahead, imagining that the precious burden was still warm in her hollow hands.

"We won't work tomorrow; we'll pray, because he's been asleep for a year."

Then the time went by, as time does, and the woman remained seated; her face no longer had the freshness of yore, but it was sad, mortally sad, and its sadness was more beautiful than beauty.

To see her so desolate in her nimbus, holding Jesus in her arms, one might have thought that the Holy Mother was thinking of destinies to come, and that she had already glimpsed the cross on the mountain.

But that was not the Ideal—never—and the master worked relentlessly.

"One of your hairs has gone white, my poor man."

Many others were whitening as well.

"There are wrinkles in your cheeks, my poor wife."

Many other wrinkles were to come.

"On Sunday, we'll be finished."

That Sunday never dawned.

"I'm very tired; would you like to go and rest by the well?"

On an evening like that one, he had met her, but now they were almost old; the wife, as they went back to town, leaned painfully on the husband's arm; she murmured:

"I can hear our child calling me."

Face to face, each on their seat, they were two phantoms: the specter of folly examining the specter of suffering . . .

Soon, the man came back alone to sit on the stone rim of the well—and the work was not finished!

He had turned it to the wall; twice widowed, by his companion and his dream, having no longer any will nor any objective, he waited to die in his turn.

That was a long time coming too—as slow as the ideal work.

One day, however, he dared to set the dolorous canvas on the easel.

He knelt down in front of it, and prayed.

How pitiful she was, the Madonna, with her poor mortal god, and how well she spoke, with her mute gaze, the somber fatality of life, and the inanity of hope, and the anguish that looms over joys! How human she was, the divine! How well she knew the eternal secret of the abyss, and how frightened she was of the oblivion promised to all dreams! One might have thought visible in her the emblem of the vain religions in which our race ecstasizes, and which death awaits, one after another, and which slowly go on their way to martyrdom, from the cradle to Golgotha.

Only one dot, there on the canvas, to extinguish that overly bright and confident light, as the last ray of daylight dies away: one point near the lip, further to attenuate that shadow of a smile, that sweetness of hope . . . and it would be the idea!

He did not dare.

But he saw the dead woman sitting in her accustomed place, who wanted to say, as before: "Work."

He took up his desiccated brushes, and with a supreme gaze, he contemplated the model. Then, getting down on his knees, he dared.

One dot, one shadow. He stepped back into the room. Night fell.

Then, standing in the silence, he recognized before him his entire soul, his entire life. The unique thought of which his life and thought were made stood up immutably, and gazed at him.

The dream had triumphed! The soul had tamed matter!

After the brushes, the palette slid from the painter's hands. Weeping his first tears of joy, he went to his beloved's seat and kissed her pious lips.

He had no more to do thereafter but depart and join them, the dear absentees, and the hour soon sounded.

In memory of them, until his last day, he kept their almost holy image close to him; when the angelus rang, he knelt down before his Madonna, uniting in the same prayer the adoration of the heavens and the affections of the earth, and the monument of glory was to him but a monument of love . . .

After the master's death, the canvas was famous for a long time in the land, for one of the honest drapers of the city, having acquired it, had written on the background: "The House of Our Lady—Probity—Confidence."

Admired by children coming home from school, the sign remained suspended over his threshold for thirty years, but the merchant's son had it painted over one day, in more cheerful colors.

HENRY DETOUCHE
(1854-1913)

Henry Detouche was and still is far better known as a painter than a writer; he contributed to several *fin-de-siècle* periodicals, including Félicien Champsaur's *Panurge*, supplying poems, articles and short stories as well as illustrations. He was a close friend of the renowned Decadent artist Félicien Rops, and some of his work shows similar influences.

"La Fiancée posthume" first appeared in *La Vogue*, novembre 1900; "The Posthumous Bride" is original to the present volume.

The Posthumous Bride

Paul Anxious lived with all his strength, so the hours went by more rapidly for him than for anyone else. He got undressed in the evening without having had time to dress completely in the morning. He only had the time to curl his moustache two or three times a week. His fingernails were broken most of the time, and he awaited the onset of baldness impatiently because he would finally arrive, by courtesy of it, at being correctly coiffed.

He was so expectant of the future in all circumstances that he never paid any attention to the present, so, when the moment had passed, he doubted the action accomplished, and that made him despair. His imagination worked quickly, more promptly than events, and when it returned from an exploration in the infinity of time, he was contrite, but remained incorrigible. The most trivial events served as a trampoline for his dreams, and visions germinated within him spontaneously and profusely.

When young, at school, while the professor spoke about science or history, he watched the expression on his face, interested involuntarily in his type, wondering quickly where he had seen such a head or a similar before, perhaps in a painting in a museum, and the location and the school of the painter in question. And the subject recounted, and listened to religiously at first, suddenly deviated for the slightest reason, and his mind then wandered in an unexpected direction, far from the point of departure, far from the professor, far from the lecture—and that mental truancy was his habitual state of mind. He saw its inconveniences, in collecting annoyances, but incessantly fell back into the same mental wanderings.

He was introduced as a possible fiancé into families that had commendable female shoots. In the homes of very amiable people, he saw, among others, three young women with flowery eyes who always dressed in bright and supple fabrics. Two were exquisitely blonde, the third brunette and beautiful, and the likeability of all of them was so equal, the charm that they emitted was so great, that he did not know what decision to make. When he left in the evening, having accepted an invitation to dinner, and he saw the group of pretty heads, radiant with so much youth and joy, his mind raced ahead, envisaging the future, seeing all those treasures of grace and beauty fade and extinguish in his hands with the years, and he hesitated over choosing and making a request.

He never went back to the radiant house.

On other occasions he was not alone with a woman for three minutes before he saw a flaw, no matter how slight it seemed, a defective feature of her face or figure, which became a deformity in his eyes. An imperceptible wrinkle became precise for him; during a kiss, the flesh softened in advance on contact with the caress, and it was the eventual being that he then had before his eyes. And that sharp thought traversed him so implacably, through and through, that his companion perceived it in the reflection in his eyes.

"What's the matter, then? What are you thinking about?"

Then he passed his fingers rapidly over his forehead, as if to wipe away an importunate vision, and replied: "Nothing."

He saw in the young woman the realized promise of the inevitable mother-in-law, the paunch and the malady possible according to the physiological indications. Nothing any longer tempted him.

He went home, into the room that had the favor of his habitual intimacy, and which was full of his entire past. There were family souvenirs there, curiosities brought back from travels, gifts from friends, and statues covered in dust, because he expressly forbade his servants to touch them for fear of accidents, and never thought of dusting them himself. Every day, therefore, brought its imperceptible gray layer, whose thickness increased.

At the same time, the large frames that contained, loosely, the photographs of women loved and disappeared, were subjected to the trepidations of the street, and the images were gradually displaced and drawn sideways, eventually lying obliquely. The pastels were disaggregated, their flower fading, and all that subtle work was done slyly, but Paul Anxious followed all its effects.

The windows of his studio initially overlooked a park. One day, in a single afternoon, the tall trees were felled, and all the tenants were consternated. A municipal laundry was constructed on the site. The odors of detergent and dirty underwear replaced the emanations of verdure, and in the place where a nightingale had been heard singing, the beating of the laundrywomen resounded, accompanying conversations of an inevitable triviality.

Two years later, builders came and erected a vertiginously high wall for a neighboring edifice, and a patch of sky was stolen from the solitary; he sensed a certain anguish in seeing the light diminished in his home, but he did not say anything about it. A year later, another story was added to a house on the other side of the road, and his second window was equally compromised. The land became so expensive that it was built on everywhere, and the azure of the firmament shrank more and more.

The years went by and he dreamed, huddled in all the past that surrounded him, circumscribed by the building works in the vicinity, hemmed in by progress, but he held firm and was obstinate, in spite of everything that his friends said, in remaining in the same house.

"No, I don't want to leave," he said. "I've been here too long; everything that is around me has been put there day by day, by virtue of a circumstance that it is pleasant for me to recall. Too many comrades disappeared forever have come to see me here. I've spent too many good evenings smoking and drinking, laughing and talking about the future; too many words have resounded here; too many pretty women have passed through here, vanished forever, but at least having left memories of their contact on every chair, a little of the perfume of their hair in the profound velvet of the cushions of the divan. The minuscule punctures of hat-pins are still visible in places on the wallpaper, because, ornamented like dragonflies, while having the waists and stings of wasps, delicate creatures have alighted here.

"I remember too, all the curiosities that it was necessary to satisfy, the incessant investigations in shop windows, bookshelves or boxes. I have too many memories of everything. Then again, hasn't everything here been furnished and decorated by life, the life of every day, and every hour? All the curtains the furniture, the frames and the trinkets are harmonized in the same atmosphere, the soiling of smoke and dust—that ashen flower made of everything, which velvets uniformly, the pitiless equalizer, gold as well as brass—has put a down on the pottery and the sculpture. The latter, on top of cupboards, thus give the impression of being lighted from below, as if by the footlights of a theater.

"In sum, all the objects, in remaining together, have lost their dissonance, nothing clashes now, all the styles are confounded in the dusty harmony, the vivacity of colors or gleams have calmed down. Everything is growing old together. Sometimes, recent objects, in a short time, want to catch up with their elders, and there's a race to fade; the dying hues arrive first. Are not beloved curiosities, things, animals and people, whatever our differences of age might be, all in the same process?

"If it becomes impossible for me to work here," he continued, "only then will I go to live elsewhere, but I won't disturb anything that is here; everything will remain as it is . . . until I die, I shall give myself the luxury of conserving intact the locale where I have spent twenty-five years of my life—the best. I shall always remain faithful to my youth. Who could truly render me the charm of this décor if I were to quit it? I feel there are the crumbs of myself and the beings that have been dear to me here, and I shall respect the walls that have collected my sighs of joy or sadness, the ceiling that my lamp has blackened as radiant and bright adolescence has fled me. Is not every house a reliquary for the soul, which feels precious therein?"

There were some among his friends who did not understand that, and others that he sensed were only putting on a semblance of understanding; they departed from his home while he delegated his disdain to accompany them to the bottom of the stairs.

And the years passed, augmenting in Paul Anxious the faculty of sensation, exasperating his desire to see everything from a height, in politics, art and literature; he rejoiced in floating radiantly above subaltern preoccupations, and it was his intimate recompense, the refuge within himself that he knew to be purified by the filtration of life. All the protests of his friends and neighbors were, to his opinions, what the current of water is that tempers steel, and he recognized that he was stronger than before.

Every new year, he put the calendar he received on his bookshelves, where he had the habit of placing it. He thus found twenty of them superimposed, with red, blue or green borders, charged with crosses that corresponded to rendezvous once awaited feverishly. They were like little cemeteries piled up. He sometimes picked up those old cardboard squares and tried to remember the significance of certain mysterious streaks, but it was often in vain, for the head no longer remembered what had made the heart beat faster. No matter; he had a quarter of a century of human life ahead of him . . .

One evening, a friend to whom he had lent some money came to visit him. After having chatted at length about various things, giving him the reason for a prolonged absence, he told him that he did not want to content himself with thanking him for his opportune aid in unfortunate circumstances, but that, knowing his eccentric mind, he had brought back something from his travels that might interest him. Opening a package mysteriously hidden under his hat, he held out to him, with a sly smile, the mummified arm of a woman, which he had removed and cut from the body of a chatelaine. The poor mutilated woman had been reposing for centuries, her feet joined, in an abandoned crypt.

Paul Anxious, after having abstained all his life, for fear of marriage, from asking for the hand of a contemporary, thus took possession of the arm of a dead woman.

Seizing the aristocratic fingers of the deceased, he looked for a long time at the fleshless ring finger, and placed a wedding ring delicately thereon.

HÉLÈNE DE ZUYLEN DE NYEVELT
(1863-1947)

Hélène de Zuylen de Nyevelt was the version of her name used on her published work by Baroness Hélène van Zulyen van Nijevet de Haar, née de Rothschild (in the famous banking family). Her early literary work, written in collaboration with Renée Vivien, was published under the pseudonym Paul Riversadale, but she went on to produce poetry, short stories, novels and plays under her own name, all of it heavily influenced by Vivien, including the items she published after the latter's death, scrupulously echoing the younger writer's Decadent and Symbolist leanings.

"Paroles des saisons" first appeared in the collection *Copeaux* (1905), much of which was probably written in collaboration with Vivien. "What the Seasons Say" is original to the present volume.

What the Seasons Say

I
The Lady of Spring

Through the foliage, I saw the uncertain smile of the Lady of Spring. As frail as an adolescent, she had the strange eyes of a disillusioned old woman. She was wandering barefoot, dispersing flowers. She was trampling them under her bare feet, throwing them to the wind with her youthful hands. She trampled them angrily and shredded them in rage.

And, having approached the Lady of Spring, I said to her: "How beautiful you are in all your youth! How charming you are in your cruel joy!"

She laughed, showing her pointed teeth, and replied: "I'm old beneath my blonde hair and the rosiness of my cheeks. I'm older and sadder than the world, under the weight of my flowers. I know the plaintive languor of convalescents, I know the dolorous ardor of the feverish, for I am simultaneously convalescent and feverish. I suffer from not knowing myself, even more than from not knowing the mysterious universe. I suffer from being young and desiring the unknown. For I love everything and nothing.

"Sometimes, I'm in love with the air and the sunlight, and songs on the road, and the sky, and me. I'm in love with existence for its own sake. The joy of breathing is sharper then than the voluptuousness of a caress. I rejoice in being and feeling.

"Sometimes, I'm sad for all my future sorrows, and I feel very old beneath my blonde hair and the rosiness of my cheeks. I cherish myself and I hate myself. I pity myself for weeping unjustly, and something in me cries: *Oh, the abominable, the hideous old woman!*

"And yet, I've been young since the commencement of the world.

"I suffer from being beautiful and loving myself. I suffer from being proud and hating myself. I suffer from everything, because I'm young. I sense that all marvels are possible for me. I suffer from wanting to be happy. I suffer from believing in happiness. How I suffer from being young!"

With her avid fingers, she tore apart the light flowers, before sighing again: "How I suffer from being young and old at the same time!"

And she looked at me for a long time, with her disillusioned eyes.

"Nothing is sadder than hope, and nothing is crueler than expectation. Memory is made of disappointed hopes, and hope already contains the bitterness of future memories."

She threw herself down on the grass, in an overwhelming languor.

"And yet, I'm glad to be alive. I'm glad that there's a sun. I'm glad that there's verdure on the earth. I'm glad to possess the senses of smell and hearing, in order to perceive living beauty, amorously."

She raised a little leaf with a slightly bitter juice to her mouth.

"When I bite this little leaf with a slightly bitter juice, it seems to me that I have the veritable taste of the universe on my lips. It seems to me that I'm eating living forests and prairies. It's by means of taste that one communicates most directly with the very essence of things. A child who bites a wild berry is closer to the primordial world that a thinker listening to the rumor of the sea or a sensualist complicating perfumes."

Suddenly, she started weeping.

"Why are you weeping?" I asked her, eventually.

"I don't know," she replied. "I'm weeping because I'm beautiful and because the sky is mild. And I'm also weeping because I have death in my soul. Oh, if only I could translate my anguish and the disquiet of my being!"

She continued, through infantile sobs: "How I envy the fever of summer, the satiety of autumn and the ennui of winter! I covet the bliss of empty hours. I covet desperately the repose of monotonous and dull hours. Who will give me blissful ennui?"

Birds were singing in the cool shade. The Lady of Spring listened to them, lying upon moss.

"Oh, the sweetness of being! How good tears are, and how exquisite terrors are! Expectations, and even regrets, are precious, since they prove that one still exists. Anything, rather than the great chill of Death. I dread slumber as a redoubtable enemy. I dread abominably the hours when I no longer feel alive.

"And yet, I'm weary of being reborn, weary of being resuscitated. I'm weary of seeing myself flourish again. I'm weary of loving, every year, with a different amour."

She was sitting under a limpid rainbow.

"I dread forgetfulness as much as memory. I'm terrified by life and by death. I'm a poor, uncertain soul, a poor disabled soul . . ."

The birds had fallen silent among the branches, and the rainbow faded away in the distance.

II
The Lady of Summer

I followed the tracks of the Lady of Summer. I followed her footprints through the dried up rivers and the desiccated plains. And I finally saw her, lying, like a fever victim, on a bed of burned moss. She contemplated me with her haggard eyes and murmured:

"I'm thirsty. I'm ill with languor and amour. The sun has consumed me all the way to the marrow. I'm burning. Nothing will ever extinguish my thirst.

"I've drunk the water of the sea in my fever, and the water of the sea has dried out my throat cruelly.

"The solitudes are afraid of my embrace; the prairies fear my implacable kiss.

"I have leaned over springs in order to smile at my reflection in the clear water, and the springs have dried up. I wanted to lie down on the fresh grass, and the fresh grass has withered."

She continued murmuring, with her ardent lips:

"I'm thirsty . . ."

And the echoes, like an invisible aerial choir, took up the plaint and the prayer: *I'm thirsty* . . .

"I've wearied that which I've loved, and I've wearied myself by my vain ardors," she sighed. "I no longer aspire to anything but a tenebrous slumber beneath the extinct stars.

"Every night I search for a peaceful river and let myself float downstream, like a dead lover. I allow myself to be borne away by the peaceful river, my eyes fixed on the glaucous light of the moon. But the moon fears my pale face, obstinately turned toward her own, for she knows that her cold mildness will never calm the bitter burning of my forehead and my eyelids.

"At dawn I flee, exasperating my wild cries, and, weary of suffering, sick with languor and amour, I rip up the clematis, I shred the honeysuckle and I crush the wild lilies underfoot.

"Sometimes, I divert myself with the drowsiness of my thought. I sit down amid the hay and the hayricks, like the peasant women, and I contemplate the red and brown landscapes without seeing them. My eyes are open, unconscious and stupid, and a bewildered torpor numbs my limbs. My wide ruminant eyes reflect the verdure of grass and the rust of spelt, I linger like that until dusk. Indolent snakes come to sleep in the pleats of my robe. I amuse myself ornamenting their living coils with emeralds and pale sapphires. But I sometimes throw them away with a weary gesture, for nothing amuses me for long.

"The imbecile crowd praises me, prefers me and desires my presence; but those who have seen me face to face fear the avid flame of my eyes. I kill those I love. I drink the sap of flowers with so much fever that I cause them to perish under my mouth. I'm like the cruel empresses and queens who kill those who love them, especially those they have loved."

She turned her thirsty and dry lips toward Infinity.

"Freshness!" she sighed. "Freshness!"

Her ardent sight was prolonged in the silence.

"Lizards and grasshoppers are my living hiccups," she said, eventually, cheered up by having seen a little greenness moving at her feet. "I've learned my most beautiful poems from cicadas. They're joyful or sad, in accordance with souls. In the times when humans had a less unquiet soul in a less weary body, an aede sang the praises of the cicada.[1] He compared it to the Gods, because it has no worries and doesn't carry the dolorous burden of human flesh and blood. Today, poets listen to its monotonous cry as a dull plaint.

"I alone am always the same, always burning with the same tormented ardor. I wander in the jungles like a lioness, and my yellow eyes pierce the curtain of the lataniers. Those who contemplate me fixedly lose their reason. I glide through the fields of rice like a furtive python. I cause paradoxical orchids and daturas to bloom in the lands where I reign solitary, for I have a despotic soul, and I want to dominate without sharing. In the countries where I reign solitary, I accord my subjects sparkling and bizarre birds, forests in which an eternal glaucous twilight lingers, and

---

1 The author probably has the ode to cicadas by Meleager of Gadara in mind, although that is by no means the only ancient Greek poetic tribute to the insect in question, and the supplementary comment does not seem to refer to Socrates' famous symbolic employment of cicadas in *Phaedrus*.

flowers, and flowers, and flowers . . . all flowers . . . the most violent and the most delicate, the most barbaric and the most complex . . ."

The Lady of Summer laughed, with an excessive clarity.

"Oh, the sunlight!" she said. "Oh, the sunlight! It flows in my veins like molten gold. It's the very substance of my flesh. It clothes me, like a royal cloak. It ornaments me with translucent jewels. It weighs upon my shoulders, like a burden of blazing metal. I'm weary of the sunlight, and yet I cherish it; for one cherishes desperately that which makes one suffer."

She stopped among the grasshoppers. She picked one up at random and admired it.

"In truth, I have the vindictive soul of the sun. I have the vindictive soul of the sun, and I give death to those who love me."

The Lady of Summer fell silent. She went in search of a little shade under the blue foliage. The chant of the springs fell silent as she approached; and the sundial, gray in the midst of red rose-bushes, ceased to mark the torrid hours. Only the cicadas were singing, untiring and monotonous.

III
The Lady of Autumn

Toward the end of a nostalgic day I went into the sumptuous orchard where the Lady of Autumn was lingering.

Beautiful fruits weighed down the branches. Apples were red-dening in their robust varnish. Pears were being gilded next to violet figs. Apricots were ambering their ripe freshness. The odor of vines soothed the air.

The pomp of colors unfurled like an Oriental procession. Red affirmed its plentitude and its profundity. It was majestic or ten-der, in accordance with the mysterious design of hues. Yellow was ardently velvety, warming up all the way to the fervor of orange.

There were no flowers in the grave orchard where the Lady of Autumn was lingering. Only the chrysanthemums were entangled eccentrically, surrendering their melancholy perfume as if regretfully.

On a bed of mown hay, the Lady of Autumn lay languidly. Vine branches ran through her loose hair, russet and brown, the color of dead leaves, and her eyes were the color of wine. Her orange robe and her red mantle brightened the shade. She was holding an empty cup in her hand. Her lips were laughing, but her eyes remained sad.

When she saw me she rose to her feet and started dancing, trampling scattered clusters of grapes. The juice of the grapes bloodied her beautiful rhythmic feet. And while dancing, she wept.

Overwhelmed by inebriation and lassitude, she finally let herself fall on to the bed of mown hay. With a hesitant hand she sought the golden cup in which she had moistened her avid lips. Being thirsty, she seized it and raised it to her lips. I followed her uncertain gestures with my eyes . . .

Being thirsty, she seized the golden cup and raised it to her mouth . . .

But the cup was empty; and the Lady of Autumn, disappointed, threw it away.

A malaise gripped me in the opulent orchard where the colors were singing. I approached the woman overwhelmed by inebriation and lassitude.

"Why aren't you rejoicing in your grape-harvest?" I asked. "Why are you weeping silently, among the heavy clusters of grapes and the weighty fruits?"

She looked at me with her sad eyes, while her mouth laughed. "I'm weeping," she said to me, slowly, "because I'm going to die."

For the first time, I perceived an indefinable odor that was exhaled by the orchard: the moist corruption of dead leaves and overripe fruit, the mortuary suavity of shredded roses, and the funereal perfume of chrysanthemums . . .

"It's in the plenitude of life," the Lady of Autumn continued, "that one senses with the greatest intensity the presence of death. It's in the blossoming of felicity that one savors with the greatest sweetness the charming bitterness of morbid memories."

Through the echoes of space, she sobbed: "I'm going to die! I'm going to die!"

She picked apart a cluster of grapes in her feverish fingers.

"Tomorrow, the whiteness of death will whiten everything. Great pure breaths will sweep away the dead leaves that are already rotting on the dried up ground. The snow will envelop with its ample folds the livid nudity of the earth. The dead wood will crack in the wind. Tomorrow, there will be the sepulchral Cold. Tomorrow, there will be the slumber of icy things. And today I am drinking to my imminent death."

While speaking, she shredded large red and yellow chrysanthemums.

"Today I've said a dolorous adieu to the heavy clusters of grapes and the weighty fruits. I've said a long adieu to the colors and the perfumes of my orchard. For tomorrow, I'm going to die."

Being thirsty, she seized the golden cup and raised it to her mouth . . .

But the cup was empty . . .

IV
The Lady of Winter

I was meditating in front of the captive fire, in which I rediscovered the redness of old sunsets; and the Lady of Winter tapped on the window panes.

She tapped on the window panes with fingers jeweled with pale sapphires; and her face appeared to me through the blue-tinted glass. Her face appeared to me, so beautiful in its sadness that I resolved to contemplate it at greater length. I followed the Lady of Winter to her palace of starry ice.

The Lady of Winter was sitting on a cathedra of ice encrusted with diamantine frost. A backcloth of stalactites emphasized her profile, rigidly sculptural. She was clad in a royal mantle of snow and crowned with a headband of glittering icicles. With her subtle and vigorous hands she was weaving, in the frame of the Frost, all the landscapes and all the enchantments of winter. She was evoking thus the boreal plains, traversed by snowy flocks of eiders and wild swans. She was evoking the blue slumber of glaciers and the meditation of mountains with limpid summits. With her vigorous and supple hands, she was weaving, in the frame of Frost, all the landscapes and all the enchantments of winter. I saw the fragile lace of branches stripped of leaves and florid with snow. I saw the black frisson of pines under the north wind. And I also saw the moon silvering the ice.

The solitary woman turned her proud and beautiful face toward me. Her hair cast the reflection of a polar sun. Her eyes harbored the glaucous azure of glittering stalactites. The North Wind was asleep in a pleat of her robe.

She said to me: "I'm the Lady of Winter. I'm the mistress of beautiful spaces. I accord, to those who love me, my aristocratic and melancholy soul. My servants are as indomitable and untamed as the storms, which also obey me."

She fell silent, and the North Wind, which was asleep in a pleat of her robe, woke up and flapped its wings. She soothed it with a sovereign gesture, and the North Wind went to sleep again.

Then the Lady of Winter said: "Ignore those who scorn you. Distance yourself from those who love you. Take refuge in solitudes, and the solitudes will murmur familiar words to you, like grave friends. They will advise you with good will. They with criticize you gently. And sometimes, they will praise you sagely.

"Distance yourself from human beings. Thus, you will contemplate the visage of your soul as if in transparent water that no other images have troubled. Learn the force of disdain. Know that men and things can do nothing against silent disdain.

"Only scorn is invulnerable. Be calm in our pride. Pride is the strongest and the most noble chastity. Pride is the savor of souls, for it drives away vulgar temptations and base covetousness. It teaches serenity throughout life and before death.

"Remember that you will die alone. Remember too that every individual ought to live as they would like to die. Prepare yourself for your solitary death by living alone.

"Do not look back. No thinking being is without regrets at the approach of evening or without remorse at the approach of night, but regret and remorse are vain things.

"Do not aspire to do good. It is a goal too high for a human soul to attain. Aspire to do as little harm as possible. The best of men and the saintliest of women are the man and woman who have done the least harm.

"Let your felicity be composed of noble sadness. Rejoice in the North Wind, ice, mists and lacy frost. The wind will be your guide, the snow your consolation."

She fell silent, and the North Wind woke up for the second time. It flapped its wings like a great wild swan. Like a great wild swan the North Wind flapped its wings and flew away into the distance. I saw it soaring above the marvelous white landscape. I followed its imperious flight with my eyes, and I fashioned myself a soul in the image of its soul, cold and tumultuous and free.

I replied to the Lady of Winter: "Like you, I am calm in my pride. Like you, I have the strength of pride and disdain. And like you, I am a friend of solitudes."

The Lady of Winter, sitting on a cathedra encrusted with diamantine frost, smiled at me. And, while smiling, she was weaving with a subtle patience . . . weaving, in the frame of frost, all the enchantments of winter.

JACQUES LAMER

Jacques Lamer contributed several items of verse and prose to *La Vogue* in its third incarnation, but no further information about the writer is readily available and the name might have been a pseudonym.

"Le Désespoir de Myrtis" first appeared in *La Vogue*, mars 1900; "The Despair of Myrtis" is original to the present volume.

The Despair of Myrtis

Myrtis and the fisherman Hylas loved one another, and that love was their sole wealth, so they had hidden it jealously, far from the envious gazes of the crowd, in a wild and solitary place. In the depths of a valley between the sea and the dry bed of a torrent, they had built a cabin with mud and reeds. While Hylas, sheltered by his white sail, fished in the open water of the blue sea, Myrtis mended his nets or went as far as the gates of the nearby town in order to sell the previous day's fish. If the days were monotonous, the nights were delightful, and, whether the nets were full or empty, Hylas' lips were always rich in kisses.

One evening, however, Hylas did not come back, and Myrtis, fatigued by a long and vain wait, having finally decided to get undressed, had to go to bed for the first time without the companion of her life. Anguish and fear kept her awake, sitting on her bed, her eyes wide open, her chin on her knees and her arms extended between her thighs. At daybreak she went down to the sea and, shielding her gaze with her hand, she scrutinized the horizon for a long time. The sea and the beach were empty. She could not hold back her tears.

Anxiously, she advanced over the wet sand. The waves curved before her and came to break and die at her feet. She walked rapidly, her gaze lost in the distance. Sometimes, she stopped abruptly, hesitated, and then set off again. The sun was already sparkling on the horizon and the sand was beginning to burn Myrtis' heels when she suddenly felt all her blood flow back to her heart. She had just perceived the body of her dear Hylas a few paces away, amid the dolorous algae and broken seashells.

She thought she would faint, and, trembling, she knelt down beside him. She leaned over his lips and his breast, searching for a breath or a heartbeat, but she could not perceive anything, and Myrtis knew that Hylas was dead.

Her despair was immense. Like a child, she started insulting the sea, the perverse and cruel water that had taken her lover from her. She picked up pebbles and threw them at it. The calm of the waves irritated her further. She was exasperated by being alone, her soul filled with dolor, in the midst of the mute and tranquil indifference of things. Folly gripped her. She took off her clothes and threw them away. Then, stark naked, clinging to the cadaver, she hugged it with her ardent flesh, between her arms and her thighs. Soon, her limbs, exhausted by fatigue, relaxed, and Hylas' body fell back heavily. Having dressed again, she crouched down beside him, and wept silently until the first shadows of dusk.

Night fell.

Myrtis wanted to take her lover's mortal remains away. The burden proved to be too heavy for her frail shoulders. She fell, and the two bodies sprawled. She had just got up again when she heard the distant plaint of jackals resounding in the mountains. Frightened, she thought of preserving the cadaver from their bites, and with her soft hands, which loved to caress so much, she hollowed out a grave in the cool sand of the shore. That concern kept her busy for most of the night. When the first glimmers of dawn appeared above the cliffs, Hylas was buried and Myrtis, her wrists exhausted and her head empty, had fled.

She did not have the courage to return alone to her cabin. She went up the valley. As she passed by, echoes ran from neighboring valleys and attached themselves to her footsteps, throwing her sighs and her sobs from rock to rock, the name of Hylas, which her lips murmured, and even the slight sound of her naked feet on the ground. Myrtis did not hear them.

She walked for a long time. She went straight ahead, aimlessly. As if to retain her, the brambles attached their long thorny arms to her body and her tattered clothing. Dogwood branches lashed her face and breast cruelly. Sharp stones bit her heels. Her feet and legs sank into the mud of marshy ground. No obstacle stopped her vagabond course.

Eventually, exhausted by fatigue, she went to sleep in the hollow of a gully, in the shade of an olive tree, her feet dangling in the fresh water of a stream. The murmuring current came to collide with the charming obstacle, and lingered there complaisantly.

The melodious sound of a flute woke Myrtis up. She looked around and saw, facing her, on the other side of the stream, a shepherd with a face so becoming that, in spite of her dolor, she felt troubled. He was clad in animal skins, but his legs, arms and breast were naked. The flute slipped from his lips and he said to the amazed and charmed Myrtis, in a very soft voice:

"Who are you, and what favorable god brought you, you who are more beautiful than Venus and more graceful than the nymphs who dance in the woods? Forgive me if I troubled your slumber, frightening with the sound of my flute the importunate swarm of charming dreams that were fluttering over your forehead. I could not resist the desire to see your eyes shine under the delicate curve of your long black lashes. Alas, I am well punished for my audacity, since my wounded heart now makes me your slave."

And Myrtis replied: "I am the unhappiest of women. I am Myrtis. I lived on the edge of the sea with Hylas, and the sea has taken Hylas away from me. I have done everything to reanimate his corpse, and I dug a grave for him in the sand of the beach. I fled, prey to the most frightful despair. Look, in my errant course I have lacerated my feet."

At those words the young shepherd descended into the stream and with his caressant hands he washed Myrtis' feet and legs. He offered her bread and fruit. Then he attempted to console her by means of soft words. He told her about his poor and solitary life on the mountain, and his magnificent dreams. Finally, he sang the pleasures of amour. There was a captivating grace in his language and his gestures. Myrtis allowed herself to be caught by the divine sound of that intoxicating music. A kiss on her arm made her shudder, but she did not withdraw her arm. The shepherd became bolder.

Gradually, the memory of Hylas faded away. Myrtis tried to resist. She did not have the courage. Soon, her mouth opened of its own accord under the shepherd's lips. An irresistible desire burned her flesh and, forgetful of Hylas, she abandoned herself.

From that day on, Myrtis no longer quit the shepherd, and in his hut, there were the same embraces, and the same tenderness, as in the fisherman's cabin. She loved him as she had loved Hylas, and her life had not changed, except that, instead of mending nets, she sheared sheep and spun wool.

GASTON DE PAWLOWSKI
(1874-1933)

Gaston de Pawlowski was an *avant garde* writer best known for his humorous and satirical writings, many of which show the strong influence of his doctoral thesis on *La Philosophie du travail* [The Philosophy of Work], especially the futuristic items co-opted into the portmanteau novel, *Voyage au pays de la quatrième dimension* (1912; expanded 1923; tr. as *Journey to the Land of the Fourth Dimension*), most of which first appeared in the periodical *Comoedia*, of which he was the editor.

"La Visionnaire," and its continuation, "Amour mort," were initially reprinted in the final section of *Polochon, paysages animés, paysages chimériques* (Charpentier, 1909) before being revised as chapters in *Voyage au pays de la quatrième dimension*. "A Visionary," which incorporates the continuation, was originally published in *Journey to the Land of the Fourth Dimension* (Black Coat Press, 2009)

A Visionary

It was in the thirty-third year of the Absolute Savants' reign, at the very moment when human science seemed to have reached its apogee, when a visionary, by means of criminal outrages contrary to all scientific wisdom, turned the world upside down at forty-eight degrees, fifty minutes and thirty seconds of north latitude and zero degrees, one minute and eight seconds of east longitude on the collective terrain A-327, at ground level.[1] (It had been impossible for some time to designate localities in any other way,

---

1 Pawlowski is using the Paris meridian, not the Greenwich meridian, as a baseline; the relevant location is in the south-eastern suburbs of Paris, probably the spot on which the author was writing.

all the towns being confused and superimposed eleven deep on the surface of our marvelous planet.)

Science now reigned alone as absolute mistress and everyone was divinely happy to live in a world organized by her. A machine had been invented, in fact, to create that belief. The horror of the first outrages was only too palpable and there was temporary anxiety about the insufficiency of the projections of iodoform designed to calm minds. It was a matter of criminal acts perpetrated on three exhibits in the Great Central Museum, and the monstrosity of those acts denoted such an aberration of mind that everyone was confounded.

For a long time, in fact, these exhibits had been the last in the world still comprised of *living animals*, the sole survivors of terrestrial fauna, which recalled those distant eras when man still shared his home with the thousands of animals from which he had descended. These curious specimens, occupying three special palaces, were three in number: a dog, a flea and a horse—but no one knew those ancient names any longer.

The first was, it was said, a bizarre creature, always on all fours, with a depressed skull, pointed ears, often pronouncing the same words—*yap! yap! yap!*—and devoid of all mathematical knowledge. It had been classified among the ferocious prescientific animals of the *anti-elephant* genre because of its hairy trunk—set behind rather than in front, as in the elephants, and designed, it was believed, to withdraw nutriments from the body.

The second animal, lodged in a grandiose palace, was scarcely larger than a grain of tobacco, but it made prodigious leaps. It was thought to date from the chaotic period during which the Earth had been encumbered with blocks of stone, which rendering walking more difficult. It was mute, as ignorant as the other, but livelier.

The third animal, finally, was of considerable size. Walking on all fours, like the first, it made a sort of whinnying sound without any practical implication, sniffed the air and struck the ground with its foot. This fashion of self-expression, analyzed by calculation, had furnished nothing intelligible. According to vague items of information surviving the second deluge, it was thought possible to baptize it with its old name, inasmuch as it could be reconstituted—the *Soliped*—even though it had four feet rather than one, as the name appeared to indicate; it was assumed, in consequence, to be a degenerate specimen: a monster.

These three animals were nourished, with great difficulty, with a synthetic artificial grass costing two thousand europeans a roll, since all vegetation had been suppressed on Earth by order of the Great Central Laboratory, the pernicious example of the loves of plants being disastrous to social order. By virtue of a laudable sentiment of scientific probity, people had abstained from teaching them to read, to calculate or to study the workings of interplanetary trains, in order to conserve them as they had once been—and also for fear that the admirable electric engraver employed for the instantaneous education of all young citizens as soon as they emerged from the *birth machine* might be subject to a fatal return of ignorance by induction.

For a long time, in fact, the reproduction of the human species had been entrusted to special biological laboratories, and sexual love, the joy of the ancient world, was unknown to the mechanically-minded citizens of the new scientific State.

The assault upon the collections of the Great Central Museum was actually committed by the son of a high functionary of that establishment: young Antimony, a descendant of the noble Stibine family.[1]

From an early age, Antimony had given evidence of a strange character, rebellious against all scientific information; it had been necessary to send him back four times to the engraver, whose fuses he continually blew by virtue of his obstinacy. When he came of age at fourteen and a half he was refused the social joys of artificial marriage in the special State workshops responsible for the necessary sample-collection. His father died of shame and his uncle Kermes fell gravely ill.[2]

---

1 "Stibine" derives from the Latin term for antimony, Stibium, which gives the element its chemical symbol, Sb.

2 Kermes is the common name of an insect related to the cochineal beetle, which was once similarly used to produce a red dye. Antimony sulfide, commonly known as antimony red, was also used as a pigment.

Antimony passed entire minutes dreaming instead of calculating. Sometimes, he spent a long time looking at his work-companion Benzamide, and asked her what reason there could be for the differentiation of the sexes. Benzamide, intrigued and quite disturbed, searched the logarithm tables for the answer, but could not find it.

A year later, contrary to all custom, Antimony had not wanted to have his brain taken out in order to have it replaced, as everyone else did, by a twelve-tier electric filing-system, and that evidence of thoughtlessness had conclusively plunged the families Sb_1O_2 and Sb_3O_4, the young man's closest relatives, into desolation.

Such antecedents foreshadowed tragic adventures.

For an entire year, Antimony became increasingly depressed; he no longer listened to the quotidian phonographs, was disinterested in the course of vibrations, and spent long hours in contemplation in front of the three living animals. Then he went out, arms dangling by his sides, to watch the chemical clouds drift across the sky between the artificial trees, spending days in the sunlight and going to bed when everyone got up at the electric dawn.

Sometimes, he wandered the streets like someone suffering from hallucinations, murmuring: "I love . . . I love . . ."—but he did not know what.

Mysteriously, in order to escape from his ennui, he then set about constructing a strange harness composed of interlaced cords and asbestos straps. Sometimes, he slipped into the deserted walkways of the Museum, went as far as the Soliped's cage, took new measurements and returned home to work in secret.

When everything was ready, he waited patiently for the great festival of Benzilic Aldehyde and, taking advantage of the general inattention, took possession of the three living animals. With frightful courage, he imprisoned the living flesh of the Soliped in a network of straps, leapt on the monster's back, succeeded in taming its wild resistance, and set about exciting it by voice and gesture. The Soliped soon bounded forwards, carrying the visionary with it on its mad course.

The anti-elephant followed, gamboling and releasing its strange and terrible cry: "Yap! yap! yap!"

As for the jumping animal, it had immediately lodged itself in the anti-elephant's fur, and let itself be carried off without resistance or fright.

The abomination of desolation then spread throughout the entire world, and a long S.O.S. of terror maddened the eleven tiers of science.

Like a whirlwind, the frightful cavalcade ran along entire autotracks, was engulfed in tunnels, launched itself over balloon-bridges, precipitated itself down parachute stairways and miraculously evaded the thousands of items of security apparatus spread by science over the entire world.

Magnetic roads were short-circuited, rivers resumed their courses, and a veritable blade of grass grew in a laboratory; thus science knew every shame.

The scientific world was then so thoroughly mechanized, in fact, that it was defenseless against an individual initiative that it had not foreseen, and the slightest dust of intelligence, lifted by the wind, was able to throw that gigantic clock out of order.

Innumerable films, taken in flight, showed Antimony smiling in his crazy course, quite transfigured, sitting up on the Soliped—which he regarded avidly—shivering and gripping its living flesh. He was seen to bound forward, then stop abruptly on the summit of some mountain, while at his feet, stretching up towards him, the anti-elephant, indubitably tame, gently licked his hands.

✳

It was not until the following evening that they were able to regain control of the disaster. It was observed with amazement that the animals had come to no harm, and they were returned without difficulty to their palaces.

As for young Antimony, even though he too had suffered no injury, it was decided his action could have had no other provenance than a sadistic counter-scientific madness of the third degree. He tried to explain, vaguely, that he had obeyed an irresistible inner desire, akin to a mysterious atavistic instinct, but he could give no reasonable explanation of his outrage and convinced himself that his criminal action had not satisfied the irrational aspirations that were devouring him.

It was decided to intern him in the laboratory where he worked and to monitor him closely for a year. Given the marvelous progress accomplished by science, the prisons and dungeons of old were long gone, and it is understandable that the new world took great pride in that reform, which placed men on a par with gods. To tell the truth, there was no difference between the condition of citizens submissive to the superhuman State and that of ancient convicts, except that the convicts of old enjoyed freedom of thought and the spectacle of nature. Prisons no longer had any utility in such circumstances.

The strict surveillance to which Antimony was subject was scarcely favorable to him. It revealed new scandals much more dangerous to public order than his assault on the Museum collections. It was thus that the terrified Absolute Savant learned what strange questions Antimony asked Benzamide regarding the utility of the sexes. His outrage reached its maximum when it was reported to him that Antimony and Benzamide were having frequent quarrels. In the new scientific world, all discussion was, in fact, unknown, since all discord could be immediately regulated by calculation.

The danger to the State became immense, but it was necessary, in order to bring a formal accusation against Antimony, to find a pretext that would not awaken any suspicion. He soon furnished one himself by writing, contrary to all the laws, an implausible manifesto from which all equations were excluded and which rested on nothing but ideas! For a citizen of the Superhuman State, that was a work of folly.

Antimony was arrested that same evening, and the Absolute Savant breathed more easily.

✳

It was on the happy occasion of the great worldwide feast of the Acceleration that Antimony was brought to trial.

Since the already-distant hour when Kilowatt, the man with the rubber fingers, had opened the doors of the Workshop and released the radiant effluvia of the artificial sun upon the world, hundreds of citizens with phosphor-bronze brains had been hurrying madly through the arterial highways and winding venous streets crying: "Ninety-three! Ninety-three! Ninety-three!" What that signified was that the net output of the new State dynamos had attained ninety-three percent.

The scientific satisfaction was general, for everyone believed that the progress of the Superhuman State was now solely dependent on the increase of social speed. Human cells had been preoccupied with nothing else for a long time. Abundantly nourished with arsenophenol, provided with arms of bismuth, electrified brains and bacterial dust-covers, all they had to do was perform their functions in narrowly delimited conditions and their happiness, in accordance with the exact givens of science, could only increase.

The Superhuman State, by complete contrast, remained perfectible. It had been taken in the earliest days of humankind for a simple juridical fiction, but with the unbounded progress of science, its living reality soon became undeniable. The replacement of a human cell was, therefore, an insignificant natural occurrence; the death of the Superhuman State, by contrast, would entail that of all the people who could not live artificially without it.

✳

One after another, surrounded by universal respect, the members of the Central Brain arrived on the roof of the State Palace and descended by the electric elevator to the Hall of Science, where the annual ceremony of the Acceleration was held.

The one hundred and eighteen State Scientists were there, sitting at their keyboards, impassive and mute. Above them, majestically enthroned, under the direction of the Absolute Savant, were the Twenty Old Men of Yesteryear, the ancestors known to humanity by means of books now destroyed in the interests of the safety of the Superhuman State.

Everyone knew that judgment would be passed on the visionary Antimony in the first ten minutes of the session. To tell the truth, the madman's ideas hardly seemed worth such an expenditure of time, and the citizens with brains of bronze were trying in vain to figure out the true motive that might have led the Twenty Old Men of Yesteryear to interrogate the lunatic in such solemn circumstances.

It was rumored in the crowd that Antimony had been diverted from the straight path by a sojourn of three months in the disaffected deserts of ancient Europe, and his assault on the collections in the Great Museum was recalled. All that the people and the hundred and eighteen State Scientists could determine was that a capital accusation of scientific imprecision hung over him. Only the Absolute Savant and the Twenty Old Men of Yesteryear understood the disturbing gravity of the debate, for they alone knew that, thanks to them, Love was extinct in the world, and that its resurrection might bring down the Superhuman State.

A few seconds passed and the session was opened. Blue rays succeeded the red rays and Antimony appeared, introduced by an automaton and powerfully shackled by hypnoses of both feet. Briefly, his frank, clear and luminous gaze wandered indifferently to the dome, criss-crossed by the instantaneograms of the provincial journals, then settled, abruptly and ardently, on Benzamide, who was sitting on the witnesses' bench, waiting anxiously.

Suddenly, the keyboards were activated and the Absolute Savant got up to summarize the ideograph of accusation.

Antimony claimed in his manifesto:

Firstly, that a *qualitative* reasoning ought to replace the scientific methods of the State, based on the illusions of time and space, in directing human cells.

Secondly, that man, without recourse to the Superhuman State, by the cultivation of *his own will*, would be able to tame the elements, fly in the skies, float without material support, and even escape death.

Thirdly, that with the increase of that same *individual will*, man would be able to displace himself instantaneously from one place to another, no longer subject to the infantile rules of space.

Fourthly, that this formidable augmentation of individual power could, undoubtedly, *only be produced as a function of other passions, unknown today, but whose nature it was urgently necessary to research in the history of past centuries.*

As this last paragraph was read, the Twenty Old Men of Yesteryear felt themselves going fearfully pale. What, then, was this terrible force of Love that had contrived to come back to life in the cinders of an abolished world to challenge their omnipotence? Was science not the most powerful thing of all, then? It was necessary to settle the matter.

✳

When the reading of the ideograph had finished, violent emanations of protest traversed the hall, and the Absolute Savant, addressing himself to Antimony, went on, sternly: "I cannot understand why, when you were under observation, you asked that your ideas be submitted to laboratory assistant Benzamide, the daughter of the illustrious Anthracite, with whom you conducted your studies. You have affirmed that, without her approval and presence, you cannot do anything. She is here today, in front of us, and I must warn you that this opportunity to explain yourself is the last that you will be given."

A long silence descended.

Haggard, with eyes aflame, Antimony looked at Benzamide; his effort of comprehension seemed frightful. The Twenty Old Men of Yesteryear followed the scene with anguish, ready to intervene; the hundred and eighteen scientists, completely uncomprehending, stared at the accused impatiently. Benzamide, in her turn, studied Antimony with a lively curiosity, as if she were seeing him that day for the first time. The experiment was infinitely perilous; it was necessary that it cease immediately, and the Absolute Savant got up nervously.

"In the absence of any explanation on the part of the accused," he said, dryly, "we shall suspend the session for three minutes, in order to permit Benzamide to draw conclusions. She alone knows the accused's ostensible works well enough to be able to testify in his favor."

Without knowing exactly what she was doing, Benzamide shut herself up alone in the laboratory adjoining the session hall. Her ideas were in turmoil, theories and methods dancing before her eyes as if she had been seized by madness.

Violently, she tried to bring order to her thoughts, to look into herself. Fortunately, she was not in any doubt. Was not her father the glorious inventor of the system of repopulation of the artificial State that had replaced whatever primitive and outdated method had previously been in use? Nevertheless, she was not like other daughters, and strange ideas sometimes got into her head. Often, when she worked with Antimony, she had abrupt fits of annoyance when the young man employed methods that were not hers. Alone among all her companions, however, she did not like her name; she would rather have been called Narcotine or Codeine.

Two minutes went by; then, suddenly, without knowing why, Benzamide felt hot tears running down her cheeks.

Instinctively, the young woman got up, took up a test-tube and conducted a rapid analysis in the Atomometer: water, 983.0; sodium chloride 13.0; mineral salts, 0.2; albuminous matter, 5.0.

I'm going mad, she thought. *There's nothing outside science; this madman is dishonoring the State.*

The third minute having elapsed, Benzamide went back into the session hall, resumed her place, and, with a movement of the head, signified that she had nothing to say; then she looked away.

There was a click, and a see-saw motion; Antimony slid on to the iodoformed table, inert.

※

No objection having been raised by anyone—even Benzamide—and Antimony posing a danger to the State by reason of his madness, the judges, exercising their discretionary power, proceeded by themselves, promptly and without further ado, to replace his brain with a logarithmic machine in arsenic bronze, of the regulation model furnished by the State

Thus, the spectators of that tragic scene soon saw Antimony leave, a docile automaton devoid of personality or thought, to mingle with the crowd of slaves of the State outside, awaiting the scrupulously regulated mechanical impulses of the Master of the Workshop.

And while Benzamide, her head bowed and her thoughts in disarray, went back to her social father's laboratory, the Twenty

Old Men got up and went into the Privy Council Chamber. There, still trembling at the dangerous experiment they had just attempted, they looked at one another slowly, without saying anything. They alone, in all the world, knew that something immense had just been destroyed forever: something fabulous, with which ancient humanity had lived for centuries; something that might have put the State in peril simply by virtue of the pronunciation of its name.

And over Love, definitively dead, over the ashes of the Divine Suffering of yesteryear, assured henceforth of the passivity of citizens of bronze with automatic hearts, they were finally able to glimpse the colossal triumph on the artificial world, forever submissive to the claws of the Superhuman State.

In the street, the docile crowd cried again: "Ninety-three! Ninety-three!"—which signified that the net output of the new central dynamos had reached ninety-three percent.

MAURICE MAGRE
(1877-1941)

Maurice Magre was a native of Toulouse who went to Paris in 1897 in order to become a Symbolist poet and Bohemian; he joined Stuart Merrill's coterie and published several collections of Symbolist verse before directing the bulk of his effort into prose, eventually becoming a successful playwright, novelist and essayist, all of his work retaining a very strong Symbolist and Decadent influence. Almost all of his prose fiction is available in translation in a twelve-volume set from Black Coat Press issued in 2017.

"Le Premièr amour du docteur Faust" first appeared in the *Revue Hebdomadaire*, 6 septembre 1902; "Doctor Faust's First Love" was originally published in *The Marvelous Story of Claire d'Amour and Other Stories* (Black Coat Press, 2017).

Doctor Faust's First Love

Once, in a small town whose name I have forgotten, there lived a man justly renowned for his wisdom and his science, and a young student celebrated for the levity of his mind.

It is said that the knowledge of Dr. Faust was infinite. Every plant became virtuous in his hands; a cripple he had visited threw his crutches toward the heavens on the threshold of his house. Three astrologers had come from France to consult him. A rich Danish lord, mute from birth, arrived in the town one evening to the sound of trumpets, followed by a cortege of pages and halberdiers; after a short conversation with Dr. Faust he was talking like a preacher monk and haranguing the trees along the road and the birds in the sky on every subject.

Some said that such a power came from the Devil, others from God, for the judgments of men are different.

Of all the blond students who spent their time singing love songs, wooing beautiful girls under the linden trees and emptying large tankards of beer in the taverns, Fritz was certainly the most joyful, the most insouciant and the most foolish. He did not believe in either science or virtue. He had lovely blue eyes and a bold expression, and he pleased women because he desired them, without loving them in his heart. He considered that life is like a long road along which it is necessary to walk cheerfully, only pausing to pick a flower or smile at a young woman washing clothes in a stream. One friend dies, another marries; one dances and one puts on mourning. That is the course of things. God was waiting at the end of the journey, with a long pipe and yellow boots, outside the Inn of Paradise, and would judge him by the number of bottles of Rhenish wine he had been able to empty.

The student's house was opposite the scientist's. Fritz's smile and Faust's beard, wisdom and folly, were good neighbors; the world is full of such contrasts.

※

Now, when Fritz reached his twentieth year he fell in love. That happened on a fine Sunday in spring. That day, the skin of women was creamier than usual, and the beer on the threshold of taverns had an admirable color. Fritz was wandering through the streets on his own. Pipe-smoke was rising up so thickly that it obscured the sun; a mild peace seemed to possess all hearts; young women were going for walks wearing new bonnets and their most beautiful dresses; audacious clerks were following them closely, and more than one kiss could be heard in the solitary pathways.

Fritz emerged from the town and reached a small wood; he saw peasants dancing under the chestnut-trees; dusk was falling gradually and the shadows rendered the trees solemn.

The music of violins resounded in the distance in the warm air; a young woman went by, and her gaze met Fritz's. Her dress had a mysterious rustle, and she disappeared around a bend in the path. But what was the student experiencing? What had that gaze cast into his soul? It seemed to him that he discovered the trees and the sky, the beauty of the world, and that his life was beginning. He ran in time to see the shadow of the young woman decreasing on the horizon, but she was a long way off. Then he retraced his steps, slowly, sat down on a bench and, perhaps for the first time, he wept.

Fritz soon learned that the young woman that he loved was the beautiful Elsbeth, the only daughter of burgomaster Frosch. Fritz had a simple nature, and in him, action always followed dreams. He therefore ran to ask for her hand in marriage.

Burgomaster Frosch had one quality and one fault: he was moral and miserly. The student Fritz, on the contrary, was reputed to have no restraint in his conduct and to throw his money out of the window. Burgomaster Frosch therefore sent the student Fritz away, and in order to avoid the enterprises of the audacious individual, he resolved to engage the beautiful Elsbeth to one of his friends, a rich and aged lord.

The beautiful Elsbeth, like so many of her peers, hid a mediocre soul beneath the adornment of her floating hair, her brilliant skin and her pure eyes, for the ideal does not always take the most beautiful forms in nature in order to realize itself. She therefore accepted the rich and aged lord as a fiancé, deeming that she would console herself for amorous kisses with precious garments, Tibetan shawls and silks from China.

When the student Fritz learned that, he fell into a great despair, and spent the first three days getting drunk on strong wine. And as his chagrin had not eased after that time, he ran to a courtesan who was one of his female friends and spent three days with her. That time having elapsed, he was even more unhappy, because of bodily fatigue, which makes the soul wretched and weak. Then he thought that science and labor might perhaps bring a remedy to his woes. He bought books, optical instruments and poisons, and, for three further days, he studied the circulation of the blood in the human body, the transfusion of metals and the movement of the planets. His suffering only increased with his knowledge of the world. He resolved to ask Dr. Faust to cure him of the malady of amour.

✳

On the eve of his hundredth year, Dr. Faust had a dream.

In that dream, he saw himself again as he had been in the time of his youth, not too ugly in the face, curious and good, loving nature and life. Already the flame of telescopes and the mysterious design of maps appeared to him to be more beautiful than the eyes of women.

There was a young maidservant in the neighborhood named Gretchen, who put on every morning, in his honor, a well-ironed bonnet and a pink apron, and who often went past his door, carrying water, tucking her skirt up with a gesture she knew to be pretty. She loved the student Faust because she was naïve and hard-working, but he did not want to know her, and tried to elevate his soul toward the most august thoughts.

Now, the dream that haunted Dr. Faust's mind that evening represented to him a sad winter evening vanished in the past, when Gretchen's eyes had met his for the first time. Faust was alone, snow was beating the window-panes, and someone had knocked on the door. It was little Gretchen, who, blushing and bold, had simply come to offer herself to the man she loved. And Faust, without hesitation, even though he had a good heart, had sent her away, for he was also proud and he believed that he would be able to embrace and conquer the world by means of his labor. A little sob had resounded in the snow, and he had never seen Gretchen again.

And now, after so many years, Faust heard a voice that said to him: "Weep, old man, for the child whose love you rejected; weep for the joys that you have not known, ignorant individual who did not know that the greatest wisdom is to live like all men."

Dr. Faust woke up, his forehead bathed in sweat. The yellow lamplight trembled on the walls. He looked at the dusty books, the sadly lined-up flasks, the jars, the retorts, the instruments. And then, remembering, he wept bitterly.

※

It was the following day that the student Fritz, introduced by the disciple Wagner, penetrated into Dr. Faust's room. A thousand strange objects were set out beneath a high ceiling: a death's-head, placed on the table, seemed ready to cry out to the visitor: "I'm the master of the house; what do you want?" At the back, sitting in his armchair, Dr. Faust was plunged in a profound reverie.

Then Fritz recounted to him his youthful folly, his unhappy amour, and how he had resolved to extinguish the flame of his desires within him. And when he had spoken, Dr. Faust stood up, prey to a great agitation, and replied to him:

"I only know my dementia, which is the equal of yours. What! Because a woman who has pretty eyes and has pleased you is going to marry an old lord, you want to renounce life? How lucky you are to have a supple body, blond hair, to love, and even to suffer! You envy my science, child? I'm the most ignorant of men, and there is no shepherd boy in the world who does not have more knowledge than me. You've come to interrogate me? But it's me who ought to have come to you, like a pilgrim with rope sandals and a cloak the color of rust. You could have informed me about the sweetness of loving a woman and thinking about her in the evening while going to sleep in a meadow. Fortunate are the amorous, fortunate are the mad! They walk like the blind, and yet they don't fall into wells, like sages. What cheerful companions fantasy and caprice are! Give me a fool's bauble and bells, young student . . ."

Faust started groaning, and then hid his head in his hands; and the student Fritz left, full of grief, because the truth has never consoled amour . . .

Several months had gone by, and one evening Dr. Faust was meditating with even more melancholy than usual. It was winter, it was snowing, and snow gives old men sad dreams of shrouds and tombs. Then again, the bells and celebratory songs had been resounding all day, for the burgomaster's daughter was getting married. Out there, young men and young women were dancing the wedding quadrilles merrily; he was shivering by the fire. Faust's logical mind was not pleased by those contradictions.

Someone knocked several times on the door. Faust started, thinking that it might perhaps be Death that was passing by and had come to collect him. He trembled; but he was proud, and, not wanting to show any fear, he said:

"You are cruel, certainly, to come to take me away from all these good things. I was working in peace with all these dear auxiliaries of my research. But I welcome you without surprise and without fear, for I recognize your footsteps behind my door. Let me take this blue flower, this cedar stick, and I'm your companion."

Faust opened the door, and was utterly astonished to see, instead of the grimacing visage of Death, the delicate and pretty features of Gretchen, such as he had known her of old. She smiled sadly, and made him a sign to follow her. The snow was shining in the distance and Faust's mind was full of allegories. An unknown tenderness descended within him, and sweet and childish confessions hastened to his lips. "Oh, Gretchen, you whom I was unable to love, forgive me!" he cried.

Gretchen, in her white bonnet and pink apron, was still smiling, and Faust followed her through the snow. She went through the streets, emerged from the town and ran along a path. They arrived at a little wood of chestnut-trees. They stopped; the trees were beautiful and grave, and thoughts of amour were floating in the sky.

The violins that were playing at the beautiful Elsbeth's wedding were vaguely audible and, raising his eyes, Faust saw the body of the student Fritz swinging gently, hanging from a high branch. He extended his arms toward Gretchen, saying: "Look at our different follies, and how we have been punished for them."

Dr. Faust wept in the snow, and now the student Fritz, at a sign from Gretchen, descended from his tree, and a great light inundated the earth, and the landscape changed and became divinely beautiful. The trees rose up all the way to the sky, a road of blue ice descended toward a miraculous valley. Gretchen had taken Fritz's hand and Faust's hand. One had loved a great deal, the other had dreamed a great deal; there was much they had to be forgiven.

And behind the little girl with the sad smile, the young student and the old scholar entered the realm of the dead.

HAN RYNER
(1861-1938)

Han Ryner was the version of his name used after 1896—when he became a fervent Anarchist—by Henri Ner, a prolific journalist, novelist and short story writer. Almost all of his work embraces his own idiosyncratic brand of mystical "individual anarchism," derived from the Greek cynic philosophers, whom he considered to be the inventors of the method of teaching by means of parables, which he tried to continue. Samplers of his work in translation are *The Superhumans and Other Stories* (Black Coat Press, 2011) and *The Human Ant and Other Stories* (Black Coat Press, 2014.)

"Lumière-de-douleur" allegedly first appeared in *Demain* in 1897 before being reprinted in the *Revue Franco-Allemande*, avril 1901; "Light-of-Sorrow" was originally published in *The Superhumans and Other Stories*.

Light-of-Sorrow

In those days, life had become quite impossible on the frozen Earth. The last reindeer was dead and it was rare to discover any lichens beneath the equatorial snows.

A hundred humans, however, obstinately persisted in not dying. All day long they scratched in the snow searching for some edible vegetation—or, armed with enormous knives, they pursued a seal, which released lamentable, almost human squeals in its limping flight. In the evening, they came together in the same igloo, huddling together and warming one another up with their love—for they were good people. They wept when they cut the throats of the squealing seals, wondering what crimes their ancestors had committed that condemned them to kill in order to sustain their expiring existence.

Sometimes, though, in spite of their meekness, pressed by the madness of hunger, one of them would hurl himself upon another, kill him, and devour his warm limbs. Then, the horrible pangs appeased, he would recover his reason and die of grief.

Among these sad and gentle beings who were pursuing the fatality of an ending world, the saddest and gentlest of all was a man of thirty who was respected by everyone for his antiquity. There was nothing that could be known that he did not know, and every evening, he would teach his companions the science that had been rendered useless by the excessive cold. He told them about the ancient resources of fortunate humankind, and helped them to understand by means of strangely clear analogies. As his sterile knowledge made him sad, his companions called him by a musical and melancholy name that meant "Light-of-Sorrow"

※

For five days, no one had eaten. They were all wandering around in groups, searching with terrible cries, but finding nothing. Light-of-Sorrow waved his large cutlass crazily. Everyone feared being killed by his famished fury.

One young orphan, however, whose name translates as Mother's-Tears, came to scrape away the snows by his side—and the orphan child smiled at the madman, whose strange eyes did not frighten him. It seemed, moreover, that the madness was gradually calmed by the smile.

Suddenly, Mother's-Tears uttered a loud cry of joy. He had discovered a lichen under the shifted snow. Violently, unconscious of what he was doing, Light-of-Sorrow precipitated himself upon him, tore the lichen from the little starveling's hand and ate it.

And his hunger was appeased—not sufficiently that he no longer suffered pain in his gut, but enough for him to recover his senses.

The weeping child looked at him and, vanquished by pain and disappointment, he fell into the white shroud of snow. Suffering in the depths of his soul for having caused suffering to one more unfortunate than himself, Light-of-Sorrow made a strange gesture of barbaric generosity. He extended his left arm on a block of ice and, with a sharp blow of his large knife, he cut off his hand. Then, presenting the bloody flesh to the child, he said: "Eat!"

The child made no move to take the bloody flesh—and the gaze of Mother's-Tears became a fixed, implacable, dead reproach . . .

✳

That evening, with the exception of Light-of-Sorrow, no one in the igloo had eaten for six days.

"We're all going to die," someone said.

Isolated in a corner, lost in the memory of his time and the pain of his wound, Light-of-Sorrow murmured: "Life wants to live!"

In the cold night, they also heard someone move to stand up, and a woman's voice affirmed, courageously: "Life shall live!"

This bold statement had no effect on any of the dying people. No one replied. It seemed the bleak despair, heavier than before, descended upon the effort to express hope. Since the words had produced neither heat in the cold not light in the darkness, was it all over, and the silence that had fallen the final silence?

Everyone, however, turned in the same direction. Something was shining in the night: a vague aureole around a gentle and valiant female face. And the woman said: "Shall we rise up, to love on Venus?"

"How shall we rise up?" asked Light-of-Sorrow.

"I don't know. Let's go."

The people went out of the cave—and those sad and gentle beings who had suffered so much and loved so much began to rise up into the air.

Light-of-Sorrow could not go with them. He sensed that he was attached to the Earth. "The weight of the crime," he sighed. But he looked at his handless arm, raised it into the air like a prayer, and began to rise, far behind the others.

His ascension was ponderous. He would never be able to catch up with his former companions. He saw them draw away, inexorably and forever. Then he lost sight of them—and to all his other miseries was added the misery of being alone.

※

Slowly, painfully, he rose up. He rose slowly, with a horrible sensation of effort, so long as he directed his injured arm toward the heavens. The arm seemed to be opening the space above him.

When the overtired arm fell back, though, Light-of-Sorrow, motionless in the infinity of the world and his anguish, felt space close around him again—and everything became black. It was as if he were in a tomb, and he felt that he was dying.

With an effort that became more painful every time, he lifted up his weary arm again, and began rising again into the suddenly brightened sky.

He rose up for millions of years.

※

He arrived on Venus. Venus resembled the Earth when he had left it. He did not find any trace of his companions there, or any trace of any living thing. Already, Venus was a dead world.

Light-of-Sorrow understood. Weighed down by his incompletely-expiated crime, he had remained *en route* for too long.

"I can ask no more than to suffer all the necessary suffering," he said—and, with his mutilated arm pointing directly at the heavens, he resumed his ascension.

He rose up for millions of years.

※

He arrived on Mercury—and he found that Mercury was a dead world.

I can ask no more than to suffer all the necessary suffering, he thought—but he did not say it, for he could no longer find words to express his thought.

He understood. In the long interval since he had last spoken, he had forgotten the words.

He did not weep, for he thought: *What use are words, since I'm alone? When I have found humans, they will teach them to me.*

And, with the liberating stump upraised toward the heavens, he resumed his slow ascension.

He rose up for millions of years.

※

As he rose up, it seemed to him that the sun was emitting less heat and light. Then the sun became no more than a kind of enormous moon. Light-of-Sorrow conjectured that the sun had become a habitable planet, doubtless inhabited. Perhaps he would find his companions there.

Surrounded by former planets that had become dead satellites, the sun-planet was probably rotating around a star in the constellation Hercules.

That was one of Light-of-Sorrow's last vague thoughts. Having lost words, he gradually lost thoughts.

Then he almost lost consciousness of himself; he was no longer anything more than an elevatory instinct.

※

He arrived on the sun, which was indeed a habitable planet. There he saw trees as stout and high as mountains, and animals that resembled moving hills.

In the midst of this gigantic vegetation, he recovered the consciousness of his distinct existence. He reflected, and recovered his memories.

On this warm and fecund planet the living was easy, especially for a being as tiny as a terrestrial human. Fruits were abundant, and the smallest fruit could feed him for a month.

Having a great deal of time to himself, he observed the new world as a child might, and ended up understanding life in the part of the sun where he was.

Among the unexpected creatures that he saw, some were particularly attractive to him. Even though they were very different from himself, and even though none of the words recovered from his memory were capable of describing their strange form, he understood that they were the humans of the sun. Often, by the variously soft light of the stars, they came together in the benevolent coolness and chatted.

At first from a distance, and then at closer range, hidden behind a leaf or between two pebbles, Light-of-Sorrow accustomed his ears to the thunder of their voices. He ended up understanding a few words of their language, and eventually understood everything that the articulated thunder was saying.

One night, by the variously soft light of the stars, someone whom Light-of-Sorrow understood, by distant analogies, to be respected for his antiquity said mysterious things.

These are the mysterious things that the respected old person said, and which Light-of-Sorrow, hidden within the calyx of a white flower, heard:

"According to the ancient sages, the planet on which we live was, for a long time, a star: a great fire lit in space. Uninhabitable itself, it gave light and heat to satellites that were the living planets, which our birth has killed.

"Again according to ancient tradition, the last inhabitants of the satellites migrated to our world. Traditions vary as to the nature and form of these beings, agreeing only in representing them as very small. Some books compare them to various species of our wingless insects.

"There is one other point on which all accounts agree: our ancestors, who were frightful barbarians, could not bear the proximity of rational beings of too different a form, and killed them all.

"Whether or not they carried out this murder, it is certain that the first humans of the sun committed many crimes. It is in punishment of those crimes that we have so much trouble slowly discovering incomplete truths.

"Perhaps the traditions regarding the emigrants from Mercury, Venus, the Earth and even further afield are themselves merely ingenious myths expressing the evident truth already suspected by our primitive ancestors: the eternity of life. We shall never know. The voyages to the satellites proposed by certain scientists will tell us nothing about this subject: any trace of life has long since disappeared from those frozen worlds."

Then, as if speaking to himself, the old person added: "Oh, to know, to know! I would gladly give my life for my people to know the fraction of truth contained in these myths."

✳

In the scented calyx of the flower, Light-of-Sorrow waved and shouted with all his might. He shouted: "Those old traditions are true. Look! I am a man of Earth!"

No one noticed the flower-head move slightly. No one heard the feeble insectile murmur.

The enormous beings could not hear the loud shout of the tiny creature, because their ancestors had killed rational beings whose bizarre forms displeased them.

Light-of-Sorrow could not shout loud enough to make himself heard by them, because his egotistical folly had killed Mother's-Tears.

✳

He died of his futile effort. The next day, a bird found his little cadaver in the calyx of the flower. It carried him away in its beak and gave him to its chicks to eat, because the dead must make the living, and because it is inappropriate for corpses to be rotting in the scented calices of flowers.

THE ABSENTEES

This anthology only contains translations of texts that are in the public domain. Several individuals active in the Symbolist Movement who produced prose work that I would have been delighted to include did not die until after 1947, the necessary cut-off date for inclusion at the time of writing. The most important are Édouard Dujardin (1861-1949), André Gide (1869-1951), "Rachilde" [Marguerite d'Eymery, later Madame Vallette] (1860-1953), "Gérard d'Houville" [Marie de Heredia, later Madame de Régnier] (1875-1963), and "Tristan Klingsor" [Léon Leclère] (1874-1966). There is little prospect of my living long enough to compile a further showcase anthology somewhere down the timeline, but if, by some miracle, my mind and I survive for another decade or two, and publishers still exist in that distant future, who can tell what might yet transpire?

A PARTIAL LIST OF SNUGGLY BOOKS

LÉON BLOY *The Tarantulas' Parlor and Other Unkind Tales*
S. HENRY BERTHOUD *Misanthropic Tales*
FÉLICIEN CHAMPSAUR *The Latin Orgy*
FÉLICIEN CHAMPSAUR *The Emerald Princess and Other Decadent Fantasies*
BRENDAN CONNELL *Metrophilias*
QUENTIN S. CRISP *Blue on Blue*
LADY DILKE *The Outcast Spirit and Other Stories*
BERIT ELLINGSEN *Vessel and Solsvart*
EDMOND AND JULES DE GONCOURT *Manette Salomon*
RHYS HUGHES *Cloud Farming in Wales*
JUSTIN ISIS *Divorce Procedures for the Hairdressers of a Metallic and Inconstant Goddess*
VICTOR JOLY *The Unknown Collaborator and Other Legendary Tales*
BERNARD LAZARE *The Mirror of Legends*
JEAN LORRAIN *Masks in the Tapestry*
JEAN LORRAIN *Nightmares of an Ether-Drinker*
JEAN LORRAIN *The Soul-Drinker and Other Decadent Fantasies*
CAMILLE MAUCLAIR *The Frail Soul and Other Stories*
CATULLE MENDÈS *Bluebirds*
LUIS DE MIRANDA *Who Killed the Poet?*
OCTAVE MIRBEAU *The Death of Balzac*
CHARLES MORICE *Babels, Balloons and Innocent Eyes*
DAMIAN MURPHY *Daughters of Apostasy*
KRISTINE ONG MUSLIM *Butterfly Dream*
YARROW PAISLEY *Mendicant City*
URSULA PFLUG *Down From*
JEAN RICHEPIN *The Bull-Man and the Grasshopper*
DAVID RIX *A Suite in Four Windows*
FREDERICK ROLFE *An Ossuary of the North Lagoon and Other Stories*
JASON ROLFE *An Archive of Human Nonsense*
BRIAN STABLEFORD *Spirits of the Vasty Deep*
TOADHOUSE *Gone Fishing with Samy Rosenstock*
JANE DE LA VAUDÈRE *The Demi-Sexes and The Androgynes*
JANE DE LA VAUDÈRE *The Double Star and Other Occult Fantasies*
JANE DE LA VAUDÈRE *The Mystery Of Kama and Brahma's Courtesans*
RENÉE VIVIEN *Lilith's Legacy*

CPSIA information can be obtained
at www.ICGtesting.com
Printed in the USA
LVHW01s1723160418
573654LV00004B/880/P